Re

The Case of the Sexy
Shakespearean
by TARA LAIN

"I think with the subject matter and solid characters Tara Lain has created, this is a new series with great potential. I, for one, am curious to see what other mysteries will entice Llewellyn and Blaise."
—The Novel Approach Reviews

"*The Case of the Sexy Shakespearean* triumphs, both as a mystery and a romance. Chalk up another successful start to a new series for Tara Lain."
—Kimmers' Erotic Book Banter

"Thank you, Tara, for introducing me to Llewellyn and Blaise and for reminding me that "myself" is the best person I can be."
—Rainbow Book Reviews

By Tara Lain

Hearts and Flour

ALOYSIUS TALES
Spell Cat
Brush with Catastrophe
Cataclysmic Shift

BALLS TO THE WALL
Volley Balls
Fire Balls
Beach Balls
FAST Balls
High Balls
Snow Balls
Bleu Balls
Balls to the Wall – Volley Balls and Fire Balls
Anthology
Balls to the Wall – Beach Balls and FAST Balls
Anthology
Balls to the Wall – High Balls and Snow Balls
Anthology

COWBOYS DON'T
Cowboys Don't Come Out
Cowboys Don't Ride Unicorns

DREAMSPUN BEYOND
#15 – Rome and Jules

DREAMSPUN DESIRES
#5 – Taylor Maid

LONG PASS CHRONICLES
Outing the Quarterback
Canning the Center
Tackling the Tight End

LOVE IN LAGUNA
Knight of Ocean Avenue
Knave of Broken Hearts
Prince of the Playhouse
Lord of a Thousand Steps
Fool of Main Beach

Published by DREAMSPINNER PRESS
www.dreamspinnerpress.com

By TARA LAIN

Published by DREAMSPINNER PRESS
www.dreamspinnerpress.com

TARA LAIN

THE CASE OF THE VORACIOUS VINTNER

DREAMSPINNER
PRESS

Published by
DREAMSPINNER PRESS

5032 Capital Circle SW, Suite 2, PMB# 279,
Tallahassee, FL 32305-7886 USA
www.dreamspinnerpress.com

This is a work of fiction. Names, characters, places, and incidents either are the product of author imagination or are used fictitiously, and any resemblance to actual persons, living or dead, business establishments, events, or locales is entirely coincidental.

The Case of the Voracious Vintner
© 2019 Tara Lain.

Cover Art
© 2019 Kanaxa.
Cover content is for illustrative purposes only and any person depicted on the cover is a model.

Mass Market Paperback ISBN: 978-1-64108-138-2
Trade Paperback ISBN: 978-1-64080-841-6
Digital ISBN: 978-1-64080-840-9
Library of Congress Control Number: 2018940596
Mass Market Paperback published April 2019
v. 1.0

Printed in the United States of America
∞
This paper meets the requirements of
ANSI/NISO Z39.48-1992 (Permanence of Paper).

To my honey, who shares everything
with me, including the fun of the central
coast wineries. Here's to us!

ACKNOWLEDGMENTS

SPECIAL THANKS to Lynn West for guiding me through the rocky shoals of a romantic cozyish mystery.

AUTHOR'S NOTE

OVER THE years I've spent some very fun times visiting the wineries of California, both the famous Napa and Sonoma wineries and the lesser-known but fantastic central coast vineyards. In this book I've had fun taking my readers with me as I revisit some of these special places—and weave in a healthy dose of mystery.

CHAPTER ONE

Bo Marchand sipped the delicious wine provided by their host for the evening, Jeremy Aames, owner of Hill Top Wineries. It took all Bo's self-control not to sigh just thinking about Jeremy.

Bo glanced quickly around the big restaurant and wine tasting area, which was packed with the members of the Central Coast Vintners' Association, but there was no sign of their host. He was probably overseeing the kitchen. Hill Top was one of the few wineries that served a full menu, which made it popular for their vintners' meetings. Still, Jeremy not being present might be good since the glorious Jeremy made Bo drool, and that could be damned bad for his illustrious image if his fellow winemakers caught on. He'd worked hard to be a leader in his industry despite his youth. No giving that away. He'd paid too high a price.

He made one more survey of the room from his seemingly relaxed position near the wall. No Jeremy, but quite another target for his attention. Standing next to the wine tasting bar, deep in conversation with two men Bo didn't know, stood Ernest Ottersen, the central coast's new golden boy—or he would have been if his hair wasn't black as midnight. Same color as his heart, most people said. Bo took a sip of his cabernet franc and forced his eyes away from the snake.

Genevieve Renders separated herself from the boisterous crowd and sashayed to the corner where Bo had sequestered himself, all the better to gaze at the object of his affection without interference—if he could find him.

"Why are you being so antisocial? Come drink with us. The guys need your opinions."

He pushed away from the wall. "Sorry, darlin', I didn't mean to be an outsider. After that spread Jeremy provided, I'm just full as a tick and needed a little lay-by."

She snorted. "Where do you get those expressions?"

"Deep in the heart of Georgia, darlin', you know that."

"California's gain, dear." She took his arm and pulled him to the largest group of arguers, made up of her husband, Randy—a name which suited him; Ezra Hamilton, the deacon of the local born-again church and mighty proud to be it; his wife, Marybeth, maybe not quite as reborn as Ezra; and Fernando Puente, owner of one of the largest wineries in the Paso Robles area—and he never let you forget it.

Randy stuck out an arm and gathered Bo in closer. "Here's the man. You gotta help us out here, Bo. Ezra and Ferdinand"—the name Randy insisted on calling Fernando—"had been saying that Ottersen's bound to win top prizes for central coast wines this year. Hell, he's aced half the contracts with Napa since he opened." His words sounded slightly slurred. For a vintner, he couldn't hold his alcohol, but at the same time, Ottersen made people so mad they could chew barbed wire and spit out a fence, so drinking too much went with the territory.

Bo smiled tightly. "I know no more than any of y'all and have just as much to lose. Sorry." That wasn't entirely true, since Bo's growing methods separated him from the pack somewhat, but still. Ottersen threatened them all. Especially Jeremy Aames, it seemed.

Bo took a quick glance around, trying to spot Jeremy. Since he had two or three inches of height on even the tallest guys in the room, it gave him a decent vantage point, but no luck.

Ezra said stiffly, "I notice Ottersen is talking to strangers. He must be getting the message that none of the other vintners like him."

Bo noticed movement near the far wall, glanced up, and had to control the slam of his heart as Jeremy Aames walked out of the kitchen with that easy grin of his, talking to a young guy who seemed to be his assistant.

Marybeth followed Bo's eyes. "Not sure what Jeremy has to smile about. Hell, Ottersen's taking the biggest toll on his profits."

Bo's lips turned up on their own. "Jeremy always smiles."

A waiter hurried out of the kitchen, grabbed Jeremy's arm, and he rushed back through the door with the assistant in tow.

Ezra raised an eyebrow. "All those gay boys smile a lot."

Bo glared at him, but not much got in the way of Ezra's righteousness.

Marybeth slapped his shoulder. "Ezra, when will you learn to be PC?"

"Never. PC's for Democrats." He raised his wineglass and drained it.

Bo wouldn't have minded giving Ezra a fist to the jaw but had no right. He'd never declared himself out of the closet, partly because it might really give his mother the heart attack she was always claiming was imminent, to say nothing of the collapse of his sisters' imagined social standing. He kept saying when he had a relationship, he'd come out, no matter what it cost him, but not coming out meant it was doubly hard to meet someone since gay men assumed he was straight. It also meant women still thought he was fair game— with a lot of encouragement from his mother. Vicious damned cycle for a twenty-six-year-old man, but in his family, gay men were still "confirmed bachelors who hadn't met the right woman."

Ezra glared at the spot where Jeremy had disappeared into the kitchen. "Ottersen'll wipe that smile off Aames's face soon. Apparently, he's already reverse engineered Aames's latest vintage and snapped up a big contract that Jeremy was counting on from Shields' brokerage."

Bo frowned. "He just unveiled that blend. No one could have reverse engineered it that fast."

"Yeah, well, those are the facts." Ezra's smile was nasty.

Bo's hand clenched into a fist, but Gen squeezed his arm, a little too close to her chest. "How's the family, dear?"

He dragged his eyes away from Ezra before he laid him out. Ezra was an asshole, but he had a lot of power among the other vintners. No use getting Jeremy in more hot water. He forced a smile. "Well, thank you." He gently extricated his limb on the excuse of checking his watch and sipping his wine.

"Your mother's health?"

He wanted to say *Way better than she thinks it is*, but that wasn't fair. "Mama's doing fine, thank you, Gen." He stepped back. "Excuse me, please. I'm seeking a rest stop."

She flashed teeth. "You're so cute."

Ezra grabbed Bo's arm. "You're still heading the dry farming committee, right?"

"Yes." He glanced at Ezra's firm grip, but the man didn't take hints easily.

"You've got to keep Ottersen and his cronies off that committee. He doesn't need any additional advantages."

Bo shrugged himself free. "I can't do that, Ezra. If he applies for an open seat and is voted in, I can't keep him off." Bo smiled. "But we don't happen to have an opening at the present moment in time."

"Excellent." He smiled big and nasty.

"Excuse me." Bo walked away from the group and threaded his way through the crowd, trying to look focused on his goal since he knew most everyone in the room and they all had something to say to him. He walked down the hall toward the kitchen and peeked in. Controlled chaos reigned inside. Cooks and waiters loaded hors d'oeuvre plates to carry out to the picky guests.

Jeremy Aames had only come to the valley a little over a year before when he bought one of the smaller wineries from a retiring old-timer. Jeremy had made a name for himself not only by enhancing some of the winery's blends right away, but by adding a very

creative kitchen that gave his tasting room enough ca-
chet to compete with full-scale restaurants, at least for
lunch.

Since Bo's winery was the only other in the area
that served serious food, people had assumed they'd
be vicious competitors, but so far Jeremy had coex-
isted with Bo quite comfortably, recommending Bo's
Marchand Wines almost as liberally as he promoted his
own brand. As a result Bo returned the favor, and they
sent business back and forth so patrons never got bored.

Bo glanced around the kitchen. Jeremy's cute
young assistant directed waiters around like a five-
foot-six-inch general, but Bo didn't see Jeremy. Bo
sometimes wondered if the assistant was more than an
assistant. That thought made his stomach clench. He
stretched his neck to the side so he could peer into the
corner of the kitchen. *Come on, just one glance.*

"Bo, is there something you need?"

The soft voice came from behind Bo, and he froze
and then turned slowly. "Uh, hello there." *Dear god of
wine, what a beauty.* Jeremy would have been handsome no matter what—his beautiful bone structure and
wide blue eyes assured that. But on top of nature's gifts,
Jeremy had chosen to grow his dark blond hair past his
shoulders, where it hung in a thick curtain that made
Bo want to sink his fingers into it. Like Brad Pitt in
Legends of the Fall, the hair took a great-looking man
and made him a myth.

A grin spread itself across Jeremy's sweet face like
maple syrup on pancakes. "Hi." For an instant they just
stared at each other, Jeremy looking up since, like most
people, he was a few inches shorter than Bo. Then Jeremy took a breath. "Can I be of help?"

Don't sound like an idiot. "Just spying. Looking for insider tips." Bo was told that his dimples were an unfair advantage, so he used them.

Jeremy laughed, just a *ha* or two. "I'm sure there's not one thing I can teach you, Mr. Marchand."

Oh, he's so wrong.

Jeremy's pretty face sobered. "But I sure understand. These days we all need every competitive advantage we can get."

Bo frowned. "He's takin' a toll on your business, I hear."

Jeremy nodded. "He's copied every vintage and bought up vineyards near me so his blends taste as much like mine as possible."

"Damn the bastard!"

Jeremy glanced up, startled. "Thank you." He shook his head. "I'm told he's installing a kitchen."

Bo nodded. "I've heard tell."

Jeremy smiled, but it still looked sad. "I'm glad your dry farming protects you. He can't duplicate your unique flavors."

"At least not this year." Bo stared at the polished concrete floors. "Maybe we can do something to stop him, or at least slow him down."

"Really?" Jeremy looked skeptical. "He seems to have an awfully big bankroll or backers with deep pockets."

"Yes, but if we put our heads together, we just might find a plan." The more the idea wormed into his brain, the better it sounded.

"Uh, are you talking about all the other owners, or, uh, just you and me?" He glanced up quickly, then away.

"Trying to get this whole herd of cats movin' in the same direction would be harder than pickin' fleas off a sheepdog. I think a smaller ship can turn more quickly, if you'll forgive the mixing of metaphors."

Jeremy stared at Bo for a long count, then started to laugh. "When would you like to plan trying to get this canine in the water?"

"I could give you my phone number. We could text."

Jeremy held out his hand and wiggled his fingers. "Gimme."

Bo tried to not look as excited as he was while he handed over his phone and watched Jeremy type in numbers. Jeremy handed it back. "Text me yours, okay?"

Since no words were coming out of his dry throat, Bo nodded as he took the phone and glanced at the number.

A crash sounded from inside the kitchen. Jeremy looked over his shoulder, wide-eyed. "I better get in there before they burn down the place." He glanced back at Bo. "Can't wait to hear from you." He cleared his throat. "Uh, about your ideas for countering Ottersen."

Bo watched him disappear through the swinging door.

Oh my heavens, did I just find a way to spend time with Jeremy Aames?

BARELY FEELING the chill of the February evening, Bo floated out of his car and through the kitchen door of his family home. Well, now it was the family home. When he'd left Georgia to start the winery, he'd been independent. Then everything changed. The ranch house Bo had bought for its open concept and huge bedrooms now groaned under the occupancy of his mother, two sisters, aunt, uncle, and grandfather. Their opinions took up as much space as their bodies. *More.* He released air between his teeth. But he loved them.

Trying to hold on to his elation, he walked quietly through the kitchen and into the long hall that bypassed the vaulted great room, open dining room, and kitchen, where whoever was still awake would likely be clustered.

Halfway down the hall, the floorboard squeaked—a move worthy of a murder mystery—and his mother's voice called, "Bo, darlin', is that you?"

Could he pretend he didn't hear?

"Bo?" His sister Blanche's head popped around the corner. "Hi, dear."

"Oh, hi."

"We're just having a quick glass of wine before bedtime. Come join us, darlin'."

Caught. "Sure. Coming." Daydreaming about Jeremy had to wait. He followed Blanche back into the great room, a space he'd loved more before his mom tried to turn it into Tara. It had started out all slate and stone and distressed wood. Now the couch was covered with flowered chintz, white sheer curtains hung beneath velvet drapes, and ceramic angels decorated the end tables. "Evening, Mama." He walked over to where his mother sat in her floral dressing gown—Mama did love flowers—rocking in her favorite chair, sipping her beloved white zinfandel, and kissed her on the cheek.

He always added a mental footnote to the gods of wine, Dionysus maybe, that he didn't produce the white zin; they bought it at the supermarket.

He nodded at Bettina, his oldest sister, divorced and living back with Mama, which meant she lived with him. Her red hair contrasted with the brown of

Blanche, him, and their mama. Bettina looked more like their dad, who'd passed on four years before, throwing care for the family onto Bo's shoulders, though he'd only been twenty-two, one year out of college and nine months into his life's dream of owning a winery. *Boom*, instant head of family. Both his sisters were older, but according to the gospel of his family, sisters weren't in line for the honor of supporting everyone who shared a particle of your DNA. That was a man's job.

Stepping to the sideboard, he poured himself a glass of real zinfandel, the red kind for which the central coast was known. He didn't need more wine that evening, but they'd all rag him for being unsocial if he declined. He settled into the chair opposite his mom, resigned to be social. "So what did you all do this evening, darlin's?"

Bettina got a funny expression. Kind of guilty. "We went to a gathering of the Junior League."

"Ah, doing good for the community." He took a sip.

Blanche giggled. "Oh yes, we did lots of good for our community."

"What are you two up to?" He glanced back and forth between the sisters.

Bettina tossed back a drink. "Three, darlin', make that three."

He turned to his mother. "Mama, what are you planning?"

"Only my responsibilities, dear. A mother's job never ends."

Gripping the bridge of his nose, he sighed. "Who is she?"

Bettina snorted a very unladylike sound.

His mother seemed to be reading the dregs in her wineglass, had there been any. Bo turned to Blanche, his closest ally in the family, though not the world's most functional human. "You'll tell me."

Blanche shared her sweet, slightly vacant smile. "Well, dear, she's a lovely lady, although she is a Californian. You know how they are."

"Do I?"

She waved a hand. "Somewhat—liberal."

His mother pressed a hand to her own chest. "Blanche, what a terrible thing to say. She's a charming young woman of great accomplishment. A bit modern for my taste, but you don't seem to like old-fashioned girls, so we believe Sage will be a perfect choice."

"Sage?"

"Yes, isn't it unique?" His mother smiled.

"Positively spicy."

Another snort from Bettina didn't improve his mood. Bo said, "Where'd y'all dig this one up?"

His mother crossed her arms over her still decorative chest—at almost sixty his mother was still a beauty, if a very round one. "We do not 'dig them up.' Sage is new to the central coast."

Blanche said, "She took a job doing PR for one of the wineries."

"Which one?"

Blanche shrugged. "I'm not sure she said. If she did, I didn't hear it."

Oh well. A couple of dates with some new woman would give him cover for another several months. Maybe by that time, he could get somewhere with Jeremy. *Yes, and what in the Lord's mercy will I do then?* Good gods and little fishes, that made his stomach turn.

He wasn't really a coward. Hell, he'd broken away from everything he knew to come to California and brave one of the toughest businesses around. He'd fully

planned to come out and live his own life. His father's
death at fifty-six not only curtailed Bo's youth, it dressed
him in his father's skin, and he'd been wearing it ever
since—like a fucking zombie. Suddenly his "dream job"
had become a frivolous pursuit that didn't provide a lav-
ish lifestyle for supporting his new dependents. Still, he
did well enough to get by comfortably. On a long breath,
he said, "I'll look forward to meeting her."

"Excellent. She's coming to dinner day after tomorrow night." His mother smiled beatifically.

Of course she is. Leaving his wineglass half-full,
he stood. "I have some paperwork to complete, if you'll
excuse me." He stepped over and kissed his mother's
cheek. "Good night, ladies."

As he walked toward the hall that led to his bedroom—aka sanctuary—Bettina called after him.

"Oh, Bo, I remembered who Sage said she worked
for. Ottersen. I recall because I love those little animals."

Bo nodded and tried to keep his face neutral. *Animal* was right. But the less he worried his family with
the problems of the winery, the more peace he had.
Still, her place of employment could mean he was looking forward to meeting this woman called Sage even
less—or maybe, even more.

CHAPTER TWO

"BO, LLEWELLYN and Blaise are here."

Bo turned from stocking the shelves in the tasting room to face RJ, his favorite waiter. Or maybe he should say his customers' favorite waiter, which made RJ Bo's favorite as well. RJ was handsome as a movie star, with teeth that shone like they'd been polished with a diamond file, and a sweet nature that wasn't totally without a brain to back it up. When RJ asked a woman what she'd like, the array of potential answers always wrote itself across her face, while his manly charm made him popular with men as well. He was a treasure, pure and simple. Blaise Arthur, one of Bo's favorite customers, called RJ "El Cutie Pie-o," and Bo could only agree.

"Thanks, RJ."

Despite a night of limited sleep thanks to dreams of Jeremy, worries about Ottersen and the future of the winery, and the imminent dinner with some unknown woman, Bo still smiled as he walked out to the patio with its spectacular view over the valley. Llewellyn and Blaise numbered among the customers dearest to his heart. He would have called them friends if he'd chosen to be a bit more honest about himself and his life. They were even planning their wedding at the winery, which thrilled Bo more than he could say—literally.

Llewellyn and Blaise sat near the wall holding hands, sipping one of Bo's dry whites, and gazing out across the scene.

"Afternoon, gentlemen. So delighted to see you."

Both Blaise and Llewellyn turned. Speaking of movie stars, Blaise certainly qualified as a golden god, while Llewellyn's quiet nerdiness snuck up on a man until it bit him in the drawers.

"Bo, hi, darling." Blaise jumped up and gave Bo a hug.

Llewellyn held back as was his way, then extended a hand for a shake. "H-hello."

"Did y'all come for a bit of wedding planning?"

Blaise sank back in his chair. "No, just for a brief respite. Between solving history's mysteries and a few real ones, Llewellyn hasn't had a break in weeks. Plus the English department finally decided I really was a teaching assistant, aka indentured servant, and they have me assigned to half the classes in the curriculum." He fanned himself.

Llewellyn chuckled. "Well, at l-least a third of them."

"Coming to the winery is the closest we can get to a vacation without traveling more than thirty minutes." Blaise laughed and sipped his wine. "This is amazing, by the way." He raised his glass. "Do you have a minute to join us?"

"Love to." Just hanging out with a happy gay couple made Bo's chest get warm with both joy and envy. *One of these days.* He sat opposite Llewellyn. "So what kind of mysteries are you solving?"

"I-I'm delving into m-mystery cults. Mostly Dionysian. So m-much isn't known about them."

"Fascinating."

Blaise said, "Actually, Llewellyn's little foray into law enforcement was so successful, the police have been asking his opinion on different issues. He hardly has time for his real work."

Bo frowned.

Blaise asked, "What is it? A problem?"

Bo shook his head. "I was just thinking how the local growers could sure use a mystery solver." He gave a short laugh.

"W-what kind?" Llewellyn looked genuinely interested.

"Oh sorry. I didn't mean to make it sound like such a mountain. It's just that Ernest Ottersen seems to have a mysterious ability to delve into other wineries' secrets and beat them at their own games. He's putting people out of business."

Blaise raised an eyebrow. "Sounds like plain old-fashioned industrial espionage to me."

"Probably, but nothing anyone has been able to suss out."

"Is h-he impacting y-your business, Bo?" Compassion showed all over Llewellyn's face.

"Some, but I'm less impacted than most. Since I dry farm, it's hard to replicate my process overnight, and the technique produces a unique flavor you either love or not."

"We love it." Blaise grinned and took a drink.

"B-but others are suffering?" Llewellyn seemed automatically attracted to mysteries.

"Yes." Bo tried not to look too distressed. After all, he didn't want to create a panic among their customers. "Mostly losing contracts with the Napa and Sonoma vintners. It's a primary source of income."

"Who's hardest h-hit, Bo?"

Bo breathed out softly. "Randy and Ezra are somewhat affected. But mostly, uh, Hill Top Vineyards. Ottersen seems to have a target on Jeremy Aames's back."

Llewellyn pressed a hand against his chest. "Oh no. We love H-hill Top second only t-to you."

"Me too." Bo glanced up. "I mean, I think Aames has done an amazing job for having been here such a short time. He adds value to the valley." There, that sounded professional. "But business is business, I suppose."

"Fuck that!" Blaise made a rude noise, and Bo laughed.

"Don't hold back, darlin'. Tell us how you really feel."

Blaise leaned forward. "Seriously, Bo. Anything we can do, just holler. You know how much we love you and the whole central coast wine country. We hate to see it threatened by some asshole. Right, dear?"

Llewellyn nodded, a slight crease between his deep, intelligent eyes.

Bo stood. "Enough of my silly problems. Let me get you glasses of something new I just blended, and we'll talk about ideas for your reception. I can't wait to hear if you and Helen worked out a date." Helen Firenze, his catering manager, had been trying to find a day that fit into their busy schedules and the winery's heavily booked event schedule.

As Bo walked through the doors into the tasting room, he glanced back and saw Blaise and Llewellyn talking way too seriously to be discussing a wedding. Five minutes later he went back with RJ beside him carrying a tray of Brie, grapes, and crackers, along with three glasses of wine.

One glance at RJ was enough to make Blaise smile, while Llewellyn looked a little less pleased. Despite the fact that RJ had a girlfriend, he did seem to smile extra big at Blaise, and Llewellyn didn't miss much.

Bo took the tray. "Thanks, RJ." Yes, that was a dismissal. RJ delivered a laser-beam grin right at Blaise and walked back into the tasting room. For a straight man, those hips did have a sway.

Bo cleared his throat, placed the plates and glasses on the table, and then sat back down. "Okay, darlin's, let's talk wedding."

Blaise put a hand on Bo's arm. "Before we plunge in, is there a chance you could invite Llewellyn and me to a vintners' event? Someplace we can meet the local players without being super conspicuous?"

"What an idea." Bo smiled. "I'm sure that can be arranged."

There was a chance he might actually sleep that night.

"Bo, DARLING, where are you going looking so very fine?"

Bo checked his watch and paused in the hall of the house to kiss his mama's cheek. "Thank you, ma'am. However, if that's true, it's totally wasted since I'm simply going to a business meeting."

"You spend too much time working. You should be taking some leisure."

He really wanted to sigh loudly. "I have responsibilities, Mama."

"Yes, I know." She *did* sigh loudly. "And if your daddy hadn't left us so suddenly, you could enjoy your youth without the burden of a family." All that was missing was the back of her hand to her forehead.

"It's my pleasure to serve the family. But I have to go." He moved as if to pass her and got a firm hand on his arm.

"At least tomorrow night you can have a bit of social time with a lovely lady."

"Blind dates are not altogether relaxing, Mama." When she frowned, he said, "But I'm sure it will be lovely." He strode across the great room and out the kitchen door to the garage before he stopped and balled his hands into his fists. *Just take a breath. Tonight at least will be fun.*

He let himself smile, climbed in the Prius, and headed toward the restaurant in Cambria he and Jeremy had agreed upon. Yes, it was a bit of a drive, but he loved Cambria. It was charming and romantic. Plus they were less likely to be seen together there than in a local place, so he wouldn't have to pretend quite so hard.

The long, winding road toward the coast stretched out before him, devoid of cars but crowded with his thoughts. Colluding with Jeremy to defeat Ottersen was one type of partnership. Beyond that, Bo couldn't guess. Bo knew Jeremy was gay. Everyone did. No one knew Bo was gay. Should he come out and tell Jeremy? Could he trust Jeremy with a secret like that, and was it even fair to burden him with it?

Before he could reach a conclusion, he arrived at the restaurant and parked in the small lot behind it in crowded downtown Cambria. *Play it by ear time.*

Heart beating hard, Bo climbed out of the little silver-blue car and walked into the cottage-style building he knew to be a far more upscale establishment than its hippy-dippy furnishings made it appear. Jeremy was sitting on an old church pew against the entry wall when Bo walked in. Other would-be diners cast subtle glances at him—he was just that handsome—but his mane was pulled back into a strict tail at his neck, or they would have been staring openly. The smile he flashed as he stood went straight to Bo's balls—and his cheeks with a flush of heat. Bo managed to get a word past his frozen lips. "Hello."

"Hi."

Their eyes met and couldn't seem to let go. Fine with him, but they weren't even close to alone. Bo swallowed hard and glanced around at the other customers, then back at Jeremy. "So, are they ready for us?"

"Probably. They said they were getting the table ready when I came in."

Bo walked over to the hostess and used the dimples. "Hello, ma'am. I'm Bo Marchand. You're preparing a table for me and my, uh, associate, Mr. Aames. Would y'all happen to be ready for us?" Flashing all the expensive dental work seemed to do the trick.

"Oh yes, sir, Mr. Marchand. We have a lovely table for you, private as you requested." She fluttered her lashes.

He leaned in. "A very important business meeting. You understand."

"Oh yes, sir." She looked behind her. "Violet, please take Mr. Marchand to his table." She grinned and said softly, "Or anywhere else he wants to go."

Bo chuckled and waved a hand to Jeremy to follow as Violet led them to a booth toward the back of the restaurant. They slid in on either side of the table.

Violet smiled. "Do you know what you'd like to drink?"

Jeremy asked, "May we see the wine list, please?"

"Of course." She stepped to a nearby serving table and grabbed a menu. "Here you go." She glanced down. "Can I ask how tall you are?"

Bo grinned. "Just a tiny tad over six feet four, ma'am."

She giggled. "I'll be back in just a moment."

Jeremy chuckled. "You do package the charm there, *darlin'*."

Bo's cheeks heated.

Jeremy leaned across the table and angled the wine list so Bo could see. He said, "They have a few of my blends and most of your vintages."

Violet reappeared.

Bo said, "I'll have a glass of the Marchand zin."

"Excellent choice, sir." A grin tugged at her lips. She probably remembered his name. She glanced at Jeremy. "You, sir?"

"I'll have the same."

"No Hill Top?" Bo asked.

"Nah, I like the good stuff."

Violet walked away as Bo laughed. But then they were alone. *Choose something to talk about.* "Uh, so have you thought any more about how we can work together?"

A waiter walked up with two balloon glasses of red and placed them on the table. "Enjoy."

Jeremy nodded. "Oh, we will." As the waiter returned to the kitchen, Jeremy held up his glass. "To us." His Adam's apple bobbed. "Uh, to our partnership." His nostrils flared. "I mean, to defeating Ottersen."

Bo's pulse fluttered in his throat. "To all of those."

They drank and Jeremy closed his eyes, revealing long, thick lashes several tones darker than his dirty-blond hair. "Oh man, you do give good zin, my friend."

"I'm so glad you like it."

"I do. So much."

The words were simple, but they made Bo shiver, and he sloshed a mouthful of wine between his lips, spattering some on the white tablecloth. "Uh, so, ideas?"

Jeremy shrugged. "Beyond sharing some recipes and doing some cross-referral that I think we already do, I haven't come up with anything spectacular."

Bo shook his head. "We need to influence the buyers more than the customers."

"True."

Violet reappeared at the table with food menus, and they both ordered salmon. Bo opened his mouth to speak when a pretty woman rushed over to the table.

"You're the guy from Marchand Wineries, aren't you?"

"Yes, ma'am. I am."

She made a little noise almost like a squeal. "A real winemaker. I just love your place, and those sandwiches. Oh my God, I can't even say. I like your wine too, but those sandwiches." She smiled. "You're sure going to make some woman a great husband."

"Most kind, thank you." He could feel the pink rising in his cheeks.

"You must be from somewhere else. Where is that?"

"I'm from Georgia, ma'am."

"Oh my God, you're just too perfect. Are you single?"

"I am." How could he make her go away?

"Haven't found the right woman yet?"

He cleared his throat. "Something like that."

"Well, come on, the female population's waiting!" She laughed loudly, and several diners looked over at their table. "I'm Jennifer, by the way." She held out her hand and he shook it lightly, but she grasped him with both hands. "I guess I better leave you alone." She looked at Jeremy and her eyes widened. "My goodness, when have I ever seen so much pure hunkiness at one table?" She released Bo and grabbed Jeremy's hand. "Are you a winemaker too?"

"Yes, I am." He grinned and she about fainted, fanning herself with her hand.

"Wow. Have a good dinner, and I'll be coming to get some more of those great sandwiches." She waggled her fingers. "Bye now."

Glancing back frequently, she sauntered away from their table.

Jeremy smiled, shook his head, and said, "A way with the ladies."

There was the perfect opening. All Bo had to do was say the words and he'd be out to Jeremy.

CHAPTER THREE

JESUS, THOSE eyes look like jewels.

Jeremy tried to keep smiling as he stared into Bo's pale green eyes and watched some kind of war of the worlds going on behind them. *What's happening in that smartass brain?*

He wanted Bo's support. Jeremy was the newcomer to the central coast wine region. Bo, while not an old-timer by any means, had made a real place for himself with his innovation and dedication. People respected him. Why Bo wanted to be on Jeremy's side, he wasn't sure, but hell, gift horses and all that.

At the same time, Bo drove Jeremy's largely ignored hormones over the edge. Yes, Jeremy was out, but a lot of good it did him. If Jeremy wanted to meet single gay guys, he needed to hang out in San Luis Obispo or visit the gay spa over in Morro Bay, which he did sometimes. But he had so little free time, plenty of worry, and, if he was honest, a definite hang-up on

Bo. Bo who attracted women like flies to honey with all
that Southern charm. Bo who was straight as Jeremy's
road to the poorhouse if he didn't figure out how to get
Ottersen off his back.

"Not exactly."

Jeremy's eyes widened. What had they been
talking about? Oh right, women. "Looks like it to me."

Bo smiled, but it was tight. "They just like the
accent."

"Come on, you don't really think that." Jeremy
sipped. "Man, this is good stuff."

That cute pink blush crept across Bo's cheeks.
"Thank you—on both counts, I guess."

Jeremy shrugged. "You're a great-looking guy. I
personally know half the females in the Paso Robles
area are gunning for you, and some of them already
have a marriage license."

Bo frowned ferociously. "That's ridiculous. I have
nothing to attract an intelligent woman. My God, I support half of Georgia. No woman would want my family,
and I'm no prize."

"Really? Not what I hear." Jeremy grinned, and Bo
met his eyes for a lingering second and then stared at
his wine.

"Why should I take all the single-guy heat in the
valley? You're just as eligible as I am. Why aren't you
married or at least engaged?"

Jeremy shook his head. "It's tough to meet available guys. Besides, while I might not have a state to
support, I'm the one Ottersen seems to want to take
down next, so I'm a damned bad financial risk."

"God, I'm sorry." Bo put a warm, strong hand on
Jeremy's forearm, looked at it like a snake had somehow crawled onto the table, then pulled it back as if the

damned snake had bitten him. He blinked rapidly. "I thought maybe your cute young assistant might be a, uh, significant other."

"Christian? No. Just a worker bee, but man, he is that. The kid gets shit done."

"Did he come with you from—" Bo waved a hand.

"The East? No. He found me. Right out of college at Cal Poly and wanting to learn the business. I'm not sure what I would have done without him. You, of all people, know how hard it is."

Bo kind of smiled into his glass. "Yes, yes I do." He looked up. "Let's get back to the topic at hand. I was thinking, what if we went together to visit the Napa and Sonoma vintners? We could put together a real attractive package including some of your bulk wine and mine."

"What about the brokers?" Jeremy folded his arms on the table.

"Bypass the brokers at first and then, if we get interest, offer to work through whichever broker gives us the best deal."

"God, interesting idea." Jeremy chewed his lip. "Uh, can I tempt fate and ask why you want to put yourself on the line for me? You have so much to lose, Bo. I mean, you can piss off Ottersen and cause him to focus on you as an enemy. Now he may see your vineyard as too hard to compete with."

"Honestly, I just see us all as ducks in his sights. I'd rather present a solid offense and make it even harder to compete with me."

What Bo said made sense. Why did it feel not quite the whole truth? "Why not partner with another dry farmer?"

"Too monolithic. You and I can offer a variety of bulk wine and not have to compete with each other."

"Okay, I accept with gratitude." Jeremy held up a hand. "And thank you for choosing me and believing in me and—everything." He blinked hard against the heat behind his eyes.

"My pleasure."

The softness of Bo's voice sent ripples up Jeremy's spine—straight to his heart. Man, would he like to believe Bo was doing this because he cared.

A waiter arrived with a big tray and served the salmon. They both dug in, which produced smiles.

Jeremy said, "This is good."

"Um, mine too."

Jeremy had to agree. Watching Bo chew enthusiastically was very good indeed. Bo had a classic face, all carved cheekbones and a strong jaw, but his mouth didn't fit the Roman coin image. It was full, juicy, and almost feminine. Staring at those lips while Bo enjoyed his fish made Jeremy's jeans feel a size or so too tight. "So uh, when are you thinking we're going to take this wine country junket?"

"As soon as possible. Ottersen's dirty tricks wait for no man."

The idea of traveling all over wine country with Bo Marchand—alone—made his stomach flip. "I haven't been up there since the fires."

"I visited a broker soon after the tragedy. A few wineries were badly damaged, but most were unscathed."

"That's what I'd heard. It's good news."

"Yes. So why don't you check your schedule and I'll do the same."

"Yes, I will."

Bo smiled. "Do you have enough help at the winery to get away?"

"Yes, I run lean, but it's doable."

"Where's your family? Clearly they didn't follow you to California as mine did."

"Uh, no. I don't have any relatives to speak of." That was the truth. He wouldn't speak of them.

"Land of mercy, I can't even imagine what that would be like."

Jeremy snorted. "Sounds like you have enough relatives for both of us."

"And the rest of central California as well."

"A Southern thing, I bet."

"Oh yes. In Georgia people don't just want to know your name, they want to know who your grandparents were. Then they figure out how you're related." He turned those perfect lips into a half smile. "You're always related somehow. Where are you from?"

Jeremy worked hard to keep his eyes level and not look away. "New York mostly."

"Whatever possessed you to move all the way to the central coast of California? They make good wine in New York."

"I was ready for a change and nothing to keep me there." They tried to keep him there, but he got away.

"Would you like dessert?" Bo's lips curled around that word so deliciously, Jeremy could think of a lot of sweets he'd like in his mouth. He shifted on his seat.

"Uh, no, thanks. I'm good."

"Yes." They did that eye thing again, and the impact of those crystal green eyes built up in Jeremy to the point that the possibility of coming in his pants was a real threat.

Jeremy cleared his throat. "Let me get the check, okay? You've done all the serious thinking." He grinned.

For a second Bo looked as if he might demur, but finally he nodded. "Thank you most kindly. I'll get it next time."

Jeremy did like that there would be a next time. He motioned to the waitress for the bill.

Bo said, "Did you always want to make wine?"

Amid all the shit he couldn't tell the truth about, that was an easy question. "Yes. When I was a little kid and other rug rats were downing Cokes and cheeseburgers, I was reading the labels on wine bottles and scanning my mother's cookbooks for exotic recipes. I didn't know I was gay until I was about twelve, but I knew I was different really young."

Bo got a funny expression on his face. Kind of sad.

Jeremy gave him a smile. "No need to feel bad for me. I've always loved being weird." That was pretty much the truth.

Bo smiled. "I understand. I'm quite the black sheep of my clan as well."

Jeremy held up his glass with a last splash of wine in it. "Hard to imagine for such a pillar of the community, but here's to all us freaks."

Bo laughed—a deep musical sound—and extended his almost empty glass. "And all our freaky works."

They clinked and downed the last of their wine.

Bo said, "By the way, I have some friends who have taken an interest in our, uh, problem. Perhaps they can learn how Ottersen is getting information on other vintners' secrets. What we need is an opportunity for them to meet the winemaking community without, uh—"

"Tipping our hand?"

"Exactly."

"How about a reception to celebrate"—Jeremy shrugged—"something."

"Yes. We could meet at my place, and then it would be logical that my friends would attend. Maybe—" His face lit up. "Maybe the Dionysian Festival in March. That's a logical celebration of wine. It gives us a few weeks to plan."

The waitress brought the check to the table, and Jeremy handed her a card. As she walked away with it, he said, "I don't know about any Dionysian Festival."

"That same friend mentioned the Dionysian mysteries recently and made me think of it. We'd likely need some kind of theatrical presentation, since that's part of the festival historically."

"Like what? A rock concert?"

Bo laughed—what was that word? *Indulgently.* "No, like theater. The festival celebrated comedy, tragedy, and satire."

"Maybe we could get the Cambria theater group to perform?"

"No. It would take them forever to get something together. More time than we have."

Jeremy grinned. "I did a bit of playacting in school."

Bo smiled, and that familiar blush painted his cheekbones. "I was in a little theater group as a boy. Before I went to college."

"Perfect, we can work out a scene together. You want to pick something, or shall I?"

"You can."

"How about *Romeo and Juliet*?" Jeremy waggled his eyebrows. No point in pretending he wasn't gay.

Bo's eyes widened. "Uh, that's okay. I'll pick something."

Jeremy chuckled, but he had to admit to some disappointment.

The waitress brought back the check to sign. "Thank you so much for coming by. Hope to see you again."

They slid out of their booth and walked toward the front of the restaurant. As they approached the door, Bo stumbled and turned slightly gray. Jeremy followed his gaze. *Well, shit.* Ezra and Marybeth Hamilton sat in a corner booth and Ezra stared directly at Bo—and then Jeremy.

Jeremy took a deep breath. "Best defense, man." He walked straight across the space separating them. "Well, hi, folks. Fancy seeing you here. You're not planning on opening food service in your tasting room too, are you?" He grinned. Not as devastating as Bo's dimples, but a guy had to use what he had.

Ezra frowned. "What? No. I don't muddy my brand with food. I'm a vintner, not some bloody restaurateur."

"Good. More for us, then."

"What do you mean?" Ezra glanced over Jeremy's shoulder, where Jeremy could sense Bo's warmth.

Jeremy glanced back. "Bo and I check out restaurants for recipes and food service ideas."

"You're in collusion?"

Bo stepped forward, frowning. "Collusion, Ezra? Since when did two vintners having a meal together constitute collusion? Where the hell is your head?"

Ezra looked startled and blinked rapidly. "Of course, sorry. It's just all these terrible competitive disasters are taking their toll."

Bo put a hand on Ezra's shoulder. *Nice touch.* Jeremy wasn't sure he could have brought himself to touch the SOB. Bo said, "For all of us, Ezra."

Jeremy said, "Bo, why don't you stay and talk to Ezra and Marybeth? I need to get going. Good to see you both. Thanks, Bo." He shook Bo's hand and gave him a significant look. *We have nothing to hide.* Jeremy winked.

"Yes, thanks, Jeremy. Next restaurant we review, I'll pay." He winked back.

Jeremy walked away chuckling.

CHAPTER FOUR

THE DOORBELL rang.

Bo's mama flashed a hand toward Blanche. "Get it! Get it!"

Blanche scowled, but their mother's favorite expression was always "Will you do that? You're younger than I am." Since everyone was younger than Mama except Harvey, Bo's grandfather, she seldom got up.

Blanche moved at half the speed their mother would have liked toward the door to fetch the elusive Sage, who was officially a half hour late. She'd texted to say she was dealing with a business emergency and would be there as quickly as she could get away. She'd said not to hold dinner, but since the whole purpose of the meal was to seat Sage next to Bo, there was no likelihood of that happening.

Bo stood at the bar cart pouring wine but looked up to see an attractive dark-haired woman, probably in her late twenties or early thirties, which made her older than he was. She wore a denim pantsuit that seemed about the right level of formal for central California business, with a thick scarf around her neck that she unwound as she walked in. "Oh my God, how can I ever apologize for keeping you all waiting? I'm so terribly sorry. It was one of those drop-in-your-lap emergencies, and I couldn't leave until it was resolved."

Mama bestirred herself and rose from her rocker, extending her hand. "Think nothing of it, dear. A busy girl like you has so many responsibilities. We were happy to wait."

Mama was never happy to wait, but she sounded charming, if not convincing.

Bo walked to his grandfather and handed him a glass of wine as his mama said, "May I present my father, Harvey Walshman."

Harvey gave Sage a smile. "Always delighted to meet a pretty girl."

Sage smiled back. "I have a good idea where all the fabled Marchand charm comes from."

Harvey gave Bo a slap on the arm without getting up from his recliner. "She's a cutie."

Mama said, "I'm sorry you don't get to meet my sister and her husband, but they're out this evening. So I think I only have yet to introduce you to Bo." She swept her hand in a grand arc as if showing off a new car.

Sage gave Bo a direct gaze. "Sage Zilinsky. I'm pleased to finally meet you, Bo. I've heard so much about you."

And wouldn't he like to know all the details? "I hope it was all good." He shook her hand and tried to smile genuinely.

Her hand was strong and warm, her handshake firm. "It was appreciative, I assure you."

He barked a little laugh, and she grinned. He asked, "Can I get you a glass of wine? A cocktail? Something softer?"

"In this home I must ask for wine. Red, please. You choose." She looked up at Mama. "And please don't hold your meal another moment for me. I know how hard it is to keep things warm."

"That's very thoughtful of you." Mama looked through the arch to the dining room where the big table was set for six. "I'll just check with the cook." She walked toward the kitchen.

They didn't always have help, but his mother preferred not to cook and Bo's sisters were awful at it. Unless his Aunt Cortina wanted to take on the job on any given day, they often ate takeout. So much for the Southern reputation.

Bo poured zin from the cocktail cart for Sage and handed her the glass where she sat in the flowered chair between the sofa and another empty chair obviously left for Bo. He accepted the cue and sat. "I assume your emergency was handled successfully?"

"Yes, thanks. Everything hit the proverbial fan about four, so I had a little time to deal with it." She looked down at her suit. "No time left to change, however."

"You look great." Which was pretty much true. Her face, while not beautiful in a traditional sense, was interesting, with almond-shaped eyes, a strong nose a little too big to be cute but quite classic, and full, lush lips. Her style complemented her bold features.

"Dinner, everyone," his mother called from the dining room.

It took a few minutes to get Grandpa Harvey settled at the head of the table, Bo's mother on the other end, Bettina and Blanche on one side, and Sage and Bo on the opposite.

His mother said to Blanche and Bettina, "Help get food on the table, please."

Sage hopped up. "Let me help. It's the least I can do after making everyone late." She bustled into the kitchen, with B and B, as he called his sisters, looking a little shame-faced behind her.

Bo rose too. "How about I help also?"

His mama gave him that disapproving crease between her brows. "Not your job."

He grinned. "Not theirs either." He walked into the good-sized kitchen. He'd always planned to rip down some walls and make the living, dining, and kitchen areas more open, but his mama liked the separate rooms, and he did admit it was nice not seeing the mess. Leaning around Bettina, he grabbed a platter of roast beef.

Blanche laughed. "I think we just moved the party in here."

Sage had donned kitchen mitts and had a serving dish of vegetables in each hand. "Make way, I'm feeding the multitudes."

Bo laughed. He liked her—so far.

With that much help, it only took minutes to serve all the food. Bo refreshed everyone's wine, then sat as his mother raised her glass. "To new friends who fit right in the family." Subtle much?

Sage smiled and nodded graciously. "Thank you. Most kind."

As they dug into food, Bo said, "I understand you're new to the coast."

"Yes. I'm from Chicago."

"I guess I don't have to ask why you left."

"What? You mean because there it's eight degrees and here it's sixty-eight?" She chuckled. "Actually, I love the big city, but I couldn't pass up the job opportunity."

"You do PR, my sister said."

She nodded, then looked at Bo's mother. "This is delicious."

"So glad you like it."

In case she hadn't changed the subject on purpose, Bo said, "Did you do PR in Chicago?"

She smiled. If she was wary, he couldn't detect it. "Yes, but for a large manufacturer. I've always been interested in the wine industry, and this was a chance to get in on the front lines." She sipped from her glass. "And I get to live here surrounded by the very best wines." She held up the balloon glass. "You do achieve the most unique flavors with your dry farming."

"Thank you." He chewed and swallowed so as not to look too inquisitive. "Ottersen sells mostly in bulk. I'd think that would be a, shall we say, PR challenge."

"Consumers are vastly different."

Bettina said, "Are you thinking of joining the Junior League?"

"I thought you were already a member," Bo said.

"No. I was invited to the meeting as a guest. Sadly, I probably won't be joining. I have limited time outside of work, and I need to get involved in the trade associations."

"So you'll be joining the local vintners' group?"

She nodded. "For some events, I guess. I gather some are for owners only."

"Yes."

She leaned closer. "Of course, those are the very meetings I want to attend."

Bo laughed. "You're not missing a lot." He glanced at her. "But I doubt we'd want our silly obsessions and petty jealousies to appear in social media."

She raised her brows. "Oh? Are they all so petty?"

Bo's words got stuck in his throat. He wanted to ask, "What have you heard?" but swallowed hard. "I guess not to us. They often feel very serious."

"I'm sure." Sage turned to his mother and started talking about the best places to shop—not that his mama would know.

Bo took the break to swallow a couple of bites of food, but he couldn't settle down and enjoy the taste. Was Sage being purposefully provocative? He'd give a lot to know what Ottersen had said to her or what she'd heard through exposure to the community. A newcomer's view would be worth a lot. Still, his brain wouldn't settle on the best way to broach that subject. He also had to focus on the fact that she'd probably come there expecting to be asked on a date.

"Bo?"

He glanced up. "Yes, Mama?"

"You were a million miles away."

"Sorry."

Bo tried not to be distracted as the women talked and finished their meals until finally his mother said, "I thought we might take coffee and dessert in the living room."

"Oh yes." He rose and held the chair for Sage, then did the same for his mother. Blanche and Bettina were already up, knowing they'd be expected to help.

This time Sage didn't volunteer but instead stepped behind Harvey's chair and leaned over with a smile. "Would you escort me in, Mr. Walshman?"

"I'd be honored, my dear." Harvey was a canny old duck, but he seemed quite beguiled by Sage. He stood and offered his arm, which she took with great formality.

"So you're from Georgia?" Sage smiled as they walked to the living room together.

Bo's mother took his arm and whispered, "See. What did I tell you?"

"Umm. She's good at PR." He grinned.

"Bo Marchand, behave yourself." She gave him a light smack on the arm.

"Always, Mama. Always." Sadly, he behaved a lot more than he wanted to.

After what felt like a year of chitchat, dessert was finally over. Sage turned to Bo. "I'd love to see more of your beautiful home."

The woman did have an interesting way of manipulating the people around her. "I'd be delighted to show it to you."

They both rose, and Bo led the way down the hall toward the back of the house. "There's not a lot to see. The place started out with various sitting rooms and amenities, but most everything is a bedroom these days. I do still have a sitting room and office if you'd like to see that."

"Love to."

He pushed open a door on their left, and she passed him into the big room with its high ceiling, stone fireplace, cushy leather furniture, and big messy desk. Bookshelves lined the walls, crammed with everything from winemaking references to novels of the Old West. Fortunately he stashed his gay romance novels in a secret box on a high shelf in his bedroom, along with his porn.

She stopped and smiled wide. "Finally, something in this house that looks like you."

He'd have laughed, but it hit too close to the heart. "When my family moved in, it was so close to my father's death, I felt it was important for them to be able to feel at home."

"That's very nice of you. I'm not sure I would have been able to do it." She strolled to the bookshelf and looked at titles.

"I didn't want to move back to Georgia, so I guess they brought it to me." This time he did chuckle.

She turned abruptly. "Would I be correct in thinking that your family railroaded you into being here for this dinner and you have no interest in dating me?" She didn't sound angry. More neutral.

"You're a direct person. I like it, although it's a shock to my Southern system." He smiled.

"Sorry. It's my Southern way. Southern Illinois, that is."

He crossed to the leather couch and perched. "You're correct that they did set this up and insist that I be here. On the other hand, I like you and think you're attractive. I even like your directness. But I must confess to having a certain unrequited fancy for another. If I seem less than wholehearted, that might account for it."

"An unrequited fancy." She barked a laugh. "You do have a way with words."

"So I've been told." Bo looked at his hands. He hadn't said anything untrue. He did like Sage, and she was attractive—if not attractive to him. The unrequited fancy part was gospel.

Sage sat on the couch next to him. "Here's the deal. There aren't a lot of eligible men in the valley."

That was sure as God-made-little-fishes true.

"Certainly there aren't any bachelors as connected to the community as you." She flashed some teeth. "Or as attractive." She leaned back on the couch, making him do the same. "I'm assuming that your unrequited fancy doesn't provide you with an appropriate social partner. I'm not looking for romance. Maybe we can help each other out?" She glanced at him sideways.

"I don't currently have a lot of time for social partnering."

"Me either. But there are those occasions where it would be nice not to show up alone."

She had a point. It would also provide him with cover, but— "You may be aware that your employer's not particularly popular with the other vintners. If we start appearing together, it will cause talk."

"Um, yes. I'm aware of his controversial reputation. I guess people could think you're revealing secrets to me under the influence of my charms."

He couldn't help but grin. "Or vice versa."

She slapped her knee. "Perfect. You can tell them I talk in my sleep!"

"How much of your motivation comes from a desire to be privy to some of that inside information as a result of being my date?"

"Oooh, who's being direct now?" She gave him a little push. "I guess the answer is some. Don't misunderstand. I'm not digging dirt on you or anyone. I'm just interested in knowing the news of the community as soon as it happens because it's important to my doing a good job."

"You may hear unflattering things about your boss."

"Yes, I know." A small crease appeared between her brows. "While I'd love to counteract the negative publicity, Mr. Ottersen hasn't asked me to do that. In fact, he hasn't discussed the issue with me or made it part of my job." She shrugged. "I'm certainly not going to publicize it, so I have nothing to gain."

That seemed unlikely, but a secret gathering could go both ways. "Perhaps we can try it. If the reaction is too negative, we may have to pull back."

"I'm up for that."

He shifted on his seat cushion. "And you really don't care—"

"That your heart's engaged elsewhere? No, I really don't, although I'll admit to being fascinated by the identity of the lucky lady."

Bo gave a small smile.

Sage stood. "So you'll call me?"

"If you give me your number."

She recited her phone number, and Bo keyed it in to his phone, then stood beside her. He said, "There will be a wine tasting event coming up. Perhaps we can go public at that time."

"Sounds great."

He walked to the door of the room, and she followed him. She crossed through the door, then turned back. "So tell me the truth. How much of your motivation comes from the chance that I might spill something about Ottersen's plans?"

Bo met her eyes. "Why darlin', why would you think of something so devious from little ol' me?"

They both laughed their way back to the living room.

CHAPTER FIVE

"Bo, WHERE are you going again?" His mother leaned forward in her rocking chair.

"I'm getting ready for the festival, Mama. There's a great deal to do."

"It just seems like you're gone an awfully lot."

"Maybe Bettina, Blanche, or you would like to help?" The thought made him twitch, but the chances she'd take him up on it were—

She waved a hand. "I'm sure we'd only slow you down."

Right. Chances—zero. "I'll get done as soon as I can."

"Why haven't you asked Sage out yet?"

"There hasn't been an opportunity."

"What opportunity? You have to eat. So does she."

"We'll work it out in our own time, Mother. She's busy and so am I."

She must have realized he was running out of patience because she said, "Very well, dear. You know best."

He kissed her cheek and walked out of the living room. Not until he stepped into the garage did he let himself feel excited. Scared, actually. *Stupid. Purely stupid. You're just going to rehearse a scene from a play, not have wild, pornographic sex.*

He actually clutched his belly at the thought, then let out a slow breath as he slid into the car. He'd like to find a way to tell Jeremy he was gay, but it was a risk. First, Jeremy might not be interested, even though he seemed to flirt a lot. But interested or not, Jeremy was an out and proud gay man. It could be hard for him to understand the shitstorm coming out would be for Bo—with the vintners who could think he lied to them, and especially with Bo's family. Not that Jeremy would openly gossip, but things could slip.

Bo pulled out onto the dark road that wound through the wine country, turning right toward Paso Robles. Then there was the possibility that Jeremy could misunderstand Bo's offer of help. If he knew Bo was gay, would he think Bo's business assistance was contingent on sex? Bo hated that idea. He honestly liked Jeremy and felt like the guy was getting a rotten deal from Ottersen. Jeremy had worked hard and deserved to succeed. It made business sense for Bo to help him— period. No contingencies. Would Jeremy believe that? *Fuck. All too complicated.*

In fact, telling Jeremy he was gay could be crazy, but when he saw Jeremy, he went a little crazy. More than a little.

Twenty minutes later Bo parked behind Jeremy's winery. Elvis once sang about shaking hands and weak knees and being shook up. Man, he related to that song. The back door of the tasting room opened and Jeremy stood there with his mane flowing over his shoulders. Men had killed for less beautiful sights.

Smiling because he had no choice, he climbed out of the car. Damn, it was chilly. He waved a hand toward Jeremy. "Go inside. It's cold out here."

Jeremy just grinned as Bo walked up to him. He said, "Just looking at you keeps me warm."

Bo sucked in air but hoped Jeremy didn't hear it as they walked through the doors into the service kitchen. The gleaming appliances shone in the light filtering through the windows from the small parking lot.

Jeremy grasped his hand and led him through the maze of prep tables and counters. Bo was tempted to stumble just so Jeremy wouldn't let go of him. Inside the tasting room, just the lights over the bar had been turned on, and two glasses of white sat side by side, a slight sweat of condensation gleaming on their sides.

"No reason not to enjoy while we work, right?" Jeremy picked up one of the glasses. "To our success, uh, in discovering the secrets of the vicious vintner."

Bo raised his glass. "The voracious, vicious vintner." Bo held up his wineglass and stared at the color against the light. "Where's your assistant tonight?"

A little crease popped between Jeremy's fair brows. "Are you interested in him? Trying to hire him away from me, maybe?"

"What? Oh God, no." *Talk about backfiring.* "I just know you said he works long hours."

"I do let him rest sometimes."

Why did that answer not make him feel entirely better?

Jeremy met Bo's eyes. "So what have you picked out for us? Antony and Cleopatra? Stanley and Stella?"

Cute. "Who'd play Stanley?" Bo gave Jeremy a raised eyebrow, but his heart still beat in his throat.

"Why, me, of course." He leaned his head back and bellowed, "Stella!"

Bo clutched a hand to his chest and accentuated his drawl. "He was as good as a lamb when I came back, and he's really very, very ashamed of himself."

"Hell. I didn't know Stella ever said anything in that whole play."

"True. Blanche gets all the juicy lines."

"So if not *Streetcar*, what?"

Bo handed Jeremy one of the two sheets of paper in his pocket, then recited Falstaff's line. "Now, Hal, what time of day is it, lad?"

Jeremy cocked his head and read, "Thou art so fat-witted, with drinking of old sack, and unbuttoning thee after supper, and sleeping upon benches after noon, that thou hast forgotten to demand that truly which thou wouldst truly know. What a devil hast thou to do with the time of the day? Unless hours were cups of sack, and minutes capons, and clocks the tongues of bawds, and dials the signs of leaping-houses, and the blessed sun himself a fair hot wench in flame-colored taffeta, I see no reason why thou shouldst be so superfluous to demand the time of the day."

Wow. "That was damned good."

"Thanks. I really like Henry the Fourth."

"I think the other winemakers will get a kick out of this speech."

"Especially all the hot wenches." Jeremy's cheeky grin popped into place.

Bo frowned, and the words slipped out. "I'm not interested in wenches, hot or otherwise."

"Really?" Jeremy looked half-surprised and half-fascinated.

"Uh, I mean there aren't any women among the winemaking community who I'm interested in." He felt an opportunity slip out of his hand. At the same time, Sage's face flashed in his mind. *I'll explain that later.* "Shall we read the rest?"

Jeremy nodded, all that fair hair rippling, and Bo plunged into his next line just for the distraction. "Indeed, you come near me now, Hal, for we that take purses go by the moon and the seven stars, and not by Phoebus, he, that wand'ring knight so fair." His heart tripped. *Knight so fair.* He groped for his wineglass, hit it awkwardly, and tipped it right over onto Jeremy's arm. "Damn! I'm so sorry."

Bo grabbed the glass and hurried around the bar for a rag of some kind. He found a roll of paper towels and dabbed madly at Jeremy's soaked shirt, the wine creeping up the cotton fabric toward his shoulder. "That was so careless of me."

"No problem, really. I always keep a shirt close at hand for just such accidents because they seem to happen several times a day. The red's the worst." He walked behind the counter near where Bo stood, opened a narrow closet, and pulled a white shirt off a hanger. Then, as Bo tried to keep his tongue in his mouth, Jeremy proceeded to strip off his wet garment and drop it in a hamper, also in the closet. He pulled another shirt up from it and laughed at the huge red stain on the front. "See what I mean?"

Dear blessed God. His comparing Jeremy to Brad Pitt washed back into Bo's brain, this time the lean, hard body of *Fight Club*. How did a normal person get abs like that, below shoulders and arms like that? *Whoa.*

With no apparent hurry, Jeremy sidled to the bar sink, took some towels and wet them, and began to wipe the wine off his glistening golden skin. Bo would gladly have volunteered his tongue for the job. Jeremy held out a fresh wet towel to Bo. "Would you mind? The wine seems to have seeped up onto my back a bit."

Catatonic. For a second he thought he'd embarrass himself by being unable to move, but he managed to pull it together and take the towel from Jeremy. Jeremy turned and presented a masterpiece of shoulders and triceps for Bo's careful inspection. Bo's dick pronounced Jeremy flawless. "You're very fit."

Jeremy glanced over his shoulder abruptly, and for an odd second, he looked—what? Worried? Guilty? Why?

"Uh, yes, I used to be into working out." He turned his head, but his shoulders had tensed a little.

Taking a breath, Bo wiped the wet towel over Jeremy's smooth skin on his shoulder and down the side of his back. His hand faltered more than once at the heat penetrating the wet paper and the overwhelming desire to drop the towel and just touch that vanilla crème texture. Thank God Jeremy was turned backward because Bo's erection threatened to take over the tasting room like Godzilla in Tokyo.

Okay, he couldn't resist, and probably Jeremy couldn't tell. Bo let his fingers slip off the side of the paper and slide across Jeremy's back. Not perfectly smooth as it looked. There were little variations in texture here and there, tiny moles or freckles, like a living, breathing human. Oh dear God, that was more disturbing than perfection. The need to lean in and rest his cheek against all that strength flamed through him.

Suddenly Jeremy made a funny, snuffly sound, as if he was stifling a moan and a sigh at the same time.

Bo froze. *Fuckity frogs and fishes!* Swiftly and efficiently, he wiped the last dregs of wine from Jeremy's flesh, dropped the towel on the bar, and walked out toward the opposite wall, taking deep breaths so there was no chance of Jeremy spying his boner. "How are you thinking we should present the scene? With full blocking and costumes?"

Jeremy cleared his throat and when he spoke, it sounded strained. The possibility that it could have anything to do with Bo's touch both thrilled him and made him want to run. Jeremy said, "It would be hard to get Elizabethan costumes on short notice. What if we just rent hats and do the scene from stools. We could probably add a few stage directions here and there, but no scenery or anything."

Still turned away, Bo nodded. "Yes, I was thinking pretty much the same thing."

"Good."

"Yes." Bo glanced down. At least his jeans didn't look like there was a live animal trying to escape. He turned and plastered on a smile. "So shall we taste just our wines or be more ecumenical?"

Now fully shirted, Jeremy leaned on the bar. "Adding other vintners' wines to the selection would give us a good excuse to taste some new vintages before they're available."

"Excellent plan." Bo finally felt calmed down enough to walk back to the tasting bar and lean on it, safely across from Jeremy. A new glass of white stood on his side of the bar. "So you trust me with this?" He grinned as he picked up the glass and sipped the dry chardonnay.

"I'm taking a big chance. I don't have any more shirts in the tasting room. After this I have to go nude."

Jeremy's glance could have been flirtatious, or maybe that was more wishful thinking.

Bo saluted with the glass. "We'll have to risk it."

"So do we include Ottersen in the tasting?" His lopsided grin was full of mischief.

"I think in the name of democracy we have to, don't you?"

"Oh yeah."

Bo stared at the smooth wood of the bar and tried not to think of Jeremy's skin. "I happen to know someone at Ottersen's I can ask to provide the wines."

"You do? Most excellent. How do you—" His cell buzzed somewhere on his person. Jeremy dug in his jeans pocket and pulled out the phone. He glanced at the screen and looked—conflicted. Like hopeful and worried at the same time. "Hello?" He listened for just a second. "Yeah, hi. Great to hear from you. Why are you—" All hope drained from his face, leaving a bleak disbelief. "But I thought we had an arrangement. We shook hands. We're reviewing the contracts now and should have them back tomorrow. If it's a question of price, I'm sure we can discuss—"

A flash of anger seared across his face. "There's nothing he can do for you I can't match. Do you realize what he's trying to do? You're going to find yourself with no suppliers and—" He listened, and anger resolved into despair. "I understand. Yes, I'm sorry too." He clicked off and stared at the phone.

The sick feeling in Bo's stomach threatened to push up his throat. "Bad news."

"God damn him to hell!" Jeremy raised his phone, looked at it, dropped it on the bar, and picked up his glass. With one Major League hurl, he sent it smashing against the wall in a gazillion shards.

"Ottersen?" *Damn the man.*

He nodded. "I had one good bulk contract for zin that was going to help keep us afloat until I could develop some new blends." He snapped his fingers. "Gone." He dropped his forehead to his hands, then lifted his head again. "That's two this week. They didn't confirm it was Ottersen. When I said "he," my customer—my former customer—pretended he had no idea who I was talking about. They decided to go another way. Blah, blah, blah." He sighed so loudly, the pile of paper cocktail napkins rustled.

Bo walked to Jeremy like a moth to a flame, or maybe the flame to the moth. He put a hand on his shoulder. "I'm so sorry, Jeremy."

In one move Jeremy stood straight, turned, and threw himself into Bo's arms. "Oh God, why? Why is he doing this to me? I'm the new kid. I've never done anything to him. Why does he hate me so much he wants to put me out of business?"

Breathlessly, Bo patted Jeremy's back like he was on fire and Bo was about to be burned to ash. *Great truth there.* "I-I don't think it's personal, Jeremy. You're low-hanging fruit to him. You don't have as many long-established customers that won't leave you."

Jeremy burrowed his head into Bo's shoulder, and his back convulsed. "It feels personal. And he's winning. He's going to put me under, and I've worked so hard. Given up so-so much. I d-don't know what to do."

Well, shit. Bo quit battling his desires and tightened his arms around Jeremy's slim, hard-as-iron body. God, even swamped by the heat and scent of Jeremy, Bo marveled at the whipcord strength of the man, like some martial artist or ultimate fighter. "I think we keep doing what we're doing. We'll try to find out how he's getting his information, and meanwhile we'll make our brands as unique as we can. If you need a loan, I'm here."

Jeremy's strained face popped up. "My God, why are you so nice?"

Words pushed against Bo's lips about caring and sharing, but he just smiled and said, "Must be all that Southern hospitality."

"Well, thank heaven for you. I can't tell you how much I value your friendship. It feels like my only port in a storm." He leaned up and kissed Bo's cheek.

Every fiber in Bo's chest felt ripped apart. Yes, he loved being Jeremy's port, but that word "friendship" hung like a sword above Bo's head. Did you lust after your *friends*? And if you did, did your *friend* think you had ulterior motives for helping him? *Damn, what a tangled web and all that deception crap.* "My pleasure."

Jeremy's gaze connected with Bo's like he'd touched the third rail, and just as fast was gone. Jeremy took a breath and blew it out as if practicing yoga. "I'm going to choose to be optimistic because you told me to."

He wasn't sure that's what he'd said, but Bo nodded. "Good. So let's make a list of all the things we need to do for the Dionysian Festival."

"There's an awful lot to do in such a short time."

"Yes, but truthfully, I've thought about having our own local wine tasting for a while, so I've done some of the legwork. I'll just put it into action sooner than expected, plus I'll tell my friends to get ready to snoop."

"I can't wait to meet them."

"You're going to love them. They say they already love your wine, so you might have met them and not known it."

"Even more reason to be anxious."

Bo slid into friend mode, Jeremy cleaned up the glass, and they settled in for an hour of steady, fully clothed planning. *Dammit.*

CHAPTER SIX

JEREMY WAVED out the door at Bo as he drove away. The driving away part was a bitch. There for a few minutes, with Bo's fingers skimming his skin, Jeremy had thought maybe, maybe he'd been wrong about the guy. *Oh please, let me be wrong.* But then Bo had been so strong and supportive. No way Jeremy could compromise that kind of help by coming on to the guy when he almost certainly didn't welcome it. *Shit.*

He stepped back in the door, closed it, and leaned against it, head hanging. In all the years he'd been planning his escape and finally getting away, there hadn't been anyone who'd interested him enough to get his brain, cock, and heart involved. Hell, even two out of three wouldn't have been bad. But nada. Then he came to Paso and took one look at Bo Marchand. *Ding. Ding. Ding. We have a winner!*

"Jeremy?"

"Holy shit!" Jeremy jumped a foot and whirled, then slapped a hand against his chest. "Jesus, Christian, you about scared me out of my jeans."

Christian grinned and waggled his brows. "Ooh, I'd like to see that."

Jeremy frowned slightly. Unlike Bo, the one downside of Christian was that he did try to step across the "colleagues" line from time to time. *Not gonna happen.* But the kid was a big asset. Of course, *kid* was a misleading term, since Christian was only a couple of years younger than Jeremy. "I didn't know you were here."

"Sorry. I would have told you, but you were entertaining the hunky one, and I didn't want to butt in or make him uncomfortable."

How much did Christian see? "So did you hear my phone call?"

"Uh, no. I was working in the office the whole time. I heard his car pull away through the window. Who called?"

Jeremy sighed, crossed the tasting room, and picked up Bo's glass.

Christian said, "I'm not going to like this, am I?"

"Sheffield withdrew their contract."

"Bullshit."

"Yeah." He swallowed the last mouthful of chard—from right where Bo had put his lips. "Look, I don't want you worrying. I've got some plans that will help make up this loss."

"You do? Tell me." Christian leaned on the bar top and stared avidly at Jeremy. He really was involved in the success of the company, which impressed the hell out of Jeremy.

Jeremy took a breath and stopped. He didn't have permission from Bo to share this with anyone. Bo might not want other people like Christian aware that his friends were going to be snooping. "I better see how things develop before I talk about it, okay? I will tell you that Bo Marchand and I are going to host a Dionysian Festival coming up, so I'm going to need your help."

"A Dio-what?" Christian cocked his head.

"Dionysian Festival. You know, the Greek god of wine?"

"I'll take your word for it." He raised a skeptical eyebrow.

"Apparently the Greeks had this big festival where they put on plays and drank a lot of wine. Bo and I were looking for an excuse to put on a festival locally and thought the Dionysian Festival would be an appropriate reason for a wine tasting. It's a lot to do in a short time, so we need to put together an invitation list fast. I think it's going to be at Marchand, but we didn't exactly decide. Will you get our names together tomorrow?"

"Sure. Sounds like fun. We won't let 'em see us sweat, right, boss?"

"That's exactly right. To quote another cliché, nothing succeeds like success—or the appearance of it, anyway."

"I'll get on it first thing." He'd draped a coat over one of the barstools, and he picked it up and put it on.

"By the way, what were you working on tonight?"

Christian screwed up his face. "The Sheffield contract."

Jeremy slowly released his breath. "We'll get past this. At least we still have Frenfield."

"Yeah." Christian ran a hand through his spiky hair. "Look, I'm so sorry this happened, but I believe. We'll have the best damned Dio-whatever party the world has ever seen." He raised an arm heroically. "See you tomorrow." He walked to the front and out the door—although the employee parking lot was in back. Someone must be picking him up. *Maybe Christian has a boyfriend.*

Jeremy carried the dirty glass to the sink and gently ran a finger around the rim. *Christian believes, but do I?* Bo might not think the attacks on Jeremy by Ottersen were personal, but that was hard to accept. Ottersen was a big-time thinker. He was after some of the plum contracts available from the big Napa winemakers. Why would he single out little Hill Top Winery for destruction? *Just because he can?* The Sheffield contract would be petty cash to Ottersen. More of a nuisance than a profit, but to Jeremy it had meant a way to pay his employees for a few more months.

Trying to square his shoulders, he washed the glass in the hot water, rinsed, and set it to drain. Like Christian said, nobody was going to see him sweat. At least not until he went fully down in flames. For whatever reason, Bo seemed determined not to let that happen. *Just as long as I don't take him down with me.*

The weight of it all pressed against his neck, and he hung his head over the sink. Damn, he'd dreamed of owning his own winery since he was little and spent those wonderful summers with his grandfather. Those weeks were like a light in a deep well of darkness and pain. He'd worked so hard to make that light his life, and now—*Fuck! No way I'm giving up without a fight.* Bo Marchand was willing to throw his weight combined with Jeremy's against Ottersen. Jeremy wouldn't look that amazing gift horse in the mouth—he let himself grin. Or the gorgeous ass either.

Jeremy walked to his racks of wines and began mentally sorting the vintages and blends he wanted to include in the tasting. Maybe they could even get a couple of the local wine judges to come and give a prize or two. Yeah, the vintners would love that. Anything for another award they could brag about.

He cocked his head. *Hey, that's a damned good idea.*

He'd call Bo in the morning and suggest it. The thought of having a reason to talk to Bo so soon made his chest warm and his cock peppy.

Okay Dio-whatever party. Let's get the planning on.

BO FLOPPED back on his still unmade bed, a smile on his face and phone to his ear. "That's a great idea, Jeremy." He ran a hand over his skin from the waistband of his sleep pants to his chest and back, enjoying the bounce of his dick every time Jeremy said something in his silky voice. "Who do you think should approach the judges?"

"I can ask Christian to do it. He's putting together our guest list."

Bo sat up. "No."

Pause. "Sorry?"

"Uh, I mean judges should only be approached by the most senior people. It should be you or me."

"Based on those parameters, it should be you, then." He sounded a little gun-shy.

"Yes, sure. I'm happy to do it." Bo ran a hand over his face. "Look, I didn't mean to be so emphatic. I just think it's better if we keep a lot of the details of this party and our other plans to ourselves. We don't know who's going to say what to whom. I don't want any more of your secrets being leaked."

Jeremy made a little snuffling noise. "God, man, you're so right. I'm sorry. Christian does so much for me, I just assume he needs access to everything, but I should be more careful. Me of all people."

Bo smiled against the phone. "It's not your nature to be sneaky."

There was a little sound like a hard swallow from Jeremy. "I'll be more careful. No point in undoing all the wonderful help you're giving me." He paused. "And by the way, I don't know how I'll ever thank you or repay you."

The myriad of images that flashed through Bo's mind made him blush from both embarrassment and shame. *That's not what Jeremy means, you pervert.* "I'll call some possible judges right away. I really think that's a great idea. We can start small and, if it goes over well, make it an annual event."

Jeremy sounded cynical. "If I stay in business."

"Don't worry, you will." *Damn, I hope I can make that come true.* "As soon as the festival's over, we'll head out to speak to the Northern California vintners."

"How about inviting some of them to the party? They probably won't come, but at least it's exposure."

"Another great idea. Hell, we can even head for the New York wineries too. They often buy California bulk to enrich their own blends. Maybe Ottersen hasn't hit them yet." There was dead silence on the line, just for a second, but enough to give Bo a little shiver. "Jeremy?"

"Sorry. Someone came in. Yes, but let's walk before we run. One question. Since we're inviting judges and giving prizes, do we still want to invite Ottersen?"

"I thought about that, and I vote yes. It's a level playing field. If we by some chance beat him, it's a clear indication that he's winning these contracts through financial manipulation or something else, like espionage. If none of us win, nothing's lost."

"And if he wins?"

"I guess those are the chances we take."

"I guess so." He sounded uncertain.

"Hey, speaking of walking and running, we don't even have the judges lined up yet. Let's not get our hounds ahead of our foxes."

Jeremy snorted. "You did not just say that."

"Sorry. You can take the boy out of the country, et cetera."

"Do you really hunt?"

"No, sir. Foxes are way too cute."

Jeremy laughed. "So are you. I'll get to work and report back soon. Let me know about the judges."

Bo's brain was still back on the "so are you" part. "I will. Don't worry."

"I'll try."

He hung up and flopped back on the bed again. He'd happily spend another hour lying there jerking off to dreams of Jeremy. That would be plain foolish, plus the noises from the house suggested that others were already thrashing about. Time to get up and at 'em.

An hour later, he'd showered, dressed, and talked to two potential judges who had enthusiastically agreed to participate. A third had refused, but from scheduling conflicts, not disagreement with the concept. *That was a damned good idea Jeremy had.* Now Bo just needed to secure a third judge and they could move ahead with the contest.

Hunger drove him out of his office to the dining room, where breakfast had been set on the sideboard in old Southern style. He loaded his plate with some scrambled eggs, bacon, and grits, poured black coffee into a cup, and gathered it all for a return to his office.

Just as he was picking it all up, his mother walked in, still dressed in her housecoat. "Oh, you're not leaving, are you? Stay and keep me company."

Sigh. "Yes, ma'am." He sat at the table as she selected items on her plate. Mama was a grazer. She plopped down in a chair beside him. He smiled. "Are you going somewhere fun?"

"I get my nails done every week at this time. You should know that."

He gave her a half grin. "Why? Are you likely to forget and need reminding?"

"Oh, Bo." She swished a hand at him. "You seem quite busy today. What's going on?"

"I'm planning a wine tasting event with another vintner. There are a lot of details."

"Ooh, I like wine tasting. Am I invited?"

"Of course you are, if you want to be. But you only like white zinfandel, Mama, and I don't make that. Neither do any of the other vintners on the central coast."

She frowned. "Yes, why is that?"

"I've explained to you, but you don't like the explanation."

"I forget." She gave him a challenging look.

He grinned. "Because the central coast is known for red zin, and there aren't enough high-quality grapes available for both. White zin requires lesser-quality fruit, and many winemakers don't consider white zinfandel to be real wine. It's thought to be one step above wine coolers."

She stuck out her lip. "But I like—"

"Wine coolers. I know. But that doesn't make it wine, dear."

"Your sisters like wine tasting, and they drink *real* wine." She sipped her coffee, laced with heavy cream and three heaping teaspoons of sugar.

"Sometimes, yes. And I'll certainly ask them if they'd like to come."

"Good."

They ate in uncomfortable silence for a minute. He waited for her other bedroom slipper to drop.

Finally she said, "I notice all your busyness has prevented you from having a date with Sage. After your sisters and I went to so much trouble to introduce you."

Oh sweet Jesus. Will she never let up? Still, he hadn't actively pursued his arrangement with Sage since he'd started working on the festival with Jeremy.

She was on a roll. "She's a lovely girl. Just the sort of person you should be seeing rather than spending all your time with your nose in your business."

The tendon in his jaw jumped. "If I don't spend my time with my nose in my business, as you say, this family doesn't eat."

She narrowed her eyes and shook her finger at him. "Beauregard Marchand, if you had taken advantage of your father's contacts and dealings, you wouldn't be scraping together pennies from this absurd business, and you'd have time for the right kind of women. So don't tell me about putting food on the table. Your father and I slaved to make Marchand Enterprises a success, and you let it fall into ruin."

The flowered, gold-flaked, curlicued cream pitcher his mama favored sat on the table in front of him. He stared at it as if it might rise up and bite him, and he wanted so badly to throw it against the wall that the muscles in his hand jumped. "Mama, the business was overmortgaged and overextended. We were lucky to get out with our shirts. I've tried to explain that." His throat worked, and he wanted to scream and pound the table. "In fact, I'll be taking Sage to the wine tasting event."

"You will?" She squealed. "Why, honey, that's wonderful." She beamed at him, and anyone watching would not have believed she'd accused him of destroying her life only moments before.

He stood, grabbed his coffee cup, refilled it without slamming it against the table, and walked out of the room. In his office he closed the door, snapped the lock, and leaned against it. *Mama only lives the way she was brought up. It's not her fault. Not her fault. Not—damn.* It was hard to constantly forgive her.

Just breathe.

He slipped a hand in his pocket, grabbed his cell, stared at it, and finally dialed.

"Well, hi, stranger." Sage's voice managed to not sound accusatory.

"Hi. It's been a zoo."

"I'm similarly behind bars." She laughed softly.

"In fact, I'm calling for a quasibusiness reason."

"Seriously? I'm all ears."

"I'm going to have a wine tasting event. I'm putting on a wine festival, actually. There will even be judges and prizes with several of the local wineries entering. I wondered if Ottersen would like to participate."

"Really? You want us?"

He smiled. "Ottersen is one of the prominent wineries of the central coast—"

"Can I quote you?"

He laughed. "Seriously, want to participate and maybe help out with the event?"

"Well, yeah—"

"And attend as my date?"

"Hell yes!"

"Okay. Decide what wines you want to enter, get a guest list together. We'll figure out the rest as we go."

He could hear the grin in her voice. "Need some help with PR?"

"Wow." *Hell no.* "Maybe later. We, uh, I don't have the details worked out yet."

"Send me whatever plans you do have, and I'll work up some announcement suggestions."

"Like I say, maybe later."

"Hmmm. Would I be correct in assuming that you'd like Ottersen's wine but, uh, how shall I say it? Nothing else?"

"It's not you—"

Her voice lost its teasing edge. "I understand, Bo. Honest. I'll send you some guidelines, okay?"

"Thanks, Sage. That would be great. Talk later." He hung up. Okay, Sage now knew there was an event, which meant Ottersen knew it too. *Nothing else. Good. Let the fucker guess.* As for Sage? She was very smart. Was Ottersen using her to gather information from Bo? Was she genuinely neutral or even a little pro-Marchand? Or was she just trying to forward her own agenda, whatever that was?

We'll see.

CHAPTER SEVEN

JEREMY POURED a little wine into both their glasses and returned the bottle to the bar.

Bo sat back in his chair and ran his fingers through his hair. "What are we forgetting?"

Jeremy wandered back to the table and sat. He ticked on his fingers. "The judges are ready, we've sent out the invites, your staff and Christian have got the decorations going, we're ready to do the scene, the wines are entered, you've got the people to run the tasting, and you did that amazing press release. I was damned impressed."

Bo's eyes veered away from him, and pink touched his cheekbones. "Uh, thanks, I used a template."

"It was really good." *Funny that he's embarrassed about that.*

A knock on the door made them both look up. Bo stood. "That should be Blaise and Llewellyn."

"Oh good. I'm looking forward to meeting them."

Bo walked to the door and let in two great-looking men. One, the shorter of the two, was a real movie star, all golden hair and lean, lithe muscles. The other was very slim and gangly almost to the point of gawky, handsome in a nerdy, understated way, with fiercely intelligent eyes. Bo hugged them both and brought them to the table.

"Jeremy, this is Blaise Arthur and Dr. Llewellyn Lewis."

Jeremy extended his hand to shake. "I've heard so much about you."

Blaise grinned, and it was like someone turned on the lights. "We love your wine."

Llewellyn smiled shyly. "And your f-food."

Bo waved them to the two empty chairs at the table as he walked behind Jeremy's tasting bar, grabbed two more glasses, and filled them from the bottle Jeremy had left on the bar. He brought them back to the table.

Blaise said, "Thanks." He tasted, smacked his lips, and held the glass to his nose. "On one of our recent trips to the valley to eat at Bo's winery, we discovered yours and became instant fans."

Jeremy pressed a hand against his chest. "I'm honored." He wasn't kidding.

"In fact, we're planning our wedding at Bo's winery in a few months and wonder if there isn't some way that we could have Hill Top wines there too."

Llewellyn nodded. "Now that we see the t-two of you working on this event t-together, we thought you c-could do that for us." He smiled. Definitely a gift.

"So what can we do for you?" Jeremy looked back and forth from Blaise to Llewellyn.

Blaise smiled. "Work together on our wedding. It would still be at Bo's winery. We love that view. But maybe you could collaborate?"

The whole idea swamped Jeremy for a second. These two beautiful, discerning gay men wanting to include his winery in an event he could only dream about and envy from afar. He swallowed hard and blinked. "If Bo wants me and I still have a business, I'd be honored beyond measure."

Bo put a warm hand on his arm, which almost completed doing him in. "There's no question of that. Wanting you or you still being in business. You deserve to succeed, darlin', and we're gonna see that you do."

Jeremy's heart still hung back on *no question about wanting him*. Man, he'd give a lot for that to be true.

Blaise stared at both of them, frowning. "Is it that bad? Are you really in danger of going under?"

"From Ot—Ot—" Llewellyn shook his head.

Jeremy sighed. "Ottersen. Yes, sad but true. The asshole has managed to copy all my most successful blends and has offered bulk wine at a fraction of my price. He has to be taking a loss, but I can't match it."

"W-why?" Llewellyn speared Jeremy with his bright gaze.

"That's the shit of it. I don't know why." He squeezed the bridge of his nose. "It's so frustrating. Why would some person I don't even know lose money to put me out of business? It's not like I'm a threat to him."

Bo said, "Ottersen took out one big winery first before the valley got wise to him. One of the other vintners was decimated by a very convenient fire that destroyed his processing plant and many of his fields."

"Has anyone established a connection between the fire and Ottersen?" Blaise asked.

Bo shook his head. "No. It was hard to get the police to take the possibility seriously. Ottersen's become a pretty big player in a short time, and no one was willing to believe he'd stoop to anything that low."

"And th-then he w-went after you?" Llewellyn glanced at Jeremy.

"Yes. And believe me, I'm in a whole different category than those other vintners. I was expanding some and starting to make a little money, but I'm a mom-and-pop shop compared to a lot of other wineries in Paso Robles. I've got no idea why he'd choose me."

Blaise barked a laugh. "A mom-and-pop shop minus the mom."

"Yes, maybe that's my problem." Jeremy looked up. "Do you think it is? Does he hate gay men?"

Blaise wrinkled his nose. "That seems like a lot of trouble to go to. Jesus, he could hire two guys to gay bash you on any Saturday night and not lose money doing it."

Jeremy shuddered. "Jeez, thanks."

"Sorry. But sadly true." Blaise looked at Llewellyn. "We'll snoop at the party. See if we can come up with anything."

"W-who else shall w-we watch for?"

Bo ticked off his fingers. "Fernando Puente is a big player."

Jeremy nodded. "Weirdly, Ottersen seems to have left him alone. At least so far."

Bo added, "Ezra and Marybeth Hamilton are pretty successful."

"They're real church-oriented and have no love for my sexuality, but I don't think they like Ottersen either." Jeremy looked to Bo for confirmation.

"I agree. Ezra seems to really believe he's next on Ottersen's hit list. I got the impression he's genuinely worried."

"There's Randy Renders too. But he's so busy chasing other people's wives, I doubt he's got time to plot against obscure wineries." Jeremy sighed.

"Is th-there a ch-chance Ottersen is just eliminating low-hanging f-fruit before moving on to b-bigger targets?" Llewellyn's mouth curved up just the tiniest bit. "You should p-pardon the p-pun."

Bo snorted, then leaned back and crossed his arms. "Then why did he take out the big guys—or guy—at the very start? No, most sadly I must agree with Jeremy in sayin' the attack feels focused and targeted."

Llewellyn angled his body toward Jeremy. "Wh-who wants to hurt y-you?"

Jeremy felt his eyes widen and coughed to cover it. "Uh, I don't know. I haven't been here long."

"Fr-from your p-past?"

He shook his head. *Think fast.* "There's no one who'd want to destroy me that I know of." He swallowed. "I haven't been in touch with any relatives for many years. I had people who didn't like me in college, I guess, but I haven't seen anyone from my past for a long time. And I'm from the East. Few people even know where I am."

"Wh-where are you from?"

"Uh, New York."

Llewellyn's stare didn't waver. *The man's intense.*

Blaise asked, "Do you think someone is giving Ottersen information about your wine, or is he guessing?"

"Possibly reverse engineering," Bo said.

Thank God for the change of topic. "Truthfully, they've done an amazing job of matching my blends, and I have a lot of them."

"How do you know?"

"One of my customers—" He couldn't help the frown. "—former customers gave me a few to taste."

"So you th-think it's more than t-talented guessing." It wasn't a question.

Jeremy nodded, then took a breath. "Let's talk about something more fun, like the wedding." He smiled.

Blaise took Llewellyn's hand, held it against his chest, and then kissed it. "I proposed at Bo's winery, and we can't wait to be married there."

Llewellyn's soft smile made Jeremy's chest squeeze. "He hid m-my ring in a glass of w-wine."

"Good thing he doesn't like to chug champagne, or we'd have had to wait a few days to get engaged."

Llewellyn snuffled a laugh, and Bo and Jeremy joined in, cutting through the tension that had been growing through the whole conversation.

"We have a guest list of about two hundred right now, so we'll need to do a buffet. Maybe serve inside and decorate the patio so people can enjoy the view at night. After the ceremony, of course."

Jeremy's gaze crept to Bo, who smiled at Llewellyn and Blaise with affection and—something else. Longing? That raised the question, would a straight man get all misty-eyed over a gay wedding?

Blaise rose, still holding Llewellyn's hand. "Let's get Jeremy's situation settled and we'll make our final plans. What time shall we be at your place, Bo?"

"Come early, like four-ish. We're going to circulate the idea that you're setting up your wedding and are looking for the wines you want to serve."

"Sounds true-ish." Blaise laughed. He hugged both Bo and Jeremy. "We'll see you tomorrow."

Jeremy walked them out, then went back into the tasting room where Bo was still sitting at the table, turning the almost empty wineglass and staring into it like it held the secrets of the universe. "Everything okay?"

"Um, yes. I was just thinking about our conversation with Llewellyn and Blaise."

"They're great, by the way." He sat next to Bo. He would have liked to put a hand on Bo's arm, but he mentally shrugged. *Better not.* "Uh, I don't want you to think I'm horning in on your wonderful clients at all. Please just tell them that it's best if all the wines for the wedding come from Marchand. That it's more efficient or something."

Bo looked up. "Why would I do that? They want wines from both our wineries."

Jeremy shrugged. "They were just being nice."

"I don't think that's true at all."

Jeremy forced a grin. "Actually, I think they made their invitation based on, shall we say, a false assumption. They just need to understand that we're only friends and business associates, not—more."

Bo's ears turned brilliant pink. "I don't think they made false assumptions. Hells bells, they were all prepared to ask me to include your wines before they even got here, I know they were."

"Oh God." *Too much.* Jeremy buried his face in his hands.

Bo's warm touch settled on the back of his neck. "I understand this all must be so hard. I honestly didn't realize how targeted Ottersen's attack on you has been. I guess I hadn't fully realized it until you started explaining it to Llewellyn and Blaise. Dear God, you must feel marked for extinction."

"That's exactly how I feel." He looked up. "As if he's devoted to putting me out of business, no matter what it costs him." He dropped his head back into his hands.

A warm hand curved around Jeremy's cheek, the fingers coaxing his chin to rise. "No one's going to put you out of business while I'm around."

Bo's eyes gleamed pale green like the Mediterranean, and Jeremy would happily drown. "I believe you. I don't know why you want to help me, but I'll happily open a vein to try to repay you."

"No blood required." He smiled, but Bo's eyes didn't waver from Jeremy's.

Whoa, maybe I am drowning—in the idea I could lift my head and taste those lips that should be declared illegal, they're so fucking sexy.

Talk about how to lose a friend in one easy lesson. *Don't be self-destructive. But oh man, it would be so easy and almost worth it and—*

Bo stood, nearly bumping Jeremy in the nose. "I better get home. We've got a big day tomorrow." He looked embarrassed but also conflicted.

"Are you okay?"

"Jeremy, I should talk to you. I mean, you should know—"

Jeremy's phone started to ring. He grabbed for it to turn it off, but—hell, it wasn't that phone.

Bo shook his head. "Not me. Wrong ring."

"So you were saying—"

"You need to find that phone, Jeremy."

"I'm pretty sure it's Christian's phone. He must have left it here."

The ringing stopped.

Jeremy looked anxiously at Bo. "So tell me."

Bo clutched his shoulder. "It's not a good time. We'll talk after the party."

"No. I'm fine. I have time."

The phone started to ring again.

"Well, shit."

Bo laughed. "Obviously the stars are against us, darlin'. Find that phone, and I'll see you tomorrow." Bo walked to the door, turned back, smiled so sweetly Jeremy's heart cracked, and left.

Jeremy pressed a hand to his heart and flopped back in his chair. The phone stopped ringing, but Jeremy didn't care. He already knew what was ringing was his "in case of emergency" burner phone, and it could only be bad news.

CHAPTER EIGHT

"BETTINA, PUT those glasses over there, please." Funny that contrary to his expectations, both of his sisters had volunteered to help.

Bo set some of the other wineries' bottles, wrapped to obscure their labels and color, out on the tasting table. The judges would review the wines first, then the guests would taste. The guests would vote in a separate contest that would be labeled "Sampler's Choice," but the coveted trophies—or at least he hoped the competitors coveted them—would be awarded by the five judges. They'd started with three, but then a couple of the candidates he'd phoned first and not reached had called back and offered to participate.

Christian bustled over. "So how many entries did we end up with?"

"We capped it at twenty-five white and twenty-five red. We filled every opening, and no winery was allowed more than three total entries."

"That's fantastic."

Bo glanced over his shoulder. "Where's Jeremy?"

"He got tied up. He sent me over ahead and said he'd be here soon. How can I help?"

"You can make sure all the forms are on the judges' table and that the tasters' materials are out for the guests. Is all your food here?"

"Yes, in the kitchen, and I brought my few staff to help out."

His staff? "Great. Can't wait to taste it."

Christian waved a hand idly. "As if we'll have time for a bite." He laughed as he hurried away.

Bo smiled to cover his uneasiness. He and Jeremy hadn't seen each other a lot in the last few wildass days. They'd split up the tasks involved in putting on what was turning into a very big event in a very short time. That had them running in multiple directions. Still, the one time Bo had seen Jeremy, he'd seemed restless and jumpy. *I guess it makes sense. I'd be jumpy too if Ottersen was bearing down on me.* Bo wanted to ask Jeremy just how hard-hit Hill Top Winery was financially, but he didn't really know him that well. Of course, that could just be his own Southern reticence to discuss money.

Christian's voice came from the door to the tasting room. "Oh, I'm so sorry. You're just a bit early. I'm going to have to ask you to come back in two hours."

Bo glanced over. *Hell.* He hurried across the big room. "Christian, stop. These are my friends, and I invited them to come early." Llewellyn and Blaise stood by the door.

"Oh, sorry." He still looked a little suspicious. "I take my job too seriously."

Bo said, "Christian, this is Dr. Llewellyn Lewis and Blaise Arthur. Jeremy and I will be hosting their—"

Christian clapped his hands together. "—wedding! Oh my God, I'm so happy to meet you. I'm thrilled to be working on your wonderful event. I have so many ideas I just can't wait to show you."

Llewellyn looked neutral as he said, "Wh-who are you, Christian?"

Bo had to bite his tongue to keep from laughing. If the Wonderland caterpillar had asked, "Whooo arrre yooouuu?" it couldn't have been more pointed.

Christian glanced at Bo, but damn. Let the dude get himself out of this.

He extended his hand. "I'm so sorry. I let my excitement get the better of me. I'm Christian Fallwell, Jeremy's assistant. He told me about the opportunity to work with both of you on your lovely event, and I'm thrilled."

Llewellyn nodded and Blaise shook his hand, but neither gushed back. Blaise said, "Yes. We're excited about having our wedding at Marchand"—if there was a slight emphasis on that word, it might have been accidental—"and having Jeremy partner with Bo on the planning of the event." Again, the careful pronunciation of *Jeremy* didn't necessarily represent a rebuke to Christian's overzealous ownership of the reception.

"Yes. Jeremy's just brilliant at event planning." He turned and placed both hands on Bo's arm. "Bo too, I'm sure."

When no one said anything, Christian had to cover his own gaffs. "Well, back to work. Sorry for being the gate guard. Good to meet you both." He turned and practically ran away.

Bo watched him go. "He's just young and officious. I hear he's efficient as a beaver in a dam, bless his heart." Blaise snorted, and Bo turned and gave them both a hug. "I'm so glad you're here. Come have a sit and we'll talk."

They followed him back to his office. When Llewellyn and Blaise had come in and taken seats at his tiny conference table, Bo glanced up and down the hall, then closed the door. "Lord, it feels odd to be peering into shadows." He took a seat at the table.

"D-do you expect Ottersen to t-target you?" Llewellyn stared at him.

Did he? Or was he just trying to spend time with Jeremy? "Yes. I mean, why shouldn't he? My wines are harder to duplicate, but money talks, sugah. People aren't gonna buy my bulk if Ottersen sweetens the pot enough. He'll get around to me."

"Especially if he sees you helping Jeremy." Blaise glanced at Llewellyn.

Llewellyn nodded but said, "B-but you d-don't have to be t-too obvious about it t-today."

Blaise said, "Stay low-key. Just make it a business thing until we know more."

Bo's head snapped up. "It-it is business."

Blaise waved a hand. "Sure. Just more business." Noise from the hall got all their attention. Blaise stood, and Llewellyn rose beside him. "Sounds like the vultures are circling. We'll get out there and report back later."

"Thank you both so much. I'll be out there in a second."

They walked out, and Bo took a breath.

A head popped in his door—his favorite head. "Hi. Sorry to be late. What can I do to make it up to you?" The smile was genuine—genuinely devastating, complete with dimples, sparkling blue eyes, and rippling golden hair.

"Uh, come in for a second." Bo stood.

The smile tightened, so Bo must have sounded serious. Jeremy stepped inside, closed the door softly, and said, "What's up?"

"Llewellyn and Blaise are suggesting that we downplay our, uh, friendship, at least for purposes of this party. We teamed up because—" He waved a hand. What was a good reason?

"Because we both have food service, and we wanted to make the event about food as well as wine. Maybe we're considering adding a culinary prize next year?"

"That sounds like a reasonable explanation."

Jeremy nodded and extended a hand. Bo cocked his head but took the offered handshake.

Jeremy said very seriously, "Good doing business with you there, Beauregard."

Bo laughed, then assumed a serious demeanor. "And with you, uh, Jeremiah."

"Just Jeremy." He grinned.

"Okay, just Jeremy. My pleasure."

Jeremy's whole face transformed into something soft, gentle, and sensual. "And I'll be forever grateful." He stepped forward, stretched the inches it took to reach Bo's cheek with his lips, and planted a sweet, soft kiss right on the edge of Bo's mouth, complete with—maybe, or it might have been a dream—a hint of tongue.

Bo gasped loud enough for both of them to hear. His penis, always stimulated around Jeremy, leaped to attention. Jeremy's gaze drifted from Bo's face downward. Maybe his lips turned up a fraction more; then he stepped back and opened the door. "See you outside." *Boom.* Gone.

Bo leaned against his desk to hold himself up. *I have to find a way to tell him.*

Maybe I just did.

JEREMY STRODE down the hall and into the wide-open tasting room. *God, I should stop flirting. Bo's my Obi-Wan Kenobi. My only hope. If I piss him off, I'll get what I deserve.*

Guests were pouring in the doors, and the big room was starting to not look empty. *Wow.* He headed toward the kitchen to check the food.

Truth? It was so hard to quit teasing Bo. Jeremy really liked him, and *liked* was a euphemism for some complex stew of lust, admiration, affection, and gratitude. Obviously, from the substantial boner in Bo's pants and other evidence, he responded to Jeremy's come-ons. Did that make Bo gay? Bi? Probably some label like that. But if Bo hadn't admitted that to himself, forcing him to face his feelings could get Jeremy one-eighty from where he wanted to be.

Walking through the kitchen door acted like a wipe to his brain. Instant focus on the moment at hand. Christian ran over. "Jeremy, the avocados are crap!"

Jeremy followed Christian's quick steps to the butcher block counter, where a young chef of Bo's stood with his hands raised and a slightly panicked expression. Yep. The avocadoes he'd been slicing for crostini looked grayish and had an odd texture. "How do they taste?"

The chef held out a slice. "Pretty good. Much better than they look."

Jeremy took a bite. "Someone froze them. Damn." He looked at Christian, who shrugged.

"We never had them. I have no idea."

The chef shook his head. "They went into our storage shed. No one's touched them."

He scowled. "Someone did." His hands wanted to shake, but he squeezed them into fists. "Okay, turn the avocadoes into guacamole, add lots of sour cream, tomatoes, and lemon. It'll taste good. Make bruschetta from the crostini."

Christian did his hoppy thing. "Brilliant!" He looked at the chef. "You got it?"

"Yes. And honest, I never—"

Jeremy smiled. "No one thinks you did. Just work your ass off, and we'll make this even better."

"Yes, sir."

He turned to Christian. "I want you to keep an eagle eye on every detail in here, got it? Nothing else needs to go wrong."

"Yes, I understand."

"All of our wines got here?"

"Yes. Both for the tasting and the party wine." His eyes were wide. He looked freaked.

"Good man." Jeremy forced himself to smile and put a warm hand on Christian's arm. Then he turned and sped out of the kitchen.

Outside, the room was full with people munching and sipping.

"Hi, Jeremy."

He smiled at Genevieve Rendell, not as flirtatiously as she grinned at him, as he trotted by. He reached out and squeezed her extended hand. "Excuse me. Got to see to the wine."

"Oooh, we wouldn't want to get in the way of our libations."

When he got to the tasting bar, Bo was behind it. Jeremy slipped in beside him. "We need to check our wine, especially the bottles in the tasting."

"Why?" A crease marred his usually smooth forehead.

"Someone tampered with the avocadoes."

"You're kidding."

"I wish."

"What should we—?"

Jeremy held up a hand. "Handled."

"You're brilliant."

"Come on." Jeremy grabbed Bo's arm and pulled him toward the judges' table. As they passed some of the guests, they got pats on the back.

Several people called out, "Great party, Bo."

Even Ezra stopped Bo as they walked past. "Excellent idea, this whole festival thing. We should discuss how more of us can get involved."

Bo smiled. "Thanks, Ezra. Most kind. I just wanted to prove the concept, and Jeremy was brave enough to take the chance with me."

Ezra glanced at Jeremy. "Yes, well—"

"But as sure as God made little fishes, Ezra, we're wanting this to grow into something bigger, and your good advice could surely take us there."

"Well, good. I'd suggest—"

"Ezra, we want to schedule a sit-down with you and Marybeth to discuss how we can make this a community-wide event, but right now we need to be sure this one is running like butter on a cookie sheet."

Ezra chuckled. "You do have a way with words."

Jesus, Bo invented charm.

Ezra cleared his throat. "But when you have a minute, I'd really like to know how you got the inspiration for this event."

"Hold that thought, Ezra, and we'll discuss it."

Jeremy headed for the wine table, and Bo followed him. Jeremy murmured, "Ezra's probably horrified that we're celebrating some pagan deity in our festival."

"That's the least of our worries at the moment."

Jeremy stopped in front of the bottles lined up for the judges' consideration.

Bo waylaid him. "We can't touch the bottles."

"We're running the contest."

"Doesn't matter. We can't tamper with the validity of the contest if we want people to take this seriously."

"We've got to check, Bo. What if someone messed with the bottles?"

"Seriously, do you think it could have happened?"

He nodded.

"Okay. I'll go to the judges."

Bo made a straight line to Genna Greenstein, the most influential of the judges. She looked up and smiled. "Hi, Bo."

"Genna, would there be any objection to Jeremy and I checking our bottles before the tasting begins?"

She frowned a little. "I suppose not. It's your event, after all. Is there a reason?"

Bo held up a hand. "We don't want to compromise the validity of the tasting in any way, but—" He sighed loudly. "You know how there have been a few uh, un-explained happenings going on?"

"Yes, sadly I do."

"Well, we just want to be sure none of that occurs here. So what if we rescue our bottles and then you taste them along with a bottle we each approve. You decide if maybe something is, uh, different?"

"Yes. I'll do that for sure. I'm sick of this crap." She crossed her arms over her elegant chest.

Fifteen minutes later Bo and Jeremy had gathered their entered bottles plus a bottle they'd each tasted and established as good. Two of the judges opened the sample wines, poured and tasted, then tried the approved bottles.

Jeremy held his breath and almost grabbed Bo's hand, but that would have been a shitty idea.

Bo flashed his dimples at Genna. "So what's the verdict? I feel like a jackrabbit in a porcupine cage."

Genna frowned and looked at the sheet from the other judge again. "Your wine is fine, Bo."

"Well, good. That's a relief."

Her gaze crept up to Jeremy. "Yours is total junk. Nothing like the sample. The entry was laced with something. It might actually have been vinegar, but subtle, so we could have thought it was supposed to taste that way."

Jeremy pressed a hand to his eyes.

"I'm really sorry, Jeremy. Please enter the bottle we tasted." She looked up sharply. "Maybe you should save that bottle that's been tampered with."

Bo said, "Isn't it possible Jeremy's bottle could have gone bad?"

Jeremy stared at him. *Why the fuck did he ask that?*

Genna scowled. "Not a chance. I know the difference. It was tampered with."

"Thank you, Genna." Bo smiled. "Your expertise is deeply appreciated. If you detect anything fishy during the tasting with any of the other wines, please signal me. We want to be as fair and equitable as possible."

"You can count on me."

"I do."

As they walked away, Jeremy said, "You wanted her unbiased opinion."

"Yes, sir."

"Thank you, Bo."

They walked into the big room, packed with people shoulder to shoulder. Jeremy looked up and froze.

He heard Bo's indrawn breath.

Through the front doors of the tasting room, with an attractive dark-haired woman beside him, walked Ernest Ottersen.

CHAPTER NINE

JEREMY COULDN'T resist this time. He grabbed Bo's hand.

"Easy, darlin'." Still, he dropped Jeremy's hand, which sadly left Jeremy free to punch the bastard. He gritted his teeth.

Ottersen looked up and surveyed the room like some predator sniffing the air for small furry creatures. Sickly, Jeremy could detest the guy and still think he was hot as shit, all that slick black hair and deep, evil eyes.

Ottersen's evil eyes connected with his. For a second Jeremy tensed because it looked like the asshole was staring at him. Then, from the corner of his eye, he saw Bo plaster on a huge smile—*plaster* was the word.

Ottersen stepped into the room—leaving behind the pretty woman—walked directly forward, elbowing through the tight crowd, and extended both his hands as he approached. "Bo, darling. You're brilliant and creative. What a fabulous event."

"Thank you, Ernest." Bo took his hands, and they did some kind of double shake.

Ottersen turned his head. "Jeremy. Delighted. I know you played a role in this as well. Congratulations."

"Thanks." *Smile, idiot. Everyone's watching.* He managed to turn up his lips.

Bo said, "Thank you for contributing to our wine service, Ernest."

"Least I could do."

Bo looked beside him. "Oh, Ernest, may I present my good friends Llewellyn Lewis and Blaise Arthur. They're both professors at Middlemark University."

Blaise stuck out a hand with his smile that launched a thousand beating hearts. "Llewellyn's the professor. I'm just a wannabe."

Llewellyn said, "B-but I'm very interested in w-wine and h-how it's made."

Ottersen lit up. "Really? Are you a science professor?"

"N-no. H-history."

"Really. We'll get you to write a history of the central coast wine country."

"F-fascinating idea. Wh-who was the first wine grower?"

Bo said, "Excuse me please. We have some details to handle." He put a hand on Ottersen's shoulder. "I'll leave you in good hands."

Bo walked away, and Jeremy followed. Jeremy muttered, "I forgot I'd actually be seeing him in the flesh."

"You did great. Let's get the wine tasting started."

"Do you think he'll look surprised when the judges don't toss my wine down the sink?"

"Probably not."

"I sure hope Llewellyn and Blaise find out something we don't already know."

"Don't get your hopes up, darlin'. No one's even been able to prove Lucky's fire wasn't an accident so far. I doubt we'll crack the case tonight."

"Hope springs eternal and all that." Jeremy stood back a little as Bo approached the judges. He knew them better. Man, he liked it when Bo called him *darlin'*. Of course, he called lots of people that.

Bo walked to the judging table and picked up a hand mic. He tapped it, which Jeremy could barely hear over the noise of the boisterous crowd, but it must have been live because Bo said, "Ladies and gentlemen, the judges will begin their tasting. Results will be announced later in the evening. We have fifty wines in two general categories being tasted. Since this is our first Dionysian Festival, we've kept it very simple and will be awarding only first, second, and third places in red and white wines. Think of it as a best in show in each type of wine. If everyone enjoys the event, we'll consider expanding the contest next year."

The judges moved behind the table, and the sommelier began uncorking the first white and serving small tastes to each of the five judges' glasses. Each judge had a spittoon, a glass of water, and a basket of crackers for clearing the palate in preparation for the next wine.

For about fifteen minutes, most of the guests, who now numbered in the hundreds, clustered around the table, gazing at the judges' expressions as they tasted the wines and guessing at their reactions. That game lost its appeal pretty quickly, and people drifted away to get more food and drink.

"When shall we do the scene?" Jeremy glanced at Bo.

"Soon, I think. People won't leave until the wine tasting results are in, but they're likely to disperse right after." He nodded across the room. "Ottersen seems to have moved on from Llewellyn and Blaise, and I'd sure love to know if they learned anything useful."

Jeremy followed Bo's line of sight. In a small alcove where Bo kept a display of very specialized wines, Ottersen stood huddled with Ezra and Marybeth, talking intently. Ezra smiled and rested a hand on Ottersen's shoulder. "Damn, look at that."

Bo raised a sculptured brow. "For a man who says he hates Ottersen, he's certainly doing his share of sucking up."

"Yeah. I wonder what he hopes to gain."

"Maybe to have Ottersen turn his attention to others and leave his business alone." Bo shrugged. "Or maybe he's just pretending, like you and I were when Ernest came in."

Marybeth waved at a friend and left the group, at which point Ottersen and Ezra really bent their heads together, and their expressions became more serious but not angry. "Man, they sure as fuck don't look much like enemies."

"No. They sure as fuck don't."

Christian rushed up like his feathers were on fire— as usual. "The judges are halfway through, so you better get on with whatever your big performance is, or the natives will get restless waiting for their prizes."

Jeremy dragged his eyes from Ottersen. "True. Shall we wax Shakespearean, Mr. Marchand?"

Bo bowed in a true courtly manner. "My pleasure, Mr. Aames."

Christian waved a hand. "You two better take this show on the road."

They walked over to the small dais they'd set up with two stools. Their velvet hats, complete with feathers, lay on a side table, and two mics were positioned in front of the stool.

Jeremy gave Bo a slap on the shoulder, though he'd rather have hugged him. "Do your thing."

Bo tapped on his microphone as he perched on the stool. "Ladies and gentlemen, gather round." It took a minute of repetition, but most of the guests, except the most dedicated drinkers, did huddle up to the small stage.

Bo said, "As you know, this is our first annual Central Coast Vintner's Dionysian Festival. The original celebrations in Greece not only included massive amounts of wine—" People clapped and were drunk enough to cheer and whistle too. Bo laughed. "As I say, they not only drank wine and ate food, but also celebrated theater with performances of comedy, tragedy, and satire." He looked at Jeremy, and Jeremy would have liked to describe it as *fondly*. "Jeremy and I put this event together on pretty short notice." More clapping. "So we weren't able to give the theater bit full attention. Instead, we've created a scene for you featuring us two celebrated thespians." He bowed, and Jeremy hopped from his stool and did the same. "We promise you, this scene from *Henry IV* by William Shakespeare will be a comedy."

Jeremy snorted. "And likely a tragedy too."

Everyone laughed as Bo and Jeremy pulled on their hats, struck a pose, and plunged into the scene.

The next few minutes were ridiculously fun. Jeremy gave his part of Prince Hal lots of swagger and sass, but Bo! The man was a wonder. With only his few lines, he turned from a tall, elegant, almost beautiful young man into a fat, scratching, wine-besotted drunkard with a keen wit. The audience laughed and screeched and applauded every time he opened his mouth. By the time they finished the short performance, the guests were stomping, and some of the drunker men moved forward and lifted both Bo and Jeremy on their shoulders for a short stint across the floor before they got too heavy and were plopped back heavily on their feet. To say it was a wild success would be far below the mark.

When they hit the floor, Bo didn't even hesitate. He gave Jeremy a huge hug—which didn't last long enough to suit Jeremy but was way better than a handshake. Besides, one more second in that clinch and Prince Hal would have been Prince Half-Mast.

People patted their backs and congratulated them as the whole group seemed to gravitate toward the judging area of the room.

Ezra appeared out of the crowd and grabbed Bo's arm. "When can we have that talk? I'd really like to know more about the inspiration for this event."

Bo smiled tightly. "Soon, Ezra. We just need to get this event behind us, and then we can talk about the next one."

Ezra frowned but said, "Of course. Of course." He melted back into the mob as Bo walked beside Jeremy toward the wine tasting.

The pretty dark-haired woman Jeremy had seen with Ottersen when he came in walked up to them with a smile. "You two were fantastic. You definitely should add performance art to your resumes."

Bo smiled but looked uneasy. Made sense since the woman had something to do with Ottersen.

She extended a hand to Jeremy. "We haven't met. I'm Sage Zilinsky. I do PR for Ottersen Wines."

"Oh. I see." God, it was so damned hard to smile, but somehow he managed it. "Jeremy Aames."

"Of course, I've heard so much about you. And I love your wine." Her smile seemed genuine, which still made him shudder. "I'm so anxious to see the results of the wine tasting. This was a great idea."

Bo nodded. "Yes, we need to get over there." He struck out at speed, leaving Jeremy and Sage behind. Jeremy glanced at Sage, who smiled. He made a little bowing motion and let her go first.

By the time they got near the front of the packed crowd, Bo had picked up the mic. "Ladies and gentlemen, the tasting is concluded. Enjoy another glass of your favorite while the judges compile the winners and prepare the awards. Good luck to all." He set the mic aside and walked out to where Jeremy and Sage stood, still side by side.

Sage said, "I'm assuming you both entered. Are you nervous?" She giggled in a throaty way. "Being a newbie, this is all pretty exciting and nerve-racking to me."

Jeremy shook his head. "This is very small potatoes. The big wine tastings that publish their results in the wine magazines make the real difference."

"Oh yes, I understand that, but they're so impersonal. This is hometown triumph, and it's always a big deal, don't you think?"

Actually he did, but he didn't want to say so in front of anyone connected with Ottersen. Jesus, what if Ottersen won? It would clearly suggest that all his winning of new accounts was on merit and not some kind of subterfuge or espionage—even though that would be bullshit!

Sage gave a deep sigh. "Bo can do anything, don't you think?"

Jeremy tried to control his frown and probably failed, but Sage was too busy staring at Bo like he was made of gold. Jeremy muttered, "Yeah." He was saved from having to say anything more by the crowd that surged forward as one of the judges placed the two first-place trophies on the table. Bo and Jeremy had agreed that getting the fanciest, classiest trophies possible would up the ante on the desirability and reputation of the contest, so they—meaning Bo—had invested a bundle in them.

Sage said, "Those are beautiful." She put a well-manicured hand on Bo's arm. "How about I show my support for all you've done here by sending out an announcement email to my entire PR list of wine publications and blogs—no matter who wins."

Bo smiled, but there was some uneasiness behind his pale green eyes.

Jeremy said, "We'd get to approve it, right?"

"Of course. Don't worry. And I assure you, my list is bigger than yours. I know bloggers and thought leaders you won't find if you ask everyone in the valley." She grinned.

Bo nodded. "That would be very nice of you."

"Great." She took a deep breath. "Let's see who wins." She crossed fingers on both hands like a little kid, which Jeremy had to admit was kind of cutely clueless.

Blanche, who'd been helping greet people and making sure they knew where the wines were being poured, bounced up beside Bo and gave Sage a hug. "Oh I'm so glad to see you, Sage." She grinned at her brother. "About time you got busy. Mama will be so happy." She gave him a smack on the arm, flashed her teeth at Jeremy, and walked off.

What the hell? Jeremy wanted to follow her and ask what she meant. Of course, he didn't.

The judges stood in a tight group, backs mostly turned to the crowd, frowning in their judgey ways.

Finally after what seemed like an hour, Genna Greenstein stepped forward and picked up the microphone. "Ladies and gentlemen, may I begin by introducing our esteemed judges."

Jeremy glanced at Sage as she pulled out a small notepad and a pencil and jotted down names while Genna recited the credentials of each judge. The judges preened as the audience members shifted from foot to foot.

Next, Genna said, "We'd all like to note that we're very proud as a result of judging this contest to say that we live and work in the central coast wine district. The quality of the wines we judged could not have been higher. With that said, I'll ask my colleague, Vincenzo Rosario, to present the runners-up in red wines."

There was a lot of murmuring among the guests as Vincenzo took the mic. Reds were the claim to fame of the central coast wineries, so the winner in this category was a big deal. Next to Jeremy, Bo's Adam's apple bobbed. He managed to look really cool, but he was sure as fuck nervous, just like Jeremy was.

Vincenzo made a big deal of announcing his winners, which was both maddening and fun. "In third place, with eighty-five points, is Midnight Wines cabernet sauvignon."

Much clapping and cheering followed the owner's trip to collect his ribbon and certificate.

"In second place, with eighty-seven points"—a quick frown passed over his face so fast it might not have happened—"is Ottersen Wines pinot noir. Congratulations."

After a slight gasp, some of the guests only managed polite clapping. Others, who were probably not in the industry and knew nothing of the vintners' troubles, cheered and whistled. That included Sage Zilinsky, who snapped photos of Ottersen as he walked up to collect his award.

In definite haste, Genna collected the mic again. "And now it's my honor to present the first-place trophy in red wines." She cleared her throat and opened the paper. Unlike for the previous award, she broke out in a smile. "The winner of the first-place trophy at the first annual Central Coast Dionysian Festival Wine Awards, with ninety-four impressive points, is—Marchand Wineries zinfandel. Congratulations, Bo." She clapped like crazy as did everyone else, and, happily, Sage also took photos of Bo.

Jeremy glanced quickly at Ottersen. The man's face was utterly neutral, which from Jeremy's point of view was as damning as if he'd been scowling. Still, Jeremy looked back at Bo's beaming face and felt like his heart wouldn't quite fit his chest.

Someone in the crowd yelled, "Fix! Fix!" But it was clearly said in jest, and everyone laughed.

Jeremy put his fingers in his mouth and whistled.

Sage laughed. "You sure seem happy."

"I love it when good things happen to good people." That her boss wasn't included in that statement might or might not have been lost on her.

CHAPTER TEN

JEREMY KEPT whistling as Bo walked back with his huge trophy. Carefully he gave him the one-armed guy hug, but he hoped it conveyed a tiny bit of his pride and joy for Bo.

Bo looked down at him, crinkles beside his jewel eyes. "Thank you. It means a lot that you're happy for me."

"Hey, you're a good man who makes great wine."

"Guess I better start fixin' to be a great man who makes great wine."

Jeremy cocked a half smile. "I don't think there's much that needs fixing."

Their gazes clung. Man, he'd give a lot to get this man alone and congratulate him properly. "Maybe we could—"

From the front, Genna said, "And now we'll move on with the whites."

Bo looked conflicted but said, "Guess we need to pay attention."

Jeremy dragged his eyes away from Bo's and caught Sage staring at them. She stepped in and gave Bo a hug, though he seemed to use the trophy as a reason not to hug back. "Congratulations."

"Thanks." Bo smiled, then turned as Genna called up another of the judges, Mrs. Winsap, to present the runners-up.

The elderly lady looked very official as she opened the winner's announcement and gave the third place to a sauvignon blanc from Ezra's winery. Everyone clapped loudly but not with the same joy as when Bo had won. Ezra's loud opinions and judgmental nature made him less popular than Bo by a long way.

Ezra looked very full of himself as he accepted the ribbon and certificate.

Mrs. Winsap said, "And now, in second place with a score of ninety—" She opened the paper, pressed her hand to her chest, and said, "Oh my. We have a tie. The second place goes to Ottersen Wines for their chardonnay."

Polite applause and some grumbling marked the announcement. Sage snapped photos again as Ottersen walked up smiling, though his lips looked tight. Maybe second place didn't suit him either.

Mrs. Winsap's smile warmed. "And also in second place with a score of ninety for their viognier is Marchand Wineries."

The cheer was a notable contrast to the lukewarm reception for Ottersen.

Jeremy gave a little hop and slapped a hand against Bo's back as he walked up.

Mrs. Winsap said, "I guess we'll have to get another certificate for you, Bo. Congratulations!" She shook his hand, then gave the mic to Genna.

Bo came back to where Jeremy was standing. "That was a big shock."

"Not to me." Jeremy flashed him a grin and tried to put a lot of warmth into his eyes, though Sage also waggled her fingers and blew a kiss. Jeremy tried hard not to make a face at her.

Genna smiled. "And now for our final award. The first-place trophy for white wine, with a wonderful score of ninety-five and congratulations from all the judges, goes to—" She paused, getting cheers from the crowd, then said, "—Hill Top Wineries, Mr. Jeremy Aames."

To say *stunned* would barely cover it. It had never crossed Jeremy's mind that he'd win. His heart beat so hard, he felt deaf. He vaguely saw Bo glance toward Ottersen, but the thrill was so huge, he couldn't even care.

Somebody yelled, "You guys sure cleaned up. Pretty fishy." Then he laughed like mad.

Genna smiled and said, "I assure you, everything was totally anonymous, and we're all completely proud of our new addition to the Paso Robles wine district. Jeremy, come get your trophy."

Bo's warm hand gave Jeremy a gentle push forward, and he floated up to Genna. She grinned as she handed him the huge trophy he and Bo had picked out from a catalog. "Congratulations."

"Thank you." His voice came out almost as a squeak, and he chuckled. The heat in his cheeks suggested he was blushing, which unlike Bo, he never did. He held the trophy aloft for a minute, then walked back to where Bo stood holding his trophy.

Jeremy laughed. "I guess this does look pretty bad."

Bo slid a strong arm around Jeremy's shoulders. "Ask if we give a shit, darlin'." He held his trophy aloft and pronounced, "Somebody take our damned picture."

Sage and about ten other people stepped up to do just that. An instant before the cameras clicked, Jeremy turned toward Bo, letting his mane of hair obscure the side of his face. *There. That should be enough.*

Jeremy couldn't stop staring at his trophy. Yes, he knew he made good wine, but that good? Good enough to win over everyone, even Bo? And even Ottersen?

Bo leaned down and said softly, "Don't look so surprised, darlin'. You make great wine."

Jeremy gazed up at Bo like he was the Oracle at Delphi. "Thank you. I honestly never knew I doubted that until this moment."

"Never doubt it again."

Sage said, "I didn't get a very good shot. Let's do another."

Jeremy waved a hand. "No, that's okay—"

Christian ran across the room, leaped at Jeremy, and ended up hanging off him like a monkey on a tree. "Ya-hooo! I knew we could do it, boss. Congratulations!"

Jeremy staggered back against his wriggling and finally got Christian's feet on the floor. "Thank you, Christian. You certainly helped make it possible."

He stepped back, hands on his hips. "You're the genius with the amazing imagination and taste for special blends. I swear, nobody's better."

"Thank you." He handed him the trophy. "Hang on to this, okay?"

"With pleasure." Christian hugged it to his chest, and Sage grabbed a photo.

"Congratulations, Aames." Ottersen's cool voice came from beside Jeremy, and he looked up into the dark eyes.

"Thanks. You too. To place in both categories is quite an accomplishment."

"I'll just have to do better next time."

Shit, that gave him a shiver.

Sage proceeded to wave her arms and line up all the winners for photos.

Jeremy whispered to Bo, "I need to go to the bathroom. Go ahead without me. I hate this part."

Bo looked surprised but didn't object as Jeremy walked toward the back office where he had a private bathroom. The chances anyone he didn't want to see the photos would actually get a look at them were slim, but still—discretion and all that. Jeremy hung out in the bathroom until the picture-taking stopped, and then he returned to that tall Southern gentleman.

As Bo predicted, people started leaving quickly after the awards. With lots of backslapping and enthusiastic thanks to Bo and Jeremy, the crowd in the room diminished.

Finally, both Bo and Jeremy leaned against a table while Christian, RJ, and various other helpers scuttled around, cleaning up. A few die-hards were still sloshing down wine, and Sage was talking seriously in a corner to Ottersen, though she kept glancing toward Bo.

Llewellyn and Blaise walked over. He'd almost forgotten about them—the whole reason they'd thought up this giant party. Funny how it had taken on a life of its own.

Blaise said, "We're going to leave." His eyes shifted toward Ottersen, then back to Bo and Jeremy. "Probably best to do a debrief after you've both gotten a good night's sleep. Maybe tomorrow or at your convenience."

Jeremy asked, "Did you learn anything interesting?"

"Not anything time sensitive."

Llewellyn nodded. "B-bits and p-pieces. B-but better not to appear t-too conspiratorial." He grinned, which in his handsome nerd face was downright cute.

Bo said. "Maybe we can come to you. Drive over to the university."

"Th-that would be great."

Blaise raised his voice. "Wonderful event. Thank you so much for inviting us. We're delighted we'll be serving award-winning wines at our wedding reception."

From the corner of his eye, Jeremy saw Ottersen glance over at that statement.

Blaise and Llewellyn left, shaking Ottersen's hand at the door. Ottersen was all smiles. As soon as the two departed, he turned again to Sage with a darkly intense expression.

Jeremy said, "Wouldn't we like to know what they're talking about."

"So true." Bo met Jeremy's eyes. "What did you start to say before we were interrupted earlier? I think you said, 'Maybe we could' and then stopped."

Jeremy shrugged. No, he didn't feel as casual as that gesture suggested. "I think I was wondering if maybe you wanted to go celebrate our wins." He smiled. "I can't imagine anyone I'd rather share a toast with than my fellow wine phenomenon." *Keep it light, Aames.* He smiled with what he hoped was a message that said *This might just be palsy-walsy, but if you're interested in more, I'm willing to talk.* Talk? *Fuck.* The way he felt tonight, he was willing to lean himself over the bar and give Bo a taste.

Bo's cheekbones turned pink, and he glanced away. *Wonder what that means?*

Jeremy inhaled and started to speak—

"Jeremy, what shall I do with leftover wine in open bottles, hmm?" Christian waggled a half-empty chardonnay bottle.

Jeremy tore his eyes away from Bo. "How about offering it to some of our remaining guests to take home?" He glanced back at Bo with what he hoped was significance. "Since we need to chase them out now so we can close."

Bo nodded, but whether out of anticipated sex on the tasting bar or just exhaustion wasn't clear.

Jeremy looked back up. "You were about to say—"

"Bo, I'm putting extra food in our walk-in." RJ flashed his amazing set of teeth. Jeremy would have liked to knock those teeth out right then. "But I'm packaging it in two parcels in case Jeremy wants some of it."

Jeremy gritted his teeth in what he hoped looked like a smile. "Thanks, RJ." He looked up again. "So what do you think?"

"Oh thank God, I'm off the clock!" Sage sailed up and grabbed Bo's arm with both of hers and leaned against him. "I'm so sorry it took me forever. Mr. Ottersen wanted to supervise every comma in my damned release." She laughed musically, and Bo wasn't disengaging her from his body, although the flame was back in his cheeks.

Sage gazed up at Bo. "So, are you done? I'm just starved, and I can only imagine how you feel. I barely got any hors d'oeuvres, and I'm sure you two got none." She must have felt the rising tension, because she said, "Oh, I'm so sorry. I just barged into the middle of your conversation." She smiled, all sunny solicitude. "Maybe Jeremy wants to join us for dinner, Bo? I'd love to hear all your thoughts on the party and the tasting and everything."

"What?" Some bubble burst in Jeremy's brain, right below the dark cloud of suspicion that formed in his mind. Of course Bo had plans. What kind of idiot made up fairy tales of gay-for-you boyfriends? Fairy tales was right. And what the fuck was Bo doing hanging out with Ottersen's PR person? "No, thanks, I have other plans." He backed up a couple of steps, stumbled, had to catch himself on the nearest table, laughed nervously, turned, and fled directly out the door.

Fuck! The cold March night air hit him, and in one instant he realized he was freezing and making a total fool of himself.

"Jeremy!" Bo called from the door.

Jeremy turned slowly, and Bo held out his coat.

Shaking his head with a rueful smile, he walked the few steps and grabbed his wool jacket. "Thanks. Sorry."

Bo glanced down at his shiny, expensive boots. "I asked her a while ago."

"She works for Ottersen. Did you know that when you asked?"

Bo glanced over his shoulder. "Yeah. I knew. I better go." He looked up pleadingly. "My mama fixed us up."

"Sure. I understand." Jeremy knew what it was like to have family expecting things from you. "See you." He turned and walked toward his car on the gravel lot.

"Do you want to go to the university with me?"

Jeremy sighed softly. "I'll text you if I can get away tomorrow."

His heels crunched on the gray stone. Family expectations were murder.

BO CHEWED his sole and affected interest in the classical guitarist playing in the corner of the small restaurant they'd come to in San Luis Obispo. He didn't usually have trouble talking to folks. He was a little shy but had always had a gift of gab. Suddenly he couldn't think of anything to say to Sage. He liked her. At the very least, he should be trying to subtly wean information out of her, but all he could think of was Jeremy's face when he'd realized Bo had a date with Sage. Recipes for a good bread pudding were less complex than his expression. Bo's heart wanted to believe Jeremy felt disappointed, but there was no doubt about the shock or disapproval on his face. Something else too. Maybe self-deprecation? Bo wanted to leap from the table, rush to Jeremy, and find out every detail of what he was feeling. He wanted to explain, apologize, tell him—what? Tell him something that would take some of the hurt from his wide blue eyes.

Sage said, "You poor thing. You must be exhausted."

"Oh no. I'm sorry. Just rehashing the events of the night."

"I had no idea when you told me about the festival that it would be anything nearly so elaborate. Honestly, it was fantastic. I think people will be talking about it for years to come, or until the next one, whichever comes first."

"Your boss didn't seem too happy." *See, he was doing his snooping job.*

She smiled and sighed at the same time. "I won't lie. He believes he should have won first place in both categories, but I guess all vintners believe in their wines."

"No. If I'd taken first place in whites, I'd have thought either the judges were amateurs or it wasn't a serious contest. My whites are good, but not as good as Jeremy's, just as the judging reflected. And neither are Ernest's."

She nodded. "Interesting."

"Ernest is a good winemaker."

"I'm waiting for the 'but.'"

Bo shrugged. "But he's too derivative. Someone like Jeremy takes big risks that sometimes don't work but often result in genuine innovation. If a vintner's wines taste too much like some other producer, good judges can tell."

"How do they know which is the original?" She looked genuinely interested.

"It takes skill, but generally the original will have nuances and notes that the copy can't equal."

"Copy?" Her eyes widened.

"The one that came second, shall we say?" He sipped the soft white he'd had with his fish.

"You're not the first to say Ernest isn't original enough. I must confess a few people said that to me at the party."

"Ernest seems to have the means to support his business, which not all of us can say. He can afford to offer product at prices less-well-off vintners can't match."

She frowned. *Damn, I've been shooting off my mouth.* She said, "You mean losing money on every transaction and making it up in volume?"

He chuckled and tried to make it sound genuine.

"But you said yourself, he's a good vintner. He couldn't have won two second-place ribbons if he wasn't."

"Exactly true." Of course, the person winning the ribbons could likely have been his reverse engineer, but Bo wouldn't say that. "So you mentioned that he wanted to read every comma of your news release."

"Yes. I'm doing two. One specifically for Ottersen Wines. Then I told Ernest that I had agreed to do a news release as a part of Ottersen's contribution to the festival."

"What'd he think of that idea?"

"Oh, he liked it. I brought the release for your approval, by the way. I hate to make you work any more tonight, but I'd like to get it to the wire service before midnight."

"Sure. I'll take a look."

She fished her phone from her purse and handed it to Bo. He read over the Word document. "This is great, and it really emphasizes the win from High Top."

She smiled. "I got the feeling that his being new to the area and new to winemaking made his win extra special. He also seemed so genuinely shocked, it was really cute."

"Do you need me to okay this? Because I like it."

"Sure. Do you want to call Jeremy and read it to him?"

He swallowed. Jeremy likely wouldn't answer. "No. Let's surprise him. He can use some good news."

"I'd think his trophy would be very good news."

"Some more good news, then."

She grinned. "I think a few people were surprised to see us together."

"Uh, yes." Damn, that was an understatement. "Did Ottersen notice?"

She wrinkled her nose. "Not exactly. He was so distracted by the contest, I don't think he paid much attention to anything else."

"Will he be upset—in light of the awards?"

She shrugged. "He's not that petty. He loves his wines and thinks they're the best, but I'm sure he respects the winners."

Bo wasn't that sure, but he dropped the subject.

Sage said, "I think your sisters were happy to see me there."

Bo nodded. "Yes. I'm sure they'll tell my mother that her matchmaking was a huge success." Which was both a good and bad thing. His mama would be all over him for the next step in their relationship.

She made a cute face. "Glad to be of assistance. I must confess you're such a doll, I can't help but wish it was all more than a date of convenience." As he opened his mouth, she held up a hand. "No worries. I'm not coming on to you. Exactly." She laughed and he did too, though his was a little forced.

As they finished their meal, Bo tried not to look like his brain was elsewhere. He even asked if she wanted dessert but was really happy when she didn't. He just wanted to talk to Jeremy.

Sage said, "I hate to cut our dinner short, but I need to send this release to the wire service so it can go out in the morning."

"Oh sure, I understand."

She grinned. "You're welcome to come watch me if you want." That was definitely fishing.

"I think I'll quit early. It's been a long day." He slid out of their booth and stood for her to walk out first.

He helped her on with her coat as she said, "But what a great one. You guys really did do an amazing job. You should be proud."

"Thank you. High praise."

They stepped out into the parking lot. They'd driven their own cars, so all he had to do was escape and he just might be able to track down Jeremy. She gave him a big hug and a kiss on the cheek.

He smiled through his blush. "Thank you again for the news release. When you suggested it, we had no idea it would benefit us personally. So our thanks as well."

She grinned. "My pleasure."

He stepped back toward his car. "So I'll talk to you soon. Thank Ernest again for his wine and contributing your services."

"Oh yeah. I'll remind him how great I am." She laughed and got in her car.

The second she drove away, he hopped in his Prius and, to the extent that a Prius could tear, he tore out of the parking lot. Despite the fact that he and Jeremy had worked on the party for three weeks, Bo still didn't know where Jeremy lived. *Damn.* That was so dumb. He pressed the pedal to the metal on the extremely long shot that Jeremy might have gone back to Hill Top after he ran out of the party.

I have to tell him that Sage and I are just friends, but what else? Do I want to tell him that Sage and I are just friends because I'm gay? He wiped his finger over his eyes. *Right, and what do I say next? I want to have sex with you.* That sounded so good his cock gave a hop.

And after that, I'll say please don't tell anyone, and when we're in public, please pretend to be my pal and put up with me going out with Sage to establish a cover.

Shit and grits!

Bo turned onto the side road that led to Hill Top Winery and began the gradual climb that the name of the winery described. When he got to the left turn into the parking lot of the medium-sized tasting room, lights shone in the windows. Could be somebody else. Could be Jeremy.

Bo kept the car far back in the big open space and stared at the soft, inviting warmth of the illumination. *What am I going to say?*

Being in the closet was crap. More than any convenient profanity, it was painful, life-denying, and cowardly. Why did he do it? The fact was, he loved his family, but they drove him mad. The idea of giving them another instrument with which to torture him made him sick. And it wasn't like his mama would be indulgent or understanding. She'd never let up, and she'd make sure his sisters didn't either. He dropped his head on the steering wheel.

Maybe I'm a coward. When his father died, it never crossed his mind that he didn't bear responsibility for his family's well-being. He'd even gone slightly round the bend one time and sought out a shrink who told him he had a choice. That he needed to recognize his choices—and he did. He chose to be the man he was raised to be.

He'd only been seven when his father had taken him into his study, just the two of them. He'd given Bo a small glass of watered wine, which Bo kind of thought tasted awful, but the honor was so great, he drank it all.

"Bo, I notice that you spend a lot of time with your sisters and their friends."

He smiled. "They're fun. They do fun things."

"Really? Playing with Barbie dolls? Please, Be-auregard." He shook his head, and Bo felt so small. "That's okay for a child—well, maybe for a very small child—but you're growing into a man. Men do not spend frivolous time with women. It's your job to take care of your sisters and your mother, just as that's my job. Women are precious gifts that must be cherished and cared for. Not played with."

Bo nodded seriously, though he had no idea what his father meant.

"I'd rather see you spending your free time playing sports. You're good at them. Your teachers tell me so."

He nodded even harder. He'd never really loved sports. The boys took them so seriously, it was no fun.

"I'd be very proud of you if you were to play foot-ball or baseball."

"You would?"

"Yes. Which do you like best?"

He shrugged. In truth, he was good at both, and the coaches had tried to get him to join the teams. "Which one do you like best, sir?"

His father leaned back and sipped his wine, so Bo did the same. His father said, "Well, I'm a Southerner, son, so football's my sport. But you choose what you want."

"Yes, sir." Two days later Bo was on the football team, and his career as a leader was well-established, all the way to his distinguishing himself as quarterback of his college team. Every personal talk he'd had with his father drilled into him the unparalleled importance of caring for the Marchand family and the Marchand name. The fact that his father left them almost worse than penniless didn't seem like the greatest care. For-tunately, Bo had received an inheritance from his grandparents when he moved to California that allowed him to start Marchand Wines. When his father dropped dead, that was all they had.

But his father's teaching stuck. Tossing off his family on the shoulders of someone else or, God forbid, expecting them to care for themselves was inconceivable. His only rebellion had been insisting that he bear his burdens his way, doing his own work, and in California, not Georgia. He'd paid the price every day with his mother's long-suffering censure.

Putting the car in gear, he rolled closer to the tasting room. He didn't know how much more he could take of life as it was. He was horny, and most of all, he was lonely. He detested sneaking, hiding, and lying. As a result he simply stayed away from all personal and romantic contact, men and women.

Fuck that! He opened the car door, jumped out, and slammed it behind him. Determinedly he strode across the lot, up the stairs of the porch, and tried the door. *Locked.* He rapped—hard.

Nothing.

Maybe the lights were just Christian and he was scared to answer the door.

He knocked again.

No answer.

Okay. What was that saying? *If a door didn't open, it wasn't your door.* Right. That's what he really needed. Inspirational sayings.

He turned and walked off the porch.

CHAPTER ELEVEN

"WERE YOU looking for me?" The voice snapped like a whip.

Bo hadn't heard the door open, but now the light shone down the porch and all over Bo. He turned. *Oh holy birds and sweet little fishes, what a shine.*

Jeremy stood in the entrance wearing jeans so low-slung it was a miracle of nature in defiance of gravity that they remained poised on his hip bones. His white, wine-stained T-shirt clung to the body that had no reason to be so staggeringly fit. The cotton revealed all six of his packs, and dear God, his magic hair hung on his shoulders like the glow from inside had pooled there. All that glory stopped at his face, which was darkened by a dangerous scowl. Bo swallowed. "Uh, hi."

Jeremy's expression didn't lighten. "Why aren't you on your date?"

The fact that Jeremy was so pissed about him seeing Sage gave Bo a minute's thrill.

"First, it wasn't really a date. We're just friends, and she agreed to make it look like a date to get my mother off my back and allow Sage to have an eligible escort to high-profile events she'd like to attend for her job. Second, she had to get back to her office to post a press release on the event. She volunteered to do one for us. That's the whole story." Bo wrapped his arms around himself because he'd left his damned jacket in the car.

Jeremy sneered, which he carried off with more venom than Bo would have guessed. "Right. You just happened to choose the one damned female associated with the person who so obviously hates me and wants to destroy me. You can't possibly be so naïve as to believe that any sweet nothings you whisper in her ear aren't going to travel by high speed back to Ottersen giving the asshole even more ammunition against me!" His voice rose and the hair on Bo's arms rose too. *Damn, he's so mad. I never thought he'd take it this way.*

Bo held up a hand. "Hold on, dammit. I'm not naïve and I'd never give Sage any piece of information to use against us. In fact, one of the reasons I agreed to be her pretend date was the opposite. To see if she'd drop something about Ottersen that could be useful to us. I happen to believe she's telling the truth about her motives, but even if she isn't, I'm careful what I say." He hugged himself tighter. "I can't believe you'd think I was colluding with Ottersen, for God's sake."

Jeremy made a snorting sound. "Ottersen has to be finding out this shit about me somehow."

Bo tried not to yell. "Right, and it makes perfect sense that I'd collude with Sage in front of you and all the other vintners. For crap's sake, Jeremy." The pressure on Bo's chest pressed against his heart and made him exhale long and slow. "Sorry you feel that way." He turned and walked toward his car in the deafening silence. *How exactly did everything get so screwed?*

One step, two, three—

"So she's just a friend?" Jeremy's voice was so soft Bo almost didn't hear it over the slamming of his pulse.

He paused but didn't turn. "Yes."

"And you're freezing."

"Also true."

Silence, then Jeremy said, "Come on in—if you still want to."

Bo turned and watched Jeremy disappear through the open door. *Do I still want to? Hellfire, yes.*

Resolutely, Bo walked into the tasting room, lit, as Jeremy seemed to like it, with only the lights over the tasting bar. Jeremy walked behind the bar and leaned on it. He stared down at his ripped forearms. "I'm crazy."

Bo barked a laugh. "Tell me something I don't know, darlin'."

"I'm also sorry." He looked up, his face flat and lined with some mixture of pain and embarrassment. "Ottersen's attacks feel so personal, and I take them personally. It's stupid and I'm ashamed of doubting you for even a minute. You've never given me any reason to feel that way." He ran a hand through his hair, pulling it off his face, then dropped it. "Seeing you with Sage... really set me off. I'm honestly sorry."

Bo nodded slowly, still standing near the door. "I get it. It has to feel like an attack, what he's doing. I was so intrigued by the combination of getting my mother off my back and snooping into Ottersen's business, I didn't really think about how it would look to you. So I'm sorry too."

Jeremy glanced up. "So there's going to be a press release?"

"Yes. I approved it, and it's going to release tomorrow morning."

"How did it sound?"

"Flattering." Bo flashed his dimples.

"That could be good if anybody picks it up."

"I agree."

"Red or white?"

Bo let his smile break free. "I think I need some award-winning white." He walked slowly toward the bar.

Jeremy poured two glasses of chardonnay. He held out his glass. "To lots of award winning."

"And may the face of good news and the back of every bad news be toward us."

Jeremy snorted. "So why does your mother get on you so much that Sage has to pretend to date you?"

One word. Two, actually. All he had to say was "I'm gay." He drew in a breath. "Uh, because I just can't find somebody I like enough to want to keep around. My mama thinks I should be spending so much time wooing women that there wouldn't be a minute left to make wine."

"You should just give it up and date men." Jeremy laughed, and Bo tried to do likewise.

"You're not the first to say it."

"I'm not?" He looked genuinely surprised.

"You think you're the only gay man I know?" He stared in his glass.

"No. You're hosting a gay wedding, but I didn't know you have gay men lining up to proposition you."

"Well, it's not exactly a line." He turned up his lips.

Jeremy laughed and said, "Here's to men with good taste and to doing what we want—with a clear conscience."

Bo clinked glasses. He didn't know exactly what Jeremy meant by that, but he could get behind that idea.

Jeremy looked at his glass, then up at Bo. "Sorry I got so pissed. Stupid, really. I'd built up in my mind that it would be fun to celebrate winning with you." He shrugged. "You know, since we both won. I guess I was shocked she worked for Ottersen. I couldn't figure out what the hell you'd be doing with someone who's on his side."

"She's definitely pro-Ottersen, but she's also kind of naïve. I keep thinking she might let something slip." He shrugged. "My mother and sisters met her at a Junior League meeting. They didn't remember who she worked for, and they don't know about Ottersen anyway."

"Really? Your family doesn't know about the stress you're under?"

My family doesn't know much. "No. If Ottersen becomes a serious drain on my business, I may have to tell them. As it is, I don't like to worry them."

"But that doesn't give you any support." A crease popped out in the perfection of his forehead." Shouldn't they be helping you in the business?"

"God forbid. I get enough of them at home." He smiled but was damned serious. "My father had a business that he and my mother built together. Then it got successful, and my mother sat back and became a Southern lady of leisure. That meant she didn't know when the business started to fail, and my father never told her." Bo sighed softly. "When my father died, she expected me to give up my silly California fantasy and come back to Georgia and take over their big, thriving business. I was stunned to learn we could barely get out of it with our shirt. I tried to tell my mother without denigrating my father's memory. I think she never truly believed me." He slowly turned his glass on the counter.

"I'm really sorry. You must have been just a kid when you had to take on a family."

Bo nodded. The sweet, spicy scent of Jeremy circled his head and filled it like the smoke of a burning drug.

Jeremy grinned and poured another inch of wine into their glasses. "So on happier topics, what time do you think our press release will appear?"

Bo swallowed. "Not sure. Sage said in the morning. If it's morning Eastern time, it will be really early here."

"Great. I'll look for it as soon as I wake up."

Maybe that was a hint. "You must be very tired."

Jeremy glanced up with big liquid eyes. "Aren't you? You worked even harder than I did." Did he look hopeful?

"Sure. Yes, I'm tired too. I just—"

"Just?"

"I like your company. You energize me." He didn't meet Jeremy's eyes.

Stillness, then Jeremy said, "I'm glad." He clasped a warm hand on Bo's arm. *Whoa. No breath.* That feeling like he had two brains crept over Bo as it always did when he was with Jeremy. One half screamed *Reach out and kiss him*; the other side froze him like so many icicles.

He desperately wanted the warmth of that hand to melt the ice, but before he could move, Jeremy pulled back with a distant smile. "So I guess I better let you go get some sleep." Shit, Jeremy's posture screamed *You had your chance and you blew it.* All Bo wanted was to grab his hand and pull Jeremy back—into his arms, then into his bed—but he didn't move. Grab that hand, and everything changed. One kiss, and his relationship with his family and every person he knew would shift. Even his business. With things so uncertain, did he dare add one more layer of chaos?

With a shrug Jeremy walked around the bar, across the room, and to the door, not even looking back.

Well hell. I've just been dismissed. Bo took a deep swallow of his great chardonnay and followed Jeremy. At the door Jeremy turned, smiled, though it still looked tight, and said, "We'll talk tomorrow."

"Yes. We need to go see Llewellyn and Blaise, uh, assuming you want to come with me, of course."

"Hey, this is more my fight than yours. I need to hear."

"It's both our fights. Everyone's, really. You and I also need to plan the trip up to Napa. I've already contacted some people I know up there and floated the idea of us coming to see them. So far, so good."

"That's great." He still seemed subdued.

"So we'll talk tomorrow." Bo tried to smile.

Jeremy just nodded and opened the door.

Oh man, I don't want to leave him like this—

But he did.

JEREMY WATCHED Bo walk down the steps of the tasting room. *I should do something. Stop him. But what do I say?*

Slowly he closed the door. About the only good stuff in his life at that moment came from Bo. *Quit pushing for more. More important, quit pushing him away.*

He walked back to the bar and washed the glasses automatically. *The poor guy's got enough on his plate. But he sure keeps sending mixed signals. Would a straight guy really say, "I like your company. You energize me"? Fuck, of course, if the straight guy was Bo. He was so formal, he probably says that to all the guys—and girls.*

Keep trying to get him in bed and I'm going to screw the pooch. He barked a laugh at his own appropriate turn of phrase. That was one pooch he'd seriously like to screw.

The ring of the phone from inside the drawer beside him made him jump. Damn! He had to quit putting it off, but hell if he wanted to answer.

Slowly he opened the drawer, mostly hoping it would stop. *No such luck.*

"Hello."

"*Nipote.* Hello." His grandfather's rough voice vibrated the burner phone.

"How are you, sir?"

"Who the fuck cares? I want to know where you are."

"Sorry, sir, can't do that."

"He'll find you, and when he does, I have to know how to help you."

"No, sir. I can't put you in the position of having to choose between us."

"Bullshit! You just don't trust me."

Not altogether untrue, so he didn't deny it. He and his grandfather had a truthful relationship—up to a point. Jeremy would never have known all his father had planned for him if he hadn't asked his grandfather directly. "Did you want something else?"

The old man sighed. "Are you okay, at least?"

"I'm fine. Good, even."

"I'm glad to hear it."

The question pushed against his lips, and he let it out. "Do you have reason to believe he's getting close?"

"Not specifically, but he has…." His voice drifted off.

"What?"

"Nothing, but don't think for a minute that he's given up. And you know what kinds of resources he has."

"Yeah. Thanks for calling."

"Wait. You know I'm not without resources of my own, *nipote*. Come home, and I'll protect you."

"I can't do that, sir. It would mean giving up my life and becoming a full-time fugitive."

"Fuck! What are you now?"

"That I can't say." He let out his breath from a very tense chest. "Thank you for caring." He hung up and slowly slid to his butt on the floor behind the bar.

Here he was fighting for a business that could be gone in an instant—even with no help from Ottersen. He dropped his head to his knees.

THE RINGING of his phone cut into Bo's erotic dreams. His heart leaped. What the hell? He opened his eyes. Still barely a hint of light.

Take a breath. It's not Mama. No one would be ringing my phone about the family. They'd be banging on the door.

The winery!

He rolled over and felt for his phone on the nightstand. "Hello?"

"God damn it, why the hell didn't you tell me that the press release effectively accused me of cheating to win? How could you let that go out? Why didn't you do something? Damn, Bo, I believed you when you said

Sage wasn't my enemy. Way more important, you said you weren't against me."

"Stop! Jeremy, I don't know what you're talking about."

"You approved the goddamned news release. You told me so. Didn't you get the implications between the lines? Bo, you can't be this fucking stupid."

He flipped onto the edge of the bed, feet on the floor, and turned on the light. The clock read 5:30 a.m. "Quit this. The press release I approved was nothing but complimentary, especially to you. I'd never let something bad be said about you. I need to get up and search for the release. I'll call you back."

Jeremy hung up before Bo could.

He staggered out of bed, grabbed his robe, pulled it on over his sleep pants, and walked barefoot to his office. Inside, he snapped on the lights and hurried to his laptop. Flipping up the lid, he pulled up the search engine and typed in "Paso Robles Wineries" and "Dionysian Festival."

There it was. *Holy hound dog shit.*

The release read much like what he'd approved until he got to, *The fact that Jeremy Aames of Hill Top Wines, a newcomer to central coast winemaking and an organizer of the event, won first place in the white wine category was a cause of some controversy at the event and prompted some grumblings, despite the assurances of the judges that there had been no preference given to the organizers.*

Holy shit. He flopped back into the chair. *She changed it. Oh sweet heart of Jesus, poor Jeremy.* Weirdly, she hadn't mentioned Bo, even though his win could have been considered as much of a fix as Jeremy's.

He stood and heard his cell ringing across the hall in his bedroom. Jeremy! He ran, grabbed the phone where he'd left it on his bed, and clicked on. "Jeremy?"

"Bo, this is Sage."

He froze.

"Please listen to me. I didn't do that. Someone changed the press release after I called it in. I don't know how or who."

"Like hell you don't! Your goddamn boss changed that release, and you know it."

"He swears he didn't. Please, Bo, why would he?"

"Because he's trying to put Jeremy Aames out of business, along with a lot of other vintners. I've got no clue why. Hill Top isn't big enough to hurt him, but he's doing it anyway."

"Bo, honestly, I don't think that's true."

"Fuck, how could you do this? One good thing happens to the man, and you help your boss make it just another way to destroy him."

"I didn't—"

"Maybe not on purpose. I've got to go. I need to see my friend." He clicked off, threw on some clothes, and ran down the hall toward the garage.

His mother's bedroom door opened. "Bo, what on earth is happening?"

"A friend of mine is in trouble. I need to be with him."

"When will you be back?"

"No idea." By the time he got those words out, he called them from the end of the hall, then ran to the garage, started the Prius, and began backing. Damnation, no address.

He hit Send on his phone. It rang and rang. Finally voicemail picked up. Bo yelled, "Jeremy, dammit, pick up this minute!"

To his total shock, a voice said, "What?"

"Give me your address—now!"

"Why? You going to send me a nice potted plant?"

"Just give it to me."

Jeremy recited an address in a very upset voice.

"Thanks." Bo spoke the address into his phone and followed the directions to a remote street leading to a gravel road in the hills behind the wineries. Damn, the man did not want to be found.

CHAPTER TWELVE

BO PULLED up in front of a cabinish house made of wood, two stories on one side and a peaked single story on the other. As he crawled out of the car, the door opened. Jeremy stood there in his jeans and nothing else, his long hair matted like he'd been pulling at it, his eyes red.

Damn. Bo slammed the door, ran up Jeremy's porch steps, and didn't even think before he gathered Jeremy's lean body in his arms and held him tight, rocking. "I'm so sorry. I don't know how this happened. I swear, I saw every word, and it was different."

Jeremy's body shook. "W-why does he hate me so-so much? Why is he doing this?"

"I wish I knew." Still holding tight, he walked Jeremy into the house, kicked the door closed, and half carried him through a small entry into a sparsely furnished living room. There was a couch, and Bo aimed for it and sat with Jeremy half pulled onto his lap. On their own, Bo's lips grazed Jeremy's forehead as he rocked. Anything to make Jeremy stop trembling.

After a minute Jeremy calmed a little, and Bo loosened his grip of iron, but not by much.

Bo said, "Sage called me a minute after I talked to you. She swears she didn't do it, though she says she doesn't know who did or how."

Jeremy stiffened. "Do you believe her?"

"No." He exhaled. "Maybe a little. She says she sent the release exactly the way I saw it to the wire service last night. You know what time I got to your place. It was still way before midnight, which was her deadline. So if she sent it after she got home or to the office, there was still time for someone else to call and change it."

"Ottersen."

"Of course. And as her boss, he'd have had the authority to edit the release."

"God damn him to hell. I actually thought for a little while that something good had happened to me." His chest heaved on a gasp.

Heat filled every cell, and Bo heard rushing in his ears. They'd hurt Jeremy. Funny, smart, adorable Jeremy. He'd been bouncing back from Ottersen's blows for months, but this.... He'd been so excited and amazed at the win. Now it was worse than if he hadn't won anything. "Oh, darlin'." Bo's lips traveled from Jeremy's hairline to his cheekbone. When his lips touched the corner of Jeremy's mouth, for an instant Jeremy froze; then he turned in Bo's arms and planted those soft-as-eiderdown lips right on top of Bo's.

Oh my God. Oh my God. Oh my God. It wasn't that Bo had never been kissed. He'd been kissed the first time in middle school by a boy who headed the junior dressage team. He'd accosted Bo, who was also on the team, in the stables, and with the warm, sweet smell of horses all around them, he'd pushed Bo against the wall and kissed him senseless, his hard erection pressing against Bo's. Way too confused and turned-on to fight, Bo had tried to learn the rules before he even knew the name of the game and kissed back. Then the boy, Izzy, had whispered, "I figured you were a fag. Don't tell anybody, or I'll say you came on to me, and everyone will believe it. I'll wreck this school for you, got it?"

He got it.

Now, some piece of Bo's brain still screamed *What are you doing, idiot?* but his body knew the answer far too well. His lips parted, his cock unfolded like a flower finally reaching sunshine, and he wrapped Jeremy so tight there was no light between them.

Sweet Jesus, listen to those noises. Jeremy moaned and whimpered, and Bo's deeper grunts joined in the chorus. Bo's tongue shifted, caressing Jeremy's and battling him for who got to explore the deepest.

Suddenly Jeremy pulled back, still gasping but also frowning. Not a good look at this particular moment. "You're gay." The crease between his eyebrows got deeper. "Either you're gay, or I'm irresistible and gay-for-you is real."

"That's true." He could barely catch his breath. "That you're irresistible, I mean."

That frown was becoming unhappily familiar. "Why didn't you just tell me? We could have saved a lot of jerking off."

"All the reasons you know. My family, mostly. My business, some. With everything going on, I thought it would be better not to start something." Bo raised his shoulders and let them drop. "You could decide you've had enough of this mess and just leave. I'd lose you."

"And you weren't willing to take a chance?"

"If it meant giving up my life as I know it and losing you? It's a testament to how much I care about you that I've been thinking about telling you every time I've seen you."

"Jesus, that's why I've been picking up such mixed messages."

"Yes. Quite honestly, I also didn't want you to think that my help was contingent on you being my, uh, lover. Like I'd been buttering you up to get in your pants."

Jeremy crossed his arms across his chest. "Have you?"

Bo wiped a hand across his face. "I like you and I'm attracted to you. I can't separate them. But I do know I believe you're getting a rotten deal from Ottersen, and I think you deserve help—from me and anyone else who chooses to give it. Those are my motives."

Jeremy slid the crossed arms up until they were folded on top of his head. "It's not like I'd prefer that you weren't gay and didn't want me. Damn, I've been on the verge of jumping you since the day we met. But I don't want you getting mixed up in a hopeless cause." He sighed. "We can have sex, and you sure don't need to be my knight in shining armor to do it."

"What if I want to be?"

Jeremy buried his head against Bo's shoulder. "Give it up, Bo. I think he's won, or he's well on his way to winning."

Bo gripped Jeremy's upper arms and gazed into his face. "Hell no. Fuck no. If I have to write a message in the sky, people are going to know that the news release was a lie engineered by an enemy. I can't directly accuse Ottersen unless I can prove it, but everyone we know will understand."

Jeremy shook his head, the matted golden hair still waving around his face. "Why are you so stubborn?"

Bo sighed softly, pressing his lips to Jeremy's hair. "Because I care about you and I know you didn't cheat. I can't let you go through this mess all alone."

Jeremy snuggled his head further under Bo's chin and snuffled. Bo rocked him gently until his breathing slowed a little.

He tried mightily to just give comfort and not feel the hard heat of Jeremy's lean body, but the warmth seemed to be turning to fire. Jeremy's slow breath picked up, matching Bo's heart. His cock stretched in his pants, and he wriggled a little to keep the erection away from Jeremy's thigh.

"Bo?" Jeremy's whisper tickled Bo's neck.

"Hmmm?"

"Your messages don't seem to be mixed anymore."

"Feel free to ignore them."

"Not a chance." Jeremy raised his head and in one smooth move, captured Bo's mouth.

Oh yes, nutrition for a starving man.

Enthusiastically, Bo's tongue plundered hidden depths, and Jeremy seemed to have come to the end of his disbelief. He wrapped himself around Bo in a move worthy of a monkey, even making monkey noises.

When their lips finally parted, Jeremy whispered, "Top or bottom?"

Whoa. That inspired heart palpitations. "I better top. It's been so long since I bottomed, it'd take a year to get me loose enough to penetrate."

"Truthfully, I'm not much better."

That made Bo ridiculously happy.

"We're pretty sorry excuses for hot dates." Jeremy pressed his lips against Bo's.

Bo nibbled Jeremy's bottom lip while his own bottom throbbed. "I seem to recall from somewhere in the past that we can have sex without, uh, having sex."

"Oh yeah." He grabbed Bo's hand. "Follow my every move." He pulled Bo after him as he rushed down the hall, arriving at—*angels surely sang*—a bedroom!

Jeremy turned and backed toward the bed, holding both Bo's hands in his. His bare chest gleamed in the soft bedroom light, enhanced by the golden mane falling over his shoulders. Even better, the front of his jeans stood out like he was smuggling chinchillas.

Jeremy's jeans pulled tight across the escaping beast as he sat on the bed, then scooted back, still pulling Bo toward him. For a second, Bo wasn't sure what to do, but Jeremy kept pulling until Bo's only choice was to fall on top of him.

Then he needed no instruction. He pressed his mouth into Jeremy's while he wriggled until most of their parts fit together. While Jeremy was tall, Bo was taller, so getting cock to cock and still kissing was a challenge.

While Bo was readjusting his mouth, Jeremy said, "Too many clothes."

He ardently agreed but hated to give up those delicious lips, so he tried to keep kissing as he writhed his way out of his jeans. He managed to get them somewhere below his hips using one hand, but then he was stuck. Besides, he was still wearing his sneakers, so eventually he had to quit kissing.

Jeremy pushed his chest. "Up."

Bo obeyed, rising with his knees on either side of Jeremy's legs, though hindered by the stretch of his partly removed pants.

Jeremy moved back, sat up, and shook his head. "This isn't working. Stand up and remove those jeans, cowboy."

Bo pushed backward and slid his legs off the bed, managed to stand, then pulled up his jeans again so he could get his shoes off. After the shoes he stripped off his shirt and then slid his thumbs into both his jeans and his boxer briefs and started to pull. *Wait.* He looked up at Jeremy, who gazed at Bo with wide, avid eyes. *Hmm. Let's make this a bit more fun.*

He turned his back.

"Hey, wait a minute. I want to see."

"Oh you will, darlin'. Don't you worry." He pulled the pants and briefs down on one side, giving Jeremy a clear view of one buttock, and a pretty firm one at that.

"Oh yeah." Jeremy licked his lips, and Bo wanted to offer spots he could put that tongue, but all in good time.

He performed the same gradual reveal on the other cheek, then turned slowly. As Bo had hoped, Jeremy glued his attention to the target.

Bo slid his waistband down another inch. Jeremy grinned. This was fun. Only problem was, he was trying to tantalize Jeremy, but he was seducing himself too. His erection was so hard, it hurt.

With a smile back, he slid the elastic over one very anxious cockhead.

Jeremy licked his lips. "Hi, there. Aren't we a grown-up boy?"

Bo felt the blush creeping up his cheeks. Yes, he knew he was well-endowed, but he never much thought about it. Not since college, when his dick had gotten him a little attention, both positive and negative. Some guys just didn't want it near their butts, not that he'd been very romantically active. He'd attended a college close to home, and there had been too much chance of talk. He yanked his pants and briefs down and let the beast free. "Too much?"

"Whoa. Just enough." Jeremy smiled.

All attempts at a career as a male stripper gone, Bo stepped out of the jeans, kicked them aside, and dragged his shirt over his head.

Jeremy's grin got bigger. "Look at all that loveliness. I didn't imagine you'd be quite so fit."

Bo shrugged. "I'm a farmer. I work hard. Hey, I'm a wimp compared to you."

Jeremy looked oddly uncomfortable for a second; then the grin snapped back. "Not in the family jewels department. There you win by a mile." He pulled open the fly of his jeans and showed off their enthusiastic resident.

"More like an inch, I'd say."

"Bring that farmer's helper over here and let's do some milking." His blue eyes glinted as he slid off his jeans and lay gloriously naked, dressed only in silken hair.

Wow. Just wow. That sounded so ridiculously good, Bo could have come just from the thought. He got to lie down next to that breathing wet dream and do—something wonderful. It boggled his mind.

Still, he felt almost shy. Carefully he sat on the edge of the bed, then stretched himself out until he was lying next to Jeremy, not touching. "I barely believe I get to do this."

Jeremy scooted closer until just the tips of their dicks touched, like a little kiss. "Believe it."

Suddenly Bo's brain—the one in his head—took over. He pressed his fingertips against Jeremy's rock-hard chest. "I-I wish I could say that I'll take care of you and never let anyone hurt you again. I wish I could be—someone else, who has no qualms about—being who he is."

Jeremy touched his lips. "It's okay. I understand. I just want this so much that I'll settle for what I can get. I can't promise I'll feel that way forever, or even tomorrow, but I do now. If that's okay, I'm going to kiss you."

Was it okay? They were both desperate for sex. How would they feel tomorrow? The simple answer was he didn't care. He wanted this too, desperately, in body and soul. "Yes."

Jeremy closed the inches between them, and his warm lips and seeking tongue drove the last vestige of doubt from Bo's brain. Soft, inquisitive exploring turned to hot flaming passion in seconds, and Jeremy wrapped his arms around Bo and drew him close but didn't get on top—or pull Bo on top.

In seconds Bo knew why—as the gasp pulled his lips away from Jeremy's. Jeremy's strong hand wrapped around his own cock and then around Bo's. Well, almost around Bo's. Jeremy whispered, "When I conceived this move, I didn't quite plan on the girth of Donkey Kong down there." He smiled. "Give me your hand."

Of course, Bo's big hands went along with the size of his penis, so he was able to wrap almost around Jeremy's fist, gripping both cocks. Jeremy squeezed. Bo moaned and did likewise.

"You like?"

Nodding was all Bo could manage since his breath was being used for gasping. *Holy angels of mercy, that feels good.*

"Show me your pumping skills, Farmer Bo. And look at me while you do it."

Bo fluttered his lashes open to find Jeremy's intense blue eyes inches away, gazing into his very heart. Jeremy gripped tighter, and Bo did too. Together they began a slow pumping. "Oh God, oh God."

"Good?"

"Beyond." His eyes wanted to close.

"Keep staring at me. I want to see you go crazy." He intensified the jerking motion until Bo's hips were snapping in time to the rhythm.

"You'll make me blush."

"Good. I want it all. Your blushes and your moans and whimpers and screams."

"Oh. Oh God, you're going to get them." Bo's head snapped back, and Jeremy slicked his tongue up Bo's throat from Adam's apple to chin. Bo giggled.

"Don't look away."

"O-okay." It was intense staring into those eyes, but the heat built until he could barely see anyway. Their hands worked together. Jeremy varied the rhythm for a while, stroking long and slow and then jerking quickly. But neither of them had the staying power to take that teasing for long. Their dicks leaked profusely, and they panted like dogs in heat.

Finally, eyes glazing over, Jeremy gave up and just started pumping like a son of a bitch.

"Holy shit! Oh God, Jeremy, I won't last. Too much. Too much!"

"Just the right amount, darlin'." Emulating Bo's drawl, Jeremy grinned until his mouth flew open. "Oh, oh God. Shit. I'm—oh man—" His head dropped back, and a wail poured from his throat while the heat of his cum squished around his fingers, filling Bo's hand.

But Jeremy didn't stop jerking. He let his own cock go and used the sticky slick of the cum to pump Bo like he expected oil. "Come. Now. Come for me."

He didn't have to ask twice. *Holy streams of heaven, can a person live without the top of his head?* "Ah, ah, ah!" He didn't just come, his cock blasted off into the lower atmosphere, taking his eyesight and all the nerves in Bo's body with it. He couldn't stop trembling as more juice than he knew he had shot from him in spurt after spurt of ecstasy. "Sweet mother of heavenly mercy, is that even legal?" All the straining muscles in Bo's body let go at once, and he dissolved into noodle soup.

"Not in some parts of the world."

"The last time I produced an orgasm like that, I think I was fourteen."

Jeremy chuckled. "Sex keeps you young."

"Sex with you sure does."

Of course, worrying about what happened next would put the age back on.

CHAPTER THIRTEEN

JEREMY OPENED his eyes, smiled, stretched his arms, and felt the smile fade. *No Bo.* No, he hadn't sneaked out like some ninja. They'd done another round of creative hand jobs and, after they'd both contributed their second stream of cum to Jeremy's hand and sheets, Bo explained that he should go home since he didn't want to raise too many questions about his whereabouts, plus he wanted to get to work on dispelling the lies in the news release.

Jeremy rolled over and inhaled. The scent of Bo, all musky and fresh, filled the whole bed. *I could just stay here inhaling all day.* He'd tried to get some sleep after Bo left, but no go. Hell, it was midmorning by then.

His phone rang, and he grabbed it from the bedside table. Bo? He was actually disappointed it was Christian. "Hi."

"Oh my God, Jeremy, what the hell did that Sage woman do to us? To you? Everyone who didn't attend the event will think you cheated to win. Shit, I could cry. I was wanting to send out an email blast to all our customers bragging about how great we are." He drew a breath and actually sounded like he was crying.

"Unfortunately, I don't know. She swears she didn't do it. Of course, she works for Ottersen, so who the fuck can trust a word she says?"

"This is just awful!" It was a wail.

Jeremy took a breath. "Tell you what. I'll call Genna Greenstein and ask her for a quote to go in our email on the validity and excellence of the contest. At least that should count for something."

"Okay. Do it quick." Christian hung up.

Talk about mood killers. He pushed himself up, swung his legs out of bed, and ran a hand through the mane. Bo was addictive, but just how much was Jeremy willing to put up with? A grown man who cowered in front of his own mother? *Damn, as if I can talk. My whole life is about escaping my family.* Of course, it seemed unlikely that Bo's mama would kill him.

He stood, realized his hand was still crusty from cum, sighed, and walked nude to the bathroom. A half hour later, he'd taken a shower and called Genna, who was all outrage over the release and happily agreed to the quote, which he forwarded to Christian. Then, hair still damp, he piled into his old Toyota and headed for Marchand.

Halfway down the long dirt road to his house— yes, it had been chosen for its hideout characteristics— Jeremy's phone rang. He glanced at the screen. *Do I know that number?* It was local. He clicked it on. "This is Jeremy."

"I knew you damned well cheated." The sneering voice sounded familiar.

"Who the fuck is this?"

"It's Ezra Hamilton, and I didn't think you'd stoop so low in public."

Jeremy hissed breath between his teeth. "First, let me ask you this. Was your win rigged? Did you pay off the judges?"

"Of course not! What do you think I am?"

He wanted to ask what Ezra thought he was, but he already knew. "Well, I didn't pay them off either and neither did Bo."

"I never said Bo cheated."

"Since he and I were together planning the whole damned event, how could I have paid somebody off without him suspecting?"

Silence.

Jeremy pulled the car over at the end of the road. No driving while yelling obscenities. "The fact is, Ezra, the news release went to the wire service without a word about the casual comment that was made as a joke being interpreted as serious. Someone added it after the fact. I'll give you one clue who probably did it. Ottersen was pissed that we won. Probably that you won too. He tried to switch my wine to vinegar before the contest and Genna caught it. He clearly wanted me out of the running." He felt the muscle in his jaw jump. "Sage Zilinsky works for him."

There was a pause, then Ezra said, "You really think he'd do that?"

"Damn, Ezra, you think he burned Lucky's winery. Why the hell would he be conscience-stricken at accusing me of cheating? You know as well as I do, for some reason he's targeting me more than any other winemaker. At least since Lucky."

"I don't see why you won."

"That's your privilege, but the judges disagreed. I called Genna this morning, and she was spitting nails over the release. She gave me a quote about the veracity of the contest to use in communications with my customers. Do you want to accuse Genna of cheating? Because I'll tell her you said so."

"Of course not." He sounded sulky.

"Okay. I know you don't like me, but I don't blame you for believing the press release. The fact is, the press release was tainted by someone. I didn't cheat. I'd appreciate you not continuing to spread the story that I did."

He sighed. "All right. I don't want to help Ottersen. I'll accept your explanation."

Shit, big of him. "Thank you."

Another pause. "Uh, can you tell me how you happened to come up with the Dionysian Festival as a theme for the event?"

"Bo chose it. I think it was just a question of the date. It was close and associated with wine. We wanted a close date. But I'm not altogether sure. Ask him."

"I will." Dead air. "Uh, thanks for explaining."

"I wish it hadn't happened."

"I'm sure. We're all getting impacted by Ottersen."

"I suppose, but he seems to save his dirty tricks for me."

"It does seem that way." He didn't sound terribly sad about that.

Jeremy waited.

Finally Ezra said, "Thank you. Goodbye." The line went dead.

Well, hell. How many more calls will I get from people? At least this was probably the worst one. He pressed his foot to the gas and entered the winding, narrow road that ran through the wine country. When he'd passed most of the wineries, the sign for Marchand came up on the left, and he slowed. Not much traffic, so he crossed and started up the steep drive. Bo had as much claim to the name Hill Top as Jeremy, but Marchand was a classy name, so it worked.

What am I going to find up there? Bo still seemed affectionate and lovey-dovey when he'd snuggled Jeremy before leaving, but he'd seen his family since then. *And how do you feel about that, Mr. Aames? We'll see.*

He parked and walked into the winery that so recently had been the site of one of his happiest moments—holding aloft that trophy for best white wine and being praised and appreciated by Bo. Lots had happened since then.

He held his breath as he walked through the door of the tasting room. Beautiful RJ flashed those too perfect teeth from behind the tasting bar. "Hi, Jeremy."

"I'm supposed to meet Bo."

He smiled even wider, which could mean anything, and said, "I'll get him." He disappeared through the door that led to the back offices from which Bo and his staff ran the winery.

A couple of minutes later, the door opened, Bo leaned out, and waggled his fingers to come in. RJ walked back into the tasting room, still smiling.

Jeremy crossed in front of Bo, feeling jumpier than fleas on a hound dog, if he could quote his host. Bo didn't say anything but led him down the hall to the door on the left Jeremy knew led to his office. Inside, Bo closed the door, still looking serious. *What am I going to hear? A lecture on how this can never work?* He turned, resigned.

Bo grabbed his shoulders and hauled him in for a deep, persuasive, not-taking-no-for-an-answer kiss. *Hallelujah!*

Jeremy wrapped his arms tight around all the Bo he could reach and let his tongue and libido go to town.

They kissed until air became a crucial issue. Bo pulled back a little. "Didn't mean to bite off more than I could chew." He laughed. "But I just wanted you to know—" His blush crept across his cheeks. How could the man be so sexy and so shy at the same time?

"Thank you. Very good to know." Jeremy smiled big.

Bo's Adam's apple bobbed. "So I guess we better get going to Middlemark. I told Blaise and Llewellyn we'd be there for an early lunch if they have time."

"Perfect." He leaned up and gave Bo a soft kiss. "For luck."

A little cloud crossed his face. "If we just knew what luck looked like."

"Well, at least learning something we don't know, or confirming something we do, will be useful."

"True. Shall I drive?"

Jeremy nodded, and they walked to Bo's Prius in the parking lot.

It took thirty-five minutes to drive out to the freeway and into San Luis Obispo, but the sun shone, nice music played, and Jeremy felt comfortable in both his skin and his companionship. He'd think about the future later. Hell, when was the last time he'd gotten to just enjoy the present? Looking over your shoulder all the time didn't make for stress-free existence.

They pulled into one of several parking lots on the campus and walked across the green quadrangle to the History building. Jeremy said, "I gather that in the battle between English and History, the latter won."

Bo smiled. "I think Llewellyn has his own office while Blaise describes his space as a cubicle with a door."

They entered the History building and climbed the stairs. Jeremy stared around. "Have you been here before?"

"No. I met Llewellyn and Blaise at the winery. They're big fans. They usually come in once a week, so there's never been a need to visit their offices, although I've come to Middlemark for lectures and events. I've been to their house. It's a beautiful old Craftsman I gather Llewellyn inherited from his mother." Bo peered at the numbers outside the office doors until he seemed to find one that matched his directions. "Here we go."

They walked into a smallish outer office with a desk, a prominent table with a coffee maker and tea-pot, and most notably a brightly smiling young woman with a mane of curly dark hair and very intelligent eyes. She bounded up, revealing a curvy body clad in jeans and a T-shirt that said *Underthrow the Overground*. She walked around the desk, hand outstretched. "Hello, you must be Bo Marchand and Jeremy Aames, right?"

Bo gave her his smile. "Yes, ma'am."

She grinned. "Clearly, you're Mr. Marchand." She shook Bo's hand enthusiastically. "I'm Maria Gonzalez, Dr. Lewis's assistant." She turned to Jeremy and again clasped his hand in a firm shake. "So good to meet you both. Llewellyn's told me so much about you and your wonderful wines."

Jeremy gave her a big grin back. How great that the shy and reclusive Llewellyn Lewis had such an outgoing front person.

She waved a hand at the couch. "Please make yourselves comfortable. I'll get him, then I'll make you tea or coffee." She cast a cocky smile. "Sorry, no wine, but I'll bet you can find some at lunch." She walked to a side door that was closed and knocked. Though it was a thick, old-fashioned door, Jeremy vaguely heard a voice through it. Maria opened it and stuck her head inside. "Mr. March-and and Mr. Aames are here. I'm making drinks. Need a refill?" She nodded. "Oh, okay. Maybe later."

The solicitous sound in her voice told Jeremy that Maria Gonzalez would be his friend as long as he was Llewellyn's friend. The moment that was cast into doubt, you could have one serious enemy. That gave him both a warm and an envious feeling. *Do I have anyone that loyal to me? Yes. Bo.*

Maria bounded back to her desk, so no coffee or tea appeared to be on tap. The inner office door opened wider, revealing tall, gangly Llewellyn standing there in khakis and a cardigan sweater. If someone defined "caricature of a nerdy researcher" in the dictionary, this was the picture they'd use. Jeremy rose beside Bo and greeted Llewellyn, Bo with a guy hug and Jeremy with a handshake.

"S-so happy t-to see y-you. Blaise will m-meet us d-downstairs."

Jeremy had noticed that Llewellyn's stutter was worse when he first saw people and improved some-what later.

Bo said, "That's perfect. We can drive if that suits."

"Y-yes, it's n-not far."

Waving goodbye to Maria, they all trooped back down the stairs and out into the sunlight. Two female students walked by, and one raised a hand in salute. "Hi, Dr. Lew Lew."

"H-hi, J-Joanna." He ducked his head in a gesture that made Bo's occasional diffidence look like a model of effusive gregariousness, but he still seemed pleased.

Across the street ran Blaise, descending on them like a movie-star-handsome puppy. "Hi, you guys. How great to see you." He stepped to Llewellyn and gave him a quick but very proprietary kiss.

Whoa. Talk about upping the envy quota.

In Bo's car, they all chatted casually about wine, Llewellyn's research, and Bo's classes. At Blaise's instruction, they pulled into what looked like a health food luncheonette, the healthy part being communicated by a certain earth mother, midcentury vibe.

Inside, the place had clearly been a diner at one time, with rows of booths and a few tables, but a glance at the menu proved it was a lot more gourmet than might have been suggested by the hand-lettered signs for that day's specials.

Jeremy looked up at Bo. "Hey, this place might give us some good ideas."

Blaise nodded. "We thought you'd appreciate it. The soup's especially good."

They all ended up ordering the day's special black bean soup and a huge crunchy cabbage salad with a delicious vinaigrette dressing.

Finally Blaise leaned forward. "I think it's time to get to the elephant in the room."

Jeremy shivered.

CHAPTER FOURTEEN

JEREMY TRIED to adopt his most inquisitive and disingenuous expression. *Do I want Ottersen to be guilty or not? If he's not, what the hell would that mean?* He was scared to know.

Bo leaned in conspiratorially. "We're very anxious to know what y'all learned."

"Since we saw you at the party, we made another contact with Ottersen." Blaise sipped the iced tea the girl brought. When she left, he said, "He invited us to his winery, I think with the goal of attracting us to hold our reception there, or perhaps giving him some of the business."

Jeremy said, "Wow. That was above and beyond the call. Thank you so much for taking the time."

Llewellyn shared his soft smile. "It's very interesting."

Bo frowned a little but said, "Tell us."

"O-Ottersen is, as you p-perceived, very ambitious. He d-does want to d-dominate the industry."

"Not just Paso Robles and the central coast," Blaise added. "He wants to spread his influence to Napa. He sees the chaos resulting from the fires as creating opportunities for new leaders to arise."

Bo shook his head. "I'm not sure there is a lot of chaos."

"That may be, but Ottersen sees a fallow field."

"B-but he p-passionately denies any involvement in the f-fire at y-your friend's v-vineyard."

Blaise nodded. "He brought it up. He said he knew that a lot of the other vintners didn't like him."

Llewellyn touched Blaise's arm. "He w-was very emphatic that he didn't have any w-wish to p-put others out of b-business."

"Did you believe him?" Jeremy tried to keep the incredulity out of his voice. The anger too.

Blaise looked back and forth between Jeremy and Llewellyn. "Oddly, yes."

Bo sat back with his mouth open. "You can't be serious. The switch of the wine in the contest, the changing of the news release."

"The cancellation of my contracts." Jeremy tried to pry his hands out of fists. "What about that suggests he doesn't want to put me out of business?" Blaise rested his hand on Jeremy's arm, but Jeremy moved back. He didn't mean to be rude, but hell!

"We did some digging. The customer who canceled your contract, Jeremy, was buying some other bulk wine from Ottersen and swears he asked Ottersen if he also had that blend. He says he asked. Ottersen told him he didn't, but he had something similar." Blaise shrugged. "The customer says he couldn't resist because the price was so good."

"Aggressive b-business practices, yes, b-but it doesn't sound like p-piracy or espionage."

Jeremy couldn't wipe off the scowl. "Excuse me, but bull."

Bo pressed a warm hand to Jeremy's thigh, which was almost enough to calm him since it felt so damned nice. Bo said, "I totally understand where you're coming from. Every sign points to Ottersen."

Llewellyn held up two fingers. "F-first, every s-sign does p-point to him." He waggled the second finger. "S-sometimes that's too m-many signs."

"You mean like a setup?" Bo's eyes widened.

Llewellyn nodded. "Only a ch-chance."

Blaise leaped in. "But if we're only staring at Ottersen, somebody else could be doing all this and we could miss them. So we're not saying he didn't do it. Only that we shouldn't close our minds to other suspects."

Jeremy felt angry words pressing against his lips and held them back. *Think, dammit. Could they be right? Even if they're wrong, you can't insult Llewellyn and Blaise. Keep your trap shut. But damn, how could they let Ottersen off that easily?*

Blaise said, "So with that in mind…." He turned to Llewellyn.

Llewellyn picked up the sentence. "Who else c-could be d-doing this?"

Jeremy shook his head emphatically.

Bo gave him a slightly chastising, slightly sympathetic look. "It's hard to think of anyone. Ezra doesn't love either of us."

Jeremy glanced up from his inspection of his tea. "Especially me. He's the bornest again of born agains and can't stand anything gayer than a Sunday paper. In fact, he called me as I was driving to Bo's to sneer and accuse me as a cheater. I told him about the press release and that someone had changed it, and guess who that someone is."

Blaise wrote a couple of words in a little notebook. "This is Ezra Hamilton?"

"You never told me." Bo squeezed his leg. "That churlish SOB, bless his little heart." He looked at Blaise and Llewellyn. "He has an ego almost the size of Ottersen's and thinks he's the best of the best."

Llewellyn got a small smile. "G-God's ch-chosen."

"For sure."

Blaise said, "Yes, we spoke with him at the festival. Pretty full of himself. He didn't like being relegated to third place."

"And he could have substituted Jeremy's wine as well or with the same difficulty as anyone, but altering the press release? I don't see how."

"The fact is, that Zilinsky female works for Ottersen." Jeremy spat it with a bit more venom than he'd intended.

"L-let's look at h-her. Sh-she's new to the area?"

Bo nodded. "She said she moved from Chicago to work for Ottersen. I had no reason to doubt her. She said she'd always wanted to be in the wine business, so she jumped at the chance. On top of that, she was very loyal to Ottersen, although she showed compassion for Jeremy's situation. I'd think if she was plotting against us, she might have wanted to appear more on our side."

"N-not necessarily. When d-did sh-she say this?"

Jeremy growled, "On their date."

"Dayum." Blaise laughed. "That's a piece of the puzzle we didn't have in our database."

Bo gave Jeremy a sideways look that almost made him laugh. Bo said, "Jeremy doesn't like her, but we're not really dating. It's just a professional relationship."

Another laugh from Blaise. "Maybe we should follow his instincts and distrust her?"

This time Bo's touch was soothing. Even more soothing than the soup that arrived at that moment along with piles of salad loaded with veggies. They paused to appreciate the robust flavor in their bowls, and it did go down easy.

"I'd love to offer soup at Hill Top." The complexity of the taste, part comfort food but with a touch of spice and exotic herbs, made Jeremy feel almost human again.

"You could do that easy, darlin'."

Jeremy glanced at Blaise and Llewellyn quickly, but they didn't even look up from their spoons. Bo called lots of people "darlin'." *Yes, and I should remember that.*

When they'd all consumed a lot of soup and Llewellyn had even asked for more, they got back to the topic while they chewed salad. Llewellyn asked, "Who of y-your employees might n-not be w-what they s-s-seem?"

The crease between Bo's brows attested to how close he was to the people who worked for him. "Most of my people were here in the area before me. RJ was born and grew up right in Paso Robles."

"Could they possibly have a loyalty to someone else and be taking it out on you?"

Bo looked really distressed. "I don't think so? Lord, like you said, I've been so focused on Ottersen, it never crossed my mind it might be someone on my staff." He looked at Jeremy, horrified.

"What about you, Jeremy?" Blaise looked up from his notes and his salad.

"I have a lot fewer employees than Bo. I'm also the new kid on the block, so I guess the people I do have would logically be less dedicated to me, but they all seem really focused on the company's success."

Bo added, "Especially that little dynamo assistant." His voice had a frosty edge. Jeremy might not like Sage, but it did his heart good to think Bo was jealous of Christian. Turnabout and all that.

Blaise said, "Is that Christian Fallwell?"

Jeremy nodded. "Yes. He's my right arm. But he's young, straight out of school, and I can't think of a reason why he'd benefit from trying to put me out of business. He'd lose a job and a paycheck."

"W-what about p-people from y-your past? S-someone who m-might wish you ill?"

Jeremy tried not to tense since Bo was still touching his leg.

Bo laughed. "I don't have any people from my past that don't live right here, mostly in my house. Lord, you'd think I transported the entire state of Georgia onto Tara or something."

Smile, dammit. Don't let them see you sweat. "No, can't think of anyone. I'm estranged from my family. I haven't kept in touch with college friends, and I didn't really have any significant jobs before I bought Hill Top."

"M-may I ask wh-where you g-got the money to buy it?" Those piercing eyes seemed to bore through him, daring him to tell a lie.

"Inheritance. My mother left it to me in her will." That at least was true. The fact that he'd had to steal it back from the thieves who'd claimed it would not be mentioned.

Bo said, "I'm so sorry. I didn't know." He looked like he wanted to take Jeremy in his arms and hug him right after he sent a covered casserole. The man was too sweet.

"It's okay. I didn't know her well. She left before she died. Anyway, that's it. No bank robberies in my lascivious past." *Not banks, anyway.*

They all laughed and finished their salads, chatting a little about Llewellyn's other mystery cults he was working on in addition to the Dionysian mysteries.

"Your n-neighbor, Ezra Hamilton, asked w-what we thought of y-you honoring the Dionysian F-Festival. He s-seemed very concerned."

Blaise set down his empty tea glass, and the young waitress hurried over and filled it from her pitcher as she passed their table. "I'd call it interested. He actually asked me if I knew if you were gay, Bo." Bo's body tightened next to Jeremy, but he didn't say anything. "Funny, while he makes a big show of his disdain for the fact that you're gay, Jeremy, I thought he was also, I don't know, what would you say, dear?"

"T-titillated."

"Perfect. He definitely has a prurient interest in your sexual identities."

Jeremy snorted. "The old hypocrite. Probably chases choirboys around the upright organ."

That lightened the mood for a minute. Truthfully, he'd had a lot of delving and could use a break, badly as he wanted to discover who was doing all the evil shit to him. But he hadn't thought about the possibility that it could be anyone except Ottersen. His father was too direct. Too ruthless. If he'd found Jeremy, it seemed unlikely Jeremy would still be alive—or at the very least, not walking around free. No, his money was still on

Ottersen—but the slight chance it could be someone else gave him the willies. Total.

Bo said, "So we should let you get back to work."

Yes, and Bo wanted to quit talking about whether or not he was gay. Damn, if he'd come out to his friends, it would have been a real commitment to wanting to be with Jeremy, but no such luck.

"I can't begin to thank y'all for the astonishing amount of work you've put in on our behalf. I think an even bigger discount on your wedding reception is in order."

Blaise held up a hand. "No need. Your prices are more than reasonable, and mysteries are our life." He picked up Llewellyn's hand and kissed the back of it. Jeremy could practically hear Bo sighing. Hell, he was too. "But you're right. I do have to teach a class in half an hour, and I'm sure Llewellyn is hot on the trail of some sexy Dionysian he's tracking down."

Llewellyn grinned. "B-but most of Dionysius's followers w-were f-female. N-not my t-type."

"Good, chase them all you want."

Jeremy snarked, "Better yet, leave them for Ezra."

Llewellyn's eyes glistened with interest. "M-must admit, it's an unusual obsession."

"If you think about it, a lot of stuff associated with this case is unusual." Blaise gathered his notebook.

Still talking, they left money for the check—Bo insisted on paying—and left the restaurant with promises to come back and try the asparagus soup.

In the Prius, Bo said, "So what's our next step? What should Jeremy and I do to carry on your good work?"

Llewellyn said, "W-we'll still help too."

"Oh, we can't ask you to waste more of your valu-able time on this, Llewellyn." Bo glanced in the rear-view mirror.

Blaise leaned forward and stuck his head between the seats. "Don't think you're getting rid of us. We're hooked on your mystery, and we won't quit 'til we've solved it."

That was both comforting and worrying, but Jere-my smiled.

"W-we will keep d-digging into b-background and following threads w-we've uncovered," Llewellyn said.

"You're both better than butter. Thank you so much."

They dropped Llewellyn and Blaise off at the cam-pus. Silence fell, and not altogether comfortable. Jere-my finally said, "So what did you think about all that?"

"Mixed."

"What's that mean?"

"I can't get my head to stretch far past Ottersen. I understand their point, but I just don't see who else has much to gain."

"I'm so glad you said that." Jeremy flopped his head back on the seat. "I think it's Ottersen. Damn the man, he's taking me out and then he'll move on to someone else. He's guilty as sin."

"Yes." He drove a little farther. "I do wonder why he chose to take you out so viciously. It tips his hand to the bigger vineyards, and yet he has relatively little to gain by bringing you down. He mostly sells bulk, and you don't. You're part restaurant, and it'll take him time to get food service going. I truly don't get it."

Jeremy frowned—and sighed. "Yeah. Neither do I."

"I should take you to Hill Top, right?"

"Yeah, lots of work to do."

Bo looked over as he turned onto the road to Hill Top Winery. "Wish I didn't have to work, though."

Jeremy smiled. The future looked full of lots of things they both wished they could do.

As they pulled up in front, Christian walked out on the porch. His face looked like someone killed his puppy and fried it.

"What's wrong?" Bo glanced toward the building.

"Christian." As the car slowed, Jeremy leaped out and trotted up to where Christian stood. "What? Tell me."

"Frenfield."

"No, dammit."

Bo walked up behind him. "What is it? What's wrong?"

Jeremy said, "What about Frenfield?"

Christian's eyes watered. "They canceled our contract."

Jeremy shook his head. "No. Come on."

"They called and said they'd decided to go in a different direction. I asked. I had to know!" His voice came out as a cry, and tears ran down his pretty face. His voice came in gasps. "Ottersen. They said they gave the contract to Ottersen." He hurled himself at Jeremy and wrapped his arms around his neck. "Oh God, Jeremy, are we out of business?"

Jeremy yanked Christian off him like a vitamin C peel. "No. No, we're not. Bo and I are going to Napa to talk to the vineyards personally, right, Bo? We're leaving right away, right?"

"Sure. Right away."

Christian wiped at his eyes and ran his wrist across his nose. "I'm—I'm so sorry. It's just we've worked so hard. I feel better now." He sucked in an audible breath. "I'll keep everything running while you're gone."

"Thanks, Christian." He gave him a one-armed guy hug. Then he looked up at Bo. Jesus, he said he didn't want to take Bo down with his sinking ship. Maybe Bo didn't want to go to Napa anymore.

Christian sniffed and glanced between them. "I'll get back to work. We've had a busy day. At least the tasting room is doing okay." He plastered on a phony smile and walked into the building.

Jeremy turned to Bo, who stood at the bottom of the stairs. "Sorry. I just wanted to make Christian feel better. I know this might not be a good time for you to take off for Napa."

"No. I think we should. It's essential to all our survival."

"Are you sure? My prospects look worse and worse."

"Of course I'm sure. I need a day to set up some appointments."

Jeremy nodded. Damn, his belly felt tied in knots. Bo was so great, and Ottersen was a fucking, cheating bastard.

He watched Bo drive away and slowly walked into the tasting room with a smile on his face that never reached his eyes.

CHAPTER FIFTEEN

Bo SHIFTED his overnight bag to the other hand and sorted through the mail that had been left for him on the entry table. Quickly he glanced at it, then looked at his watch. They had to get going. It was about a four-and-a-half-hour drive to Napa. They'd considered a train or plane, but ending up in Napa with no car didn't make sense.

He tossed the mail on the table—mostly bills he'd pay later—and walked toward the garage door.

"Bo?"

Damn. He'd considered telling Mama but had half hoped to sneak out and call her from the road. Of course, talking to her with Jeremy listening in could be embarrassing. He turned. "Yes, ma'am."

"You going somewhere?"

"Yes, I have a short trip to take to Napa wineries. I'll be back in two days."

"Oh. When were you going to tell us?" Her eyebrows rose in vast disapproval.

"I need to get on the road and wasn't sure if any of you had arisen, so I planned to call. Why? Did you have something important to tell me, ma'am?"

"Not precisely, but what if there was an emergency?"

"That's why I planned to call you. Besides, there are a lot of you here to handle emergencies, now aren't there?"

"Yes. We're so fortunate to live in the loving embrace of family."

"Yes, ma'am." He swallowed hard. "I'll see you in two days." He stepped over to kiss her cheek, ignored her less than enthusiastic expression, and walked out the door. The meter on his endurance tank hovered inches from Fed Up.

Before he could get in the car, Blanche came walking in through the garage door. "Bo."

"Hi, Blanche. Sorry, I'm in a terrible hurry. Anything I can help with fast?"

"I was wondering. I had a great time helping out at your festival thing, and I thought maybe you might have a job for me at the winery. You remember I did some marketing before…." She drifted off in her spacy way. She didn't say *before she'd seemed to lose interest in most everything except reading romance novels and dreaming about some imaginary future where she got married and had a grand house.*

Bo tried to erase the crease from his forehead. "I haven't noticed any interest in returning to work prior to now."

"I know. I guess I was in a slump there for a bit, but now I want to move on with my life." She shrugged.

The fact that the slump had lasted the full seven years since she'd graduated from college with a major in English poetry and a minor—very minor—in marketing did not bear mentioning. "I can't afford to add a new employee right now, Blanche. Every position's filled."

She frowned. "I thought your winery was doing so well."

"We're holding our own, but we won't be if I start packing on employees I don't need." He smiled to soften the blow. "I love that you want to get your life together, but maybe start at another winery or one of the companies in Paso or San Luis."

She screwed up her face. "But I'd feel more comfortable getting some experience with you before I try my skills out on another company."

"Why not apply for an internship? Most of them aren't paid, but it would give you a chance to hone your skills without having too much expectation piled on top of you."

Her face lit up. "Perfect! I'll be your intern."

"We don't have an internship position, Blanche, and—"

"You can create one, right?" She hopped up and down like a kid rather than a woman of twenty-nine. "Oh I'm so excited. When can I start?"

"I'm going to have to talk to my staff. You can't have an internship without a supervisor, and that means someone has to be willing to do that. I'll be out of town for two days, and then I'll see what they say." His insides were rebelling, and he wanted to scream.

"Where are you going?"

"Napa."

"Can't you stop on the way?"

"Blanche, was there something about 'I'm in a hurry' that wasn't clear?"

Her face crumbled in woundedness. "You don't have to be mean."

"First, I'm sorry, and second, if you want to go back into the business world, you'll have to toughen up." He let out air. "I'll try to contact my marketing manager by phone and float the idea."

"Oh thank you, thank you!" She leaped up and kissed his cheek, which drove him directly into the car where he applied pedal to metal.

Speeding out onto the main road, he hurried to Hill Top. The faster he got away from home, the better.

Good God, what kind of wild hair had gotten into Blanche? Years of being the Queen of Luxury Living, second only to Mama, and now she wanted to be a worker bee? Why? The idea of having her that close to his business, where she could observe and report back to the family, made him damned nervous, and not just about the threats to his winery. What if he wanted to escalate things with Jeremy a bit? He'd never have any privacy anywhere. Blanche might be an airhead, but she had two eyes.

Just plain shit.

The only consolation was that there stretched ahead of him two whole days with Jeremy—and two whole nights. Anything could happen, and he'd brought the condoms and lube in case that *anything* included a breach of his nether regions that he'd been stretching just in case. Of course, Jeremy might not be into it. He'd been kind of distant sometimes, and Bo couldn't blame him. Hell, who wanted a lover who was in the closet? More than in the closet. Under his mother's thumb. *Good Lord, is it just a Southern thing, or am I a complete wimp?* He sighed. *Maybe I shouldn't answer that.* Yes, his mama had lost everything—her husband, her business, her community—but was there a line in the son contract that said he had to be the one to make all that up to her? He'd accepted the role without question. Now the questions flooded his brain.

He turned on the road to Hill Top, the early-morning sun shining through the windshield. *Okay, quit. Focus on your trip and the time with Jeremy. Who knows how many more of such times there will be.*

As he approached the building, the whole scene with Christian played through his head. Clearly, the guy seemed dedicated to Hill Top—*and to Jeremy, I suppose.* But losing the contract? No matter how Bo turned it in his mind, Ottersen's seemingly single-minded dedication and focus on putting Jeremy out of business didn't add up. Bo didn't know how big the contract Jeremy lost was, but compared to what he knew of Ottersen's deals, it had to be small. Was Ottersen really expending all this vicious energy against one of the smallest vineyards on the central coast when big fish like Fernando Puente and Randy Renders kept operating? Yes, they'd lost a little business, but not much more than seemed normal when facing an aggressive competitor. And because of Jeremy's experience, they were all on their guard. It wouldn't be as easy for Ottersen to take them out.

Jeremy walked out on the porch, his expression still subdued, but he carried a small bag over his shoulder. Christian walked out behind him lugging a big box that was probably wine samples and bottles. Bo had already stocked the car with his bottles and a laptop and PowerPoint he'd had his marketing manager put together. He hopped out, opened the trunk, and then held the passenger door for Jeremy. Jeremy said, "Thanks, Christian. Keep a good thought for us."

"I will. I can barely think about anything else."

Bo just nodded and crossed to the driver's side. It was hard for him to like Christian, which clearly wasn't fair since the guy worked his ass off for Jeremy. Just jealousy.

He got in and looked over at Jeremy's beautiful face, hair pulled harshly back to show off his cheekbones and the firm line of his jaw. Interesting. The hair feminized him, but without it, his face was quite masculine. *Still handsome as warmed sin.* Bo said, "Let's forget all the shit and have a great trip. What do you say, darlin'?"

Jeremy nodded. "I'll try. Honest."

"Are you hungry?"

"Yes, actually. I had so much to do to get ready, I never ate this morning."

"How about we stop and have a filling breakfast that will hold us until we get to Napa for dinner? Or not. I'm sure we'll be mightily tempted by every restaurant in San Francisco." Bo chuckled, trying to lighten Jeremy's mood.

"Sounds great." *Ah, my first genuine smile.*

Bo headed out Highway 46 toward Paso until they found the Springtime restaurant that served good omelets and pancakes. It was a favorite of people in the wine country. He parked, and inside the hostess gave them a booth toward the back.

They settled in, ordered omelets, and then Bo reached in his windbreaker and pulled out his list of notes on their appointments. "I emailed over most of these, but I've added a couple of new ones since then."

Jeremy glanced up. "I must have missed the email." He looked over the list carefully. "You've got some pretty big targets here. Are we up to it?" He didn't sound really skeptical, just inquisitive.

"I think since it's both of us, we can offer them some serious packages. If they want more, we can always call one of the other small wineries like Yellow Sky or Golden Cellars."

"You wouldn't include Randy or Fernando?"

"They're so big, they might try to commandeer the deal. Maybe not even on purpose. Just by the breadth of their offerings. I don't think they need our help right now."

Jeremy nodded and leaned back as the waitress served the meals. She also refilled their coffee, dropped the check, and left, so they both pounced on the food. Jeremy glanced at Bo's list again. Swallowing and chasing it down with a sip of coffee, he said, "Man, we're even talking to Strausburg."

"Um." Bo chewed. "It's a long shot, I know, but they need grapes and they make some blends other than bubbly, so what the hell. And I love wandering through their caves."

"I've never seen them."

"What?" Bo set down his cup. "You can't visit Napa and not see those amazing caves. They're the only winery in California that riddles their wines by hand."

"Clearly, I've got to see that."

"A must."

They chatted through the rest of the fast meal, both of them aware of the long drive. Dropping money on the table that Jeremy insisted on adding to, Bo slid out of the booth and headed toward the front. As they approached the first row of booths, Jeremy gasped so loudly Bo froze, expecting to see a snake crawling from under a table. "What? What is it?"

Jeremy's jaw muscle jumped, he swallowed so hard his Adam's apple bobbed three times, and then he nodded toward a booth ahead of them.

Facing them was Sage Zilinsky and, with his back turned but identified by the ink-black hair, sat Ernest Ottersen. Worst of all, they couldn't leave the restaurant without passing him.

Bo grabbed Jeremy's arm. He was shaking, and his hands gripped into fists. Bo whispered, "Just walk past. You don't even have to look at him. Let me talk if anything needs to be said."

At that moment Sage looked up, and her glance connected with Bo. She smiled big. "Hi. Fancy seeing you here. Ernest, look who it is."

Damn, why did she say that? Jeremy vibrated so hard, it was visible.

As they got almost to their table, Bo said, "Hi. Sorry. We're in a terrible hurry. We have to get back to business for an, uh, appointment." *Do not let on where we're really going.*

They came level with the table. Jeremy still stared straight ahead. *Good man.*

Bo said to Sage, "We'll talk soon." Then he turned his head slightly and nodded at Ottersen with a small, polite smile.

Ottersen gave him a big tooth-flasher. "Bo, how's tricks?"

"Good."

He started walking but, of course, the damned cosmic joker couldn't let it be.

Ottersen said, "Hi, Jeremy. How's business?"

Match, meet powder keg. Jeremy's head snapped toward Ottersen, and he snarled, "You ought to know, you cheating son of a bitch."

Ottersen's dark eyebrows dove for his nose. "It's not my fault if you can't stand a little competition, so don't accuse me of cheating."

"My ass! Your idea of competition is stealing my formulas and copying them. I'd say that qualifies as espionage, not competition."

Bo muttered, "Quiet, Jeremy." But he was too far-gone.

Ottersen half rose from his seat, blocked by the table. "I've stolen nothing and you know it. If you were a better businessman and a better winemaker, I wouldn't be able to attract your customers. Hell, I don't even have to ask them. They call me. You can't blame me for taking advantage of offered business."

"Bullshit."

Bo grabbed Jeremy's arm.

"It's the truth. That's why I know you cheated to win that damned contest. If your customers aren't even loyal enough to stay with you, I know you don't make the best white on the central coast."

"Liar! God damn you, lying bastard." Jeremy pulled himself away from Bo and leaned into the table toward Ottersen. His voice turned into a hiss, but it was still loud enough to carry to all the surrounding booths. "You steal any more of my formulas and I swear I'll kill you."

Somewhere nearby, a woman gasped. Sage slapped a hand to her mouth.

Holy shit! Bo grabbed Jeremy's bicep and put all his superior height and weight into dragging him away from the table. "Enough!" He glanced back toward Ottersen, who stared at Jeremy with narrowed eyes and a half-open mouth. Bo said, "Sorry. He's just upset."

With force he hauled Jeremy through the front of the restaurant, trying to ignore the blatant stares of the other diners. Most of them must have been able to hear at least part of the argument, but likely not that last threat. *Thank the Lord.* A thing like that got around to too many tourists and they'd walk into Hill Top, take one look at Jeremy, and turn and run.

Outside, Jeremy shook his arm, but not hard, until Bo let him go. "I'm okay now."

Bo walked to the Prius and held the passenger door for Jeremy, who slid in, looking a little contrite.

When Bo got in the driver's side, Jeremy said, "I'm sorry. That was so stupid. My temper finally got the better of me."

"I understand." Not entirely true. Why did a civilized man say he'd kill another person? Was it just an expression, like saying "I'd kill for a cup of coffee"? Maybe, but it sounded deadly serious. "It was really unwise, though."

Bo carefully drove around the restaurant and exited onto the side street, then made his way through back streets to the 101 freeway just so Ottersen wouldn't see them driving away from Paso Robles rather than back toward the vineyards.

Jeremy didn't speak as long as Bo was looking for the freeway, but once on it, he sat back, sighed, and said, "How badly do you think I blew it?"

"Fortunately, I don't think many people heard that last part, even if they heard the rest of the argument."

"Your friend Sage did." The word *friend* might have had a bit too much emphasis.

"Yes, but she knows a bit of the story and will take it with an appropriate grain of salt."

"I sure hope so. Man, that was so stupid. I don't even know why I said it."

"Don't worry about it anymore. We got out of there without anyone being able to tell we were heading north. Sit back, close your eyes, and relax."

"Thanks. I think I'll take you up on that."

Right. Let me do the worrying for both of us.

CHAPTER SIXTEEN

"JEREMY?"

"Wha—?" Some light filtered in as his lids fluttered; then he managed to pry his eyes open. He raised his head. *Ouch. Neck hurts.* Bo was leaning over him.

"Time to wake up, Sleeping Beauty."

"My turn to drive?" He leaned forward and cocked his head from side to side.

Bo chuckled. "Time for you to get out of the car and bring your stuff into the cabin."

Jeremy raised his head. Right. They were sitting in the parking lot of—someplace. "Where are we?"

"Napa."

"You're kidding?"

Bo just smiled.

"Why didn't you wake me?"

"You looked too peaceful. Not a problem. Come on."

Jeremy glanced around at the row of cabins set forward and back from each other and bordered by a line of tall trees. "Did you already check in?"

Bo pulled out the key card. "Yep." He pointed to the cabin on the end. Number six. "That's us."

"Nice."

"We'll see."

"I mean, it's kind of private."

Bo grinned at him. "That took a little work. I told them I had a sleep problem and couldn't stand noise."

Jeremy walked to the trunk as Bo opened it and grabbed his bag. Jeremy said, "You didn't tell them that you wanted to make noise?" He looked up and laughed at the bright pink on Bo's cheekbones. But he grinned, and Jeremy could interpret the expression as hopeful.

Inside the cabin, they walked into a small living room. It was comfy and homey if not plush. Beyond the living room was a bedroom with two double beds. Bo shrugged. "Had to make it look convincing." His cheeks flushed again.

"Hey, we can mess up one and sleep in the other."

Bo grinned. "Sounds good to me." He unzipped his bag. "But as you may recall from our list of potential customers, we have a winery to see this afternoon before they close. It was one of my last-minute additions, and this was the only time I could fit them in."

"Hey, I got four hours' sleep while you drove." He unfastened his own bag and pulled out the few things he'd brought, stashed them in the drawer, and hung up the sports coat he'd carried in a garment bag. "We're here for business, so let's go get some." He slid the jacket over his dress shirt and jeans.

"Let me make a quick pit stop."

Jeremy sat on the bed while Bo peed and brushed his teeth. He'd managed to sleep despite his horror at what he'd done with Ottersen. Old habits and training died damned hard, but he'd gotten so angry, it was like he was back at home, fighting for his life. Hopefully Bo was right. It would blow over.

After Bo washed up, he donned his own coat and they took off for Reynolds and Reynolds, a small winery in Sonoma, a half-hour drive away.

Jeremy watched the huge fields of vines stretched out on both sides as they drove. Funny, he felt oddly nervous. A lot depended on this trip, and he really wanted it to go well. Despite his fury and the fact that he knew in his gut that Ottersen was a big fat liar, his words still rang in Jeremy's head. "Bo, do you think my customers really called Ottersen and offered him contracts?"

Bo glanced at him, then back at the road, but his face radiated compassion. "It would align with what Llewellyn and Blaise told us—that Ottersen passionately denies going after your clients. At least one client agrees. They did seem willing to at least countenance the idea."

"I think he's a fucking liar." He hadn't meant for the words to come out that angrily.

"I know. You made that clear, and I'm inclined to agree, but you asked."

"I'm sorry for snapping at you." He rested his hand against Bo's warm, strong arm. "Ottersen's strategy is like water torture. Every new drop takes another layer off my nerves."

"I know, darlin'. It's pure hog crap."

Jeremy finally smiled. At least they could agree on that.

Bo pulled into the drive of the Reynolds and Reynolds winery and crunched the short distance to the tasting room on the gravel drive. "We go in the side door to the offices."

Jeremy took a huge breath. *Showtime.*

An hour later he walked out smiling. "Man, that went well."

Bo grinned. "As slick as cat poop on linoleum."

Jeremy snorted. "I can't believe you said that. But seriously, it would be a smallish contract, but we can promote it to other wineries."

"Yes, and we'll work out the details of our relationship."

I'd like to work out some relationship details. Jeremy glanced at Bo, who seemed clueless on what he'd said. "Right."

"So how about we go eat and drink lots of wine to celebrate?"

"Sounds perfect." *As long as that double bed follows closely on the heels of wine.*

"And then we can go to bed early." The blush accompanied a sexy little chuckle.

"I'll drink to that."

After a short drive from the winery, Bo navigated them into the little town of Healdsburg and found a parking spot near the town square. Jeremy climbed out of the Prius and stared around at the trees and benches all surrounded by shops and restaurants. "Uh, excuse me. When did I enter this storybook?"

"Amazing, isn't it? This is one of my favorite towns."

They walked across the square into a small, intimate bistro that Bo also identified as a fave of his. The man had even called ahead for a reservation, though when he'd had a moment to be that plan-ahead thorough, Jeremy didn't know. Funny how, despite Bo being cagey about their relationship, he still made Jeremy feel cared for. Not something Jeremy'd had a lot of in his life.

The maître d' walked them to a booth in the back, which reminded Jeremy uncomfortably of their breakfast, but once settled he loved the quiet ambiance, the comfortable low-key leather seats, white tablecloths, and crisp white napkins. Before the host left, he said, "Can I have the sommelier bring you a wine list?"

Bo nodded. "Absolutely."

"Right away, sir."

Bo smiled. "How about we start with champagne and then graduate to something redder?"

"Sounds perfect."

Five minutes later he'd order a bottle of Strausburg Brut to be followed by a pinot noir.

"I picked Strausburg since we're seeing them tomorrow morning. We might as well get prepared."

"I'll get prepared on champagne any day you choose."

When it arrived, was poured and tasted, and they were alone again, Bo leaned forward with his flute. "To us and our adventures."

While Jeremy would have liked to define the *us* part more clearly, he could totally toast the *adventure* part.

They ordered duck for Bo and sea bass for Jeremy, preceded by Caesar salad and mushroom bisque. When the first course arrived, Jeremy tasted his soup, which was amazing, then filled his spoon and held it out to Bo. "Here. Try."

Bo looked startled, glanced around to see as Jeremy had that no one could observe them in their private little space, and leaned forward to take the soup into his mouth.

"Oh, delicious. My salad is great, but you got the best thing."

"Always." Jeremy grinned, then slowly took the bowl of the spoon into his mouth and licked, showing lots of tongue. He chuckled when Bo swallowed hard.

What followed was a yummy meal full of as much tantalizing sexual tension as food. Little touches, lingering looks, and shared bites of everything had Jeremy's cock so hard it made it difficult to get enough energy away from his groin and into his stomach to digest his food. At one point Bo picked up a piece of succulent duck and held it in his fingers to Jeremy, who sucked them into his mouth, exploring every surface as he planned to do with other appendages very soon. As an afterthought, the duck tasted good too.

By the time the check came, they were salivating for different things. Bo slapped down a credit card. Jeremy tried to hand him cash, but he refused, and that ended up in a competition as to who could force the other to do what he wanted. Bo won and they slid out of the booth, laughing. Jeremy led the way toward the front of the now-crowded restaurant, and when they turned the corner toward the door, Jeremy came face-to-face with a man standing at the maître d's desk.

Jeremy froze. *Do I know this man?* Medium height and stocky, he fell into the fireplug category of body types, but the face—pockmarked, some of the skin an odd color like maybe it had been burned, but most of all, his eyes showed no light or warmth.

Bo said, "Is everything okay?"

"Y-yes. Thanks. Fine." He walked by the man, trying not to look like he was in a hurry. He desperately wanted to ask Bo if the man was staring at him, but he didn't. Outside, he glanced back. The restaurant had small windows, and lights in the parking lot made it hard to tell if anyone was looking out.

When they got in the Prius, Jeremy said, "Would you mind driving around the back so I can see how they've set up the service bays? It's such an old building, it must have been a challenge."

Bo gave him an odd look but nodded and exited the long way round. At least if that guy was watching Jeremy, he wouldn't see him leave the lot—unless he followed.

Come on, I'm spooking myself. How can someone who happens to be in a small restaurant hours from where I live be looking for me? Stupid. But man, those eyes gave him the willies.

Bo directed that glance at Jeremy again. "I seem to be saying this a lot, but is everything okay?"

"Yes." Tell some of the truth. "I freaked when we were leaving the restaurant and saw someone I thought I knew from, like, my childhood."

"Not the terrifying-looking man at the desk?" He sounded shocked. Good instincts.

"Yes, actually. He resembled a man who was an, uh, acquaintance of my father. But it makes no sense. What would such a person be doing here?"

"Excellent question. Would this man or your father have business in Sonoma?"

"Don't think so." Jeremy tried to keep his voice light. "But as I told you, I'm estranged from my family, so I don't know what he's into."

"What work did he do when you were at home?"

Do not go there. "Businessman. I'm not too sure. You know how those details are fuzzy to kids."

"When was the last time you saw him?"

You mean before or after he locked me in a room? "Three years ago, I guess."

"Why are you estranged, if I can ask?"

Jeremy shifted in his seat. "He was a cruel SOB to my mother and to me. My mother died. Nothing to keep me there." *Not after I escaped.* "I don't really like to think about it." He slid a hand onto Bo's knee. "Especially not when I have much more exciting things to contemplate." He hated treating sex as a distraction— he was deeply excited about their night together—but he had to change the subject. Not only because thinking about that face in the restaurant convinced his erection to go into hiding but also to avoid any more questions about uncomfortable subjects.

Bo PULLED into the parking lot at the motel and glanced at Jeremy, who seemed to be staring in the side mirror outside his window. Jeremy had been super jumpy ever since he saw that man in the restaurant. Hell, that was easy to understand. The guy looked like warmed-over menace. But why did Jeremy think he knew a man like that? As much as Bo wanted to accept Jeremy at face value, nothing added up on that face. He was only twenty-four, but he'd come to the central coast with enough money to buy a winery, and yet he said he was estranged from his family and seemed to hate his father.

Back at the festival, Bo had thought Jeremy was avoiding the cameras, purposefully turning his head when someone snapped photos, especially Sage. Bo had convinced himself he was crazy and making that up, but after the episode at the restaurant, maybe not. Jeremy sure didn't seem to want to be recognized. Even funny little things intrigued Bo. Why was Jeremy so fit when he didn't seem to be a gym rat, and where did that streak of violence he demonstrated to Ottersen come from?

"You're thinking awfully hard." Jeremy's voice was light. Why did it sound wary?

"Just replaying our visit to Reynolds and Reynolds to consider what we should do tomorrow."

That answer seemed to satisfy him. He took one last glance in the side mirror, then said, "Strausburg's a real long shot."

"Agreed, but their caves are so much fun, I can't resist taking you. If we make a contact, that's gravy."

"I can't wait." He turned his head and smiled. "No, hold on. That's not true. I want tonight to be as long as possible."

That made Bo catch his breath, so he smiled and busied himself parking the car in front of their end cabin as warmth spread from his chest to his groin.

By the time they got inside, that warmth had turned into a pretty substantial fire, and his jeans felt too tight, the rough denim rubbing hard enough against his briefs that he could feel it on his cockhead. *Good.* It was the only thing that would put a damper on the beast.

Jeremy disappeared into the bathroom. Bo took off his shoes, but then lost his nerve and sat on the end of the bed. *What if Jeremy doesn't want to have sex when he comes out?* But he heard the shower running, and that made him smile. *Good idea. I'll do that next.* He pulled his shirt out of his pants and sat back against the headboard. He only waited a couple of minutes.

When Jeremy opened the bathroom door, steam escaped and Bo snorted. Jeremy struck a pose, one arm behind his head and a towel, unequal to the task, tucked around his waist. The white terry cloth gapped over his thigh and gave Bo a peekaboo view of golden pubic hair. But speaking of hair, his shiny mane fell around his shoulders, perfectly dry.

"How did you keep your hair from getting wet?" Bo flashed a dimple or two.

"I wrapped my head in a towel."

"Oh darlin', I wish I'd seen that."

"Definitely looked like the Queen of Sheba."

Bo slid off the bed. "My turn in the bathroom?"

"Sure. The turban awaits."

Bo ran his hand over his well-cut auburn hair. "Probably not required." He leaned in toward Jeremy. "You smell better than an apple pie on the windowsill, darlin'."

Jeremy turned his back and gazed over his shoulder. "Come and get yourself a piece, *darlin'*."

Oh my. First he had to keep from having a spontaneous orgasm just looking at Jeremy. Bo escaped into the bathroom before he forgot about the grime of the day and the much-needed shower and went down on Jeremy right that second.

Stepping under hot water—amazing Jeremy had left any after the steam bath he'd created—he quickly washed his pits and then paid special attention to his privates, not rubbing too hard for fear of losing his proverbial shit right there. Moments later he stepped out and grabbed a towel. *Yes, I'm anxious, thank you very much.* Bracing a foot on the edge of the tub, he dried his leg, stood, and caught a glimpse in the mirror.

He stared. *I wonder what Jeremy sees.* To his own glance, Bo looked like a young man with old eyes. Back

in college, girls had always said his green eyes were his
best feature. Now he seemed wary and... what? Bur-
dened? Sad? No, not sad, exactly. He wasn't sad about
taking care of his family. So, what? Bo leaned against
the wall, still staring in his own eyes. *I'm sad to be
living my life by someone else's rules. There. Said that.*

The sound of Jeremy moving around in the other
room brought a slow smile to Bo's face. *But not tonight, Mama. Tonight I get to be all Bo all the time.*

CHAPTER SEVENTEEN

UH, WHERE is he? Jeremy shifted against the bed pillows and glanced toward the bathroom door—then blinked as it opened like he'd said the magic word. *Oh my.* Bo, dressed only in a towel, made saliva collect in his mouth and flashes go off in Jeremy's brain. Delicious and worthy of cover-model status. So tall. So broad in the shoulders above everything else that was lean, baby, lean. Bo's legs were so long they forced pornographic images of them wrapped around Jeremy's back or straining beside his hips as they fucked. "Hi."

Bo returned his smile. *Hmm.* Bo's expression was—confident, saucy even. Not quite as haunted as he sometimes looked. That shower must have been dispensing chutzpah. Jeremy patted the bed. "You look delicious."

Bo's beautiful lips curved upward. "Then get ready to eat."

Jeremy laughed, letting his head fall back against the headboard. "You're in a sexy mood."

"You have no idea." He took a couple of steps forward. "I've been stretching with a butt plug."

Jeremy felt his eyes widen. "You're kidding?"

"I'd never kid about my ass." He sat on the edge of the bed, then scooted a bit toward Jeremy.

Oooh, feisty. Jeremy leaned forward and met Bo partway. "Guess what? So have I."

Bo chuckled, low and dirty. "Shall we flip for top or bottom?"

Jeremy unfastened his towel and rolled backward all in one move. He grasped his legs, allowing himself to expose all his most private parts to Bo's inspection. "I already flipped. I won."

"Well, damn." Bo took an audible breath. "Supplies?"

"Just look in that bedside drawer right there." Jeremy flicked his eyes to his left.

Bo lost his cool and scrambled to the table. *Totally cute.* The sound of packages ripping made Jeremy smile even bigger. "Uh, I can only assume this acrobatic and highly, shall we say, revelatory position for so long."

"Oh right. Sorry." Bo scampered back to the mattress.

Jeremy almost released his position but stopped. What was that? A soft fluttering caress, like a butterfly or a kitten's tail, tickled his butt. He peeked around his own ass and saw Bo kissing it. Nice, but—holy crap! Bo's whole tongue stroked over Jeremy's right cheek, then moved to the left and repeated, and then, oh yes, Bo pulled apart his cheeks and slid the warm, soft, wet intruder between.

Jeremy gasped so loudly Bo stopped.

"No! Don't stop, please." No one had ever done this to him, for him. What started as tickles turned to full sparks of electricity that shot straight from Bo's tongue into Jeremy's balls, prompting little squeaking cries that were kind of embarrassing, but he didn't care. "Oh! Oh! Yes. There."

Bo moaned low in his throat as he pressed more deeply into Jeremy. Oh yeah, moaning was in order. Jeremy moaned too, but it came out a little whimper instead as a shock of pure pleasure lit him up, turning his shaft into a lightning bolt ready to fly. It bobbed against his own chest, looking for attention, but the pleasure in his butt consumed everything and he couldn't move his hands.

Bo's tongue slid away and, just as Jeremy was ready to yell in protest, a sticky, slick, cool finger slid into the well-oiled channel, pressing deep and then—

"Oh my God!"

Bo chuckled, low and sexy. "Don't we just love prostates more than cornbread and grits?"

Jeremy tried to answer, but his breath stopped as Bo did that curly thing with his fingers again and jolts of a whole new level of sensation, almost too intense to call just pleasure, rocked him. "Mmm fttt yahhh."

A second finger must have gone in because he felt even fuller—but not full enough. "G-getting all the goodies. Fuck. Fuck me."

Bo leaned over him, his fingers still delving. "Truth is, darlin', I'm so hot for you I don't expect to last too long, so I want to be sure you're ready."

"Ready? I'm a fucking incendiary device. Get that dick in—therrrrre!" His last word accompanied the hard/soft slide of a big dick into his hole, and then a fast pull out and harder thrust, driving the monster so deep Bo's balls slapped against Jeremy's ass.

He couldn't cry out or move. Hell, he could barely breathe as Bo set up a rhythm and thrust in and out of his body, making deep grunting sounds that vibrated through Jeremy's whole being. Like heaven with a little edge of burn that made the sweetness even better. It wasn't just that it had been so long since he'd had sex. It was that he'd never had sex like this. Sex with Bo. No, he wasn't a better lover than other men. In fact he was a little awkward and puppyish. But it was the look in his eyes, so full of things Jeremy both ran from and wanted more than anything, that made each thrust reach all the way to Jeremy's heart.

"Oh my stars, Jeremy, this is so wonderful. So wonderful."

Bo's words were sweet, but that big cock did beautifully nasty things to his insides, and Jeremy's whole body woke up and took over, rising up to meet each thrust like an overanxious lover. Their skin slapped and squished with sweat despite the coolness of the night outside.

As each dive hit bottom, a flash of light lit up Jeremy's brain, then plunged to deep blackness between, letting him see the heavens, then taking them away, then back to the stars. His breath came in pants and he hung, suspended on the edge of explosion, as Bo whispered, "Oh Lord, I'm close, so close, so—are you?"

"Ummmm-hmmmmmm!" His body froze, his brain exploded, and Jeremy became the stars he'd been seeing, vaguely aware of hot fluid shooting out on his chest, onto his chin, and one shot right in his eyes. He laughed and yelled at the same time. "Holy shit!"

"Jeremyyyyyyy!" Bo's long strokes devolved into bunny hops as his head strained up, all the cords in his long neck standing out. His body froze, then began to shudder.

It took minutes before they stopped shivering in aftershocks of pleasure; then Bo, who'd been holding himself on his forearms, flopped to the side, still breathing like a coal train. Jeremy missed his weight instantly.

Bo kind of giggled—in baritone, which sounded funny. "You know, that was so worth waiting for."

Amen to that, baby. Jeremy let his barely movable fingers sift through Bo's deep red hair. Such beautiful coloring. The hair like flame. The eyes like sea glass. Clearly he'd drunk some kind of sappy Kool-Aid, but he couldn't quite bring himself to care. "I agree."

Bo rolled to his side and gazed at Jeremy with way too much affection pouring from his eyes. "If I'd known what I was missing, I'd have been sneaking up on you in the vineyard rows."

Jeremy gave a snort. "Ah, but would you have practiced buttage?"

Bo gave a howl, laughing at Jeremy's pun on the French word for the practice of covering vine grafts with dirt to protect from frost. "Definitely, and I'll never do it again without laughing."

Their chuckles quieted, letting Jeremy wonder if their sex had been earth-shattering enough to make Bo come out, but he refused to spoil the mood by bringing it up. Not like him to be so nonconfrontational, but their sex had been pretty revelatory to him too.

With a shove Bo rose up, slid off the bed, and padded to the bathroom, giving Jeremy a front-row seat to the flexing of a spectacular ass. Bo disappeared, and then Jeremy heard water running. A moment later Bo emerged with a warm washcloth in hand, his own groin shining with moisture from what must have been a quick wash. Bo sat on the edge of the bed and gently wiped the fresh terry cloth over Jeremy's chest, scrubbing a little to get off the pool of fast-drying semen, then applied his ministrations lower to Jeremy's relaxed and sensitive cock. When he finished he sat back and just gazed. "You're in such remarkable shape. You make my hour workouts at the gym four days a week seem pretty slothful."

Don't tense. Don't look guilty. "I was quite a gym junkie back in college. Now I'm lucky to get in as much exercise time as you do." He shrugged. "But it's easier to keep it than to get it."

"Well, it sure looks pretty. The first time I saw you bare-chested, I thought you looked like Brad Pitt in *Fight Club*—but with the hair of *Legends of the Fall*."

"Yikes. Not sure I can live up to that comparison."

Bo touched Jeremy's chest with a finger and said musingly, "Actually, you're better-looking. Even more classic. Not so boy-next-door."

"I guess all I can say is thank you. I'm glad you think so."

Bo blinked like he'd been somewhere else for a minute. "You looking for some sleep?" His devastating dimples flashed. "Before we try that again?"

Jeremy laughed, though he glanced at the fairly small bed uneasily. "Sounds good, but we may have to try a variation later since my poor behind is out of shape."

"I'd never say that, but I'm happy to offer up mine next time. Let's sleep first, though, okay?" Bo took the washcloth into the bathroom; they took turns peeing and brushing their teeth, then snuggled into the sheets Bo had straightened while Jeremy did his ablutions. Bo sighed deeply and gathered Jeremy into his arms.

It took all his focus not to tense. He'd always shied from sleeping with anyone. Too intimate. But this was Bo, and Bo was the exception to a lot of rules. Jeremy released his breath slowly, laid his head next to Bo's on the pillow, and amazingly, fell asleep.

What's that? Jeremy's eyes flew open and his body froze—too many years of too much vigilance. Bo softly snuffled, pressed tightly against him. One big man and one medium-sized man in a double bed didn't leave a lot of extra real estate. *Is that what woke me?* It should have, but every nerve and well-honed instinct said no. He glanced at the clock on the bedside table. One a.m. He'd been asleep beside Bo for an hour and a half. Why would the proximity wake him now?

With a glance at Bo, he slid from his side of the bed, feet hitting softly on the chilly floor. He'd taught himself to walk without sound when he was really little. It had allowed him to sneak out of the house when he needed to get away. Hell, it had allowed him to buy a winery.

The uninspiring motel drapes were pulled tight across the windows, but like most blackout curtains, the thickness of the plastic lining created a small gap. A tiny beam of light, so fast and so small it might not have happened, flashed against that gap and was gone. *Damn, is there any way out the back?* He wanted to bang his head against the wall. He never entered a space without checking for exits. He'd been so anxious to have sex he'd lost all his training. Bo made him stupid.

"What's wrong?" Bo's sleepy voice came from behind him.

Shit! He turned and plastered on a mildly concerned expression. Speaking softly, he said, "It sounds like someone's walking around the outside of the cabin, real quiet-like."

"Might be a maintenance man." But he'd lowered his voice.

"At 1:00 a.m.? Really? This cabin's set apart, so I don't see why anyone would be walking past to get to or from their car."

"A kid sneaking out?"

"Maybe, but they've got a flashlight with a tiny beam."

Bo sat up on the edge of the bed and wiped a hand over his face. The fact he was stark naked reminded Jeremy he was the same. Bo said, "Why would someone want to sneak around spying on us?"

Jeremy shook his head but said, "Wait here." He grabbed the closest thing he could find that had any weight—the TV remote—and handed it to Bo. "If someone comes through the door, smash them."

"Holy shit, Jeremy." In the almost nonexistent light, Jeremy's adapted eyes could just make out a hint of the frown on Bo's face.

"It probably won't happen." He crept softly to the closet, grabbed his jeans and sweater he'd tossed in earlier, and pulled them on as he tiptoed to the bathroom. He remembered a window in there but had no idea if it opened. The flicker of the thin light jiggled across the window, and Jeremy turned into a statue.

Just that fast—gone.

He waited. No more light. Stepping back out the bathroom door, he saw Bo crouched by the front windows, staring at the front door like a cat at a mouse hole. A naked cat. He almost laughed, but no time. The tiny, almost imperceptible blink of light reflected on the drapes. Bo turned quickly toward Jeremy, and he nodded at him.

Okay, fast. Jeremy hurried across the bathroom, stepped into the tub, and faced the frosted glass window. It had an old-fashioned lock, which he unfastened. *Here goes.* Taking a deep breath, he grasped the bottom of the window and shoved up. Nothing. Might be painted closed, but he gave it one more heave. With a sharp cracking sound, it raised an inch.

Damn. He waited. Nothing happened, but that didn't mean much. He could open this window and come face-to-face with a guy holding a gun. But now there was an inch gap at the bottom of the window, so he had to go one way or another.

What the hell? He pushed up. The cold night air struck his cheeks, but no gunshot.

He poked his head out a couple of inches and looked both ways. *Super quiet.* Hooking a leg over the sill, he slid out, and his bare feet hit the damp, rocky ground. He barely noticed. Quietly he pulled the window down, not quite to the bottom, but far enough that you had to be right next to it to see it wasn't closed tight. With another quick glance around, he scooted back into the bushes to hide. If someone tried to open that window, it wasn't entirely clear what he'd do about it, but he couldn't search the neighborhood for a loose tire iron. He did glance around and find a good-sized rock he could hold in his palm to increase the impact of a blow.

Then he held still, barely breathing, and waited. God willing, Bo wouldn't suddenly shove his head out the window and shout. Even more than that, Jeremy's fingers were crossed that no one broke in that front door.

Minutes passed in total silence. He listened so hard it made his ears hurt.

Crack.

He held his breath as a soft step sounded near the corner of the building. The little beam of light played against the tree branches for a moment and then—*poof.* Blackness. It was like some Harry Potter said the opposite of *Lumos.*

Something about the quality of silence that followed spoke of his being alone with no one sneaking in the bushes, like the trees and bushes had been holding up their transpiration and now returned to normal. He waited another moment, then skittered to the window, raised it, and slid inside.

He gasped at the big body standing in front of him—until he realized it was Bo. "Holy shit, you scared me."

Bo full-on frowned. "Where were you?"

"I went outside to try to catch the person who was snooping around."

"Since you're not hauling someone by their ear, I'm assuming your quest did not succeed." He crossed his arms.

"No. I didn't see him either, but there was definitely someone there. I saw his flashlight."

Bo sighed, turned, and walked back into the bedroom. Jeremy leaned against the doorframe since he needed to wash the dirt off his feet. Bo said, "It really could have been anyone, Jeremy. Why do you think they were spying on us in some way?"

"I don't know exactly. Jumpy over all Ottersen's dirty tricks, I guess." That was close enough to the truth.

In the near darkness, Bo's inhale sounded shaky. "Maybe somebody, like some horny teenager, heard us having sex and came to check it out."

That was actually a possibility. "I don't think it was a kid. The steps were too heavy, and there was no giddiness. This felt focused and stealthy."

"Maybe it was someone who hates gays and tried to spy on us so they could call a cop or something."

"Cop? Come on. Gay sex isn't illegal."

"Never stopped them before." Bo looked pretty worried.

He pushed away from the doorjamb. "Seriously, Bo. Nobody in California wine country is going to try to get a gay couple put in jail for sodomy, although I guess there could be some crazed born-againer wanting to break in and shoot us." He jerked his chin toward the bed. "Get under the covers before you freeze. I'm going to wash the dirt off my feet." He turned, then looked over his shoulder with a grin. "After I'm done, let's give them something to talk about, shall we?"

Trying to keep his steps jaunty, he walked to the bathroom. This thing didn't make sense. Would Ottersen go so far as to have them followed? If so, who told him where they were going? If it was someone from his family—hell, it couldn't be. No way they'd just watch. *What the fuck is going on?*

CHAPTER EIGHTEEN

BO DROVE up the hill toward the parking lot at Strausburg. Jeremy hadn't been kidding about the "something to talk about" part. Lordy, they'd sucked and rubbed and rolled so far on the bed they fell off, laughing in a heap on the floor. Whatever had spooked Jeremy—and that seemed considerable—he'd thrown caution to the proverbial winds after he came back into the cabin. But Jesus, Mary, and Joseph, had he overreacted much to a little flashlight in the dark? Damn, he'd even had Bo scared. Sitting there naked with a deadly remote in his hands, staring at the door as if a velociraptor was coming through at any moment—it'd be funny if it weren't so flaming stupid.

"Wow, this is pretty."

Bo blinked himself out of his worried reverie and glanced around at the beautiful vineyards and grounds. Strausburg was one of his favorite wineries. "Yeah. America's champagne maker." Not really, since nothing made outside of the Champagne region of France could legitimately be called champagne, but Strausburg used authentic methods and got as close to the original style as any "sparkling wine" could. He found a space and parked.

As they walked toward the side entrance to the offices, Jeremy said, "I'm surprised they agreed to see us. I thought they used only their own grapes."

Bo nodded. "I was a little surprised too, but I'd heard a rumor that they sometimes buy a small amount of specialty grapes or blends for a few of their second-label wines." He smiled. "I mostly wanted an excuse to see the caves."

"Can't wait." Jeremy smiled back.

Inside the bright, modern offices, a receptionist greeted them with an efficient smile. "Yes, gentlemen, Mr. Fieldstone had an emergency meeting. He said you should go ahead with your cave tour, and he should be ready to speak with you right after. I've asked Peter, Mr. Fieldstone's assistant, to be your guide."

An older man, short with white hair, rose from a nearby desk. Not at all what Bo had thought of when he heard the word *assistant*. He walked forward, hand extended to Bo. "Peter Fieldstone."

"Oh, hello. I'm Bo Marchand, and this is Jeremy Aames."

"Marchand. Sounds like we might have a Southern influence." He smiled charmingly.

Jeremy gave a little snort, since talking to Bo was like a lesson in speaking with cornpone in your mouth. They all laughed as Peter led them out of the offices toward the entrance to the caves. They bypassed a group of tourists milling about waiting for the next guided adventure and stepped into the relative dark of the caves.

Peter said, "Not sure how much you know about the winery, but these caves were built in the 1880s, and there are over 35,000 square feet of them. The caves maintain a constant temperature and humidity for our fermenting wine. We keep a couple million bottles in here, in various stages, for two to seven years."

Jeremy stared around, his eyes wide. "What an amazing amenity to have for your winery."

Peter smiled, obviously proud of the company. "We're the oldest winery in Napa, so the original founder had a lot of land to choose from. It's a perfect environment for sparkling wine."

They walked farther into the long, rounded caves, most with smooth, finished stone walls, but a few still boasted the rough-hewn rock.

They entered a big cavern with rack after rack of bare bottles, their necks slanting slightly downward. Bo nudged Jeremy. "This is what I told you about."

Peter nodded. "Yep. People seem to remember the fact that we hand riddle better than anything." He walked over and looked at a schedule on the wall. "Sorry, no riddling is planned in the next few minutes, but the bottles each get turned according to a specified schedule. A lot of wineries do it by machine, but we're proud of our hand riddling that gives us more control."

Jeremy bent down and looked at the rack full of bottles. "Do they always get turned the same amount?"

"Nope. Different amounts and shifting from clockwise to counterclockwise. It helps us impart a unique flavor to the wine." His cell rang, and he pulled his phone from his pocket. "Excuse me." Holding it to his ear, he said, "Yes? Oh right. Be there in a sec." He clicked off. "Would you excuse me a couple of minutes?

Best not to wander far. You can actually get lost in here. I'll be back in five." He strode away.

When Peter turned a corner at the end of the hall, Jeremy grabbed Bo's hand and pulled him backward into the passage at the rear of the cavern, where some rough stone gave Bo an archeological explorer feel. Like there could be cave paintings any minute.

Jeremy wasn't spelunking, however. He backed into the rough wall and pulled Bo after him. "Need a coffee break." Wrapping both hands around Bo's cheeks, he cocked Bo's head and came in for a deep, exploring kiss.

Umm, maybe he was spelunking after all.

Bo was happy to participate, wrapping his arms around Jeremy's lean body and pulling him tight so he didn't scrape his back on the unfinished wall. Oh Lordy, what a great mouth. Unlike some men who kind of nipped and nibbled but never got down to it, as if kissing were just an hors d'oeuvre, Jeremy made kissing a serious meal. His lips enfolded Bo's, sealing their mouths together; then his tongue went to work, caressing its opposite number as well as delving deep into Bo's mouth. *Whoa!* He even slid between Bo's teeth and lip in that super sensitive spot that no one ever seemed to give any attention.

Bo's lips responded, but so did all the other erogenous zones, and his cock hardened so fast it robbed his brain of blood. That was the only explanation for his hand that unfastened Jeremy's fly all on its own and dug into the folds of shirt and briefs to grasp an equally swollen playmate. Ripping his mouth away, he reached in his pocket for a handkerchief—old-fashioned as it was—pulled his own dick from his pants, and squeezed the two together, pumping like a madman. They likely only had minutes. Maybe seconds, and he had to come or he'd die. Here. Now. With Jeremy.

Jeremy caught the fire, wrapped his own hand around the package, and helped with the rhythm, staring wide and glassy-eyed into Bo's soul. "Oh shit. Hurry. Hurry!"

Both their bodies jerked up and down to help their hands. Bo gritted his teeth and saw the tendons in Jeremy's jaw standing out as they jacked like madmen. "Close. Close."

"M-me too."

"Sorry to take so long. Be right there." Peter's voice echoed through the caves.

"Oh God." Jeremy looked wild.

Bo tightened his grip and upped the pace. "Oh. Oh Lord. Yes, yes."

Jeremy nodded frantically, then his eyes literally rolled up in his head, his mouth opened in a silent scream, and cum gushed into Bo's hand, lubricating his last jerk that brought his own orgasm racing down on him. "Shit. Shit!" The words came out in a hissing whisper.

"Mr. Marchand?"

Jeremy grinned as Bo wiped their dicks and his hand. He tucked himself in and zipped up so fast he caught his shirt but quickly righted it. "This is amazing in here. It looks like there should be cave paintings." He walked away from Bo toward the cavern, giving Bo an extra second to finish wiping.

Peter said, "Yes, aren't they remarkable? A lot of the walls were still like that when the current owners, the Seatons, took over back in the sixties."

Bo stashed the handkerchief in a crevice of the wall to cut down the smell of sex surrounding him. He grinned. *Glad it's not monogrammed.*

He backed out from his hiding place, staring at the truly amazing details of the cave. "I could explore these caves forever."

Peter smiled. "I'm glad you got to look around, because Henry's ready to see you now."

As they walked out of the caves, Jeremy glanced at Bo and gave him a wink. Funny. Jeremy made him want to do crazy things. Crazy, but they felt more authentic than the life he lived every day.

Jeremy was saying, "I can't help but notice the same last name. Are you and Henry related?"

Peter chuckled. "Yes, I'm his father. I used to do his job, but I wanted to semiretire, so I became his assistant."

"How's that working out for you?" Jeremy shared his big smile.

For an instant a frown washed over Peter's face like one of those illusions in a funhouse. Then he showed his teeth. "Great. I get to share my wisdom—" He coughed loudly, and Jeremy laughed. "—without working all those hours." But something about the frown gave Bo a shudder.

When they got to the office again, they were met by a man slightly taller, substantially less silver-haired, but otherwise the image of Peter—if you didn't count some quality in the eyes. Not mean, exactly. More like afraid, cornered. *Odd.* Nonetheless, he smiled and shook their hands. "Henry Fieldstone. Hope you enjoyed the tour. Sorry I wasn't ready when you got here."

Bo displayed the dimples. "We enjoyed it very much." He had to work to keep from laughing. "No problem at all."

After they thanked Peter, the younger Fieldstone led the way into an inner office and asked them to sit.

He stepped behind a big desk, glanced down at a sheet of paper, and crinkled his brow. "I'm sure you know that we buy very little bulk." He slapped on a phony smile. "I guess it's not right to call it bulk, then, is it?" He laughed at his own joke, and Bo and Jeremy forced smiles. "However, since you have your dry farming product available in small quantities, I think we would be interested in arranging a contract."

Bo really smiled that time. "Thank you. We'd be honored to supply Strausburg. We have some unique blends between the two of us and—"

Fieldstone held up a hand. "By *us* are you referring to you and your associates at Marchand Wineries?"

Bo frowned. "No. I mean Jeremy and me, of course. What we're offering is a package of our unique wines and blends in bulk. I thought that was clear from my emails to you."

"Well, it was." He gave an indulgent smile. "But I assumed you'd be interested in selling us your wines, Bo, separate from Mr. Aames, because—" His eyes flicked to Jeremy and then away. "—we're not interested in his wines at all."

Bo's brain scrambled. He'd give a fucking lot to be able to say he sold bulk wines to Strausburg. It would be an amazing implied endorsement. But they'd started out together, they'd crafted their contract to include bulk from both vineyards, and no way he could just abandon Jeremy, who sat there looking blank. Bo could feel the anger seething. He said, "Uh, I'm sorry, but—"

Jeremy leaned forward. "Of course it can be set up that way. I totally understand that the dry-farmed grapes have that hard-to-duplicate flavor. I know Bo would be honored to be your supplier. Who wouldn't?"

He stood. "Perhaps I'll just step out while you two discuss the contract."

"Jeremy—" Bo reached out to touch him, but he stepped back, shook Fieldstone's hand—although how he got the balls to do it, Bo could barely understand—and Jeremy was out the door.

DON'T FREAK. Don't cry. Jeremy clenched and unclenched his fists. He smiled at the receptionist with practiced slickness, pushed open the door to the parking lot, and started breathing in air the moment he felt the sun on his face. *The bastard. The bloody, stinking bastard.* He didn't really mean Henry Fieldstone, but he'd include him in the bloody, stinking package.

He stopped walking when he got away from the building and under some trees. *Shelter from the storm—as if. Maybe it's time to quit. Damn, I hate to let Ottersen win, but I could end up taking Bo down with me, and that would be a tragedy. Breathe.* Heat pressed behind his eyes, which was so fucking stupid, but even thinking about all the good shit Bo had tried to do for him made him feel warm, fuzzy—and guilty. *God, I should lie down and become his concubine to try to pay him back, because the way things are going, I'll never pay him back any other way. At least not and survive.*

"I'm really sorry."

Jeremy's head snapped up, but it wasn't Bo. Peter leaned against a tree trunk.

"Uh, thanks, I guess." He inhaled. "So you knew." It wasn't a question.

"Yeah. He doesn't do much without consulting me. Usually he'll listen to my advice, but this time he was determined to make this stupid decision." He pushed away from the tree, crossed his arms, and shook his head. "If it's any consolation, I think your blends are brilliant and would be good for us."

"Wish you still held the position." He turned his lips up.

"Well, if I did, I'd be getting the pressure Henry is, and, of course, I'd refuse to be coerced, which means I'd lose my job and we'd be right back where we are now, right?" He smiled ruefully.

"Ottersen?"

"Who?"

"Ernest Ottersen. The dude who's pressuring your son."

Peter scrunched his eyebrows. "I don't think that was the name." He shrugged. "But it could have been, I guess. Or maybe he's got a go-between. Anyway, son, I'm sorry. I think you've done an amazing job, and when I met you and saw how young both you and Marchand are, I was doubly impressed."

"Thank you, Peter. I'm grateful."

"Wish I could put some money where my mouth is."

"Me too."

Bo came out of the office door, frowning ferociously, looked around, then powered over to where Jeremy stood.

As Bo approached, Peter shook Jeremy's hand. "Sorry again."

Jeremy nodded but tried to put on a happy face for Bo.

Bo walked up. "Stupid bastard."

Peter nodded and chuckled mirthlessly. "Amen to that."

"Excuse me, sir."

Jeremy said, "At least you got a contract. Some good came of this pooch screw."

"I told him to shove that contract where the sun don't shine."

"No way!"

Peter pumped a fist. "Well done."

Jeremy felt like his mind was at war. Half a brain crowed that Bo had stood up for him. The other half cringed from the idea. *My fault. My fault.*

"That whole thing was a crock of horseshit," Bo snarled. "I made it very clear what we had to offer. That little twerp wants to see if he can turn us against each other. Well, he can take his sparkling wine and drown in it." He glanced at Peter. "Sorry for speaking ill of your family member, but he's an idiot."

Peter nodded. "Sadly, that's sometimes true."

Jeremy said, "I wonder how Ottersen got to him?"

"Yes. I wondered at first why he wouldn't have just refused us both, but I'm guessing this was a way to point out that you were being discriminated against. It wasn't just that he didn't have a use for our wines."

Peter scratched at his cheek. "You know, I still don't think Ottersen's the name I heard."

Jeremy sighed. "Not *we*, Bo. Me. He's discriminating against me. He's trying to put me out of business."

Bo shook his head. "I just don't understand why." He waved an arm toward the business office. "And I don't even know how he learned we were going to be at Strausburg, for Lord's sake."

"I don't know how the fucker knows anything he does."

Peter put a hand on Jeremy's arm. "I'm terribly sorry this has occurred and that my son has been a pawn in this crap. If I hear anything useful, I'll call you, okay? And if I remember who Henry said he spoke to." He shook Bo's hand and walked away.

Jeremy looked up at Bo. "Tell me the truth. Do you think tomorrow's appointments are going to be any different?"

The crease between those beautiful eyes got deeper. "Let's get back to the motel and I'll make some calls."

"Thanks, Bo." Jeremy started walking toward the Prius. "Thank you for everything."

CHAPTER NINETEEN

JEREMY STARED out the window as the miles of highway sped under the wheels of the Prius. *Last chance. Last effort. Shot. Fuck.* True to his word, Bo had called each winery with which he'd made an appointment. *Oh yes, Mr. Marchand, we look forward to seeing you. Yes, we're interested. What? Oh no. We assumed we could rewrite the contracts to exclude Hill Top wines. Surely you're not inflexible on this point? Oh, you are? Sadly, then, we have nothing to talk about. Sorry to waste your time.*

Jeremy tried to convince Bo to relent. He couldn't do this to himself. Bo had a chance to prevail against Ottersen and make some much-needed sales. He couldn't afford to stand on principle. But of course, this was Bo. Mr. Principle. Except for one or two little staying-in-the-closet details, but still.

"Jeremy?"

"Hmm?" He kept looking out the window.

"We're going to think of something, darlin'. Don't give up hope. I hate seeing you look so dejected."

It wasn't fair, but Jeremy wanted to scream *"You haven't been rejected by every customer on the West Coast. What would you know?"* He didn't. Instead he turned his head and smiled, though it probably didn't make it to his eyes. "I don't know why you don't give up, Bo. On me. Obviously this is a hopeless task. For some weird reason, I'm being driven from the business."

"Shit on a stick, it doesn't make sense." Bo glanced at his phone and clicked it. The speaker in the car burst to life and started ringing.

After a couple of rings, a voice answered. "Hi, Bo. I've got Llewellyn here too. Can I put you on speaker?"

"Sure." The sound became more echoed.

"H-hi, Bo."

"Hi, Llewellyn. Sorry to bother you guys on the weekend."

"N-no problem. We w-wanted to talk to you."

Bo sighed. "We're getting desperate, and I just wanted to know if you've uncovered anything."

"Why? What's happened?" Blaise's voice was intense.

Bo detailed their trip, from the one promising appointment at Reynolds and Reynolds to the total strike-out at the others. Strikeout for Jeremy and Hill Top, that was.

Llewellyn spoke thoughtfully. "Y-you made the appointment at R-Reynolds at the l-last minute?"

"Yes." He glanced over at Jeremy.

Son of a bitch, Jeremy hadn't thought of that.

"S-so whoever spoke t-to the w-wineries wasn't informed about the f-first appointment."

Bo nodded as he changed lanes. "I see that now. Sorry, this has been so upsetting, we're not thinking real clearly."

There was a pause. Blaise said, "Uh, Bo. We haven't been able to find any evidence that Ottersen is behind all this."

Jeremy shook his head disgustedly. "He's just a damned good liar."

"Th-That may b-be, Jeremy. But y-your clients swear that they c-called him. Not the other w-way around."

"When we ask them why," Blaise added, "they get evasive. Better prices. More inventory. More popular types of grapes, but the fact is, they couldn't have known that in advance unless someone told them."

"Right, Ottersen!" Jeremy tried not to sound exasperated, but no matter how he weighed it, he couldn't figure out a way to lay this on his craptastic father.

"We just can't prove that." Blaise sounded really skeptical.

"It's not going to matter much longer anyway, guys. I'm going to have to put it on the market. Wineries aren't all that easy to sell. Unless, of course, that's what Ottersen's wanted all along. Maybe he'll buy it from me—at a rock-bottom price."

Bo put a warm hand on his thigh. "Have you learned anything else?"

Blaise gave a funny snort. "Kind of, although it probably has no significance."

Shit, none of it did. Jeremy wiped a hand across his eyes.

Bo said, "What is it?"

"On Llewellyn's research—"

"On Dionysus?"

"Yes, exactly. He keeps hearing rumors that there's some kind of Dionysian group or society in the wine country."

"Our wine country?" Bo looked at Jeremy with raised eyebrows.

Llewellyn said, "Y-yes. And it s-seems to be very, um, shall we say prurient in n-nature?"

Jeremy frowned. "What?"

"The rumors s-suggest the s-sexual aspects of the Dionysian m-mysteries, and there are m-many."

"Where'd you hear this?" Jeremy and Bo glanced at each other in amazement.

"Llewellyn heard it through some people in the history department who apparently were asked to join."

"Y-yes. They demurred d-due to a d-disinclination to have s-sex in public."

"What the fuck?" Although why Jeremy should be surprised at anything the central coast vintners did, he wasn't sure.

Llewellyn gave a dry, little chuckle. "P-precisely."

"But how might that affect Jeremy and me?"

Blaise said, "We don't know. It's just another twisted thread running through that community of yours."

"Wonders never cease." Bo passed a truck, one of many that loomed in their way as they tried to get home a day earlier than expected. "Thank you again for all you—whoa!" A black car that had been in front of the truck pulled into the lane directly in Bo's pathway. He slammed on the brakes and leaned on the horn. "Asshole!"

"What happened?" Blaise sounded concerned.

"Just an idiot driver that clearly got his license at Walmart." Bo exhaled. "As I was saying, thank you again for all your help."

"W-we haven't g-gotten m-many results."

"But not for lack of trying, darlin's, I can tell. We deeply appreciate it."

"We're not giving up, Bo."

"Thank you. Thank you both. We'll talk again soon."

He clicked off and wiped a hand along his eyes. "They're so great."

"I agree. I hope I didn't sound too frustrated."

"I'm sure they know how terrible this is for you."

Jeremy gave a tight smile. "Which is Southern polite speak for 'You were an asshole but they'll likely forgive you.'"

"No, honestly. You behaved as I'm sure they'd expect from someone being so mistreated." He looked over. "Why don't you lay your head back and rest? We've got another few hours to go."

"I want to take my turn driving."

"I'll wake you in an hour if you fall asleep."

"Deal." He rested his head against the door and got as comfy as Prius physics allowed. His eyes closed, and Bo turned on some soothing music that encouraged him to drift. Nothing much he could do until he got home. Hell, nothing much he could do....

"Jeremy?"

Bo's voice cut through his foggy brain.

"Jeremy! Wake up!"

"What?" His eyes fluttered as his body slammed against the doorframe, then hurdled back and banged into the console, his head actually grazing Bo's shoulder. "What's happening?"

"They're running us off the road!" Bo slammed his foot on the gas and sped forward, but the black car—the same black car—pushed into their lane and wouldn't let Bo get ahead. On Bo's left, the road shoulder fell away into a drainage ditch.

"God damn!" Jeremy powered down the window, stuck his head out, and screamed, "Get the hell in your own lane, you idiot!"

"Jeremy, get back in here, for God's sake. They could have a gun or something."

Jeremy's eyes widened as the side of the black car came straight at him, and he yanked his body back in as a thud rang out, signaling that the black coupe had grazed the side of the Prius. *Oh fuck, this is serious. Not some drunk but a real attack. Jesus H. Christ.* "They're after us, Bo."

"I know." They careened ahead as Bo stomped the gas, and they burst around yet another truck. Bo started to pull to the right when Jeremy spied the Highway Patrol car. He leaned over and pressed down on the horn.

Bo yelled, "What the—" Then he saw the cop too and pressed his hand on top of Jeremy's. The policeman looked over, and Jeremy waved wildly behind them.

Bo glanced at the mirror. "Wait. Shit!"

"What?"

"The car's gone. They must have seen the cops too."

Jeremy fell back against the seat, a combination of pissed, scared, and relieved.

As expected after their comic opera, the patrolman waved them over. It took a few minutes at high speed, but finally they were able to change lanes and pull to the shoulder of the road.

Still breathing hard, they waited for the cop to walk forward from his car; then Bo opened the window. "Thank you, Officer. I think you saved our lives." As he tended to do when being charming, Bo's accent accentuated so it came out as "saved ahr lahves."

The officer frowned. "License and registration, please. And explain what you mean."

Jeremy leaned over. "A black coupe, something like a Camaro, I think, with blacked-out windows, was trying to run us off the road."

"What? Why?" *Skeptical, thy name is policeman.*

"We don't know exactly, sir. Earlier the same car tried to enter our lane, and I honked at him. Maybe he was drunk and saw a chance to get even."

Jeremy snorted. "Yeah, well, he was sober enough that when he got one look at you, he disappeared."

The cop might not have believed them, but they hadn't done anything wrong except wave and honk at a highway patrolman, which hadn't made it onto the Thou Shalt Not list of driving yet, so he just told them to be careful and left.

Bo said, "Do you think he'll even report that?"

"Nope. He thinks we're wackadoodle."

"Can't say I blame him. If it hadn't happened to me, I'm not sure I'd believe it either."

"What do you think happened?"

Bo exhaled long and slow. "I guess what I told the cop. The guy got pissed because I honked at him, and he chased us down and tried to run us into the ditch."

"Seriously, you think that's all it was?"

"What else could it have been?" But his frown was deep.

"I'm gonna leave you to imagine that for yourself." Jeremy dropped his face into his hand and rubbed between his eyebrows. He had to admit, this maneuver could plausibly be someone other than Ottersen. *Maybe I need to think about getting out?* God, just the thought made him nauseated.

Bo sighed, stared intensely in his side and rear-view mirrors, actually turned around and checked the oncoming traffic, then pulled out fast into the moving stream of cars. No menacing black coupes.

When they were whizzing along, Bo glanced uneasily at Jeremy. "That was really scary."

"Yeah." He could hear the "but" hanging in the air.

"Maybe not a reason to jump to too big a conclusion."

Jeremy shrugged. What point in pushing his agenda? He was the one on the receiving end. Of course, Bo would have been just as injured or even killed as Jeremy if the car had driven them off the road. Plus Bo's business was being impacted as well. Not as much as Hill Top, but the blowback from his support of Jeremy could be costly. "You're probably right." He forced a smile. "Hey, aren't I supposed to be driving?"

"No. I'm jumpier than a cat in a room full of rocking chairs. I'd never get any rest. I might as well drive."

"Let me know if that changes."

"Will do."

Jeremy closed his eyes, just so he could think. Did Ottersen really send that car? How? Not everyone had contacts willing to kill or injure someone for you. Yes, Ottersen was crappy and deceitful in business, but stealing customers and killing people were pretty far apart. And what would he have to gain? If Jeremy died, Ottersen didn't get anything more than he could acquire without the risk. Maybe he was just trying to scare Jeremy into selling, and the guy in the car went too far? Possible.

With all that said, what am I going to do?

"Jeremy?"

His eyes flew open. That was conditioning from the last time Bo called his name. "Yes?"

He must have sounded scared, because Bo smiled. "Nothing's wrong. I could just smell the grits burning, you were thinking so hard."

"Yeah, sorry."

"I was thinking too. What if I loan you the money, or maybe buy a piece of your winery?"

Jeremy tried to keep his frown from looking disapproving. "I'm not a good risk at this point, Bo. I might never be able to repay the debt, and the winery isn't worth much with no customer goodwill." He glanced out the window. They were getting closer to home.

"I'm thinking if Ottersen knows I'm investing, he may realize he hasn't got a chance against both of us. The land and vines have value. We can hold the vineyard until he gives up and then build back up the customer base."

Jeremy's heart beat so hard it made his chest hurt. Here was Bo willing to go out on an even bigger limb for him. "Why?"

"What?"

"Why would you do this for me, Bo? I know the land's valuable and it's decent collateral, but you haven't got money to burn with half the state of Georgia to support. Maybe you like fucking me, but you're not even out. Not like it's going to do you much good. It's not that I'm not grateful. Hell, I could open a vein for you. But I just want to understand." He wiped a hand over his neck. "Maybe I'm not a nice enough guy to get this?"

Bo held up a finger and took the next exit into San Luis Obispo. At the end of the off-ramp, he turned right and pulled into a supermarket parking lot, where he took an empty space. Then he turned to Jeremy.

"Okay, first off, you're about as nice as guys get, which is one of the reasons I like you. In fact, a lot of people like you, not just me. But I admire you. I mean, I know what it's like to come to a brand-new place and try to make your way. You've managed to fit in and stand out. That's not easy. You've put together a fine business, you deserve to succeed, and I don't think it's fair that someone's trying to defeat you by cheating." He idly ran a finger across his own lips, but it made Jeremy shiver—in a good way. Bo said, "There's a whole lot more that I reckon I've not earned the right to talk about, but what I already said are the reasons I'd want to help you, without any other considerations."

Unprepared. Water sprang out of Jeremy's eyes like oil from a geyser, and he slapped a hand to his wet cheek so fast he could have killed a spider.

Bo put a big, warm hand on his arm. "What are those tears about?"

Jeremy shook his head. "Not many people around to tell me I did anything well." He wiped at his eyes and swallowed hard. "Not even me." He let his gaze rest on Bo's sea green eyes. "I really appreciate it."

Bo raised his hand to Jeremy's cheek. "So think about my offer."

"I will." He inhaled deeply. "Now here's another invitation. Want to come to my place tonight?"

Bo smiled, slow and sweet. "If I spoke twelve languages, I'd say 'hell yes' in every one of them."

CHAPTER TWENTY

Bo DIDN'T go home. If he did, no way he'd get out of there. He'd said he would be gone two days, so they wouldn't be looking for him. Since he had his overnight bag, he carried it into Jeremy's. Walking in this time, he noticed more, like how very spare the furnishings were and the almost total lack of decoration except for one or two pretty but generic paintings. It showed none of the style and spirit reflected in Hill Top Wineries.

Jeremy must have noticed him looking because he said, "I've been pretty focused on the business since I moved here. I haven't put much energy into this place." He walked into the good-sized living room and turned on lights.

"It's a great place." Remote as hell, but that had advantages. "Do you own it?"

His eyes skittered away from Bo, then back. "No. I rent. I wanted to be sure I liked the house and location before I bought anything."

"Sure. That makes sense."

Jeremy pointed down the hall. "Want to put your bag in, uh, the bedroom?"

"I'd be delighted."

"You know where. Uh, want something to eat?"

"Sure. I could eat. I'll help after I put this away." Bo started down the hall. Jeremy had acted very sure of himself when he issued the invitation, but now he seemed uncertain and a little shy. Hell, the guy had been beaten down until it was a wonder he was still standing.

Bo hadn't quite recalled from his last intense visit, but Jeremy's bedroom was even plainer than the rest of the house—a big bed with white sheets, carefully made, with a comfy blanket at the foot, bracketed by some nightstands. That, plus a dresser and a chair, constituted the total décor of the room. Not a single picture hung on the walls or photo decorated a tabletop. Spartan.

Bo opened the closet—*whoa*. A few things hung on the racks, but two smallish bags sat against the back wall, open and obviously neatly packed. Did he just return from a trip—other than the one they'd just taken? Bo closed the closet, feeling a little like a snooper, tossed his bag on the floor next to the chair, and went into the bathroom to pee and wash up. When he got back into the kitchen, the placed smelled amazing. "Wow. What's that?"

"Chicken veggie soup and grilled cheese, tomato, and pesto sandwiches."

Bo collapsed into a kitchen chair. "That sounds better'n almost anything—except sex." He grinned.

Jeremy gave him a glance over the shoulder. "That's dessert."

"Jeremy Gelato?"

"With Beauregard Crème Brûlée."

The idea gave Bo's shaft some pretty peppy ideas, but this evening wasn't really about sex—even though they said it was. Ever since those tears in the parking lot, Beau knew the night needed to be about comfort and letting Jeremy know someone cared about his plight and was there to help. He stood, walked closer, and wrapped his arms around Jeremy's waist, then softly kissed his neck. "Thank you for cooking."

"My pleasure." He arched his neck back and gently kissed Bo's available lips.

The food also turned out to be a pleasure, showing that original zest that Jeremy's house decorating seemed to lack. After they'd cleaned up the dishes, they held hands and walked down the hall. Some quick toothbrushing later, they left their jeans and sweatshirts they'd changed into after their appointments on the chair and crawled into bed. Like an old married couple, they leaned against the headboard and held hands.

"Bo?"

"Hmm?"

"I've thought a lot about your offer."

"Good. I hope you decide to accept it."

"I realize you're trying to take care of me."

Bo shrugged. "Maybe a little."

Jeremy let out a long exhale. "I can't begin to tell you how much I love that you feel inclined to do that, but you need to quit."

"Why?" Bo tried to smooth his own brow.

"Because—" He held up a finger. "—you don't need any more damned people to take care of."

Bo smiled. In truth, Jeremy had a point. "But I actually like taking care of you."

"The thing is—" He sighed loudly, and Bo tensed. "—people are going to notice, Bo. For a guy who wants to stay in the closet, that's not a good thing. Your family will realize you're making special efforts and concessions for me, and they're going to want to know why. Same with the other growers. Someone like Ezra is going to put his finger right on the truth." He looked up and met Bo's eyes with an intense stare. "If you don't want that, you need to stop taking care of me."

He was right, of course. "I'll tell you what. How about you let me worry about that?"

"But—"

"Shh." Bo stopped Jeremy's lips with a kiss. The soft kiss turned to slow, gentle lovemaking, both of them too tired and too sad for anything more fiery. Maybe what Jeremy had said about no longer taking care of him gave their embraces an extra edge of poignancy. Bo had to make a decision. As the old expression said, it was time to shit or get off the pot. That was his last inspiring thought as he fell asleep.

Bo's eyes opened suddenly. *What time is it? Was that my phone?* He raised his head and stared into the dark. There was no moon tonight, and out where Jeremy lived, no light shone in from the street. Bo felt for his phone on the nightstand and glanced at the screen. *Text from Llewellyn?*

He didn't want to shine blue screen light in Jeremy's eyes when his soft breathing said he was sleeping so soundly. Slipping out from under Jeremy's arm, he slid to the side and reached his foot to the ground. He had to feel his way. After a couple of seconds, he managed to find the chairs. The jeans on top proved to be Jeremy's—too small for Bo—so he grabbed the next pair, then pulled on a sweatshirt. The hood testified that

THE CASE OF THE VORACIOUS VINTNER   211

it was Jeremy's, not Bo's, but it was big enough it didn't matter. Patting at the wall with his hands, he found the door and crept out into the hall, then walked into the living room. Outside was probably the best place for this so as not to wake Jeremy.

Quietly he opened the front door. *Good thing Jeremy doesn't have a dog. Hmm. Wonder if he'd like a pooch. I'd kind of like one.* The quiet night struck him. Usually there were crickets or frogs, even in the early spring, but not tonight. So silent. Like a held breath.

He looked down at his phone. Odd that Llewellyn would be texting him so late, although in truth, he and Jeremy had crashed fairly early after their long drive and upsetting morning. Poor Jeremy. To sit there and have someone say so matter-of-factly that of course they didn't want his wine. The unique blends he'd slaved over. Sweet Lord, like a slap in the face.

He clicked on the text, but it hadn't downloaded. He glanced up like he could see the bad reception, then walked a few feet off the porch to get into a different position. Sure enough, his bars increased by two and the text clicked in. He bent over it.

Background data on Jeremy sketchy & inconsistent. Don't want to overstep, but needs investigation. Be careful.

He felt the strain of his own scowl. His instant reaction was to fly to Jeremy's defense. The second thought was this wasn't anything he hadn't considered himself. Jeremy blatantly didn't discuss his past. Sure, Bo got not wanting to dwell on an unhappy childhood, but to never mention a family experience, bad or good, seemed amazing—especially to a Southerner.

But how do I bring it up without—?

The scuff of a step behind him registered in his head one second before something way beyond hard smashed into it.

OH LORDY, does my head hurt. Bo tried to crack open his eyelids, but the searing flash of light against his eyeballs should be sold to the CIA as an interrogation tool. He'd tell them anything to make it go away. He squeezed his eyes closed and tried to put a hand over them, but something dragged against it and hurt when he moved.

"Somebody close that curtain." The demanding voice shivered through Bo—in a good way. *Jeremy.* Some light directly above Bo went out and the general illumination on his eyelids seemed to soften. *Better. Maybe.*

He tried again and managed to get a crack in his lids, though he cringed a little from it.

Near his face, Jeremy said, "You scared the holy shit out of me."

Bo finally made his lips work. "T-tell me so I can be scared too."

"Beauregard Marchand, you stop trying to be funny and rest. You've experienced a great trauma."

Mama. That was not comforting. He managed to force his eyes open and faced his mother, with the rest of the Marchand clan hanging in the doorway. Apparently someone had told them they couldn't come in the room but hadn't managed to control the access point. Bo sighed softly. "What kind of trauma?" He tried to move his arm to touch his head again, but this time could see he was hooked to an IV. *Lord Jesus, how bad off am I?*

His mother frowned daggers toward Jeremy. "Mr. Aames believes that someone intended to accost him and mistook you for him. Apparently that sweatshirt you were wearing was one he loaned you?" She might have been saying Jeremy killed baby seals in the garment before forcing Bo to put it on and then beating him over the head with a lead pipe. He'd have laughed if he didn't feel like crap.

He spoke softly to Jeremy, who stood next to the bed, his back half-turned toward Bo's mother. "So you think someone was after you?"

"Of course. Don't you?"

"You mean—?"

"Who the hell else?" He looked bitter.

"But why? He's done a pretty effective job of neutralizing any threat from you. Why would he need to—" He shrugged. "What? Warn you off? Physically harm you?"

There was a tap on the door. Bo forced his head to move. A tall, thin man with dark hair and light eyes stood inside the door, Bo's family clustered behind him. "Mr. Marchand, I'm Roberto O'Hara with the Paso Robles police." He glanced around at the crowd. "I wonder if I can ask you some questions about this event."

"Yes."

"I'll have to ask your, uh, guests to leave."

Bo waved his free hand. "Come on everyone, scoot, please."

His mama got up huffily and walked out to the rest of the family. Jeremy started to follow, but O'Hara put a hand on his arm. "You're Mr. Aames?"

Jeremy nodded warily.

"If you wouldn't mind remaining."

Jeremy appeared to be considering leaving but nodded again. When Mama had made it fully out the door, O'Hara closed it.

"So who called you, Mr. O'Hara?" Bo cocked his head. "Is this for certain some kind of crime?"

O'Hara extended a business card to Bo, then sat in the chair Mama had vacated, leaving Jeremy standing beside the bed. "You were thinking perhaps someone hit you hard enough to give you a concussion for fun?" He pulled a notebook from his pocket. "And it's Detective O'Hara."

"I'm sorry. I don't exactly know what happened. One minute I was looking at my phone, and the next I was here."

"Where were you when you were on the phone?"

"Outside Jeremy's house, uh, a few feet off the porch."

"And you, Mr. Aames?" O'Hara had big blue eyes with a lot of white around the pupil. He focused them on Jeremy.

"You mean where was I when Bo was outside my house? Asleep, I guess. He was, uh, staying with me since we'd just gotten back from a business trip. We were tired and went to sleep early."

"You didn't hear him go outside?"

"No. Sound asleep."

"So you found Mr. Marchand unconscious?"

"Yes."

"Where?"

Jeremy glanced at Bo. "About half a mile down the road from my house."

"What?" Bo's head snapped up, and he was instantly sorry. *Ouch.* "How did I get down there?"

"You don't remember being pulled, carried, or dragged?" O'Hara sat with his pen poised.

"No. I told you, I was just standing there. I heard a crunch behind me and—that's it. That's all."

"What was your impression, Mr. Aames?"

Jeremy shook his head. "I didn't know. At first I thought Bo had decided to go home and collapsed somehow. But that made no sense. His car was parked in front, and he was wearing my sweatshirt while his clothes were, uh, in his bag at my house. Mostly I was scared I couldn't wake him and called 911."

Bo said, "So you didn't call the police?"

"No. I mean, I asked 911 for an ambulance. Like I said, I was really scared for you. I thought there was a reasonable explanation until I found out you'd been hit very hard. Then—" He shrugged.

"Then?" O'Hara glanced up.

"Then I thought someone must have been after me and mistook you for me in the dark."

O'Hara frowned. "The ER called me when they discovered Mr. Marchand had been struck with a blunt weapon, dragged, and abraded. And why would you think someone would want to do that to you, Mr. Aames?"

"I, uh, didn't exactly. I just have enemies in the valley, and I thought maybe one of them was trying to scare me or threaten me in some way. I didn't realize it was quite that serious."

"And now that you do?" O'Hara's big blue eyes never wavered.

Jeremy shrugged but didn't exactly meet O'Hara's stare.

"Doesn't it seem likely that someone might have dragged Mr. Marchand to a vehicle thinking he was someone else? You, for example? And then upon discovering his mistake, tossed him out on the road?"

"I suppose." Jeremy really frowned.

Hell, so did Bo.

"So would you care to supply the names of your enemies, Mr. Aames?"

"I'm not sure anyone would have it in for me quite that much."

"Perhaps not, but nonetheless, the enemies list will be important."

"I don't want to point fingers at innocent people."

Bo looked at Jeremy. When did he get so concerned about Ottersen's possible innocence?

O'Hara handed Jeremy a piece of paper and a pen. Jeremy looked worried but sat on the edge of the bed and wrote his list. Finally he looked up and handed the paper to O'Hara—reluctantly, it seemed. "The first person on the list has screwed me out of a lot of contracts lately, and I've been pretty pissed about it. The others don't like me because I'm gay, but I doubt they'd beat me over the head for it."

"Wouldn't be the first time." O'Hara raised an eyebrow.

Bo grimaced.

O'Hara tucked away the paper. "Thanks. Neither of you leave town without letting me know first, okay?" He pulled cards from his pocket and handed them each one. "And call me if you remember anything else pertinent. We'll be scouting around your house, Mr. Aames, so stay away from the area where you found Mr. Marchand unconscious so that you don't inadvertently damage evidence."

"I have to drive down there to get to work."

"That's fine. Just don't linger."

Jeremy nodded, and O'Hara opened the door. Like an equal and opposite reaction, Mama rushed back in, with the family behind.

Bo stared after O'Hara with a brand-new certainty. Jeremy wasn't completely convinced that it was Ottersen who hit Bo. Bo might not have an idea who else it could have been, but he'd bet Jeremy did.

CHAPTER TWENTY-ONE

BO STOOD from the wheelchair they'd made him ride in to get out of the hospital. Instantly his uncle Davey slid an arm around his waist while his mama and Bettina clucked in front of him. Despite a passionate desire to swing his arms in a wide circle and swat them all like flies, he restrained himself. They just wanted to take care of him. He held up a hand. "I'm fine. Honest. Aside from my head hurting, I'm good as new. I need to talk to Jeremy for a minute. Please get in the car."

His mother planted hands on her considerable hips. "Beauregard, the doctor clearly said you're recovering from concussion and need to rest."

"Yes, ma'am, which I will do as soon as we get home. But first, as I said, I need to talk to Jeremy."

His mother's glare could have killed grizzlies. "I would think that *Jeremy* had done enough."

Bo just sighed, and his mother gave it up and slid into the front passenger seat of the "family" Honda—a car that Bo paid for like everything else but everyone used, while he kept the Prius for himself. That would be the Prius still parked in front of Jeremy's.

Bo walked the few steps to where Jeremy stood leaning against his car. "Thank you for coming to the hospital."

Jeremy shook his head and gave a tight smile. "You're something else, man. I about get you killed, and you're thanking me? Get serious. Your mother's right. I'm worse for you than this year's flu epidemic."

Bo cocked his head away from the car and grinned. "And I had my shots, right where they did the most good."

Jeremy snorted.

"But I'm worried about you, darlin'." His face sobered, and he so badly wanted to reach out and touch Jeremy's cheek. "Whoever hit me almost certainly was after you. What's to stop them from trying again?"

"A whole lot of cops, as far as I can tell."

"Wish that made me feel better." He took a breath. *Pull the tiger by its tail.* "Do you really think it was Ottersen who hit me?"

Jeremy raised a light eyebrow. "No. I think it was somebody Ottersen paid a bunch of the money he stole from my contracts."

"Seriously, I just wish I could figure what he had to gain by doing it. He'd have to realize you'd suspect him immediately."

"Yeah, and that I'd have trouble proving it."

"But where you found me suggests whoever hit me was planning to abduct me. Or actually, abduct you. Why would Ottersen do that?"

Jeremy stared at his shoes, then up at Bo. "I don't know, but then, why has he done any of the shit he's done to me, Bo?" His voice rose in exasperation and, from the corner of his eye, Bo saw his mother stare from the car.

Bo nodded and fought the intense desire to hug Jeremy. Yes, he was hiding something. Maybe a lot of somethings. But he was also frustrated, horrified, and hurting like hell. "It's gonna get better."

"From your lips to God's ears, baby." He gave a really pained smile and slid into his car.

Bo watched him pull out and drive away, then walked slowly to the back seat of the Honda. As Davey pulled away from the curb, Bo said, "Take me to the winery, please, Davey."

His mother shrieked, "You most certainly will not! You're going home, young man, and straight to bed."

"Yes, ma'am, right after I look in on my staff and make sure everything is okay. They may have heard all sorts of things about what happened to me, and I don't want them to worry unnecessarily."

As he'd hoped, that excuse made sense to her. "Very well, but just for a minute and no stress."

It took a few minutes to drive into wine country, but Davey finally turned onto the steep road up to Marchand. Bo itched to get inside. With everything so topsy-turvy, he couldn't get the feelings of unease to die down. Yes, he'd been hit on the damned head, which wasn't an everyday occurrence. But even beyond that, things just didn't feel right.

When he opened the door to the tasting room, the usual calm that soothed him in the winery was shattered by yelling voices coming from the kitchen. *What the hell?* He powered through the swinging door to find Blanche standing in the middle of the floor with her hands on her hips, hollering in a voice that would have done credit to his mama, and an immovable RJ facing her with folded arms, his perfect movie-star jaw clenched, shaking his head. He was speaking in a low, tight voice to match the jaw. "Bo says we don't have the resources or personnel to be able to make money on catering. We're not a full kitchen."

Her back was to Bo. RJ looked up and saw him, but Blanche didn't. "And I'm telling you, we're going to cater that event and get some exposure with the best of local society. Bo put me in charge, and you'll do—"

"I most emphatically did not ever put you in charge of anything in this winery, sugah, including bussing the goddamned tables."

She whirled. "Bo!" She crossed her arms over her chest and looked guilty, then sucked in breath and courage and said, "Well, damn it, I'm family and part of this winery is mine, and when I'm here I should be second-in-command to you."

Had it. Up to here. Bo's eyes narrowed like the space in his heart for her. "None, I repeat none of this winery belongs to you, Mama, Bettina, or anyone else except me. You want to order people around?" He pointed at the door. "Then get out there, go to work, and earn the right, because you don't have it here. Mama and the rest of the family are in the car outside. Go get in that car and tell them I'm not coming. Now get the hell out of my business. Do you understand?" His head throbbed, but he stood his ground.

Blanche stared at him with her mouth literally hanging open. "But I only wanted—I—" Tears burst from her eyes, and she turned and ran out the kitchen door. Somewhere outside, a glass hit the floor, and RJ rushed toward the sound. By the time Bo got there, Blanche was gone, and a single wineglass lay in shards on the floor as RJ pulled the dustpan from under the sink.

Bo tried to relax his fists. "I'm powerfully sorry about that, RJ. She came to me just as I was leaving and asked if she could be an intern for the winery. I told her I'd talk to Annette about supervising her, and then I plumb forgot to call her. I didn't put Blanche in charge of dusting up."

"I didn't think so, boss, but she came in right after you left and said you'd made her your supervisor. I told her I already was and so we'd have to speak with you about how to divide our responsibilities. She didn't much like that and started, well, shoving her weight around."

"Truly sorry." Bo sighed.

RJ frowned. "She really wanted to know every detail of the business. She asked to see your books!"

"What?" What the hell was she up to?

"I told her I didn't have access to that information. I didn't tell her I wouldn't give it to her if I did." He flashed the solid sunshine smile that made Marchand as much money as their best vintage. *Well, almost.*

"Thank you, RJ. You're worth your weight in gold."

RJ dumped the broken glass into the trash as Bo looked out the window. The Honda was gone. Good, because family murder was frowned upon in the state of California.

"So why the hell were you in the hospital?"

Bo sat to give RJ a highly expurgated version of the previous night's events, while still trying to figure out what the hell he was going to do about his family.

An hour later he sat back in the tasting room, saying hi to some of their best customers after checking in with his vineyard supervisor and marketing person. Blanche had cut a wide swathe in only a few hours. Fortunately his staff knew him well enough that they had taken her with a half a salt shaker, but still, they hadn't wanted to tell a member of his family she was full of shit. Why did she do it? Why the sudden power grab, and above all, why had she starting snooping into his business? Jesus, Mary, and Joseph, the world was tilting on its axis.

Everything Blaise and Llewellyn had told him played through his mind. No evidence about Ottersen. Jeremy's background couldn't be verified. And— "RJ?"

RJ polished glasses behind the tasting bar, having just served a couple sitting out on their deck admiring the view. Most guests sat outside, since Marchand had a unique site with the best overlook of the rolling hills of the wine country and the ocean far beyond.

"Um-hm?"

"Have you ever heard anything about a Dionysian society or a Dionysian group of some kind here in the central coast wine country?"

The pause was brief but very pregnant. "Uh, you mean like the festival we did?"

Bo looked up at RJ, who seemed to be carefully inspecting the nonexistent spots on the glasses. Bo nodded. "Sort of. Same name. But I heard a rumor that there's some kind of group with similar roots in the Dionysian mysteries or some such fable somewhere around here."

"Where'd you hear that?"

"Gee, I don't exactly remember. Maybe somebody said something at the festival since it happened to be by the same name." Bo carefully kept his voice casual and his eyes averted, because RJ seemed much too alert.

"Um, not sure. Maybe. Like at the same time as you. Someone asked me at the festival, I think. Asked where we got the idea. I said I didn't know."

Bo smiled. "Right."

"Where *did* you get the idea?" That was a question he really seemed to want answered.

"Oddly, I think it was from Professor Lewis."

"Our Professor Lewis?"

"Yes. I think he mentioned that he was studying the Dionysian mysteries, and Jeremy and I wanted a wine-related excuse for an event. The historic Dionysian festivals of Greece happened to be in March, so we chose it."

"Oh. So that was the only reason?" Again, the question seemed more important than it should have been.

"Yes. As far as I know."

"So you're not, like a, uh, fan of Dionysus?"

"Fan?"

"You know, like, a worshipper or something?"

Bo pressed a hand against his chest and adopted his thickest Southern drawl. "Good Lord, RJ, I'm a Georgia Baptist. One word of Dionysus and my mama would die in her grave on the spot." He laughed and RJ joined in, but his expression remained quizzical, like maybe Bo was lying and really was a follower of Dionysus. *Okay, let's add a bit more uncertainty.* "Of course, I guess anyone who's been called to start a winery since they were a child must be a secret disciple of Dionysus on some level, don't you think?"

RJ laughed, but the smile never touched his gorgeous eyes.

"Give me another one?"

The bartender, Russ, stared at Jeremy through narrowed eyes. "You've had way more than usual."

"Need another one." Jeremy pointed at the empty shot glass. "I took an Uber over." Not a hundred percent true, but Russ was a good guy. He'd help a friend out.

"What's a matter, kid? You got troubles?" Russ filled the shot glass with beautiful, life-giving amber liquid.

"Yeah. Troubles." He grabbed the glass, sniffed it, stuck his tongue in for a moment's evaluation of the scotch whisky, then slugged it back since it did, after all, taste like medicine. Not at all like beautiful, complex, wonderful wine. *Damn.* Oh God, he loved wine and he'd miss it so much. He'd miss his vines and all the fun mixing and blending to achieve complex and brilliant tastes that startled and soothed the tongue.

And—shit, I'll miss Bo.

"Gonna miss Bo, Russ. He's my good friend who tries to take care of me, even though it's too hard to do and he shouldn't even try, but he does anyway."

Funny how the big, handsome Southern gentleman had wheedled his way into Jeremy's no-access heart. The idea of walking—no, running—away and never seeing him, never talking to him again, never sharing the joy of wine or the joy of sex…. He sighed. The joy of Bo.

"Haven't seen you in here for a bit, Jeremy." Russ wiped the bar in front of him and slowly slid a cup of coffee toward Jeremy.

"Oh, subtle. So subtle." He snorted, but he picked up the cup and blew in it, making little waves in the dark liquid. "Yeah, I been busy."

"With your friend Bo?"

"Some." Jeremy looked up. "Oh, but not like that. He's not gay, but he's my friend. Not like that. Dammit." He half giggled, half snorted.

This place, the low-key Backstreet Bar, was the closest to a gay bar the area had, and when he'd first moved to the area, Jeremy had spent a couple of evenings a month there looking for friends with a benefit or two. Then he got a good look at Bo Marchand and changed his idea of friendship.

"I gather from your mood today that your busyness ain't happening anymore."

Jeremy let his head drop to his arms. "Right."

A warm body slid onto the seat next to Jeremy, causing him to raise his head and slide his arms closer to his coffee. Russ glanced at the person and said, "What'll you have?"

"Do you have white wine?" The voice was soft and light.

Jeremy had to turn his head. What guy ordered white wine in the Backstreet Bar when the wine country was next door?

The man had dark hair and, as he turned with a smile, his light green eyes made Jeremy's heart leap. He said, "Hi. I'm Sean."

"Jeremy."

"Can I buy you a drink, Jeremy?"

Russ slid a cloth between them. "He's not drinking. Want more coffee, Jeremy?"

"Hit me with a double, Sam."

Sean leaned in, and the breath from his pink lips touched Jeremy's ear. "We could go somewhere else where the bartenders aren't so high-handed."

Tempting. Damned tempting. "Thanks, but Russ is high-handed on my side. I better stick with caffeine." Still, his head felt stuffed with cotton.

Sean looked disappointed, but he smiled and sipped his wine. "So what do you do, Jeremy?"

"Uh, I make wine."

He pressed a hand to his chest. "You do? Oh my, I just love wine."

The words leaped onto his lips. "Seriously. Then why are you drinking that crap?" He slapped a hand to his mouth as Russ gave him the evil eye from a few steps down the bar.

Sean laughed charmingly. "Because I hate whiskey and beer and I needed an excuse to buy you a drink, so any white wine in a storm."

That was cute. "Okay. Forgiven." He sipped coffee and tried not to wish it were stronger. Plus the damned stuff was going straight to his bladder. "Would you save my seat? I need the men's room." Behind him, the bar had filled up.

"I'll fight off all comers." Sean grinned, and Jeremy turned on his stool and elbowed through the throng of those trying to get Russ's attention. A guy pushed past, and Sean's voice rose above the din. "Sorry. This is saved."

Somebody said, "Aw, come on."

"No. I swore on my mother's life."

Jeremy chuckled as he made it to the far wall and pulled open the men's room door. A couple of guys waited, but it was otherwise an oasis of calm. He propped his butt against the wall and tried to think of something besides needing to pee while his turn came.

The world was full of cute guys like Sean. *Why have I been ignoring them in favor of a closeted mama's boy?* Man, that, the meaning of life, and the source of world peace were the questions. Still, just thinking about pushing Sean or someone like him up against the wall made Jeremy's stomach turn, and that wasn't just the whiskey talking. *Face it, dumbass, you've got heart involvement going here. Something you swore you could live without.* But Bo got to every one of Jeremy's heartstrings. He loved wine. Was as passionate about it as Jeremy. Super easy on the eyes and charming as a snake in Eden, the bastard was still shy and self-effacing. And most of all, Bo cared—for people and, it seemed, for Jeremy. He couldn't exactly say no one had ever given a shit about him in his life, but close. Jeremy's mom had cared a lot for herself and a little for him. Enough to have left him that money he'd had to steal to finally get. And his grandfather? Yes, he cared, but somehow the love always seemed tentative. After all, he was Jeremy's father's father. Sayings about acorns and trees came to mind.

"You're up, man."

A guy pushed away from the urinal, weaving a little, and Jeremy finally whipped it out, his appendage a little fuller than normal just from thinking about Bo. He finished in relief, washed, and pushed back into the crowd. *Stop thinking about Bo. There lies madness.* He couldn't make wise decisions while his heart yearned to stay right here where Bo was. Hell, he couldn't make wise decisions at this moment anyway. A little more coffee and he should be ready to drive. Thank God for Russ.

Jeremy slid back on the stool, getting the stink eye from several potential claimants.

Sean did that hand-against-the-chest gesture again. "You have no idea what I've had to battle for you."

"In that case, I at least owe you another glass of craptastic wine." He waved a hand at Russ. "Hey, Russ, another round. How come you don't serve my wine here?"

"Don't own the place. I would if I did, believe me, buddy." He warmed up Jeremy's cup and poured more into Sean's glass from a bottle of cheap commercial white.

Jeremy tossed some bills on the table and sipped the bitter brew that would allow him to get home.

Sean leaned in. "Shall we finish this and go to your place?"

Whoa. Not quite the speed he'd anticipated on the come-on. "Can't. Lots of people there." He neglected to mention the people were the police.

"Umm. Well, I'm a visitor, but my hotel's not too far away." He smiled slowly. "Or we could rent a hotel room around here."

Jeremy held up a hand but smiled to soften the blow. "Sorry. I've just got to finish sobering up, and then I need to get home."

"Where the people are?" Sean raised an eyebrow, and his smile lost just a touch of its warmth.

"Yes, sadly. Those people are expecting me. But why don't you visit my winery while you're in town? It's not far, I can give you some really good award-winning wine, and we can go from there." The missing information was Jeremy wouldn't be there.

"Ooh, can we go now?"

Jeremy snorted. "Uh, it's really late, and about the people I mentioned?"

"Oh right." Man, this dude looked disappointed.

"Seriously, all you have to do is sit here for three minutes after I go, and you'll have more than your share of companionship." Jeremy patted Sean's slim shoulder. *Hmm.* Harder-bodied than he'd imagined. Probably a city guy who worked out in the gym all the time. Jeremy took another big mouthful of the now lukewarm coffee.

Sean stuck out his lower lip. "But I want you." Leaning closer, he whispered, "Seriously, don't you know how drop-dead gorgeous you are? You look just like—"

Jeremy nodded. "Yeah, yeah, *Legends of the Fall* and all that. I gotta go. Good to meet you." He slid off the stool, his feet hit the floor, and his knees wobbled. Shit! The more coffee he drank, the drunker he got. He waved at Russ, checked his pocket for the phone in case he needed to call Uber after he hit the air, and took off across the room. The door looked a long way away.

Fighting through bodies and a growing fog that just wouldn't lift, he got to the entrance, pushed opened the door, and—

—the stone of the floor rose up to meet him.

CHAPTER TWENTY-TWO

THE BANGING echoed through Jeremy's brain like someone pounded on him with a mallet. *Shit.* Just getting his eyes to open constituted an act of bravery.

Wham. Wham.

He managed to lift the heavy lids and was greeted by sunshine barely creeping into his own fucking living room.

Wham. Wham. The front door shuddered from a fist outside.

Flopping his feet to the ground from his couch, he pulled himself to sitting and almost puked. "Hang on. Give me a damned minute!" *Ouch. Do not yell again.* He pressed his hand against his temple.

At least the banging stopped.

Oh man, how did this happen? He was well on his way to sober when he left the bar. He swallowed and grimaced. The awful taste in his mouth spoke volumes about something a fuckload lot stronger than the coffee he'd been consuming. Rohypnol? Who? Not Russ. The guy had lots of opportunities to drug Jeremy over the last year and never had. Probably Sean. *But why? And how the hell did I get home?*

Wham!

"Okay. Coming." He staggered to his feet, almost vomited again, but managed to lurch to the door and open it.

O'Hara stared at him, a stormy expression on his cop's face. "You've redefined the term 'Looking like shit.'"

"Good morning to you too." Jeremy pressed a hand to his mouth. "I gotta barf. Come on in." He ran to the bathroom, hearing footsteps clomping into his living room behind him. After tossing practically no food and a whole lot of sour liquid, he wiped his mouth, peed, washed up, brushed his teeth, and plodded back to the living room, where he flopped onto the couch.

O'Hara had taken the most comfortable chair. "You must have tied one on."

Jeremy nodded. "Did but was drugged."

"What?"

"I went to a bar I go to sometimes, drank too much but was nearly sober when this guy started talking to me. I was drinking coffee, but I went to the john. He must have slipped me Rohypnol."

O'Hara raised an eyebrow. "For a regular guy, you sure attract crap."

"Tell me about it."

"How did you get here?"

"That's what's most weird. I've got no idea. Is my car outside?"

"Yes."

"Curiouser and curiouser. I don't feel like I was, you know, violated." He shivered. "I guess the guy from the bar could have checked my wallet—" He patted his hip. "—which I have, by the way." He pulled it out and started looking through it. Nothing seemed to be missing. "So maybe this guy drugs me, figured out where I live, and somehow found my car and drove me home, dragged me in here and didn't bother to fuck me or even rob me after slipping me a mickey, and then called a cab to take him back to the bar or to his hotel—stop me when I've exceeded the bounds of credulity."

"Yeah. Way back there."

Jeremy put his wallet back in his pocket. "My only other theory is the bartender—Russ saw what this guy was doing, stopped him, brought me home in my car, then called somebody to get him. He's a good guy. But I don't know why he wouldn't have just dragged me to the couch in the office and let me sleep it off."

"I believe we'll be asking him. Would he have known where you live?"

"Driver's license, I guess." Jeremy wiped a hand over the back of his clammy neck. "So why are you here?"

"For permission to search your house."

"What? Why?"

"It's possible whoever attacked Bo Marchand could have come in here."

"Seems unlikely. Nothing's been disturbed or left out of place."

"Still, we'd like to."

If O'Hara carried a sign saying he didn't trust Jeremy, it couldn't be more obvious. *Wise man, our O'Hara.* Jeremy's fake credentials could stand up to pretty intense scrutiny, so few worries there. But still, cops had instincts. No point asking if O'Hara planned to get a warrant if Jeremy refused. Why give him more reasons to be suspicious? "No, I don't mind. I just need to get cleaned up and get to work."

"We'll try to stay out of your way."

Right. Jeremy nodded, lay back on the couch, and watched the police making their damned selves at home. Yes, he hated this. He'd spent a year being ridiculously private, and now here they were. *Try to look relaxed.* At least they didn't have much to confuse them. He'd kept his life as spartan as possible.

"Going somewhere?" O'Hara stood at the end of the hall looking into the living room holding Jeremy's escape bag, the duffel he kept packed with essentials he'd need if he had to leave in a hurry—like now. It contained jeans, sweatshirts, sneakers, a windbreaker of special importance, and a warm jacket, but nothing incriminating. Money and fake IDs—make that faker IDs—he kept in a metal box in the woods behind his house.

Jeremy shrugged. "I was planning a weekend in Big Sur." He sighed loudly. "Before I lost my last contract. I just didn't have the heart to unpack."

O'Hara crossed to the chair beside the couch and sat. "So this guy Ottersen on your list of people who dislike you has really done a number on your business, I understand."

"Who told you that?"

O'Hara glanced at his notebook, but Jeremy held up his hand.

"Right. Who didn't tell you that? Yes, he's managed to gyp me out of a lot of contracts. He seems to be able to copy my blends about five minutes after I develop them and offers them to my customers at prices that have to be losing him money."

"Why? What'd you do to the guy?"

"Not one fucking thing. I barely know him." Jeremy sucked a breath. "He's taken a toll on other wineries, but I'm his fave."

"And you think he arranged to have you, what, mugged? And they somehow got Mr. Marchand instead?"

"Could have. I don't honestly know." He ran a hand over his hair. "I just know I won't be able to survive much longer."

"I assume you mean businesswise and aren't referring to your mortality."

Jeremy gave him a look. "Hopefully."

O'Hara looked at Jeremy from the side of his eyes. "How were you able to afford a business this large to begin with, young guy like you?"

"Inheritance. But I used that up to start the winery. For a time it did well—until Ottersen set his sights on my destruction." All those lines were practiced but still based on truth.

"And your relationship with Mr. Marchand?"

Ha. Tricky. "Bo's interested in seeing the central coast thrive. Centering all the power in the hands of one vintner is bad for all of us. So he's been trying to help me."

"He seems like a very good friend." Every word rang with a question, but Jeremy didn't bite.

He nodded. "Yes."

"And he chose to sleep on your couch rather than going home to his own bed because—" O'Hara stared at Jeremy with dark, glittering eyes.

Jeremy let his annoyed frown show. "He didn't want to wake his family, plus I think they kind of drive him crazy. They weren't expecting him for another day, so he took advantage of a night without them breathing down his neck."

O'Hara got a small smile and flipped his notebook closed. *Good.* What Jeremy said must have agreed with what Bo told him, or maybe even others. O'Hara said, "So another reminder. Don't go anywhere without letting me know, okay?"

"I won't and I've got a card, thanks." Jeremy glanced at his watch. "I'll be going into work soon."

"It's still early." He half smiled. "And you look like you could use some sleep."

"I know. My stomach thinks I've swallowed a porcupine. But I've got destruction to oversee." He was only half kidding.

"Your funeral." O'Hara walked toward the door. "We'll be working on the road for a while."

Jeremy nodded and watched O'Hara and the rest of his crew clear out. They'd surprised him by showing up at the crack of dawn, literally. Still, he didn't think they'd learned much. Which meant they knew about as much as he did. But unlike O'Hara, Jeremy had his suspicions—and fears.

He walked to the front windows to be sure they were done, then pulled out his phone and dialed. It rang twice. At least it was later there.

"Yeah? Hi."

"Hi." Jeremy's stomach lurched at the old familiar voice. "I'm probably going to need another package."

"Sorry to hear that, man."

"Yeah, me too. I may have to wait a while to pay."

"No issue, you know that."

"Thanks. A lot."

"You need details?"

"Probably best."

"Shit. I really am sorry. Two days. Usual place."

The phone went dead, and Jeremy pressed it against his chest. Fuck, he hated giving this all up. Like letting go of a dream. Yeah, he was young and maybe after people died, he could create another dream. Pressure built behind his eyes, and he pressed the back of his wrist against the sockets to make them shut the fuck up.

Where will I ever find another Bo?

He forced himself to take a shower while he made coffee, then dressed, laced the strong black brew with cream and called it nutrition, and headed out the door. Driving down his road, he had to pass the police crew sorting through the leaves. Interesting that they were taking Bo's potential abduction so seriously. Time Jeremy took his own abduction even more seriously. He glanced toward the trees and shuddered.

He nodded at O'Hara and headed for the winery, the sun just making its presence known. He wanted to beat Christian and his staff, what was left of it, in the door so he didn't have to spend the next two hours explaining every detail of his abortive trip, as well as why his eyes looked like he was bleeding internally.

Despite the oppression of the day, he felt the familiar leap of his heart when he turned toward Hill Top. Damn, he loved his business. The thought of walking away and leaving it behind made him sick. At least he didn't have a lot of debt to make his staff worry. He'd vanish, they'd spearhead an orderly shutdown, and that would be that. End of a dream.

He pulled behind the building and parked, then laid his head against the seat and closed his eyes. Nothing made sense. Why had Ottersen targeted him? Was there any chance Ottersen or one of his henchmen had hit Bo thinking it was Jeremy? As everyone pointed out, Ottersen didn't need a blunt force instrument to get rid of Jeremy. He was being quite effective just outmaneuvering Jeremy from a business perspective. He slowly released his breath. Right now, thinking Ottersen was behind the attempted abduction might have been a relief—at least compared to the alternative. *Fuck! Why can't they just leave me alone?* Of course, he knew the answer. The millions of answers.

He lifted his head from the upholstery. Wouldn't it be great if he and Bo could just escape? Go somewhere no one knew them? Be together for a long time? Maybe forever? He sucked a little breath.

Shit, had he really used that *F* word? Bo Marchand was a family man so far to his core he couldn't reach it with a Pilates reformer. And while Jeremy honestly believed that Bo cared for him enough to compromise his business and his success, he'd never leave his family—even for Jeremy.

Get on it.

He slid out of the car and crunched across the gravel. Using his key, he let himself in the back of the admin offices. Quiet. Smelled kind of astringent, like somebody overdid the bathroom cleaner.

He opened his office and then slid up the window to let it air out after two days closed up. *Um, good.* Really fresh morning.

Flipping on the computer, he signed in and started his system through its laborious start-up. If he got the coffee in the tasting room going, his crew would love him forever. They'd all want some as soon as they came in. Contemplating such a simple routine almost made him tear up. Loss gnawed a hole in his heart.

Leaving his PC still opening his browser windows and his email, he walked out toward the tasting room, opened the door, and grabbed his chest. *What the holy shit?*

The smell hit his nose and his unsettled stomach at the same time, and he had to rest his hands on his thighs while he breathed to keep from vomiting or passing out. Trouble was, breathing was a double-edged sword. What was that smell?

He backed out and closed the door, then just stood there, sucking wind. His stomach gripped and bile burned his throat, not just because the smell made him sick but from dread.

He didn't want to walk back into the tasting room. From his own personal experience, he knew the smell of death. He could pray, hope, grovel, and wish that he'd walk in there and find—what? A dead raccoon? Fat fucking chance. Who—not what—was dead in his tasting room?

His hands shook and his belly gave up the fight against the smell. He retched, heaving onto his floor. Not carpeted, thank God. He had nothing to vomit but coffee, so it was over quickly.

Don't want to know. Don't want to see. Want to run.

He gasped. Wait—no, what if it's Bo? Both his fists slammed into the door, and he ran headfirst into the tasting room. Sticking around the edge of the bar on the polished concrete floor were legs clad in dress pants. A man. *Odd clothes for Paso Robles.*

Oh God, maybe not Bo. Probably not Bo.

He crept forward, bent like a frightened animal, and peeked around the corner of the bar. The male body lay facedown.

Jeremy's mouth opened. "Fuck." He straightened up, put his hands on his hips, and stared.

The face of the dead man was hidden, but no one could possibly mistake that head of shining patent-leather black hair. That was Ernest Ottersen.

A weird snort erupted from Jeremy's nose, followed by a giggle that turned into a bray of hysterical laughter, and then he was crying. Tears ran down his face while he kept making strange giggly noises.

A shriek pierced the air and rattled the windows. "Oh my God, Jeremy! What have you done?"

Jeremy sank to the floor while Christian jumped up and down, waving his hands and screaming.

CHAPTER TWENTY-THREE

B0 TIED the laces on his shoes, looked in the mirror, and smoothed his dress pants and white shirt. *Back to work. Enough of this invalid crap.*

The rap on his bedroom door raised his hackles like a dog. Who had the nerve? Not Blanche.

He crossed and opened the door. *Of course. Mama.* "Yes?" He didn't step aside to let her enter.

She crossed her arms defensively over her chest. "Beauregard, I want to know why you've been so rude to your sister, who only wanted to help in your hour of need."

"Bull."

"Excuse me?"

"Blanche did not just want to help me in my so-called hour of need. I told her we might consider her as an intern at some date. She went into my business knowing I was gone and trying to tell my employees what to do, a job for which she has no experience or, likely, skill. There was nothing altruistic about the move."

She scowled. "But she's family."

"I don't care. I don't run my business on DNA. We make it because I hire the best people, pay them what they're worth, and expect a great deal. When Blanche fills that description, we'll talk." Staring into her horrified face, he took a breath and held strong-ish. "When I have a moment, I'll speak to my staff about the possibility of an internship."

She nodded once abruptly. "And what's happening with your friendship with Sage?"

"Mama, not that it's any of your affair—" Her eyebrows shot up, and he instantly felt bad. Damn. "Sage and I are just friends and, with all that's going on, we have no immediate plans to get together."

The woman knew no fear. "You speak of 'all that's going on,' but what I observe is just you spending an inordinate amount of time with Mr. Aames that has done nothing but get you into trouble."

This time he let out his breath noisily. "You don't understand my business or my friendships, Mother. Both are my concern."

"So I should butt out?" Her jaw stuck forward.

"I have to get to work. Thank you for your interest." He reached to his dresser, picked up his phone and wallet, and closed his door behind him as he stepped into the hall beside her. "What do you have planned today, Mama?" Glancing at his phone, he realized he'd turned off the ringer. *Damn.* He flipped it back on.

"Not that it's any of your concern, but I plan to get my hair done." She glanced up at him and at least had the good grace to curve the hint of a smile.

"I'm sure it will be lovely." He smiled at her as they entered the breakfast room, where his grandfather, two sisters, aunt, and uncle were all gathered, eating bacon and sipping OJ. His uncle read the paper while Bettina texted on her phone, getting glares from Mama. Blanche gave him a look that could kill more than foxes and averted her eyes. *Hell.*

He walked over and kissed the top of her head. "Sorry. I've been under some stress lately. I apologize for being rude."

"Okay." She sniffed.

His mother sat in her usual seat at the head of the table. "Have something to eat before you go, Bo. You don't want to lose any weight."

"Yes, ma'am." He picked up a plate on the sideboard and shoveled some scrambled eggs onto it.

"Have some bacon. I asked for it special."

Dutifully he placed a strip on the plate and sat in his seat, trying not to bounce his knee. He wanted to get to work and call Jeremy. Hell, he'd call him from the car. Not anxious or anything. It felt like they had a million obstacles between them, but all he wanted was to hear Jeremy's voice and know he was safe. Well, that's not all he wanted.

"Penny for your thoughts," Bettina said dreamily.

"Oh. Nothing."

"Sure looked pleasant." She giggled.

He took a bite of bacon, and his phone rang. His mother frowned since she discouraged cell use at the table, but—he glanced at the screen. RJ. He stood and clicked to answer. "Yes, RJ?"

His voice sounded strident. "Bo, I just got a call from the police looking for you."

"Oh, okay. O'Hara?"

"Yes. God, Bo, there's been a murder."

"What?" His heart slammed against his ribs as he pictured whoever had hit him coming back to Jeremy's to finish the job. *No, God, no.* "Not Jeremy!"

"No. Bo, it's Ottersen. Somebody killed him in the Hill Top tasting room—and Jeremy Aames was arrested for murder."

Bo's butt hit the chair. "No. No."

"Beauregard, hang up until you've finished your breakfast."

"Be quiet, Mother." He stood. "Where is he?"

"I don't know. O'Hara said to call him and you know the number. Damn, boss, do you think he did it? He sure hates Ottersen, and I don't blame him a bit."

"Of course he didn't do it. Manage things for me. I'm calling O'Hara."

"Will do, boss. Keep me posted."

"Thanks, RJ."

As he clicked off, Bettina said, "Ooh, was that the dreamy guy from your winery?"

"Yes." He stared into all their curious faces. "I have an important call. I'll see you later."

His grandfather said, "Something wrong, son?"

"Yes, sir. Very wrong. I can't stop to explain. Don't worry." He ran from the room straight to his car, dialing his phone at the same time. It only rang once.

"Bo? H-hi. What's up?" Llewellyn sounded concerned.

"I just heard that Ernest Ottersen was murdered."

"N-no shit?"

Bo almost laughed since Llewellyn so seldom swore. "Apparently his body was found at Hill Top Wineries in the tasting room and—and—" His voice broke.

"J-Jeremy's b-been accused." He didn't say it as a question.

"Right. O'Hara has called me, and I have to call him back. I wondered if you could find out anything before I do. I know it's a long shot, since I won't have an excuse to wait more than a few minutes to phone him."

"I h-have an idea. G-give me a few m-minutes."

"Thanks in advance, Llewellyn, even if you can't find out anything."

For fifteen minutes Bo drove slowly toward Marchand and hadn't heard from Llewellyn when he got there, so he circled a couple of the local wineries. Finally his phone rang. He grabbed it.

"Llewellyn?"

"It's Blaise. Llewellyn says he takes too long to get words out, so he asked me to call you."

"Bless him."

"Here's the deal we found out from our contact in the San Luis police department. Apparently Jeremy showed up at his house somehow this morning not remembering how he got there. He claims, anyway. He says he was at the gay bar in Paso last night, and he was drugged by some guy he calls Sean. He remembers trying to get to his car, then nada. He woke up on his own couch this morning with nothing stolen and no violation perpetrated to his adorable body as far as he can tell. Then he goes to work and finds Ottersen on the floor. That idiot twink who works for him comes in and starts screaming bloody murder, saying Jeremy did it. Somebody called the cops."

"Wow." Funny how, after all that, his heart still hung back on the fact that Jeremy had been at the gay bar with a guy named Sean. *Idiot.* "Do they know what time Ottersen was killed?"

"Sometime between 2:00 and 5:00 a.m."

"How?"

"Strangulation. I hear that O'Hara's going to be questioning the bartender at the Backstreet Bar about what happened to Jeremy before he left there."

"Okay. Thanks so much, Blaise. I'll never repay you guys."

"No repayment needed, Bo. Take care and keep us in the loop."

"Yes." He clicked off, pulled to the side of the road, and searched on his phone. When he found Backstreet Bar, he hit Send and prayed, though he knew God would wash his hands of this mendacity.

"Backstreet. This is Russ."

"Russ, you don't know me, but I'm a friend of Jeremy. My name's Bo Marchand."

Russ chuckled. "Yeah, I heard about you." That made Bo cringe. Russ said, "How's our boy? He sure tried to tie one on last night."

"Uh, he's in some trouble. I don't have much time, but I need to find out how he got home last night."

"Sure. I took him."

"Oh thank God."

"You sound relieved. Were you worried about that pervert who tried to pick him up?"

"Yes."

"I saw Jeremy getting worse when he should have been getting better, so I grabbed him before he hit the floor, shoved him in his car, waited until my shift ended, and drove him home with a buddy following. I used his keys to leave him on his couch. I didn't stay since he was sleeping really sound and I, uh, had a friend waiting."

"What time was this, Russ?"

"A little after two. My shift ends at 2:00 a.m. and I closed. What kind of trouble?"

"Somebody's trying to pin a crime on him. I can't say more, but I sure thank you. The police will be there soon to question you."

"Good to know. I'll neglect to mention this conversation."

"Thank you. Sincerely."

"I hear you've been a good friend to Jeremy. Glad to help."

"I need to call the police too. Again, thanks from the bottom of my heart." He clicked off and dialed O'Hara's number.

"O'Hara."

"It's Bo Marchand." He wanted to find out as much as possible before he volunteered anything.

"Took you long enough."

"Sorry. I had a concussion, remember? I turned off my ringer. I forgot to turn it back on."

"I need to talk to you. Can you come in now?"

"I gather it's important?"

"Vital."

"I'll be there in a half hour." He clicked off, turned the Prius, and started driving to Paso Robles, concocting his story as he went.

Twenty-five distracted minutes later, he pulled into the police department parking lot and walked resolutely in to the desk and asked for O'Hara. When the detective showed up, he redefined frowning. "Thanks for coming. Get in here."

Bo followed him through the door to the busy department and entered the room O'Hara directed him to. Yes, it did have a mirror on one wall, thank you.

O'Hara pointed at a chair. "Sit. Need coffee, water?"

"No, thanks."

O'Hara sat opposite him. O'Hara's interesting mix of tan skin, probably from some Hispanic blood, and light blue eyes made for a startling combination. Those eyes fixed on Bo. "Where were you last night?"

Bo matched O'Hara's frown. He did get right to it. "I was at home in bed until somewhere around two, and then I got worried and drove over to Jeremy Aames's house." Dear sweet God, he'd done it. He'd just lied to the police.

"What the hell did you do that for?"

"I'd tried to call him, and he didn't answer. Since I figure whoever hit me probably thought I was him, I got spooked and couldn't sleep. I drove over to check on him." He shrugged, real noncommittal.

"And what did you find?" O'Hara looked plenty skeptical.

"I knocked and got no answer. The door was unlocked, which scared the fuck out of me, so I went in. I found Jeremy passed out cold on his couch. I tried to wake him, but he didn't even stir. Then I smelled the alcohol and guessed he was dead drunk. He was still wearing his jacket, so I figured he might have been out, got drunk, made it home and inside, and collapsed."

O'Hara's eyebrows pressed against the top of his eyes. "What did you do?"

"I was still worried, so I left, locked the door, and sat in my car for quite a while. I think I fell asleep for a bit but finally woke up, drove home, and slept a couple hours before I got up and went to work."

"When you woke up, was Aames's car still there?"

"Yeah. I was blocking it, so he couldn't have moved if he'd wanted to."

O'Hara sat back and folded his hands across a flat stomach. "Is this the truth?"

Bo adopted his best confused face. "Uh, sure. Why is this odd?" His heart beat to the rhythm of *liar, liar, pants on fire.*

"Because." O'Hara leaned forward and propped his forearms on the table. "Most people don't get up in the middle of the night because they're worried about a random friend. You got hit, maybe in his place. I'd think that would be an excuse to stay far away. Not go hanging around where it could happen again. So why should I believe you?"

"I don't understand why my motivations are even in question by the police." There. That sounded convincing.

"Because, Mr. Marchand, as I suspect you very well know, Mr. Aames is being questioned on suspicion of murder. A murder that was committed sometime last night."

Bo leaned forward, scowling, and it was no pretense. "Fuck that, sugah. Jeremy Aames wouldn't kill anyone, and I'm here to say he didn't." He sat back. "Who's dead?"

"Ernest Ottersen." He gave Bo that sidelong glance again. Bo just nodded. O'Hara said, "You don't seem surprised."

"If you think Jeremy had a reason to kill someone, it makes sense it'd be Ottersen."

"So you think Aames had a motive for Ottersen's murder?"

Bo shrugged. "I know Jeremy was distraught over all the crappy tricks and deals Ottersen was pulling, most of them focused on Jeremy's business. And you know that too, I'm sure. In fact, I was there in a restaurant when Jeremy got so angry he said he'd kill Ottersen, so yes, I expect you might think Jeremy had motive. But as I say, Jeremy would never kill anyone.

Plus I happen to know where he was last night, so I think that's that." His heart felt like it was beating in his mouth, so he shut it.

"Jeremy threatened Ottersen?"

"Ottersen made a snarky remark to him, and Jeremy lost it." Bo shrugged expansively. "Anyone could have said it, in my opinion."

"And you say he was asleep on his couch at home?"

"That's what I saw."

"What time did he get there?"

Bo shook his head. "Don't know."

"Did he drive himself home?"

"His car was there and no one else, so I guess so. But I don't even know if he went out. I only know he was wearing his jacket."

"You willing to write all this down and sign it?" O'Hara reeked mistrust.

"Sure."

"Mr. Marchand, why are you doing this?"

Bo narrowed his eyes. "You asked me to come here and answer your damned questions. I'm doing that." He met O'Hara's eyes. "Are you going to let Jeremy go?"

He fiddled with the papers in front of him. "Probably. We were just holding him for questioning, and our time will be up soon anyway."

"I could take him with me."

"It will take more time than that."

"If you call me, I'll come and get him." Bo stood.

O'Hara gathered his stuff and stood across from Bo. "You certainly are a dedicated friend."

"Is there a problem with that?"

"Probably not." He smiled coolly. "I'll call you when he's ready to go, unless he chooses to contact someone else."

Bo nodded and walked to the door. O'Hara reached around him and opened it, then led Bo to the entrance. Bo said nothing as he walked out into the early-afternoon sunshine. His sterling reputation as an upstanding pillar of the community just shattered in a gazillion pieces.

But maybe, just maybe, he'd gotten away with that.

CHAPTER TWENTY-FOUR

"AGAIN, MR. Aames, can you prove where you were last night?"

Jeremy leaned back in the chair and sighed—loudly. "Is there something about 'I was passed out' you don't understand? I remember nothing, absolutely nothing after I felt myself falling on the porch of the Backstreet Bar."

"No idea how you got home? If you drove yourself? If anyone saw you?"

"No. If I thought someone could corroborate my story, don't you think I'd be yelling it at the top of my lungs? Yes, someone might have seen me. There were an assload of people in that bar. But I have no idea who." He grabbed the bridge of his nose and squeezed. A whole day sitting in an interrogation room had not ranked on the top of his favorite things list. Suddenly he looked up. "Hey, since I presumably had means, motive, and opportunity, why aren't you charging me?"

"Who says I won't? Do not leave town without informing me first, understand?"

"Yeah."

"So your friend"—he said the word with emphasis—"Bo Marchand offered to pick you up when you were released. Since you didn't request someone else, I called him. You can call him off if you act quick." He handed Jeremy back his phone that had been confiscated under some made-up rule of no cell phones in the interrogation room.

"How did Bo know I was even here?"

"I called him in for questioning."

"Why?"

"You're not the only one who hated Ernest Ottersen."

"Actually, Bo owns one of the least affected wineries in the region. His growing methods are hard to duplicate. Plus you can't believe that sweet man would ever hurt a sugar cookie."

"Speaking frankly, to defend you, I don't think there's much he wouldn't do."

Jeremy coughed to cover his own indrawn breath. "He's a protective kind of guy."

"Is Bo Marchand your lover, Mr. Aames?"

Jeremy frowned. "Bo's straight, more's the pity."

"I've been unable to determine any long-term relationships he has with women."

"You've been asking?" He stared daggers at O'Hara.

"It's my job."

"To pry into people's love lives?"

"Love lives are frequently connected to murder."

"Bo's my friend. I never said I don't wish it were more." He put his wallet in his pocket. "Can I go?"

"Yes."

Jeremy stood. Jesus, he felt like he'd been sitting forever. O'Hara marched him out to the lobby of the building. Bo sat in a chair, flipping through his phone, looking better than ice cream. It took almost more will-power than Jeremy had to keep from running to him and planting a kiss on those patrician lips.

Bo looked up, smiled, visibly adjusted his expression to one of concern, and stood to his considerable height. He walked forward. "Are you okay?"

"As good as can be expected. Thanks for coming to get me. I could have called Christian."

O'Hara, who stood behind Jeremy, snorted. "Considering how certain he was that you killed Mr. Ottersen, you might want to question your relationship."

Bo gave O'Hara a scathing look. "The man's a twit."

O'Hara actually laughed. "Couldn't have said it better myself, but don't quote me." He nodded to Bo. "Don't either of you—"

Jeremy wanted to strangle O'Hara. "—leave town without informing you. We know!"

"Just checking."

Bo gave O'Hara a head bob back, then took hold of Jeremy's forearm with his big, strong hand and guided him toward the door. Outside, the sunlight felt like heaven, but not as good as that warm body beside him. He wanted to hurl himself into Bo's arms and get hugs and kisses. Fat chance with half the Paso police watching—or maybe it was just O'Hara, but same thing.

Bo's Prius looked like a port in a storm. Bo beeped the lock as they approached, and Jeremy walked to the passenger side and got in. Bo was already behind the wheel. Without even looking at Jeremy, he pulled out of the police department parking lot and headed toward the wine country. *Oooooookay. Doghouse city.*

"Are you pissed at me?"

Bo held up a finger toward Jeremy and kept driving. *Hmm.*

When they'd left the town proper and pulled onto Highway 46 toward the wineries, Bo seemed to take a breath and lighten up—a little. Before Jeremy could say something else, Bo made a sharp right-hand turn onto one of the more remote tracks off the highway, bumped down the road a short distance, slammed on his brakes, turned off the car, and reached for Jeremy all in one move.

One moment Jeremy was forming his lips to ask a question and the next those lips were consumed by Bo's hot, demanding mouth. *Oh, much better than talking.*

Jeremy wrapped his arms tightly around Bo's wide shoulders and tried to crawl across the console. Clearly getting the idea, Bo hauled Jeremy onto his lap, simultaneously pushing the seat as far back as it would go. Still, it was a Prius, and neither of them was teeny. The laws of solid geometry were being tested. Jeremy didn't care. The tighter the better. He straddled Bo as best he could manage, both legs awkwardly bent in the tight confines of the seat, but he still succeeded in splaying his thighs enough to get their cocks into proximity; then he just leaned forward and rode hard, never releasing Bo's mouth.

Bo moaned and slid a hand between them until Jeremy got the message. He leaned back enough to let Bo slide down his own zipper while Jeremy did the same. Bo dug inside Jeremy's fly and released the ravening beast to meet his own big cock, then wrapped a paw around them and pumped, attacking Jeremy's mouth again.

For a minute Jeremy let Bo explore his tongue and the soft insides of his cheeks, but the divided sensation overwhelmed him, and he pulled back. "Too much." He wrapped a hand partway around Bo's package and increased the speed and pressure until his dick was ready to power into outer space beside the Falcon Heavy. "Oh damn, Bo. Can't last much longer!"

Bo rummaged in his back pocket with his free hand and brought forth his cloth handkerchief that he wrapped around the leaking heads of their penises. He gazed deep and intently into Jeremy's eyes with that crystal green gaze and hit the blastoff button.

Both of them breathed so hard there had to be an oxygen deficit in the car. Their grunts and moans just spurred on the jerking and the thrusting of their hips. Hell, he loved this. Like healthy young animals in heat, desperate for release.

But somewhere under the lust, that other *L* word lurked. *Think about that later.*

Jeremy threw back his head and surrendered to the fire in his loins and the bolts of electricity shooting out from his balls until one shot turned to orgasm, and his body froze as waves of pleasure washed over him, exploding the top of his head into the stars while juice spurted from his cock.

Another shout, Bo's this time, joined the chorus, and his body shook and trembled against Jeremy's thighs.

When Jeremy stopped shuddering, he opened his eyes and stared at the now soaked handkerchief. *Oh man, maybe I can save it forever.*

Bo let his head fall forward against Jeremy's. He wiped their softening shafts with the cloth, then tossed it on the floor, pulling Jeremy close against his chest. He spoke softly against Jeremy's ear. "Are you okay?"

"Yeah. At least I didn't have to spend the night in jail. Although to tell you the truth, I'm not sure why they let me go."

Bo got very still.

"What? What did you do?"

"I, uh, lied to the police."

"What?" He sprang back, hitting the steering wheel and honking the horn, which made them both jump.

"Llewellyn and Blaise found out the bartender from the Backstreet brought you home, and I learned the murder occurred sometime between 2:00 and 5:00 a.m. I said I was worried about you and came to your house, your door was open, and you were sleeping on the sofa wearing your jacket." He grinned. "Nice touch, right?"

Jeremy frowned at him and shook his head. "I can't believe any of this. What else?"

"I said I sat in my Prius and fell asleep, but I was blocking your car, so you couldn't have sneaked out." He shrugged. "So I left a little before six, went home, slept an hour, and then got O'Hara's call to come in."

"And none of this is true?"

Bo shook his head like a guilty puppy. If ever there was cause for kissing— "I figured the story gave you an alibi, but you didn't have to know anything about it. Plus I don't believe anyone in my family can say I was or wasn't there. I parked my car last night by my bedroom. There's a small back door I use sometimes, though not often since Mama considers it antisocial. I've got to confess, I've got my fingers crossed on that detail."

The battle between kissing and killing raged in Jeremy's chest. "So you risked yourself lying to the police to protect me?"

Bo looked up, met Jeremy's eyes for a second, and then stared at the console.

The magnitude overwhelmed him. He dragged himself off Bo's lap and into the passenger seat, his now very flaccid dick still hanging from his fly. "What are you? Nuts! Sweet freaking Christ, every time I breathe I get you into more damned trouble!" He threw his hands in the air. "How do you know I didn't pretend to be drugged, drive to Ottersen's, kill him, and take him to my tasting room?" The idiocy of what he'd just said struck him. "Okay, so maybe I found him in my tasting room and got so incensed I shot him."

"He wasn't shot."

"Hit him with a hot poker. I don't know, dammit, but you can't go risking yourself on the chance that I didn't do it."

"There's no chance you did it."

"How do you know?"

"I just do." He set his very masculine jaw in a very stubborn line. "And even if there were, why on earth would you leave his body in your own tasting room?"

"Drunk?"

"If you were sober enough to kill him, you'd have been sober enough to dump him in the creek or the ocean or someplace." Bo looked up, very serious. "O'Hara didn't really believe my story. He as much as said so. But he used it as an excuse to let you go because he also knows it makes no sense for you to dump your victim in your own damned winery. He doesn't think you did it."

"Couldn't have proved it by me."

"I figured you'd maybe want to help me discover who did kill Ottersen and give 'em a thank-you note." He gave a sideways smile.

"Now that's a plan." He shared the smile but looked away. Unfortunately he was getting scared about who murdered Ottersen and why. He didn't want Bo anywhere near involved. "But truthfully, I'm not sure either one of us should be poking around in police business. I could end up in jail with you beside me."

A frown flashed across Bo's face. *No wonder. He's got to believe I'm wimping out on him. Still—*

The car got very quiet. Some kind of internal battle seemed to be raging in the driver's seat. Bo skewered Jeremy with a stare. "Why did you go to the Backstreet Bar?"

Jeremy sighed. "I wanted to get drunk. I just felt so defeated. All I could think about was drowning my sorrows."

"I told you we'd work it out together. I said I'd find a way to make this all okay."

Jeremy shook his head like an emphatic cow. "No, you can't do any more for me. Somehow I've got to work this out for myself."

"Did you go there to have sex?" He spoke softly and stared at the gearshift.

"No. Of course not. I haven't had sex with anyone since I started mooning over you." Jeremy gripped the bridge of his nose—again. Headaches seemed to be a part of his status quo.

Suddenly Bo's head snapped up. "I've been thinking…."

"About what?"

Bo took a huge breath, let it out slowly, and then met Jeremy's eyes. "I know you don't trust me, Jeremy, and I don't blame you. I'm a chickenshit mama's boy, and you can't believe I'm serious in my feelings for you if I persist in this cowardice."

"Sweet Jesus, Bo. I should polish your boots with my tongue, you're such a good and generous person. I have no right to ask anything from you."

"Yes, you do. You have the right to ask a man who's your lover to be honest with you and with the world about who he is. You've honored me by allowing me to be your lover. I need to keep up my part of the bargain."

Jeremy's heart beat in his throat, and he couldn't speak.

Bo inhaled. "I'm going to go home and tell my family that I'm gay and that I have a boyfriend—if you'll have me."

If Jeremy's ears had turned solid gold and filled with myrrh, the sound of those words couldn't have been any sweeter. But if Bo Marchand was his boy-friend and everyone knew—"No, don't." Bo looked like he'd been slapped. Jeremy grabbed his arm. He couldn't help it. "It's probably not best to rock any more boats until this whole murder thing is solved. If you confirm our relationship, O'Hara's going to doubt you twice as hard."

"I think he already knows." He still appeared con-fused and sad.

"And if you say we do have a relationship, he'll be sure you lied, and he'll move heaven to prove I'm guilty."

"Yes, I suppose so."

Oh God, I'm so sorry. Jeremy took Bo's hands in his own. "I'm so touched and happy that you'd do such a thing for me. I can't tell you how much it means to me. You've done so much for me, Bo. Of course, I trust you. And you don't need to ruin your life with your family and your friends to prove that you care about me. Dear God, no one has ever done a tiny fraction for me what you have."

"But—but Jeremy, how can we be together if I don't come out?"

Bo looked so wounded, Jeremy wanted to carve out his heart and lay it at his feet. He tightened his grip on Bo's hands. "We'll find a way, dear." *Man, I'm such a liar.*

Bo quietly took his hands back. *Yes, don't blame him.* "So what's next?"

"I guess I should go home, clean up, get my car, and go to the winery so my staff can stop worrying about me."

"What about the little shit?"

Jeremy snorted. "In his defense, when Christian walked in on me with Ottersen's body, I was laughing hysterically, so he might have had a reason to believe I'd just killed the asshole. I'll admit to being of two minds, because the man's an idiot, but he gets shit done. Still, I won't have to fire him if he decides he betrayed me and doesn't show up for work. I really can't afford to keep anyone who's not actually growing grapes."

Bo crossed his arms. "I don't think you're safe in that house by yourself."

"I lay on that couch helpless last night and nobody killed me."

"But who the ruddy fuck drugged you?"

"Some asshole named Sean. He was hitting on me, and I wasn't cooperating. I think he decided to use chemical persuasion. But it sounds like Russ saved me. I've got to seriously thank him." Except he'd never see Russ again.

Bo leaned down and started the car with its funny whirring, clicking noises. "I'd feel better if you came and stayed at my house. No one would dare take on my mama."

Jeremy burst out laughing, and the tension in the car lightened. It only took a few minutes to cover the short distance to Jeremy's house. Jeremy found himself gazing at Bo's beautiful face as he watched the road. So this man was willing to not only jeopardize his business, his wealth, and his friends for Jeremy; now he wanted to transform and threaten his relationship with his family, around whom his life revolved, so he could be with Jeremy. Giving back a gift of that magnitude ripped Jeremy's heart and shattered his spirit. Even if he survived, there'd be nothing to survive for.

At his house Jeremy hopped out and gave Bo a kiss through the window.

"Will you call me when you get to Hill Top? I want to know what happens with Christian."

"You bet." He kissed him again. "You're a miracle from heaven, my friend. I must have had some really saintly past life to have earned the right to know you in this one." He forced himself to smile.

Bo swiped at his eyes. "Can I see you tonight?"

"Yes." He pecked his lips against Bo's patrician nose, then stood back.

The tears that rolled down his face as Bo drove away were left to dry on their own as Jeremy ran to the living room, grabbed the emergency travel bag, double-checked to be sure the windbreaker with the credit card sewed into the elastic waistband was in there, grabbed a shovel, then headed for the woods behind his house to get the rest.

Couldn't think about what he was leaving behind. *You always knew the day might come. Don't bitch.* Still, the tears kept flowing as he ran toward the big tree with his shovel and tried to prepare his heart to dig in the soft dirt he'd hoped never to have to disturb—or at least not until he was planning for his own wedding. Crap, that made him cry harder, like some kind of frigging drama queen. The tree still loomed a few yards ahead, but his vision blurred with tears, and he fell to one knee and buried his face in his free hand.

This time the blow with the butt of the gun landed on its intended target.

CHAPTER TWENTY-FIVE

DAMMIT, ANSWER. Bo pressed the phone to his ear for the third time in fifteen minutes and listened to the ringing. *Nothing. Damn.*

"Bo, want to try the 2013?" Luther, his winery supervisor, held out the glass with a sampling of red wine.

"Yeah, thanks." He stashed his phone, buried his nose in the glass, and inhaled deeply. That made him smile. He took a sip, swished it in his mouth, and then spat it out in the receptacle they kept for such purposes. He licked the inside of his mouth. "Wow."

Luther shared his mouthful of teeth. "Good one, right?"

"Yeah." Bo took another careful mouthful, and this time he swallowed. "I think we've got a winner."

"We've missed the San Francisco competition, but I'll bet we could enter it in LA, the Critics Choice, and some others."

"We'll make it so." Bo handed back the glass to Luther, then looked at his phone.

"Everything okay?"

Bo glanced up and tried not to look frantic. "A friend who'd had some troubles. I can't get a hold of him, and I'm worried." He shoved the phone back in his jeans pocket. "He probably just left his phone off or something." He waved and walked toward the door of the big processing room. "Thanks, Luther."

Outside, he dialed Jeremy's phone again. He actually gasped when the thing went straight to voicemail without even ringing. "Jeremy, it's me. You're kind of freaking me out. Call me, please, so I know you're okay."

He hung up and stared at the phone. *What's going on?* Without even forming the thought, his finger pushed the number for Llewellyn's cell.

"H-hello, Bo."

"Hi. Can I come talk to you?"

"Y-yes. Shall w-we come there?"

"No. Too many prying eyes. When and where shall I meet you?"

"My house as s-soon as you can get there."

"I don't want to break into your workday."

"N-not a problem. B-bring wine." He chuckled.

"Will do. See you soon." He hung up and walked into the tasting room. RJ polished the tasting bar and chatted up two couples who were sampling wine. Bo walked behind the counter and picked three bottles he thought Llewellyn and Blaise would enjoy. RJ gave him a big, uncomfortable smile—like all the smiles he'd shared since their Dionysus conversation. At least, Bo was pretty sure he wasn't imagining a change in RJ's attitude toward him.

Bo smiled at the guests and said to RJ, "I have an appointment. If you need any help, ask Tanya to come in, okay?"

"Sure." He glanced toward the guests and turned his back to them a bit, saying softly, "Everything okay with the cops?" Everyone on his staff knew he'd had to answer questions.

"Yes. Just questions about—you know."

RJ frowned, and a slight flush touched his sculptural cheekbones. "Terrible thing. I heard they had Jeremy Aames in custody."

"Just questioning because it's his tasting room. He's out now."

RJ's eyebrows shot up. "Really." He adopted a smile, though he looked a little... what? Disturbed. "That's great to hear."

"I'll be back later, but I might miss you." Bo knelt down by the small refrigerator they kept under the counter and grabbed a wedge of cheese. When he looked up, RJ was still staring at him. As he stood, Bo said casually, "Ever hear any more about that Dionysian mystery?" He laughed.

For a second RJ looked shocked, then laughed too and shook his head. "Best get back to the guests." He hurried over and poured the next wine for each taster. "You're going to like this one. It's a light red with a lot of forward fruit."

Bo packed up his cheese, stashing it along with his wine bottles in a Marchand Winery bag like the ones they sold to visitors. Interesting. He'd thought a couple of times that maybe he'd imagined RJ's uncomfortable reaction to his questions previously, but clearly that wasn't the case. He didn't want to spook RJ. The guy was a valuable employee. But damn, he did act weird at the mention of the god of wine.

Nodding at his customers, he walked from the tasting room and climbed into his car. Reflexively, he dialed Jeremy's phone. Straight to voicemail. Which meant his phone was dead or turned off. Why would he do that?

He pulled out onto the highway, pointed the car toward San Luis, and let his brain drift. He knew Jeremy hid a lot of things—from Bo and probably everyone else. Yes, it meant he didn't trust Bo with the truth of his situation or past, but he also seemed genuinely worried that he was bringing a lot of problems, maybe even danger to Bo.

Bo sighed and flipped on music, willing his mind to relax until he could talk it all out with Llewellyn and Blaise. Mystery was their business.

Fifteen minutes later Bo pulled into the driveway of the beautiful old Craftsman-style home where Llewellyn and Blaise lived. As Bo climbed out of the Prius, Blaise waved from the big front porch. Bo grabbed the bag of goodies from the back seat and carried it up to the front door. He grinned at Blaise. "Aren't you supposed to be teaching?"

"Llewellyn told me you were bringing wine. How could I resist? Besides, I don't have a class this afternoon."

Blaise took the bag from Bo, and they walked into the entry, then the living room, where Llewellyn had his laptop on the coffee table. He perched on the couch, talking on his phone. "Th-thank you, Tick. Tell us w-when you c-can have dinner." He listened and nodded. "Y-yes, soon." He clicked off, looked up, and smiled at Bo. "W-welcome."

Blaise held up a finger. "Bo, please sit. I'm going to serve this wine and amazing-looking cheese. Say nothing until I return. Clear?"

Even though he was antsy, Bo chatted with Llewellyn and forced himself not to stare at his phone screen until Blaise walked in carrying a tray with three glasses of red, some sliced apples, and a big plate of cheese. He set the tray behind the laptop, offered a wineglass to Bo and then to Llewellyn, and finally grabbed his own glass and sat next to Llewellyn on the couch. He sipped, and his eyes widened, then closed. "Oh wow. Nobody makes wine like Bo."

"Thank you, kind sir."

Llewellyn savored a swallow. "D-delicious."

Blaise leaned forward, wineglass cradled in his fingers. "So tell us what's happening? We know that Jeremy was released. We know he had an alibi, but not what it is."

"Me." Bo grimaced.

"W-we suspected as m-much." Llewellyn gestured with his wineglass. "G-go on."

"I told the police I was watching his house because I was worried about him and found him lying on his couch at home, passed out and still wearing his jacket. I said he couldn't have left the house by car without me seeing."

"How much of that is true?" Blaise asked.

"None. But what idiot would kill someone everyone knew he hated and leave the body in his own tasting room? Seriously?"

"M-maybe someone who w-wanted us to think exactly th-that."

Bo shook his head. "Jeremy didn't kill him, but I think he knows who did."

"Who?" Blaise glanced at Llewellyn, then at Bo.

"No idea. But Jeremy's been acting weird ever since I got hit. I know he never tells me the whole truth, but since that time he seems particularly jumpy and worried, mostly about me. I believe he suspects who might have hit me. And the worst part is, now he's not answering his phone. It's going straight to voicemail, and I'm going out of my ever-lovin' mind."

Llewellyn said, "Y-you really c-care for him."

Bo breathed deeply and nodded. "I told him I'd come out for him, that I wanted to be together."

"Oh, Bo." Blaise pressed a hand to his own chest.

"The bitch of it is, he turned me down." Bo tried to look cool but ended up wiping at his eyes. "Actually, he said we shouldn't rock any more boats right now and make the police even more suspicious of my story exonerating him. I guess that's sensible, but truthfully, I didn't want him to be sensible. I wanted him to be thrilled. How's that for an ego as big as a Georgia peach pie?" He sighed.

"It actually was sensible, but I understand your point of view." Blaise smiled.

Llewellyn slowly rotated his glass and stared into it like a deep red crystal ball. "Remember w-we told you th-that Jeremy is not who he s-says?"

"Yes, but who is he?" Bo had to stop gripping his glass so hard or he might break it.

Blaise said, "We don't know for sure. What we're finding is that his background has the look and feel of witness protection, but our contacts in the police department don't know anything about it."

"S-so we think he's disguised his identity on h-his own."

Blaise nodded. "And done a damned good job of it. He looks to the world like an orphan who started his winery on an inheritance from his dead mother."

Bo said, "I think that's true. There's a certain emotion attached to the mother story that rings authentic."

"Might be."

"H-he knows w-wine, in-inside and out." Llewellyn sipped and smiled, then said, "W-we are l-looking at the w-wine-growing regions."

"New York seems likely." Blaise gave Llewellyn that significant glance again, seemed to get an affirmation, and went on. "There's a chance of organized crime connections in New York City."

Bo's heart practically broke his ribs it slammed so hard. "Mafia?"

"Yes. Italian probably rather than Russian, since some have legitimate wine-growing operations in upstate New York. Of course, so do the Russians."

Bo put down his glass so hard he almost tipped it. "That means the mafia might have killed Ottersen?"

A crease between the brows made Llewellyn look even smarter. "Y-yes, but why?"

"Because they kill people!" It was a wail.

Blaise said, "Maybe they thought Ottersen was hurting Jeremy, so they killed him?"

"If J-Jeremy was h-hiding from them, why w-would they protect him?"

Bo could barely breathe. "But Jeremy may be missing. Maybe they killed Ottersen to make it hard for Jeremy to stay here so he'd have to go—where? Home?"

"P-plausible."

Bo gripped his hands behind his neck or his head might fly off into space. "Jeremy could have been taken by the mafia. Dear God." *Do not pass out.*

Neither Llewellyn nor Blaise said anything, and the weight of the silence was crushing.

"I've got to find him."

"B-Bo, you don't even know he's b-been t-taken."

"I feel like he has."

Blaise shook his head. "Maybe he ran. You said he's been jumpy. If he thought these people found him, he may have gone into hiding."

"I think he'd let me know somehow."

"It'd be dangerous—for you. He'd never do that."

"H-how would y-you find out who's after him?" Llewellyn peered at him with those smart brown eyes.

Like some harbinger of—doom? Joy? Bo's phone rang. He grabbed it so fast he dropped it to the chair cushion, it bounded to the floor, and he had to juggle it. He slammed it against his ear. "Hello! Hello!"

"Bo? Oh God, Bo." *Female. Fuck! Crying.* For a second all his brain screamed was *Not Jeremy.*

"Uh, Sage?"

"Y-yes. Sorry. Oh, isn't it awful?"

"Yes, terrible. Are you okay?" He glanced up at Llewellyn and Blaise. Blaise gestured *Shall we leave?* by walking his fingers, and Bo shook his head, then mouthed the word *Sage.*

"Yes, but so terribly sad. I just can't believe this whole thing. I mean, who does something like this?"

"Lots of people, sadly."

"I heard they arrested Jeremy."

"No. They took him in for questioning, but he had an alibi. Plus why would he kill Ernest and leave him in the Hill Top tasting room?"

"He hated Ernest so much."

Hard to argue with that fact.

She snuffled. "And the sad thing is, he shouldn't have." Bo's back stiffened, but she kept talking. "I called some of our new customers, and they told me that someone contacted them and said that Hill Top was having trouble meeting its contractual obligations. They were told they shouldn't trust Jeremy. So they gave the business to Ernest, but they wouldn't have otherwise. They said they loved Hill Top."

An arrow pierced Bo's chest. "What the hell? Who could have done that? Ernest?"

"No. They said it was someone from Hill Top. Someone they knew." She started to cry again. "So, see. Jeremy didn't even have a reason to hate Ernest."

"Jeremy didn't kill him."

"If you say so. But isn't it awful that he hated him so much?" She broke into sobs.

"I'm so sorry, Sage. Yes, the whole thing's a total mess. We'll find out who killed Ernest. I promise."

"Thank you, Bo. You're a rock. I hope I see you soon."

"You will. Get some rest."

"There's so much to do here. It's not clear who'll inherit Ernest's property since he wasn't married. His parents are elderly." She sighed loudly. "Oh, Bo, this is just awful."

"Yes. Yes, it is." He gripped the phone so tightly his fingers were getting numb. But his mind roiled. "We'll talk soon, Sage."

"Thank you for making me feel a little better."

Bo clicked off and stared into space.

Blaise said, "Anything important?"

Bo clenched his teeth. "Llewellyn, ask me that question again, about how I'd find Jeremy."

"H-how would you—"

His head snapped up, and every word felt like a bullet shooting from his mouth. "I'd find that pipsqueak, twink, asshole, Christian, who worked for Jeremy, and wring it out of him. I've always felt he knows more than he says about the whole Ottersen mess. I think I just got confirmation that it's true."

Blaise said, "Christian?"

Bo nodded.

Llewellyn nodded. "I th-think you should d-do that. Find him."

Blaise raised a golden eyebrow that reminded Bo of Jeremy. "Maybe not too much wringing. We don't want another visit from the police."

"W-we'll query our c-contacts as w-well."

Bo stood. He needed to move or he'd start screaming. *Mafia. Holy shit.*

"If you l-learn anything, d-do not act on it. Not alone. D-do you understand?"

He nodded once. "I need to get over there." He walked the few steps to the couch and hugged Llewellyn, then Blaise.

Blaise grinned. "So congratulations on coming out."

"Oh, I haven't really. You're the first to know, aside from Jeremy, of course."

"Glad to hear that part." He looked at Llewellyn like he was staring at the sun. "I highly recommend life with the man you love."

Llewellyn blushed, and Bo felt kinship. Also envy. He had to find Jeremy, make sure he was safe, and persuade him that their future was together, growing wine and making love. "Gotta find him first."

"C-call us. Thank y-you for the w-wine."

"And cheese." Blaise took a big bite on a cracker and shoved the last bit in his mouth with his finger.

That finally squeezed a smile from Bo, who blew a kiss and ran out the door.

The drive back to the wine country felt like forever, but Bo stared at the road. He'd start at Hill Top. Somebody had to know where that pretty little turd lived.

He almost missed the turn, he was thinking so hard, but he squealed the tires and drove up the hill. Hill Top, oddly, wasn't quite as high as Marchand but still commanded a great vista. Bo slammed to a stop and pushed into the tasting room. A bunch of people stood at the tasting bar and behind it—*Well, step up and call me fucking flabbergasted. Christian.* The idiot held forth at the bar, laughing and pouring wine.

CHAPTER TWENTY-SIX

Bo STORMED across the Hill Top tasting room. As he rounded the bar, Christian looked up, must have seen Bo's face, and started moving in the opposite direction. Bo was faster and way bigger. He grabbed Christian's arm and nearly yanked him off his feet.

"Let go of me, you maniac."

"Not a chance, sugah." He raised his voice and laughed loudly. "I caught you, you cute little devil. You know you can't escape your daddykins." The people at the bar, who'd been looking shocked, smiled, giggled, and went back to their wine. Bo made eye contact with a girl who worked for Jeremy part-time. He jerked his head toward the patrons. "Can you help them out while I talk to Christian?"

"Sure. Love to."

"Call the police, Tiffany." Christian wriggled in Bo's grasp.

Bo just shook his head and got a nod from Tiffany. He dragged Christian through the door to the administrative area and into Jeremy's office.

Just the subtle scent of Jeremy in the room made his heart hurt. He shoved Christian toward a chair, locked the door, and stood in front of it. Christian caught himself against the arm of the guest chair, then looked around frantically, likely for escape.

Bo crossed his arms. "What are you doing here?"

Wheels clearly turned in Christian's head. "I knew poor Jeremy was in jail, so I volunteered to come in and cover for him."

"You know full well that Jeremy's not in jail. Furthermore, you know where he is and who took him there. You're not leaving here until you tell me."

"Don't be ridiculous. How would I know if Jeremy's somewhere besides jail?" He huddled in the chair and wrapped his arms around himself.

Bo walked over and dragged a straight-backed chair in front of Christian so their knees almost touched. "Look at me."

Christian looked up, scowling. "You can't keep me here."

"Yes, I can. And to answer your question, the way you'd know is because someone paid you to spy on Jeremy."

The shocked look in his eyes confirmed what had been a wildass guess. *Okay, one answer. How about another one?* "And they paid you to help Ottersen, right?"

Strike two. Christian turned white.

"You told Jeremy's clients Hill Top was in trouble."

Christian frowned murderously.

Bo leaned forward until his nose practically touched Christian's. "Right?"

"Okay, yes."

"And you gave Ottersen Jeremy's blends?"

Christian shrugged. "He should have protected them. What a trusting idiot."

Bo clenched his fists and let Christian see them. He might not believe Jeremy killed Ottersen, but Bo might kill Christian on the spot. "Christian, you better start talking, or I'll show the police you were directly involved in murder."

"Like hell! I had nothing to do with that murder. Nothing. And I don't know who did. I was just hired to make life difficult for Jeremy by giving his business to Ottersen."

"Who hired you?"

He shrugged. "Just a name on the phone and a whole lot of money in my bank account."

"What name?"

He stuck out his jaw and his chest, not an altogether impressive posture, but a good try. "First, I want to say I haven't done anything illegal. Everyone does a bit of espionage. When Jeremy hired me, I was already working for these other dudes, so I wasn't even being immoral."

"If you have a very fluid moral code."

Christian, the asshole, shrugged.

Bo narrowed his eyes. "And I'll remind you that murder's illegal."

"As far as I know, Jeremy did it."

"You know that's ridiculous."

Another shrug.

"I can prove I didn't." He didn't look sure of that.

"So can Jeremy."

Christian sneered but looked worried. "How? By you? Are you going to tell the police you two are lovers? Because I know you are. That should compromise any alibi you give him." He crossed his arms. "Besides, Jeremy's gone."

Damn. Don't let him see you sweat. "I'll happily tell the police everything you've been doing to undermine Jeremy and suggest that Ottersen found out, confronted you, and you got angry and killed him to protect yourself. It might be disproved, but for all I know, you did do it."

His worried look turned to panic. "And you won't tell the cops what I did if I give you what I know? It's not much."

"I may have to tell them about the dirty tricks, but I won't suggest you killed him. I'm sure they're investigating you as it is."

Christian nodded and stared at the floor.

"So what was the name?"

"I get the feeling this guy on the phone could cause a lot of trouble for me."

"So can I. And tell me why you think that."

"He just sounded like someone with, you know, power. Like he was used to always getting his way." He shook his head.

Bo picked up the legs of the chair and crashed them down. Christian jumped.

"Okay. He called himself Sam, but I heard someone who talked to him while he was on the phone call him Mario or Mark or something like that."

"Last name?"

"No idea."

"Signature on your checks?"

"No checks. Just direct deposits from a bank account in the Caymans."

"Phone number?"

"Always a different number.

"Does he still owe you money?"

"No."

"Tell me what else you know."

He sighed like this was a great inconvenience, which it would be when Bo slugged him in the jaw. Bo's face must have conveyed Christian's peril, because he said, "The man had an accent, and he knew everything there is to know about wine."

"What kind of accent?"

"I don't know. Maybe a little bit of New York or Jersey and something like European. Spanish, Italian?"

"So he knows wine."

"Yeah. A real lot."

Bo leaned back, his stomach churning. "Why do you think he wanted you to do this?"

"I didn't get the feeling he hates Jeremy. He just wanted him out of business."

"So you got paid." *Another guess.* "And you take over Jeremy's winery? Is that part of the deal?"

He drew himself up in a tight little cylinder. "Not necessarily. But if Jeremy's gone, someone has to run the place. Why not me?"

Bo leaned forward and stared in Christian's twinky blue eyes like a mongoose riveting a snake. "Because I'll see that you're never welcome in the wine country again and that you'll be tarred and feathered or lynched if you come back." Christian's eyes were huge blue moons of horror. Bo smiled as evilly as he could muster. "They do that where I come from. So if I were you, I'd lay low before you have to hire a lawyer to defend yourself against a murder charge—darlin'."

Christian's expression warred between scared and pissed. Scared won. "Okay."

"So you've got no idea where they've taken Jeremy?"

"No, honest. Sam never said anything about taking Jeremy anywhere. I didn't know he was gone until you told me."

"Okay, you can leave."

He frowned. "Who'll run the winery?"

"You mean now that you're not undermining the business and giving it to Ottersen?"

"Yeah, I guess."

Bo stood to his full and considerable height. "I will. Now get out. But don't leave the area until I say you can go. If I call you to provide information to the police, you better be available. Understood? There's no place in the world far enough for you to run from me."

Christian nodded and scampered out the door like the weasel he was.

Bo watched him go. He now knew more than he had—but what did it add up to?

RIP VAN Winkle, baby. Waking up sure you've missed a fuckload of your life.

Jeremy let himself groan. After all, a log sure as hell lay on his head, and his mouth tasted like a new definition of shit. He tried to lick his lips. *God, what is that? Why does this keep happening?*

"Sorry, *nipote*, they had to drug you. You were just too much of a handful." The familiar voice ended in a chuckle—of pride, apparently.

"Where the hell am I?" He tried to sit up and re-gretted the move instantly. Pain seared his head.

His grandfather's voice sounded worried. "They hit you much too hard and will pay for that. The doctor says you may have a slight concussion, but nothing to worry about."

"Nothing for *you* to worry about. Fuck, *Nonno*, what have you done to me?"

"Saved you, I hope. You were playing into his hands. I had to get you away from him and bring you home."

"How did I get here?"

His grandfather shrugged. "My plane, of course."

What the hell? Very, very slowly, Jeremy opened his eyes and raised his head. Oooh, terrible idea, but he had to see. His grandfather, noticeably older, his white hair a bit thinner, the sunbaked lines on his face deeper, sat across from where Jeremy lay on the couch in his big den. The den in upstate New York. Jeremy glanced around. God, he'd spent most of his few happy hours in this room. "So you're the one who had me kidnapped?"

"Not kidnapped. Taken into protective custody." He laughed that familiar sound Jeremy remembered from his childhood. Reeling from his father's harsh, uncaring discipline, he'd escape to his grandfather's winery and get to actually laugh. Nonno frowned. "You were about to be accused of murder. Did you do it?"

"Of course not! Did you?"

His grandfather spread his hands and shrugged in that classic Italian gesture. "Why would I? I know little of this man except to hear of his grasping greed, but then all those California types are perverse, aren't they? It's good you're away from them."

Jeremy almost snorted. *Away from the perverse California types and home with my family of thieves, murderers, and drug smugglers. Much better.* But his grandfather truly didn't see the family that way. He somehow found their lifestyle in no conflict with his traditional Catholic values.

Jeremy laid his head back down. "So why? What's he up to?"

Leaning his elbows on his knees, his grandfather gazed intently at Jeremy. "He's having some financial issues. Life-threatening ones." *Right.* That meant he'd borrowed from nasty dudes who collected with guns and knives. Nonno said, "He's determined to find what's left of your mother's money. He's got men out all over the country. Even some in France and Italy. He figured you'd choose the wine industry, which is uncomfortably close to home."

"Couldn't you have just called me?" He rubbed the bump on his head.

"Sorry, my boy. I didn't know they'd be so violent. But I could clearly see that you didn't want to involve me in your troubles, and I was sure you'd run again. He's bound to find you, *nipote*. That wouldn't be desirable."

"But surely this is the first place he'll look." He managed to swing his legs closer to the edge of the couch seat and eased his way to a sitting position.

"No. He's looked here many, many times. I think he believes that you've cut me from your life." His voice sounded sad.

"I just don't feel right making you choose between us, Nonno. He's your son."

"Yes, but his grasping greed has gotten the better of him. I'm ashamed to call him *il mio figlio*."

"I'm so sorry we've put you in this position."

He shrugged elaborately. "It happens. Families are no guarantee." He stood, and those strong hands that used to be so steady shook a little. "Why don't I help you to your room, where you can rest? Later, if you feel like eating, you can join me for dinner."

He leaned down, put an arm around Jeremy's shoulders, and helped steady him as Jeremy managed a clumsy rise to his feet. Once he was balanced, they made slow progress from the study, down the hall to the bright room that Jeremy had occupied in his boyhood. He smiled. "Wow. It looks the same but smaller."

"Because you are bigger, *nipote*."

Jeremy flopped on the double bed, which felt really small next to his own king, and his grandfather pulled an afghan up around his neck. "Sleep now. I must chastise the men who hit you."

That gave Jeremy a shiver. "It's hard to knock someone out. You know that."

"Yes, but I was clear in my desire you not be hurt."

"Go easy on them." "Chastise" in his family's terms could be a very bad word.

"Of course." Nonno smiled and left the room, closing the door after him.

Moving slowly, Jeremy dragged himself off the bed and to the attached bathroom, sat down to pee since his legs were so shaky, and dropped his head in a hand. *Well, shit.* He really hadn't counted on his grandfather's well-meaning interference in this mess. Having two Andrettis combing the world for him was at least one too many to escape, obviously. Of course, Nonno had insider information. He knew Jeremy was in the US and involved in wine somehow, so there were only so many options. Hell, who knew how many clues Jeremy had given the old man over the last year? *And Nonno didn't kill Ottersen. Does that mean my father did?* No way. If Angelo Andretti knew where Jeremy was, he wouldn't have sent any warnings. *So who?*

Slowly he rose from the john, washed up, and returned to his supine position on the bed, pulling up the throw against the chill of the AC.

Half his brain only wanted to think about Bo. God, he must be frantic. This was exactly what he was afraid of.... *Maybe he thinks I ran—from him. Of course, I was planning to. Letting my father anywhere near Bo would top the mile-high pile of craptastic ideas.*

Jeremy dropped an arm over his eyes. He desperately wanted to let Bo know he was safe, but that was also on that craptastic pile. Bo equaled Angelo in tenacity and perseverance. He'd find a way to uncover Jeremy's hiding place, no matter what it took.

No, Nonno's kidnapping might have been a blessing. It removed the decision to leave Bo from Jeremy's hands—a decision Jeremy might never have been able to make.

So I'm here. What next? He had to persuade his grandfather to let him hide somewhere else. No matter how many times Angelo had been here, he had to know Jeremy loved Nonno and vice versa. He'd always come back for another check.

Unless Jeremy could convince his father that he had no more money. Would Angelo let him go if he knew that? Or would he want revenge for what he perceived as Jeremy's theft of the money, despite the fact that it had been left to Jeremy in the will?

Since there was no way he could sleep, he got up, took a shaky shower, shaved with the conveniently provided razor, and dressed in his own clothes from his getaway bag that were hanging in the bedroom closet. The sweatshirt and jeans wouldn't fall on the top of Nonno's sartorial favorites, but so be it. He crossed to the dresser and looked— and looked. *Huh, no phone. Maybe Nonno has it.*

He walked down the long tiled hall toward the dining room. Good smells greeted him, and he glanced in the kitchen to see old Donna Ana cooking as she had in his youth, and two other servants, a young woman and an older big man, helping. The guy looked more like a bodyguard than a butler, and probably was.

Jeremy kept walking to the high-ceilinged living room. Nonno sat in his big comfy recliner, glass of red wine in hand, *La Traviata* playing on the sound system, and two guys with the steely eyes and coat bulges of made men sitting near him, leaning in and talking. If Francis Ford Coppola had staged the scene, he couldn't have done it fucking better.

Though it made him catch his breath, Jeremy knew a man of his grandfather's background couldn't live without protection.

Nonno looked up, smiled, stood instantly, and crossed to Jeremy, both hands extended. "*Nipote*, you look so much better. Your rest seems to have restored you, and the harm of those stupid goons was not permanent." He took Jeremy's hands and kissed him on both cheeks. "Come, sit. We'll have wine and then dinner."

By the time Nonno backed away and they walked toward the sitting area, both of the men were gone. *Poof.* Vanished. "I'm sorry. I didn't mean to drive your visitors away."

"No. No. Who needs business when I have you?"

Nonno poured a glass of red at the bar cart, brought it to Jeremy, and sat opposite, back in his recliner. "Enjoy. It will further restore you."

Jeremy sipped the wine and smiled. "You do have a way with wine, Nonno. Truly among the finest I've ever tasted."

"Thank you. The highest praise."

"I wish you could have tasted some of my wines to see what I learned from you. I hope I would have made you proud."

"Ah yes. The seed does not fall far, as they say."

"I hope not. You'd love my friend's wine too. He uses dry farming techniques, and they give the wines a unique flavor."

Nonno frowned for a second, then said, "Yes. I'm familiar with dry farming. I can imagine it would be useful in California." He sipped. "But you're here now." He leaned forward and waved a hand toward Jeremy's hair. "I see you haven't cut it. Your mother would have been so pleased."

"Yeah. I know it's kind of dumb, but it's the one thing I know she liked. The only thing that connects me with her."

"Except her money, of course." Nonno laughed.

The big man Jeremy had seen in the kitchen looked in from the dining room. "Dinner's ready, Mr. Andretti."

"Thank you, Carlo." He flopped his feet to the floor. "Let's eat. I'm hungry."

"Me too."

"Good sign. Good sign."

They sat catty-corner to each other at the big table and proceeded to dig into an Italian's idea of dinner—soup, antipasti, pasta, fish, turkey in deference to Nonno's aging arteries, and finally spumoni for dessert. All through the meal, different wines accompanied the courses, and different discussions about wine accompanied the vintages. Finally they sat back with digestivos and tried to digest.

Jeremy laughed and patted his stomach. "I haven't been this indulged in a long time."

"Not indulgence. Mere subsistence." But he laughed to show his own conceit. "So, do you want to move your money to a safer place so Angelo doesn't find it?"

Hmm. Whiplash subject change. "Angelo can't find it because there's nothing left to find. I invested all the money in my winery." He turned the small glass in his fingers. "The man, Ottersen, who was killed effectively put me out of business, so most of that investment's gone." He frowned.

"How odd. Your father's under the impression that you were left over ten mil US. Surely that little enterprise didn't take that kind of investment."

"No, of course not. My mother left me ten million, but I only got three. Angelo must have used up the rest. He's being disingenuous. Probably he just wants an excuse to kill me."

"Is this the truth? My men who found you said you had a shovel."

Jeremy looked up at the frown on Nonno's face. "Of course it's the truth, sir. I keep my travel documents buried as you taught me. I was on my way to get them when I got slammed." He rubbed a hand over his head. "Did you believe Angelo?" He took a mouthful of the limoncello. "Do you think I'd have let that asshole, Ottersen, mow me under if I'd had the resources to stop him?"

"Why didn't you ask me for help?"

"If I'm not good enough to run my own business, I can't ask for handouts." He looked up. "You taught me that."

"But it sounds like these were extraordinary circumstances."

Jeremy just shrugged.

"Will you excuse me a moment, *nipote*? I need to make a call. Enjoy your drink and coffee. Help yourself to more. I'll only be a moment."

CHAPTER TWENTY-SEVEN

WHEN HIS grandfather left, Jeremy crossed to the sideboard and poured more dark Italian roast into his cup, then laced it with cream. As a child he'd been allowed a little coffee in his milk. He never got over loving the taste.

Sipping the coffee, he wandered to the old-fashioned bar tucked into a nook between the dining and living rooms and surveyed the rows of wines, most Andretti labels, but a few others. Nonno favored red, but some whites and sparkling wines had made it into the selection, as had been evidenced during the meal.

Jeremy glanced down on the lower shelves under the bar and spied a couple of California vintages. He smiled. Breaking his own rules, Nonno seemed to have shied from devotion to only New York and Italian labels.

He knelt down and cocked his head. *Wow. One of Bo's wines.* That made his heart squeeze. He wanted to pour the wine into a glass and sip it slowly for hours so he could feel like Bo wasn't so very far away. He glanced back into the corner of the cabinet and—*What the fuck?* Two bottles of his wine. Hill Top.

He stood quickly. Something about the way the bottles were hidden suggested Nonno didn't want him or anyone else to see them. Walking quickly back to the table, he took a couple of deep breaths, then sat and picked up his drink. So Nonno knew about Hill Top. How long ago did his grandfather find him? Had he been toying with Jeremy for months, pretending not to know where he was?

He took another sip. *Calm down. That'd be like him. To give me the impression that I'm on my own so I could be independent. Plus maybe he thought I'd run again if I knew he'd found me. Or maybe he doesn't know Hill Top is my winery? Possible, but unlikely.*

Nonno walked back in, smiling. "Sorry, son. As you know, winery business never sleeps."

"I do know."

His grandfather sat and leaned back in his chair. "So what if you were to become my winery manager?"

"What? Sir, Angelo would get wind of that in a second."

He waved a hand. "Hear me out. We'd use your adopted name, Jeremy Aames. If Angelo knew that, he'd have been on your doorstep before now. Obviously you'd remain here on the property. No socializing in the community, though that's a loss. But it would help me, keep you busy, and hide you in plain sight, so to speak."

The desire to ask how long his grandfather had known about his winery burned his lips, but he just smiled. "It might work, Nonno. Let me think about it, okay?"

His grandfather slapped a hand against his own forehead. "Yes, yes, of course. Here you are, ripped from your life, assaulted by nincompoops, and I'm pressing you for decisions."

"Not at all. I'm flattered by the offer." He pressed his hand over a yawn. "But I must confess to being tired. I'm not used to so much food and wine. I'll clearly get fat if I stay." He laughed. "By the way, Nonno. Do you have my phone?"

"No. Is it missing?"

"Yes, since I was struck in California. Your men must have taken it."

"I'll speak to them."

"Thank you, sir." He stood. "It's been a delightful evening."

"For me too." He embraced Jeremy and gave him the two-cheek kisses. "I'll see you in the morning."

Jeremy went straight back to his room, changed into pajama bottoms and a T-shirt, then plopped in the chair beside the fireplace that someone had lit in his absence.

I need my phone.

What exactly am I planning to do if I find it?

No clue, but at least I'll know Bo could call me and I could call him. Shit, I'll bet he's called me a bunch of times. I'll bet he's so worried and so pissed. I miss him so much.

The prospect of a life without Bo washed over him again like toxic rainwater. He curled his knees to his belly, rested his head on them, and tried to cry quietly until he fell asleep.

When his eyes opened, he was in bed and sun shone offensively in the windows. He frowned. *How the hell did I get from the chair to here?* Chances were good

Nonno had come to check on him and had one of his behemoths carry Jeremy to bed. That creeped him out.

He dragged himself out of bed and stared in the dresser mirror at his red, puffy eyes. *Damn, I'm a wuss. Can a guy blame his emotional outbursts on hormones? And if I want to say it's a broken heart, I can't claim anyone broke it but me. Bo was ready to come out for me. Nobody's ever wanted to change their life for me.*

Shit!

He rushed to the bathroom, turned on the cold water, and held a handful against his face. *No more damned blubbering. Suck it up. I've got serious thinking to do.*

He took a breath and rubbed the light stubble on his chin. He should let his beard grow. If his hair got any longer, he'd need something to establish he was a guy.

Fifteen minutes later, clean, dressed, with his spine stiffened and carrying his windbreaker, Jeremy walked into the breakfast room, one of his favorite spaces in his grandfather's house. Designed to catch the morning light, the room, with its good smells and easy camaraderie, had always made him feel ready for the day.

Nonno sat in his place at the head of the table. At least Jeremy assumed it was Nonno. Somebody was behind that newspaper. A hand slid out from the newsprint and deposited a box at Jeremy's place. The paper popped down a few inches. Nonno said, "The men say they threw away your phone. Here's a new one. It has limited access, however, to keep Angelo from finding it." The paper moved back up.

"How would Angelo find it, Nonno?"

His voice came from behind the paper. "I have no idea. I don't understand this technology shit. But my IT guy says it's so, and I don't want to take the chance."

Jeremy glanced at the phone, then got some breakfast. As he ate his scrambled eggs, he pulled out the device that looked like a regular iPhone. He turned it on and found it was already charged. His fingers just started moving, dialing, trying to get to Bo. *I'll tell him that I'm okay. I need to tell him.*

Beep, beep, beep.

He frowned. "How can I dial out?"

His grandfather waved a hand. "The usual way I suppose."

He dialed his office.

Beep, beep, beep.

"Who can I call?"

"What?"

"Nonno, who can I call?"

The paper dropped. "I don't know. He said he'd make it safe."

"Does that mean I can only call you and 911?"

He shrugged. "Maybe. I don't know."

"Can I use it for social media?"

"I'm telling you, I don't know." His white eyebrows met over his bright blue eyes, so like Jeremy's.

"I appreciate the gesture, Grandfather, but there's no point in having a phone if it doesn't communicate with anyone."

"It can call me if Angelo finds you. Clear?"

"Yes, sir. Thank you for thinking of it." As Nonno went back to reading, Jeremy ate the rest of his eggs, his mind ten steps ahead. "Please excuse me. I'm anxious to go see the winery operations."

"I'll show you around."

"No need. I remember." He bounded up before his grandfather could stop him and stepped out through the french doors in the breakfast room. Outside, he broke into a jog and headed for the closest of the vineyard's production buildings. It took a few minutes at a good clip, but he got there before anyone could interfere.

Inside the big cavern of a building, people busily moved around between giant oaken barrels and tanks. Beyond were the rooms of vessels and the blending labs. Jeremy inhaled deeply. That sweet, pungent smell was in his blood from birth, and he loved it.

"Hi. Can I help you?" A young dark-haired guy stood there looking pleasant and very curious.

"Oh, hello. I'm Jeremy Aames. I'm going to be working with Mr. Andretti here in the vineyards. I'm just taking a quick look around, and then I'll be back for an in-depth tour."

"You're a winemaker, Mr. Aames?" The pleasant look turned a little skeptical, probably because Jeremy was about the age of the guy standing in front of him.

"Yes. I've been setting up wine blending operations in California."

His eyes brightened. "Will you be doing that for us?"

"I believe so, yes."

"That's great." The pleasant smile turned enthusiastic.

"If you'll excuse me, I want to do a jog around the fields. Can you tell me the ones I should see?"

"Three, four, and ten are nearby and will give you an overview."

"Thanks. I'll see you again, probably tomorrow."

"Yes, I'd like to talk with you about some ideas I have—"

Jeremy held up a finger. "Forgive me. Please hold that thought. I have so little time right now, I don't want to rush you."

"Oh. Okay."

Jeremy ran out the door and headed toward field ten, the closest to the road. When he got to the field, he cut through the rows, slapping hands with some of the workers, then slipped out of view and emerged on the road. It was less than a mile to the nearest town, although a hamlet of 800 people didn't exactly promise lots of technology experts. Still, worth a try.

A few minutes later, he trotted into the chic and popular little town and gazed around. Even small-town people had phones. He grinned tightly. Ahead of him was a small two-story retail building, and on the second floor, like manna from heaven, a sign announced Cellular World. *Thank you!*

He ran up the stairs—his thighs would regret this whole effort later—and pushed into what proved to be a small, very messy shop. A head popped around the edge of a workstation. "Yeah?" The guy looked like he might have escaped from one of the episodes of *Jurassic Park*.

"I need some help with a phone." Jeremy smiled and went for helpless.

"Come back tomorrow."

Shit! "Sorry. Can't. Can you recommend someone else I can see?"

The guy sighed. "Okay, show me."

Jeremy rushed forward, taking the phone from his pocket. "So this may not be okay with you, but my boss gave me this phone, and then somebody must have done something to it that makes it impossible to call anyone but a couple of approved people. It's wacked, man. How the hell am I supposed to carry two damned phones around all the time so I can call my girlfriend or my mom?"

"Fuck, man. I hate that. Damned authoritarian ass-holes trying to use technology to control us."

Jeremy nodded. He'd judged his man correctly. "Fuckin' A, man."

"Gimme."

Jeremy handed him the phone.

"Go get some coffee and let me look at this thing."

"You take credit, right?"

"Sure."

"Okay. I really appreciate this."

"Yeah, well, power."

They bumped fists, and Jeremy walked out into the sunlight. A drugstore across the street caught his eye. He jogged over and found just what he wanted, a crowded little space with a single person behind the counter. Jeremy wound through the aisles until he found a pack of razor blades, pocketed them, and then discovered a restroom at the back of the store. He slipped in, occupied the only stall, pulled out a blade, and applied it to the thick elastic of his jacket. He made a small cut, ripped the hole farther, then pulled out the credit card. Just holding it in his hand made him breathe deeper.

He exited the john, paid for the blades with the card, although the cashier gave him a look over the package being open, and in a second he was back outside. He stepped into the street, looked up, stumbled, and nearly fell on his face. *Damn.* He glanced at the passing car, all tinted windows and black sleekness. Was that Angelo? No. Why would he be in Hammondsport? *He hates small towns.*

Still breathing hard from the shock, he mounted the stairs to Cellular World and went in, glancing back. *No one.*

"Hey, man, you're gonna be stoked. I got this."

"No shit?"

"Yeah, whoever did this ain't all that, man. Might think so, but he couldn't stump the bump, man."

"Bump?"

"Red Bumpchin. Me." He stuck out his hand and shook Jeremy's.

"Can I call anywhere?"

"I didn't optimize for international, but you can do that on your laptop, right?"

Wrong, but he didn't want to say that. "You're the wizard, man."

"The Keymaster."

"How much do I owe you?"

The Bump held up his hands. "Hey, man, it's my pleasure to stick it to the man. Just use it in good health."

"No, that's too much. What can I do for you?"

"Bring me back a vanilla caramel latte with coconut milk."

"You got it." He walked to the door. "Be right back." He walked out and saw the coffee shop sign two blocks down. The now presumably working phone burned a hole in his pocket and his heart, but he had to get the coffee. Clearly everyone in town had the same idea, and the line at the coffee shop stretched to the door. He wanted to tell Red that he didn't have time, but the guy had done him a huge favor.

By the time he got his drink, it was fifteen minutes later. He ran it in to Red, thanked him again, and took off like a shot back toward the winery. He didn't dare stop and call Bo. The gnawing demand in his gut to let Bo know he was safe fought with the reality of his situation. He wasn't even sure what he wanted to say to Bo. Jeremy couldn't go back to California. Not if Nonno was right about Angelo closing in. Should he ask Bo to run away with him? Be a fugitive? Hell, that wasn't even a little fair, and it would place Bo in huge danger. Plus Bo would never leave his family, so back to square one. What did he want to say?

Chugging like a train, he threaded his way into field ten and then rushed through the rows until he reached the edge of field three. There he slowed and started looking at the vines and the fruit. All told, from the time he talked to the guy in production, he'd been gone over an hour. *Have they noticed?*

It took another ten minutes, but feet came stomping up behind him. "There you are. I've been looking for you everywhere."

Jeremy turned to Nonno, who walked up to him with the guy from production and the big man from the kitchen.

Jeremy smiled graciously. "I'm so sorry, Mr. Andretti. I explained to this gentleman—" He pointed at the young guy. "—that I wanted to take a look at the vineyards. I must confess, I got engrossed and lost track of the time. I'm ready for that tour now."

Nonno seemed to realize they needed to play the game of employer and employee in public. He slapped Jeremy on the shoulder. "Of course, Jeremy. I look forward to your observations on the growing procedures." He glanced at the young guy. "Paolo, did I explain that Jeremy was in charge of running a very unique California winery? I think he can bring some new ideas to us."

"Yes, I'm very excited to be working with him." Paolo gave Jeremy a glance that might not have been entirely professional.

They toured the production facilities, which Jeremy remembered from when he was a kid and had to be careful not to say so. He got a kick out of his

grandfather's obvious pride in the winery and its product, and he creeped out over Mr. Made Man who walked
behind them with his hands in his pockets. *Man, I'm
out of practice. I forget what it's like.*

Jeremy looked around with affection. He'd love
to get his hands on this place—but not as much as he
wanted to know what was happening at Hill Top. Not a
fraction as badly as he wanted to see Bo.

CHAPTER TWENTY-EIGHT

"Nonno, I'm out of practice. Have mercy." Jeremy leaned back in his chair and clutched his over-full stomach. After another six-course dinner, he felt half-satisfied and half-uncomfortable. Actually, that described a lot of things.

Nonno laughed. "You need practice."

"I need a day at the gym."

"Ah yes, you used to be quite the fitness enthusiast."

Jeremy nodded, not mentioning that he'd done it in self-defense against the constant implied threat of Nonno's hulking bodyguards and his father's fists. "Is there still a gym in town?" He asked that super casually.

"Oh, we built one here on the property. All the latest equipment. I'll show you tomorrow." Nonno stood. "I have a business meeting this evening. Please feel free to use the theater room if you'd like."

Jeremy rose. "Thank you, but the flat-screen in my room is plenty. Plus I'm a little tired. I'll turn in early."

"Then I'll wish you good night." Nonno kissed his cheeks and left the dining room.

Jeremy ambled out of the dining room and down the hall toward his room. He'd told the truth. He was tired. Getting hit on the head, drugged, hauled to New York, and then performing his 1500-meter race that day to town and back had taken a toll. But also he had the feeling that if his footsteps strayed far from their appointed path, there'd be someone to object. As with every moment in the house, his spine tingled as if he was being watched. Chances of it being true? About 99.9 percent. Maybe not because Nonno didn't trust him specifically, but because Nonno didn't trust anyone.

He wandered into his room, flopped on the bed, and clicked on the TV. News, sports, and *Bones* reruns. None of those exactly attracted him. He flipped on his back, glanced at the door, and pulled his phone from his pocket. No way to make a call. They'd hear him. But a text?

He input Bo's number from memory and texted *I'm okay. Don't worry about me.* His fingers kept typing. *Miss you like crazy.* With a deep breath, he hit Send, then immediately erased the text from his phone history. Somebody with some IT skills could track it, but not a casual observer. He stared at the screen like a cat at a mouse hole, praying for a reply. *Shit, what can he say? He doesn't know where I am and if I lo—uh, care about him, I can't tell him. Also, he might not want to hear from me. His life has to be 100 percent easier without me in it.* Still, he couldn't help hoping.

Ten minutes of trying not to but still staring at the phone produced no reply. A piece of him refused to let go. *It's three hours earlier. He's at work. Busy. His phone might be in the office.*

Damn, he needed something to distract him. *A movie.* He swung off the bed, slipped his shoes back on, and walked out the door—then realized he had no idea where the movie room was. It had to be something Nonno had added since the last time Jeremy was here.

The most likely location was near the pool since he'd had extra space around there. Peeking into rooms trying to find a big-screen TV or someone to ask with no luck, he walked to the pool area. There was a new room, but it proved to be a gym—well equipped. He'd use that the next day.

Okay, where's the theater? Wending his way back toward the central living spaces, he stuck his head in the kitchen. Weirdly, no one was in there.

Maybe Nonno's meeting is over? Jeremy headed toward his grandfather's office. *He might even want to watch a film with me.*

As he approached the big double doors, no body-guards stood watch. *Good sign.* Probably the meeting was over. From a couple of feet, he could hear a bit of noise through the thick mahogany doors, but maybe just Nonno watching news.

He grasped the old-fashioned door handle and turned. No resistance, the door pushed open, and—

—Jeremy could hear his own gasp above the sound of Nonno's voice raised in argument with another speaker. Every cell in Jeremy's body turned to ice as all the eyes in the room turned to stare at him. That was a lot of eyes. Jeremy felt frozen in place, staring at Nonno seated in an obvious position of power on one of his grand high-backed chairs, to the man sitting in front of him, perched on a stool—Jeremy's father, Angelo. Angelo Andretti, the presumed most powerful don left in the NYC mafia.

Tingles started in Jeremy's spine as the two men peered at him as if he'd crawled from under a rock. Angelo looked over his shoulder. "Are you telling me you left no one on the door, you idiot?"

Nonno rose with a smile. "*Nipote*, I told you I had a meeting. Can I help you?"

"I was looking for the theater. No one was around." The reason was obvious. Every person Jeremy had seen in the house was currently in that room, including old Donna Ana, who somehow looked less friendly and mild sitting in a chair with her legs crossed, smoking a cigarette.

"Not a problem, my dear. Carlo will take you."

Carlo stepped away from the wall, and Jeremy stepped back. "But Angelo—" Someone against the wall moved. Jeremy looked, sucked in his breath, and turned to run. He got two steps before a giant hand clamped on his shoulder. He threw a punch, but two more huge paws got added to the mix, and he was dragged off his feet. These guys weren't hired killers because they were good negotiators. Jeremy struggled, but they clamped his hands painfully behind his back and turned him toward the room.

The words spat from Jeremy's mouth. "Why was I such a goddamned, unbelievable, stupid, gullible fool?"

The man standing by the wall trying to look inconspicuous was Sean, the dude from the bar who'd drugged him.

Nonno smiled and shook his head. "What we learn in boyhood becomes our truth, dear one. Why would you ever doubt it?"

Everything in Jeremy rebelled. No, he'd never believed his grandfather was a sweet old man or that he trusted him, but he'd honestly thought— "I believed you cared about me, at least a little."

"But of course I do, my darling." He walked forward. "That's why I worked so hard to restore you to the family. I was pleased that while you escaped from us, you never provided evidence against us. That was testament to your honor and your family feeling. You're intelligent, *nipote*, and have skills we need."

Jeremy stared around the room. Five made men including the two holding him, Donna Ana, Sean, probably also a made man though obviously serving a different purpose, and his father, Angelo, were assembled. Jeremy looked back at Sean.

"If Sean's here, that means you know I'm gay, and I don't see you taking a gay man to the bosom of the family, Grandfather. Not with your opinions."

Nonno frowned. "Yes, that was a great disappointment. I nearly told them to kill you. But then I remembered the perverse influence of those people in California and knew we only had to return you to a family of real men for you to realize your true nature again."

Jeremy narrowed his eyes. "Just to clarify, *you* would have told them to kill me? Not Angelo?"

Nonno gave an icy smile. "Well, of course, *he* would have made the call on *my* say-so."

"So you've always been the head of the family?" The ice from that smile traveled up Jeremy's spine to his heart.

"Yes. Power and leadership aren't *necessarily* hereditary." Nonno's eyes slowly glanced at Angelo with unalloyed disdain. "But I believe you've inherited much of the best of my line." He beamed.

Well, shit.

"So basically you have a choice to rejoin your family, learn the business, and perhaps take over upon my death. You'll get to do it here, in this charming atmosphere, surrounded by things you know and love."

"Or die."

Nonno's strong white teeth gleamed at him. "Is there ever any other choice?" His white eyebrows rose. "Oh yes, and return to me the ten million dollars that is rightfully mine. That idiot mother of yours knew that the only way I agreed to let her leave Angelo was to sign over her inheritance at her death to me."

Angelo's eyes widened. "What?"

"She changed it on her deathbed, apparently. I can't believe I let her live."

"You agreed to her leaving me?" Angelo stared at his father in obvious shock. "I always wondered why you didn't bring her back to me."

"Yes." Nonno sighed. "I'm a sentimental fool. I only acquired her for you because I had a, shall we say, yen for her? She was so beautiful." He glanced at Jeremy. "Jeremy looks so like her. I'm glad he never cut his hair." The brows lowered. "I suppose now I'll have to insist he cut it since it obviously makes him look like a fag, but it's sad." He shrugged. "Anyway, even after I was done with her, I couldn't quite bear to kill her, so I let her live. But the money's mine."

Jeremy took a breath. Choice. He could fake it until he could escape. Pretend to go along with the plan. Pretend to give back the money. But first he'd have to demonstrate his ruthlessness, maybe even kill people to show loyalty. If he managed to escape, he'd spend his life running, and this time without the illusion of any support. And no matter what, he'd live without Bo. Yes, he was twenty-four and had a lot of life to live, but what for? He sighed out the words. "That's all well and good, Nonno. Two problems with your plan."

"Oh? What?" The words dripped off his lips.

"First, I don't have any of Mother's money. Maybe Angelo got it or someone else, but when I took it, there was three million. Period. I used it up. It's gone."

Nonno scowled at that and opened his mouth to speak, but Jeremy said, "And second, no matter what you do, I'll still be gay."

That's when Nonno's eyes turned colder than Jeremy would have thought possible. "The first's impossible, the second is nonsense."

Jeremy only shrugged.

"Then you require persuasion to learn the whereabouts of the money?" He might as well have asked if Jeremy would like ketchup with that, he said it so matter-of-factly, but the tone disguised a reality of more pain than Jeremy could even imagine. He knew that. *Damned tough way to die.*

He shrugged again.

Nonno sighed. "I truly thought there was some hope for you, but I suppose as the son of my idiot son, you couldn't have been much better. Don't worry. We'll learn the location of the money—before you learn the meaning of the hell devoted to perverts."

Man, that did not sound fun—his brain's snarky way of covering a black pit of fear. *Just keep remembering, just keep remembering—*

A sound came from the front of the house.

Nonno looked up. "Was that a knock?" He looked incredulously around the room as if asking *Who knocks on the door of a mafia don without permission? Girl Scouts?* He pointed at Jeremy, who still stood hanging between Carlo and another thug, "Tie him." Then he looked at the sometime cook. "Donna. Go see."

She rose and left the room, looking for all the world like a sweet little old Hispanic cook. *I'll bet there's a gun under that black dress.*

One of the bodyguards tied Jeremy tightly to a chair with his handy-dandy plastic pull ties but didn't plug his mouth—yet.

Donna stuck her head back in. "Some man says he's a winemaker. He's a visitor and was referred to you by some other winemaker. I told him you're busy, but he asked for just a couple minutes since he's only in town today."

Nonno scowled. "How did he learn where I live? I don't give many friends my address."

The door pushed open abruptly, slamming into Donna's back. She fell forward.

Jeremy's mouth opened as he stifled his scream in his throat. His heart and brain exploded with one word. *Bo!*

"Mr. Andretti, you'd be amazed at how many people know your address." Bo pushed a phone to his mouth. "Now!"

"Bo, run!" Jeremy shrieked a second before the gun butt slammed into his skull. His head fell forward, but he didn't lose consciousness. Knocking someone out was way harder than most people thought. Still hurt like hell, but let them believe—

It was hard hanging his head with the chaos around him. Guns fired, glass broke, and people screamed. Then he heard what might be his favorite words of all time next to *I love you* from Bo—

"FBI. Drop your weapons and put your hands on your heads."

Holy fuck. Did that mean Bo brought the feds? Still, he kept his head down since he was tied and it would only take one shot to end him. If they knew he was awake, they'd shoot him in a minute, but unconscious he was a lower priority.

A bullet whizzed past his head. He bit his tongue not to move. *Where's Bo? Is he okay?* Shit, he had to stay alive to find him, help him, save him.

A body bumped him, landed hard on his foot, and didn't move. At all. *Fuck, who is it?*

If it's Bo, I don't want to live.

That thought almost made him gasp—bad idea but important thought. Very slowly his eyes opened.

Angelo. Totally dead. Jeremy had always had to force himself not to pray for this moment. Knowing that the misery of his life had been directed by his grandfather, not Angelo, decreased any sense of satisfaction. For a fraction of a second, some weird wish that maybe he could have known either of his parents before they were ruined by his grandfather crept into his brain. *Poof.* It had still been Angelo's fists applied to his young son's head, no matter who'd instructed it. *Good riddance.*

Suddenly somebody fumbled behind his chair, and Jeremy assumed total unconsciousness.

"Shit, these things are tough."

Is that voice familiar? Jeremy didn't move.

The hands moved away from his wrists, and lots of fumbling and swearing followed. Then they were back, cutting the plastic zip ties. "Damn, Jeremy, I can't carry you."

Holy shit! That's O'Hara. Jeremy's eyes snapped open, and he fumbled off the ties and peeked at his surroundings. Several prostrate bodies, at least one of them being an Andretti bodyguard, lay around the floor, but no one was moving.

Jeremy jumped up, turned, and threw his arms around O'Hara's neck. "What the hell are you doing here?"

O'Hara grinned. "You don't think I'd give up my case to the feds, do you? We don't get stuff this big often. I mean, hell, man? Organized crime?"

"Where's Bo?"

"No idea."

No, no, no! Jeremy took off like a bat for the door, beyond which he heard shooting, noise, and chaos.

"Jeremy, stop! For God's sake, you'll get yourself killed!"

No way. Bo's out there. He slammed the door open but had the good sense not to plunge into the hall, where bullets still flew. He peered around the corner of the door, then ducked back. Nonno, Donna, and one other guy hid along the hall's perimeter, facing away from Jeremy. *Damn, wish I had a gun. O'Hara!*

He turned into the office. O'Hara stood behind him. "Give me a gun."

O'Hara's dark brows dove over his nose. "No way, man."

Jeremy looked at the bodies, hurried to the closest one, and grabbed the 9mm Smith & Wesson lying beside what had once been a dangerous guy. Probably in it for the money like most of the remaining mafia, but the Andrettis were old-school.

Checking the chamber, he rushed back to the door and pushed at O'Hara.

O'Hara blocked the door, holding his police issue loosely. "I can't let you do this. The FBI needs your testimony against your grandfather. They've been after him for decades, and I need you in California. You can't get yourself killed."

Jeremy stared at O'Hara and hissed, "I guarantee I'm better with a gun than you. I'm also faster, more experienced with my hands, and promise you, there will be no testimony of any kind if Bo's dead and I could have saved him. I got him into this mess. I have to get him out."

"Damn it, Jeremy. It's my job to keep you safe. Bo too."

"That's the deal." He stepped forward. "Move before I hurt you."

O'Hara seemed to inhale the message in Jeremy's eyes, because he stepped aside. Jeremy dodged out the door and back in quickly. His carefully trained powers of observation might be rusty, but he was pretty sure Nonno and company had moved farther down the hall and sadly, all were still alive.

Whoa, that thought stopped him for a second. *Do I really wish Nonno were dead? Yes, because then I wouldn't have to kill him.*

Moving quickly and quietly, he slipped into the hall and pressed against the wall, but the small outcroppings didn't provide much cover. There appeared to be several FBI people at the end of the hall. More might be trying to find entry at the opposite side of the building, but Jeremy knew how hard that was. As a kid he'd always wondered why this part of the house was built like a fortress. But he and O'Hara were behind, so they could do the job.

Nonno seemed to be well ensconced in a niche in the wall and was letting his bodyguards take most of the risks. If Jeremy could take him down—or out—the others wouldn't stop fighting, but they'd lose motivation. He crept forward another couple of feet, then stopped so as not to attract attention in their well-trained peripheral vision. Sadly, the made man and the lethal Donna appeared to be better shots than most of the FBI guys. Crème de la crème, the best of Nonno's people, probably. Loyal to the death.

He just needed to get the right angle. If he missed, he was dead and O'Hara wouldn't have a shot.

Another foot forward. One more. Nonno didn't see him. The feds kept his grandfather pinned, and he was relying on the protection of his loyal subjects.

If Jeremy took another step, at least one of the feds would be able to see him. *Will they know who I am or shoot anyone they see?* No choice. He still had to do it.

One more foot. Significant parts of Nonno's body came into view. Jeremy slowly raised his hands. Took a breath—

A door down the hall opened, a person stepped through. Jeremy caught his breath. *Well, shit!* It was Bo.

Jeremy's heart slowed to a thud echoing in his chest in slow motion.

Bo made eye contact with Jeremy. Everything on his face went stunned, then burst into full panic. *Shit.*

Bo screamed, "Stop! Don't shoot him!"

Donna began to turn her head toward the spot where Bo's eyes were riveted, aka Jeremy's body. Jeremy squeezed the gun as the huge blast went off from Nonno's weapon. Bo stumbled backward, his hand clutching his chest, and fell to the ground.

"Bo!" Every cell in Jeremy's heart and particle of his soul exploded in pain and loss. He could barely stand the agony. Everything that had made sense shifted. *Gone. All gone.*

He pitched forward toward the polished stone floor, drowning in welcome darkness.

CHAPTER TWENTY-NINE

"JEREMY. WAKE up."

Like a tiny match lit in a vast stadium of blackness, Jeremy considered consciousness. Some piece of his brain said *I'm not dead. Surprising.* A memory filtered in. Bo's beautiful face contorted in pain. *Right. No reason to live.* He swallowed another mouthful of oblivion.

"Damn it, Jeremy. Open your eyes. We need to talk to you."

Who is that? O'Hara? Go away. He drifted.

Noise, voices, conversations. *Shit.* Hell was just like life. Stupid people who wanted stuff all the time.

"Jeremy." Someone shook him.

"Don't hurt him."

Thanks, whoever you are. Just leave me alone.

"He's not hurt. He passed out from shock."

What? No. I died.

"Some kind of mental breakdown, do you think?" That was a female voice.

"Come on, he's the son and grandson of organized crime leaders. You think he hasn't seen a little murder here and there?"

Not. Like. This.

"Hey, O'Hara. He's here."

"Thank crap. What have they been doing, admiring his beautiful teeth? Get him the fuck over here."

Rustling, thumping, people moving.

Leave me alone!

"Sweetheart?"

What?

"Darlin'?"

Oh shit. Oh shit. Oh shit. No, wait, some trick of hell.

"Jeremy." Lips touched his cheek, then his mouth.

Another voice—O'Hara?—said, "Did you two really think anyone believed you were just friends?"

"Well, of course, since for a time we really were."

"Yeah, well, news flash. Everyone else knew before you did, then."

A chuckle, like music to Jeremy's soul. His eyes opened and he feasted. Bo was turned toward O'Hara, laughing, his dimples like perfect little crevasses, and his teeth as white as—*okay, asshole if you say snow, you've totally given up all grasp on life and deserve to die.*

Bo looked down and the smiled increased. "Hi."

"Do you know you've turned me into a poetry-reciting, simpering sap, but the poetry appears to be *Mary Had a Little Lamb*?"

Bo flashed a quizzical half smile. "Hold that thought and explain later." His mouth descended.

Okay, I was wrong about the hell part. This is clearly heaven. He wrapped his arms around Bo's neck and accepted the best kind of mouth-to-mouth resuscitation.

"You guys get a room. Hell, get a whole hotel."

They finally pulled apart, smiling. Jeremy sighed. "With pleasure." Then he frowned, staring at Bo. "I saw you get shot. I thought you were dead."

"You saw me get two cracked ribs when your grandfather's damned bullet hit me in the bulletproof vest I'd been wearing since I walked into the room where they were holding you." He grimaced and rubbed his side. "Smarts. It knocked me off my feet and unconscious for a few minutes."

"How in hell did you get here?"

"That's a long and complicated story, my friend—"

"Which we don't have time for, because the FBI are about to pee their pants wanting to talk to you." O'Hara pulled on Bo's arm. "So get up and let's go give them what they want, so we can go home and I can have my crack at you."

Jeremy drew his eyebrows together. "Am I still a murder suspect?"

"Not while you continue to have an alibi—which we all know is fictional, but, hopefully I can't prove that because I don't think you did it."

"How about Nonno, I mean, my grandfather?"

"He'd never dirty his hands."

Jeremy waved a hand as he sat up. "Of course not. But he has lots of men he could send."

Bo shook his head. "I doubt that, but we better get to the FBI before we start trying to solve the murder of the vintner."

"The voracious vintner?" Jeremy felt the edges of his lips turn up.

O'Hara said, "What the hell are you two talking about?"

"Later. Let's go see the feds."

Three hours later he'd explained every detail of his abduction, from going to the bar, Sean trying to pick him up, getting drugged, and on and on. He explained all he knew as best he could figure it out to a room full of federal agents. "So with this you can get him on kidnapping?"

Agent McAllister, a small guy with sparkly eyes, said, "As long as you and Mr. Marchand testify, I think we've got him. But we're hoping you can give us more to convict him on murder, racketeering?" He spread his hands. "You tell me."

Jeremy shook his head. "Sadly, he hid everything from me. Don't misunderstand, I knew he'd been a mafia don, but he presented himself to me as retired. He said he'd passed everything over to my father, and anything that happened, he blamed on Angelo." Jeremy wiped a hand over his eyes. "For the last year, since I ran away, I've been feeding him information about my life that he used to find me. I trusted him—somewhat. At least I thought he loved me." He felt himself flinch at those words and saw a flash of compassion on McAllister's face. "Anyway, I believed him. My father was a meanass son of a bitch, and any chance I got, I'd run up here to be with kindly old Nonno." *God.* His hands curled into fists. "I didn't realize I was doing exactly what they wanted. What *he* wanted." Slowly exhaling, Jeremy said, "I realize now that he was constantly surrounded by made men. People came to see him for help. I was a kid. He told me they were visiting a lonely old man. As I got older, I knew these men around him were thugs, but since he'd been the head of the clan, the family, so to speak, I reasoned it away."

McAllister leaned in. "Did you ever see anything incriminating? Even small details could be helpful."

"Sure. People showed up who were really scared. So much so, one time I ran in my room and hid my head, a man was so terrified. But I have no idea who these people were or what happened to them. His bodyguards never talked around me. He'd send me to the wine processing buildings when I wanted to chatter. You can try some of those people. They might have more information than I do."

"Yes, we will. We are." McAllister jotted a note. "What about at your parents' home."

Jeremy shrugged. "A lot of yelling and hitting, loud men who sometimes acted like they were drunk. I was always afraid. But I never knew what happened behind all those closed doors." A big inhale felt good, and Bo squeezed his hand and didn't seem to mind if the FBI saw it. "Maybe my grandfather originally intended to allow me to go straight, maybe run his winery or start my own, so he protected me from any business dealings. Then, after my mother left me the money, he wanted me back. Well, he wanted the money back. Apparently he was my mother's lover. He had a soft spot for her but required that she leave her inheritance to him. She appeared to comply, somehow, but then must have changed it at the last minute. After the will was read, the money disappeared. I thought Angelo took it. He did, but it was for Nonno. I never knew that. Later, I found where Angelo hid it. I stole it. Well, it was mine."

One of the other agents said, "How did you steal it?"

"I broke into the Cayman bank and extracted my funds."

"What?"

Jeremy laughed. "Sorry. He actually hid the money in his house. Weird, right? But I think he wanted to be sure Angelo never found it. I saw him hide a suitcase. Of course, I thought he was hiding it for my father. I sneaked back and took it. But all I found was three million of the total of ten she left me. I don't know, maybe that wasn't my money. Maybe it was from something else and he hid the ten mil offshore, although he acted like he had no idea where it was and that's why he kidnapped me. Anyway, I used that up starting the winery and then dealing with Ottersen's dirty tricks." He glanced at O'Hara, who sat back in the pack of people, listening.

Bo said, "Your grandfather's dirty tricks, actually."

"What?"

"Marco hired Christian the twit to undermine you and give your business to Ottersen."

"When?"

"Before you hired him."

"Well, shit."

"He may be a twit, but he's a smart twit, and he immediately identified Ottersen as a capable and very ambitious man who wouldn't mind taking out a competitor if offered an opportunity. A seemingly legal opportunity, by the way. Ottersen didn't know he was ruining you. Christian would call your customers and lie to them, say you were unable to produce and deliver. Then he'd suggest Ottersen as a viable alternative. Your customers would call Ottersen and offer the business. So he wasn't lying when he said they contacted him. He was, however, willing to steal your blends when they were offered to him."

"Son of a bitch."

"Yeah. Anyway, we can talk about that later."

McAllister, who'd been watching their conversation with interest, nodded. "So keep thinking of any facts we could use to broaden our case against Marco Andretti now that we have him."

"I'll try."

"I'm sure you're anxious to get home."

"Hell yes, especially now that I know my customers don't hate me." He smiled and squeezed Bo's hand. "And other new things."

"We ask that you inform us if you go anywhere besides your homes and make yourselves available to testify."

Jeremy stood tentatively. He still felt shaky. "Count on it. No one wants to see the kidnapper go down more than I do, since the kidnappee was me."

Bo put his arm around Jeremy and took some of his weight. Jeremy looked up. Bo was sure working hard to prove he meant what he said about their being together. Man, that was a flat-out thrill, since Jeremy's most intense memory in life was his will *not* to live in a world in which Bo didn't exist.

It took a few more minutes, but Jeremy finally walked out of the building with Bo and O'Hara into the morning light. *Exhausted.* He looked up at Bo. "You must be tired."

"I've pulled a couple of all-nighters lately." He kissed Jeremy's temple.

"I can't wait to be awake enough to hear the whole story."

O'Hara beeped what looked like an official-issue car. "You two get in the back and sleep while I drive us to the airport."

He didn't remember much of anything except taking staggering steps between the car and the plane, and then into another car where he curled up in the back seat as they headed from San Francisco toward the central coast. *Oh boy, home.*

There was some jostling, the sensation of flying, and then—he opened his eyes to sunshine and the warmth of a strong body next to him. *Home in bed with Bo.*

If he had to have his life and future hanging in the balance, this seemed like a perfect outcome.

He breathed in the enormity of the moment. His father was dead, may he rest in whatever peace there is for people like that. There was a chance that Nonno's influence on his life—one he didn't even fully comprehend until now—could be over. Jeremy had an opportunity to restore the well-being of his business without someone undermining it.

He turned his head and watched the slow rise and fall of Bo's big shoulders as he breathed…. *And then there's Bo.* Jeremy didn't know all the things that had fed into Bo's decision to include Jeremy in his life. When he'd tried to share his feelings, Jeremy had shut him down. *Hell, I bet that hurt the shit out of him, not to have his monumental life decision respected. Damn. I never told him I care.*

Wait? Care? He gazed at the ceiling like it might open and reveal the secrets of the universe. *If I was willing to die over the loss of Bo, does it mean I just care for him? Hell, I care about my staff, but I'm not sure I'd die without them.*

His heart slammed against his ribs, harder than when he realized he was a prisoner or thought he'd lost his freedom for life. With urgency he flipped on his side and pulled at Bo's shoulder. "Bo. Wake up. Bo." Some tiny particle of gray matter said *Bo's exhausted. Let him sleep*, but this couldn't wait. "Bo!" He leaned over and kissed every spot on Bo's face.

Bo's hands came up like he was fending off a puppy, and he laughed as he tried to pry his eyes open. "I'm awake. I'm awake."

"Look at me, so I can tell you're conscious."

He opened those big sea-glass eyes. "I'm always conscious of you, darlin'."

"I love you."

"What?" He looked confused but still smiled.

"I'm so sorry I put you off and wouldn't let you tell me you were coming out to be with me. I'm so terribly sorry. It's the greatest gift anyone ever gave me, even including risking your damned life for me. I was afraid to accept the responsibility, but I want it, Bo. I'm a responsible man, all evidence to the contrary, and I want to prove that to you. That I can take care of your heart."

Bo's eyes, which Jeremy was staring into so hard, filled with tears. One dripped down and slid into his ear. Bo swiped at it with the back of his hand. Jeremy giggled. "I think there's an old song about getting tears in the ears."

Bo kissed his nose. "I love you too. In a new and different way that changes everything in my life, shifts it, and lets me see it brand-new. I'd like to be with you forever, if you'll have me."

Squealing in a way totally unlike him, Jeremy hopped up and straddled Bo. "I can't think of anything I want more."

"Okay, then we have a couple of priorities." He held up a finger. "I need to come out to my family."

"Whew."

"Yes."

He flipped out the second finger. "We've got to solve a murder, fast."

"Why can't we let O'Hara do that?"

"I've got a pretty good idea that the police will soon be able to poke holes in my alibi. Once they start talking to my family and Christian, who already knew we were lovers so he was likely spying on you, somebody's bound to say I never left the house that night."

"O'Hara doesn't really think I did it."

"True, but lawyers are messy and time-consuming." Bo pulled Jeremy's head down to kissing range and pressed soft lips to his. "And we have better things to do with our time."

"So true."

Jeremy nodded. "Before we set off on the accomplishment of those goals, we have a major priority."

"I know what one is." Bo's grin lit Jeremy up inside.

"I'd also like to know how the hell you tracked me down."

"For another time. Right now we need to dress, eat breakfast, focus on priority one, and drive to my house."

"That's a sure way to ruin my appetite."

"We'll eat light." Bo grabbed Jeremy's shoulders, flipped him until he was lying flat on the bed, and covered him with his big, hot, irresistible, life-changing body.

CHAPTER THIRTY

A BUSY, satisfying hour later, they'd both showered—separately, in deference to nerves and time—and
dressed. Jeremy served yogurt, all he could find in his
barren refrigerator. "Okay, give me a quick account of
your daring exploits."

"Right. Maybe it'll make me less nervous. It starts
with Christian."

"Seriously?"

When Bo finished telling Jeremy about how
Christian had been working against him, undermining
his business, he wanted to vomit. "Talk about being
gullible."

"He made himself indispensable." Bo grinned.
"And he had a cute butt."

"Ha."

"Anyway, some of the things he told me was the
man on the phone had an accent that sounded partly for-
eign and partly New York. He also said the man knew

everything about wine, that he didn't seem to hate you but just wanted you out of business. It occurred to me that this might be someone you knew from New York, and of course, I thought of the New York vineyards. I called a friend I know in one of the wine regions who's also very active in the New York Vintners Association. I figured he'd know everyone. I described this person Christian had described—accent, powerful, used to getting his way, very knowledgeable, and with a name like Mario or Mark, which Christian had told me. He immediately said, 'Marco?'

"I said, 'Maybe. What's the last name?' That's the first time I heard the name Marco Andretti. I re-searched and quickly discovered the organized crime connection. I called O'Hara, who knew the name. He followed up and discovered the FBI had been trying to get something on Marco Andretti for decades. We took off for New York. Fortunately they needed me to identify you in case they'd changed your appearance, so they didn't try to leave me behind. Plus I was pret-ty insistent. They spied on Andretti for a day before I got there and confirmed there was a new young guy on the property. They were pretty convinced you weren't a prisoner since you looked so at home, but O'Hara and I persuaded them to let me check. You know the rest."

Jeremy couldn't stop shaking his head. "You did all this for me." It wasn't a question.

Bo smiled softly. "Of course, I didn't have a white horse to ride in on or a saber to carry. Had to settle for the FBI."

Jeremy threw his arms around Bo's neck and kissed him until they both had to raise their heads for oxygen. Jeremy grinned. "What's coming out compared to tak-ing on the New York mafia?"

"Mama's scarier."

Jeremy laughed. "Okay, let's go, then." Hand in hand they walked to Jeremy's car and headed down the hill to the highway.

Bo looked nervous but resolute.

Jeremy glanced at him again. "What are you going to say?"

"I'll pray for guidance at the time."

"To Dionysus?"

Bo looked startled but said, "Among others."

Jeremy's stomach clenched. "Look, Bo, you don't have to—"

"Of course I do. How can we be together forever if I'm in the closet?"

"Be roommates?" Jeremy grinned sheepishly.

"Right."

"Okay, out is in!" He laughed, his heart beating a mile a minute. "Where'd you tell them you were going?"

"I didn't. I just said I had to go on a trip and they shouldn't worry."

At Bo's direction, Jeremy turned off the highway, followed a winding, gravel road, and pulled up in front of a big ranch house with incongruously cute rows of primroses arranged in beds by the front door. Bo blew out a breath and opened the passenger door, planting himself like an oak in front of the house.

As Jeremy climbed out his side, the front door opened and Bo's mom, a round but beautiful woman, came running out shrieking, "Oh my God, Beauregard, we've been so worried about you. I'm so grateful you're safe." She hurled herself toward him and clutched him around the neck.

She has no idea. Jeremy walked around the car.

"I told you not to worry, Mama."

She looked over, caught sight of Jeremy, and scowled. "You always seem to get in trouble when you and Mr. Aames are together."

Double no idea. Jeremy hid a grin.

"Mama, go inside, gather whoever is home, and meet me in the great room. I have some important things to discuss."

She fanned her hand in front of her face. "Oh my."

Triple no idea.

"Is this about—"

"You'll know what it's about soon enough. Go on inside." She bustled up the stairs, clutching at her frilly blouse.

Bo extended his hand. Jeremy swallowed, and he took it. Jeremy said, "To whatever comes next."

Bo nodded. "Forever."

When they got into the house, a weird combination of masculine ranch style and something out of a historical romance novel, people were scampering from every direction. An elderly man walked in from a hall. Bo said, "Jeremy, this is my grandfather, Harvey Walshman."

Jeremy extended his hand but had to release Bo's to do it. "How do you do, sir?"

Harvey glanced at Bo, then at Jeremy, and grinned. "Well, isn't that something? This is going to be fun." Chuckling, he squeezed Jeremy's hand. "Delighted to meet you, Jeremy. De-lighted."

Bo took his arm and escorted him into the great room, where his mother and the sisters sat on various couches and chairs, all much too flowery and formal for the house. The two sisters sat on opposite sides of their mother in a mutually protective line. An older couple occupied a love seat. Their expressions were interested and open.

Bo motioned to the couple. "Jeremy, you haven't met my Aunt Cortina and my uncle Davey."

Jeremy walked over and shook their hands as Bo's mother said tightly, "Jeremy is a colleague of Bo's."

He wanted to laugh. Nerves, but still. Talk about wishes making it so. But it was true, so he said nothing.

Bo guided him to a floral chair, which used up the available seating, so Bo grabbed a chair from the dining room and pulled it into the circle of anxious-looking family. He sat and gave them all a gaze.

Bettina said, "Come on, Bo, you're freaking us out."

Bo's mother waved a hand. "Should we have some wine?"

"Mama, it's 10:00 a.m."

Blanche laughed nervously. "Always time for wine."

Bo's chest expanded and he said, "What I want to tell you is I'm gay."

JUST SAYING the words unfurled a line of barbed wire that lived around Bo's heart.

Blanche slapped a hand over her mouth, Cortina and Davey looked at each other, Bettina gasped, and Grandpa just gaggled a laugh.

Mama narrowed her eyes. "Stop joking, Bo. It's not funny."

"No, it's not." He leaned forward and forced himself not to cross his arms. "What's not funny is the fact that I'm twenty-six years old and have never felt safe or comfortable enough with you to tell you who I really am."

Mama did cross her arms. "You're not blaming us for that?"

"I'm blaming all of us. It means you all are dependent and judgmental and I'm a coward. You have too much invested in me never changing, and I've been afraid to jeopardize your good opinion, which I value, as well as risking the scorn of others in my business life."

"Which you will receive!" His mother stared at him.

"I don't care, Mother."

Her hand clutched her chest. "How can you say that? A man has nothing more valuable than his honor and good name."

Jeremy made a little snorting sound but coughed over it. Mama shot him a vicious look.

"Mama, what I've realized is that I've internalized all the crap I grew up believing to the point I'd give up my own happiness in order to fit your pictures. I can't do that anymore. I deserve a life of my own."

"Crap?" Her eyes widened.

"Yes. All the 'the man is the head of the household, the provider, the one who must care for everything and please his family' crap. And that a gay man must spend his life as a confirmed bachelor who just never found the right girl."

For a moment there was icy silence. Davey held up a hand. "Bo, can I say something?"

Bo nodded.

"Cortina and I have been talking for months. We never intended for you to take care of us. We were grateful to be able to move with you but always planned to go out on our own. We're not old. We want to work. You just made life so comfortable for us, it's been easy to mooch, and I apologize for that, but we're ending it. We have some money saved, and we'll find a place to live in Paso right away."

Bo had to bite his tongue to keep from saying, "Don't go," but that was reinforcing everything he'd just declared he wanted to change. "I appreciate that."

"And there are more people in this family who could think about self-sufficiency as well." Davey stared pointedly from Blanche to Bettina.

Mama said, "Am I supposed to go out and push a broom or something?"

Before Bo could say something stupid like "Of course not, Mama," Davey said, "You're not an old woman, and it's time you stopped acting like the lady of the manor while your son's working his butt off to support us all."

She waved her hands in dismissal. "Why are we even talking about this? Bo has just told us that he's under the misapprehension that he's a homosexual. What do you have to say about that, Davey?"

"I'd say first, that's Bo's business, and second, that Bo's earned the right to a life he wants. Far be it from me to say what that should and shouldn't be."

Mama's mouth dropped open. She glanced at Cortina, who held up a hand. "I agree, and I already sent out a resume last week. Got a few bites too." She grinned.

Blanche pressed her folded arms tightly over her chest. "According to Bo, I don't have any skills or business sense, so I don't know why I should look for a job."

Davey leaned back in the overstuffed chair. "Eating might be good motivation."

Bettina had been staring into space. She looked up. "You're right, Davey. I've appreciated the time to get myself together after the divorce, but I need to move on. I'll start looking tomorrow."

Bo's grandfather said, "I'd like something to do. Maybe I can help Bo with his books?"

How exactly this coming out had turned into an employment discussion, Bo wasn't sure, but he couldn't complain. "My real intention was to introduce you all to Jeremy Aames, the man I love and plan to spend the rest of my life with." He reached between the chairs, took Jeremy's hand, and kissed it.

His mother snorted.

Davey said, "I'd change my attitude if I were you, unless you want to end up pushing that broom."

"No son of mine would ever—"

Bo raised a hand. "Mother, you're not going to be pushing a broom, and you're also not going to be pushing us around. I appreciate that everyone wants to return to some independence, and I applaud your choices, but they are *your* choices. I'll be living with Jeremy, whether here or somewhere else remains to be seen. For the moment all you need to do is wish us well or keep your mouth closed. I've had enough opinions to last a lifetime."

Grandfather Harvey said, "So, Jeremy, are you a winemaker too?"

Jeremy smiled. "Yes. I own Hill Top Winery."

"Oh, lovely. Bo's shared your wines with us, and they're my favorites after Bo's."

"Thank you, sir."

"Call me Harvey."

His mother raised her voice. "Are we just pretending that this is all settled?"

To his shock Blanche turned on Mama. "Oh, give it up. What do you have to say about it?"

"But—"

"She's right, Mama." Bo kept his expression soft. "There was no question in my announcement."

"What happens when you start losing business because you're a—gay?"

"Then I lose business. I've lost it before, God knows."

"But—"

"Mama!" She shut her lips in a straight line. Bo said, "If you can't be happy for us, at least stop talking. We have a lot to figure out, but I'll keep you all in the loop." He stood and extended his hand to Jeremy. "We better get to work. There's a lot to do."

Jeremy gave him a smile so sweet he could have stirred it into tea, rose, and took his hand.

Bettina smiled. "I just want to say I'm mighty happy for you both. I've always believed love is love, and I know personally how hard it is to find."

Blanche frowned. "You never believed love is love, for God's sake."

"Yes, I did. I just never told you." She gave a quick nod, like *so there*.

"I'm righteously happy for both of you." Harvey stuck out his hand. "And I'm serious about helping with the accounting."

"Thanks, Harvey." Bo grinned. "But I have an accounting team. Maybe we can find another job for you."

"Anything you need."

"I could use accounting help, Harvey," Jeremy said. "My winery's smaller than Bo's and I recently had some hard times, so if you have accounting skills, I could use you."

Harvey bent at the waist in a small half bow. "Qualified CPA, at your service."

"Excellent."

Cortina bounded up and hugged Bo. It seemed since Davey had defied his sister, none of them were as afraid of her—including Bo. She grinned. "We're so happy for you, Bo. You deserve a wonderful life."

She stepped over and hugged Jeremy. "Welcome to the family."

Bettina followed, and then Harvey and Davey. Mama wiped her cheek. Her chest expanded. Her voice sounded tight, but she said, "You know I want you to be happy. I've always wanted that. Family is more important to me than anything, no matter what the preacher says."

Bo knelt down in front of her spot on the couch. "I know how hard you worked to give me a great childhood and education. I don't want to be a disappointment to you. That's why I've never told you. But I didn't have Jeremy then. Giving him up would be far more than anyone has a right to ask—including me."

She snuffled and dabbed her cheeks with a lace handkerchief. "You could never be a disappointment to me, Beauregard." She dabbed some more. "Will there be a wedding?"

"At some point, I hope so." Jeremy gazed up into his eyes with a gleaming smile, and Bo gave him a gentle peck on the lips.

"C-can I plan it?"

He looked at Jeremy, who nodded. Bo said, "You can help."

Jeremy gave her his happy smile. "I don't have any family, Mrs. Marchand, so your help would be much appreciated."

"No family!" Like Blanche Dubois, she pressed the hand against her breast again. "Oh, you poor thing. You must be from the North. Am I right?"

"Yes, ma'am. New York."

She shook her head. "That explains it. Crime, broken families, rat race, and no appreciation for roots."

Bo wanted to laugh, but Jeremy nodded solemnly.

"Where's your mama?" She frowned, like clearly his mother had done a piss-poor job if he'd turned out gay. But then, that might reflect upon her.

"My mother left our family and then died. I never knew her very well."

"That's terrible!" The hand pressed the chest. "Isn't that terrible, Blanche?"

"Yes, terrible." She rolled her eyes.

Bettina turned. "Blanche, stop this. Bo used to be your closest friend in the family. Why are you being like this?"

"He doesn't want me to work for him." Her tight arms clutched her chest.

Bo frowned. "I don't want you trying to run the business when you have no experience. Obviously."

"What kind of job do you want, Blanche?" Jeremy squeezed Bo's hand.

"An internship." She stuck her chin out.

"That's not what you told RJ," Bo said. "And I told you, we don't have an internship set up, and I haven't had a chance to work on it."

"Tell you what, Blanche. I just lost a key employee," Jeremy said, "so we can work out an internship for you. You won't make much, but it would give you experience."

"Really?" She squealed and threw her arms around Jeremy. He hugged her back, laughing.

Mama glanced at him. "That's kind of you. Thank you." She took a deep breath. "So you're going to live here, right? After all, Jeremy needs some family around him."

"We'll talk about it, Mama. But probably we're going to want some privacy to start our life together."

"But family—"

"I know. We'll talk about it." Jeremy gave him a hand squeeze again. "Meanwhile, there's work to do."

Mama said, "Jeremy, where's your father?"

"Dead, ma'am."

Her eyes widened in genuine horror. "Oh my God, you poor dear. How you've suffered."

"Thank you for your kind thoughts, ma'am."

"Are you sure you're from New York? You certainly have the look of a Southern gentleman. So dashing with your beautiful hair."

"I'm pretty sure, yes, ma'am."

She stood and walked to him—amazing in itself. She reached up and touched his hair. "How do you happen to have all this lovely hair in these days when men chop the hair on their heads and grow it all over their faces?"

He grinned. "My mother loved it, and keeping it has helped me feel a little closer to her."

Tears filled Mama's eyes. "Isn't that the sweetest thing I ever heard?"

"It's true. I look in the mirror and think of her."

"Bless your heart."

"Thank you, ma'am."

She touched his cheek. "Darlin', call me Mama."

CHAPTER THIRTY-ONE

WHEN THEY pulled up in front of Marchand, they were still laughing. Bo shook his head. "'Call me Mama'? I feel like a fool for building this up in my mind until it was an insurmountable barrier."

Jeremy shrugged. "You're as much a product of that kind of prejudice as your mother. You were finally ready to break the barriers."

"Because I had something I wanted so much more than my family's approbation."

Jeremy put a finger under his chin. "Moi?"

"Tu."

"So how are we going to attack our other priority? How will we solve the murder before O'Hara finds out you're fibbing?"

"Not sure it'll be considered a fib. More like lying my ass off."

"And such a pretty ass."

Bo kissed Jeremy's nose. "Let's cast all our nets, hunt all our hounds, and see what we come up with. I've got a lot of questions but no answers yet."

"Maybe Christian let some hound slip to one of my staff."

"Or you could be barking up the wrong tree." They were both light-headed with relief, clearly.

They kissed softly and Bo walked into the winery, waving goodbye to Jeremy.

RJ looked up and smiled. "Hi, Bo. How was your trip?"

A laugh escaped. Thinking of that adventure as a "trip" was unexpected. "Good, RJ. Action-packed. Hey, would you see if you can get all the staff together? You don't have to bother the vineyard crew or production. I'll talk to them later."

A crease marred the perfection of RJ's forehead. "Bad news?"

"No. Not bad at all."

He grinned and ran for the back.

Bo dropped his stuff in his office, and when he walked back into the tasting room, RJ stood with the personnel from accounting, marketing, and sales, as well as the cooks and kitchen manager, which sounded impressive, but was actually Ida, Lucy, Camilla, Frank, José, Arturo, and Layton. They all looked a little worried until Lucy, his accounting manager, a sweet-as-pie earth mother type who could crunch a number like Genghis Khan, gave him a lopsided grin.

"Bo, are you glowing?"

"What?" That was not the question he'd been prepared for.

"You look like you just had a two-week vacation on the Riviera with two cabana boys."

He laughed and everyone joined in, reducing the level of tension by a mile.

Bo sucked a breath and said, "Funny you should mention the cabana boys, because the first thing I want to tell you is that I'm gay."

No one except RJ looked surprised. *What the hell?*

Lucy smiled. "Right. And?"

"Wait." Bo held up a hand. "You knew?"

"Suspected."

Camilla, who worked for Lucy, said, "Didn't care."

RJ looked around. "I didn't know. Uh, that's cool with me."

Arturo nodded. "Me too, boss. I always wondered why you didn't seem to like any of the girls who're hot for you all the time, so I kind of figured."

Bo looked at each of their faces, amazed. He felt relieved and like an idiot for taking so long to admit it. "Well, okay. I guess my upbringing made me think people would be upset."

"Oh, sweetie, what business is it of anyone's?" Lucy patted his arm. "Times have changed and this is California. I mean, we can be as assholic as the next person, but overall we're an accepting bunch."

"The other thing is, I'm, uh, in love with Jeremy Aames."

"There's the reason for the glow!" Lucy sprang at him and started a round of hugs.

RJ stared at Bo quite fixedly and with a funny expression Bo couldn't decipher. "So what does that mean, Bo?" Somebody snorted, and he blushed. "I mean, for the winery and stuff?"

"I don't know yet. This is all new. We've been do-ing a lot of collaboration with Hill Top since the two wineries are natural partners. I guess I just didn't know how much." He felt his cheeks heat. "But all in all, my trip was good and I expect business to get even better, so we have lots to look forward to."

They broke out a couple of bottles of bubbly—Strausburg, which reminded Bo to call them back—and then the tasting room opened with a few enthusiastic visitors waiting outside, so they all went back to work.

Bo sorted through emails, the warm glow of his love for Jeremy making him smile while he did it. He called Strausburg, holding his breath while he dialed.

"Peter Fieldstone."

Bo glanced at the phone. Why was Peter answering his son's phone? Probably just filling in. "Uh, Peter? Hi, this is Bo Marchand."

"Bo, good to hear from you. I have you near the top of my list to call."

"Well, likewise."

"About the contract my son offered you."

He swallowed hard. "Yes, I wanted to talk about that too."

"I want you to know we're still very interested and want to include the Hill Top Wineries bulk as well."

"You do?"

"Yes. I discovered that Henry was unduly influenced in his decisions about the Hill Top wines."

"By Marco Andretti?"

"Uh, yes. Not him personally, but a member of his, shall we say, staff? Henry was both tempted and intimidated. I apologize."

"That intimidation will no longer be an issue, I believe."

"I'm very glad to hear that. I'll send over our signature on your proposal, and then we'll draw up contracts. Agreed?"

Bo didn't think his heart had any more room to swell, but it did. "Yes, sir, that will be more than fine. Is there a chance we can promote the fact that we sell to Strausburg?"

"Hmm. We don't usually announce the outside bulk we purchase since we consider it a secret weapon, but if you've got a customer on the fence and need a reference, send 'em over."

"Thank you, Peter. I love being a secret weapon. We look forward to working with you." That didn't explain the half of it. He hung up, and his phone rang like it had been waiting. *O'Hara. Damn.*

He clicked. "Hello, O'Hara."

"Hi, Bo. Hope you got some rest. Just want to set up a time for you and Jeremy to come in for the next round of Q&A."

"Yeah. Okay."

"I'm getting a lot of pressure on your alibi. They're wanting me to delve into your family to see if anyone can verify you went out. I keep pointing out you helped the country get a case against one of the old-line mafia they've wanted to bring down for half a century, but my local guys don't care. So if you've got anything we can use, I need it."

"I can't tell you how much I appreciate your belief in our innocence, O'Hara."

"Yeah, well, that and five bucks'll get you a fancy coffee. I'm only allowed to let my instincts influence me so far."

That made his stomach clench. What if Blanche knew he'd been at home in bed all night? She was angry, despite Jeremy's olive branch, and might say something out of spite—or by accident. Or Christian, the twit. "We'll come in soon and tell you every little

detail we know. Maybe you'll find something important in it."

"Okay, Bo. Soon."

"I'll coordinate with Jeremy. We're both so busy
after being gone and, uh, everything."

"Tomorrow?"

"Probably. I'll get back to you."

"Okay, but this is serious, Bo."

"I understand, but as I sort through what I've
missed, I might learn something significant."

"Serious."

"Yes. I get it." His fingers ached to call Jeremy.
"Soon." *Jesus.* He clicked off. His finger poised over
Jeremy's number and the damned, hellacious, idiot
phone rang again. *Huh. Ezra.*

"Hello, Ezra, how are you?"

"Well, Bo. Thank you for asking."

"How can I help you?" Ezra usually called to complain about something, so Bo tried not to sound wary.

"Well, uh, I hear congratulations are in order."

Bo frowned. "Uh, I'm not sure what for."

"You and Jeremy." His voice reverberated with
forced good humor.

"What about me and Jeremy?"

"Well, I hear you're a couple."

What the hell? Ezra sounding happy about a gay
couple? "Uh, yes, that's right. How did you hear it?"

"I think it was RJ. Yes, RJ."

Clearly RJ couldn't wait to share this new revela-
tion. "I'll be honest, Ezra. I thought you were dead set
against homosexuality. Although I'm happy to receive
the congratulations."

"Well, you know, times change, and we have to
change with them."

"Glad you feel that way." *As if. What does he want?*

"You and Jeremy are both very, uh, attractive men. If you want to be together, love's love, as they say." *Okay, then.* They fell into an uneasy silence. Then Ezra cleared his throat and Bo tensed. "So I've learned a bit more about your interest in the Dionysian thing."

Bo tingled with attention. "Oh, who'd you talk to?"

"Jeremy, actually. Anyway, it happens that a few folks from the wine country get together to celebrate old Dionysus from time to time."

"Oh, is it a theater group?" Bo tried to sound naïve.

"Uh, no. It's more about the, shall we say, Bacchanalian aspects. You know, the, uh, sexual mysteries and such."

"Oh? How interesting." Oh yes, he was interested.

"We thought two attractive gay men would be a diverting addition to the group. You'd have to be of a liberal mind-set, however."

"Liberal?"

"Like days of old, activities are shared. Publicly, that is."

"Group sex?" He tried to sound neutral.

"Well, yes. Although one doesn't have to participate with people who aren't your partner if preferred, or, of course, you can sit out when you choose."

Bo waited just long enough to let Ezra sweat. "Of course, I'd have to discuss it with Jeremy, but I'd be interested, at least exploratorically, to coin a phrase. I've never done anything like that."

"Well now, most of us hadn't, and some drop out. We just ask that you not share the Dionysian secrets with others."

"Of course. I'll talk to Jeremy."

"Uh, our next meeting happens to be tomorrow night, so we'd be happy to welcome you."

"I'll talk to him immediately and let you know either way."

"Excellent. I hope you decide to participate."

"I'll call you soon." He clicked off. He was up to two people he needed to call *soon.* He slammed down on Jeremy's speed dial so fast, his fingers almost missed the phone.

"Hey, baby," Jeremy answered.

"You're not going to believe what just happened."

"What?"

"Well, two things, no, three actually. We just received a contract offer from Strausburg."

"You're shitting me?"

"Never would, darlin'."

"That's amazing. Fantastic. You mean both of us."

"Absolutely."

"Tell me all about it."

"Later. The bad part is O'Hara wants to talk with us posthaste. His colleagues want him to dig into my alibi."

"Damn. We've got to find a better suspect to hand them—besides me."

"Amen."

"What's number three?"

Bo chuckled. "You and I have just been invited to have sex in public at our local Dionysian mysteries club." He held his breath.

"What?"

"Total truth. And you know who invited me?"

"I'm going to guess Ezra Hamilton, the two-faced fraud."

"Ding, ding, ding, ding. Give that man a teddy bear." He full-on laughed.

"So, seriously? Sex in public?"

"Yep. And who knows what fascinating things we may discover?"

"Why us?"

"I suspect it has something to do with prurient interest in how gay men have sex. Gay porn in person."

"Wow."

"Yep. Are you up for it?"

"Way up."

Bo laughed again. "It's tomorrow night."

"I'll polish up my leather."

"Whips and chains." That sounded fun.

"You're thinking this might give us a clue to the murder?"

"Maybe. It's interesting that the rumors about this group have been circulating about as long as Ottersen was active in the community. I've got no idea if there's a connection, but I may have a resource to find out. I'll also call Llewellyn."

"Well, dayum, man, if we have to go through with it, can you?"

"I'm not sure. Maybe blushing all the time. Or maybe we can learn what we need before we have to perform."

"I don't know. I might relish a little kink." Jeremy laughed real dirty, which made Bo shiver in the best way. "What are you going to wear?"

"Help. I think I need your advice."

"We can head for San Luis this afternoon. There's a shop I've heard of that might cater to kink."

Bo's blushes had blushes. "Okay. I'm in your hands. See you later, boyfriend."

"I like the sound of that."

"Which part?"

"All of it. See you."

Clicking off, Bo gathered his cool and walked into the tasting room. RJ was bustling out to the patio with several plates, so Bo polished glasses while he waited for him to come back. All the guests were enjoying the sunshine outside, giving Bo and RJ the tasting room to themselves. Bo lowered his voice to make it sound conspiratorial. "So, Ezra called me."

RJ adopted a phony surprised look. "Really?"

"Yes, he invited Jeremy and me to the meeting tomorrow. Or I guess you'd call it a gathering."

"Oh, that's great." RJ smiled with wide eyes, as if they'd invited Bo to a Boy Scout campfire.

Bo leaned on the counter. "Do you know who the members are?"

"Uh, yes. Some. But we don't ever talk about that to anyone. You have to see for yourself."

"That makes sense, but I was just wondering."

"Yes?"

"I noticed I started hearing rumors about the club around the time Ottersen came to the community. I just wondered if he was a member. I mean, before."

RJ thought for a minute with a slight frown. "I guess it doesn't hurt to say he was a founding member. Really active."

"Interesting. So he was into the mysteries."

"Oh yes, he was into all that stuff."

Bo smiled. "I guess we'll have to wait to discover what *all that stuff* is. Will we see you there?"

RJ colored and shrugged. "Probably not. I don't go a lot. Other obligations."

"I'm sure. I'd guess not all women are into public shenanigans. Not like us randy guys, right?"

"Right." His cheeks flamed, and RJ wasn't noticeably a blusher usually.

"Well, thanks. That helps me decide."

"Glad I could help."

Bo walked into the back, his pulse racing. He pulled his phone and dialed Llewellyn. His day for phone calls.

"Hi, Bo."

"Hey, Llewellyn, guess what? Jeremy and I have been invited to a meeting of the local Dionysian mysteries group, but it doesn't sound like much is left to mystery. It's a kinky sex club."

"N-not surprising that people use D-Dionysus as an excuse for whatever activities they w-want to get into."

"But I discovered that Ottersen was a founding member."

"Y-you think someone from this c-club killed him?"

"Actually, I have a lot to tell you about my last few days, but for now I'll just say I've ruled out a couple of other possibilities for our murder suspect. With that said, it makes sense to me that someone from this club could possibly be involved or know something. Sexual rivalries and all that. And it's possible the police haven't uncovered this group. I can imagine they'd be pretty tight-lipped."

"S-so they asked you and J-Jeremy?"

"I think we'll feed their kink because we're gay."

"And y-you plan to g-go through with it?" He was making an effort to sound neutral. Llewellyn was very reserved.

"If we have to, but if we can get what we need without it, that would be our choice. Neither of our tastes run to exhibitionism."

"I'll send y-you some data on the mysteries so y-you can be well-informed."

"Thank you. That would be great, and I'll fill you in as soon as I can pause. The police are getting anxious."

"T-tell us all about the sex club afterward. I'm sure Blaise w-will want d-details." He laughed.

Bo's stomach clenched.

CHAPTER THIRTY-TWO

Bo STARED down at his body and felt the blush spread like honey on cornbread. *Come on. If you're blushing at this, what'll you do when you have to get naked in front of a room full of staring people?*

The door to the bathroom opened, and Bo turned. *Oh my God.*

Jeremy popped dimples. "Look at you."

"I'm a mere shadow of your glory." Dear heaven, the man was sex in a bottle, and what a bottle. The finest vintage. He'd poured himself into black leather pants—just like Bo's—that hugged his thighs and outlined his package like a Picasso, then topped it with a net shirt that showed the *Fight Club* body and soft pink nipples. His hair resembled liquid gold on his shoulders, and he seemed to have outlined his eyes a bit, which made them leap off his architectural face. "You cause the angels to weep with envy."

Jeremy thrust out a hip and planted his fist on it. "If that's true, they're giving up their halos to be with you, baby. My God, those legs make me want to stay home and fuck you till dawn. And that boy bulge?" He raised his forearm to his face. "My eyes! My eyes!"

Bo snorted and waved a hand. "Stop, you charmer." He looked down. "I sure hope everyone else doesn't show up in khakis."

Jeremy laughed. "All the better. They'll be even more stunned. I guess we better go enter the world of kink."

"After you, oh kinkmaster."

It took nearly half an hour to drive to the obscure address Ezra had emailed him on a remote street in the hills surrounding the wineries, even farther back than Jeremy's house. When they pulled up, there were a few cars visible, but they seemed to be scattered up the road so it wasn't obvious to which house they belonged. The building itself was so tightly draped, only an occasional sliver of light revealed that the house wasn't empty.

They exited the car, pulling their jackets tight to get some warmth in their thin shirts, although Bo had opted for silk rather than net. His relationship with exhibitionism was tentative at best.

Jeremy slid his arm through Bo's. "Ready?"

"As I'll ever be." If he didn't count the shaking knees, trembling hands, and sick stomach.

They walked up a dark porch, and Bo knocked. Nothing. He knocked again. "I told Ezra we were coming—"

The door flew open, and Ezra stood there with a big, phony smile. "Boys, delighted to see you. Glad you could make it. Come in and let me take your coats."

They stepped into an entry hall lit by a dim chandelier and closed from whatever living space was beyond by large double doors. They peeled their coats off. Ezra's eyes widened. "Well. You two certainly got into the spirit of the evening." Ezra wore something like a dressing gown with what appeared to be pajama bottoms beneath. "You'll more than enhance the beauty of the party, that's for sure." His eyes drifted to Bo's crotch and he startled. "Man, Bo, what an impressive, shall we say, manhood."

Bo tried to smile; it probably came off like a death rictus.

"First, let me impress upon you the need for absolute secrecy. Even if you don't enjoy the group, by entering through these doors you're still agreeing to confidentiality."

Both Bo and Jeremy nodded.

"Okay, ready?" He looked a little edgy. He threw the doors open with ceremony and announced, "Welcome to the Dionysian Mysteries Society of the central coast."

Ezra stepped aside and left them to the voracious gaze of a roomful of people in various states of undress. Bo recognized some of them, including Ezra's wife, Marybeth, clad in a floral kimono with what appeared to be a G-string under it, her opulence overflowing its tiny coverage. She waggled her fingers. Reclining on a chaise by the wall lay Genevieve Renders wearing lace panties and nothing f-ing else. On the far other side of the room, naturally, stood Randy Renders, wearing a jockstrap with a gun belt and holster improbably buckled over it, leaning on the shoulder of an unknown blonde. He put his fingers between his lips and whistled. "Lookin' good there, guys."

Most of the remaining twenty or so people were unknown to Bo. Was it better to focus on people he knew for information or those he didn't? Probably the latter.

Marybeth rose, came up, and took Jeremy's arm. "Let me get you both a drink? We actually have things besides wine." She giggled.

Jeremy gave her the teeth. "Like what, dear?"

"There's a pitcher of margaritas."

"Yum."

She looked at Bo, who smiled more tightly. "I better stick to wine."

Everything jiggled as Marybeth led them to the wine cart in the dining room. By the time they came back, people had found other sources of amusement, and serious foreplay had broken out, one couple having made it all the way to oral. Watching proved some uncomfortable combination of sexy and embarrassing.

Marybeth said, "So make yourselves comfy, guys. With each other or—someone else." She fluttered her lashes invitingly.

Jeremy said, "That's a most kindly suggestion, ma'am. But we really do like boys best."

"Oh sigh, what a waste of pulchritude, but I'll enjoy watching."

Bo looked up and frowned. "Uh, darlin', I'm wondering why there's a noose in the middle of the ceiling?"

She giggled again. "Some of our members like a little asphyxiation play."

"What's that?"

"Well, I've never tried it myself, but I guess the feeling of almost choking can be sexy, especially for guys. Ezra's really into it." She lowered her voice. "He comes every time, at his age!" Another giggle.

Jeremy leaned down and whispered, "I'm so glad you told us. We were a little worried there for a minute."

She cackled and slapped his arm. "Oh, you."

"Are we going to get to see him do it? I've never seen that kind of, uh, play."

She frowned and then seemed to force it away. "Uh, no, he's kind of cooled on the whole thing." She sashayed back to her couch and reclined.

They found an empty couch and sat, sinking into some kisses hot enough to keep anyone watching entertained. In a nuzzling break, Jeremy whispered, "Let's see if we can corner a couple of pigeons and ask some questions. I'd like to know where the jealousies were."

"We better do it before this turns into an orgy and people quit talking altogether."

"Okay, you go to the john, and I'll get more wine and see who I attract."

As Jeremy rose and walked toward the bar cart, every face turned to stare—*drool* might be the better word—except those fully buried in genitals. Bo tried to look confident when he got up, knowing his make-out session had inspired a lot of swelling in the nether regions, the sight of which he hoped might loosen a tongue or two. He found a bathroom in the hall and slipped inside, grateful nobody had claimed it for a bedroom.

His current state of, um, fullness made peeing difficult, so he sat on the toilet lid. What a weird situation. Who knew people did things like this? Back in college some pretty raunchy things had occurred in his fraternity house, but those paled by comparison.

Get on with it. He got up, washed his hands, and wiped a little water on his face, then unlocked the door and—

Whoa! The door burst open, and Gen Renders of the lace panties hurled into the small room. "Oooh, looky what I found." She pressed her bare chest against him, which, if he'd been attracted to women, would probably have been a turn-on since she had perky breasts. As it was, he backed the short space to the wall, almost tripping over the toilet. She chuckled. "Bo, who knew you were packing all this firepower?" Her hands performed a thorough examination of his crotch, and the small head definitely liked the attention no matter what gender did the stroking. "I'd love to see this on display."

He gently pushed her hands away. "Most kind, ma'am, but I must tell you, uh, Jeremy's feeling a little under the weather, so we may not be staying. Perhaps another time."

"Oooh, he doesn't look under the weather. He looks delicious."

"I agree." Bo managed to edge his way around the perimeter of the room to the door, and Genevieve pressed against him the whole way. He looked out and saw the rope again. "Uh, Gen, we were hoping to get to see Ezra doing the hanging thing before we go." He whispered, "Does it really give you a giant erection?" There. Did that sound raunchy enough?

She raised her eyes and purred. "In your case, I'd love to see that." Her brows pulled together. "But actually, we're kind of off that strangling shit."

"Oh? Why? I thought it sounded kind of, uh, kinky." He chuckled and hoped it didn't seen forced.

"One of our members got a little, uh, carried away a while back. People freaked."

"I guess that could be scary."

She glanced at him. "Scary. Yeah."

Bo saw Jeremy across the room, chatting up a buxom woman Bo didn't know. He pressed his hand against his mouth in exaggerated shock, then laughed.

Gen followed Bo's gaze and growled, "He looks pretty fine to me."

"He's a trooper, that boy."

"So you've been gay all along and we never knew."

"Yes. I'm really embarrassed not to have been more forthcoming, but where I come from, men are more reserved about such things."

"Did your family know?"

"I'm ashamed to say, no."

She ran her hands up his chest. "You sure you aren't bisexual? Maybe that's why you never wanted to declare your major, so to speak?" She shared her throaty laugh.

"I know. That's the hell of it. I'm really gay, but until I met Jeremy, I guess I never cared enough to come out."

"You two are cute."

Across the room, Jeremy waved.

Bo waved back. "I think my guy wants me."

"Hell, he's not the only one." She grinned up at him. "Think about a little show-and-tell before you go, okay?"

"I'll ask him." He smiled to cover his hard swallow. Escorting Gen partway, he waited while she settled on a couch; then he hurried to Jeremy, who slid his arms around Bo's neck and pressed against him.

Jeremy nuzzled his ear. "Did you find out anything interesting?"

"Interesting but not definitive."

Jeremy sighed. "I sure hope O'Hara can make something out of the bits and pieces we've got."

"I'm getting a lot of pressure to put on a show."

"Me too." Jeremy laughed.

"I hate to say this, but I'm afraid if we don't come through, they may not invite us back."

Jeremy's beautiful blue eyes twinkled. "I think all they want is a glimpse of that Tyrannosaurus Rex in your pants. I'm up for sucking, if you're willing to receive."

Am I? "I'm never averse to your lips on my cock, darlin'. That'd be plumb foolish."

"Well, all righty, then." He kissed Bo gently. "Let's go in the dining room and see how long it takes them to notice."

Bo sucked a huge breath. "Okay. I guess." He laughed nervously.

"All you have to do is close your eyes and pretend they're not here."

"I'll try."

Jeremy took his hand and led him into the dining room, where a few people sucked and even fucked, but it was relatively quiet. A sturdy table in the middle of the room provided a handy exhibition spot. Jeremy pointed. "Your throne, my darling."

Bo plopped his butt on the edge of the table, being tall enough to do it easily. Jeremy found a big footstool and two cushions and placed his miniedifice on the floor in front of Bo. Already, people had started to notice, and a few gathered around. *Holy cow in the pasture.* Bo squeezed his eyes shut.

He didn't watch Jeremy slowly lower his fly, but he could feel it. They'd agreed to go commando, so the breeze on his privates communicated the action. As Jeremy peeled his fly apart and pulled out his penis, Bo heard the soft gasps from a couple of people. At least they were getting their money's worth.

He cracked open his eyes, realized at least ten or fifteen people were watching, and squeezed them shut again. Then Jeremy's hot mouth slid over his cold cock. *Oh sweet mother.*

Someone in the audience moaned, and so did Bo as Jeremy slid up and down Bo's shaft, nuzzling his balls on each pass. Bo wouldn't last long at this rate. How embarrassing would it be to orgasm in front of these people?

Somebody yelled, "Yeah, suck him!"

A woman nearby said to someone else, "I've never seen a guy do it to a guy. Damn, it's so hot! I might have to watch some gay porn."

Another woman whispered back, "Do you think we can get them to fuck? That would be amazing."

Bo's brain was ripped between trying to ignore the racy comments and trying to surrender to the amazing feelings.

"What the hell are you guys doing?" A woman's voice yelled, but it sounded like it came from the living room. A door slammed.

Bo's eyes flew open, and Jeremy's lips paused, then slid off. The watchers had all frozen and stared toward the front door.

Some voices murmured, but the woman's voice got louder. "Haven't you got the tiniest shred of respect for the dead? He's not even cold and you all are back at it?"

Somebody said, "Come on, Sage, be fair."

Wow, it's Sage. Jeremy started to turn toward the door, but Bo stopped him. Bo put both feet on the floor. All around them, the club members looked at each other uncomfortably.

Sage was shrieking now, and it sounded like several people were trying to calm her, which only seemed to make her louder. "Fair? You talk about fair? Get your hands off me! For fuck's sake, you let him kill himself, dump his body like the trash, and go back to fucking in a matter of days? What's wrong with you? What kind of people treat their friend that way?"

By now a few watchers were taking furtive glances toward Bo and Jeremy. Did they all know Ottersen had been dumped at Hill Top? Had they blamed Jeremy on purpose?

Bo slid his phone from his pocket and hit speed dial. Shit and fans might just be in close proximity soon.

Ezra yelled, "Will someone shut that bitch up?"

A voice said "Hello?"

"Need help," Bo whispered, then dropped the phone into the front of his pants. *Come on, Tyrannosaurus Rex, cover the evidence.* Bo grabbed Jeremy by the hair. When he turned, Bo signaled, *Suck.*

His eyes widened, he grabbed Bo's penis and shoved it in his mouth, sucking like there was no tomorrow.

Bo didn't want to believe his own neighbors would throw him and Jeremy into the river, but damn, evidence seemed to be to the contrary. "Oh yeah. Oh God!" He bounced his hips, threw his head back, and generally acted like he didn't know or care what Sage had been talking about. Bo didn't close his eyes since he needed to move fast if someone decided to grab them, but he kept them narrow. "Oh man, you're so good. You're amazing."

Jeremy pulled his lips back for a moment and wailed, "I love your cock. It's the best thing I've ever had in my mouth. I want to suck it forever."

That was nice, even if he did wail it like a porn star.

Around them, a few people looked uneasy, but more were riveted on the action. That didn't mean they wouldn't put one of them in that noose the minute they stopped, so like Scheherazade, they'd better keep weaving tales, because also like the fabled storyteller, if they quit, they could well be dead.

CHAPTER THIRTY-THREE

DAMN. DESPITE the stress, Bo's cock seemed interested in coming, which would make him a lot less impressive visually. He pulled Jeremy's hair again and got the big eyes staring at him.

"Your lips are like heaven, baby, and I want to love you into next week."

Jeremy tossed his hair like a pole dancer. "Yes! Do it. Do it." He rose, still thrashing his head, and began to unzip his skintight leather pants.

A quick peek at the group revealed if someone like Ezra tried to stop them now, he'd likely be lynched. Riveted eyes watched the slow striptease. Meanwhile, Sage seemed gone. Hopefully not permanently.

The only thing that could pull the watchers' eyes from Jeremy's flashing hair was the sight of his world-class ass being revealed inch by breathtaking inch. He seemed to have purposely leaned forward and parted his legs enough to give a clear view of his balls showcased between muscular thighs. Through Bo's narrowed eyes, everyone appeared transfixed, the men with seeming envy and the women—well, drooling was on tap.

With a hip waggle, Jeremy shook the pants farther down. He bent forward slowly, giving the onlookers a better view of his butt. Several people moaned—loudly.

A soft thunking sound caught Bo's attention, but it didn't seem to be anything threatening, and Jeremy's antics still enthralled the group, who stared glassy-eyed, riveted on Jeremy's amazing assets.

A woman drawled, "Oh my God."

Bo smiled, but then Ezra's voice came from behind him and off to the side. "What the hell? Why hasn't someone gotten hold of these guys?"

It might have been Randy who said, "Seriously? You won't get anyone to help you until after they're done. Hell, I'd kind of like to see it myself. Plus I'm not sure they even heard. Don't go off half-cocked, man." He laughed. Definitely Randy. He said, "You should pardon the pun. Seriously, if these guys disappear, lots of people will notice. Not like… you know."

"And what option have we got?"

"Shit, I don't know."

"They wouldn't have told anyone where they were going. We don't have to worry."

Sweet mother! Keeping his cock hard enough to be riveting was Bo's primary challenge, right after figuring out how to keep both of them alive.

Someone gasped, and Bo realized Jeremy was caressing himself. Theatrically. Bo joined the performance. "Oh God, you're so hot." He used his best performance voice, but that didn't make it any less true. Despite the considerable distraction, he had to think. There were at least twenty people in this room who seemed to have reacted to what Sage had yelled. Would they go along with Ezra, and if so, could he and Jeremy find some way to escape? Hell, he'd like to stay alive to be with Jeremy, but if it came to a choice, protecting Jeremy was all he cared about.

Wrapping his hand around Jeremy's so they were jacking him off together, Bo glanced at the part of the room he could see. A door out at back of the dining room probably led to the kitchen, that probably had a back door to the outside. A lot of probablies. He and Jeremy were young and fast. Could they escape the whole Dionysian pack? It could come down to trying. Nobody seemed to be coming to save them.

Bo leaned over Jeremy's back, wrapped his arm around his waist. The crowd was going crazy, yelling obscene encouragement. Bo threw his head back and yelled, "Are you going to come?" He leaned close to Bo's ear and said loudly, "Come for me, baby," then whispered, "When I pat your butt, run for the door and try to get outside."

Raising up, he grabbed a handful of Jeremy's hair, dragged his head back, leaned forward, and kissed him.

Some woman yelled, "Oh my God! They're killing me."

Just as long as they don't kill us.

Bo took a breath and slapped Jeremy's right buttcheek. Before the lookers could realize it wasn't just a passionate move, Jeremy dragged up his pants and ran like a rabbit.

Bo heard gasps as he took off behind Jeremy and made it through the dining room door with no signs of pursuit. *Damn!* He was in a weird space like a butler's pantry or a scullery. He saw Jeremy disappear through the door at the end of it and ran at full speed after him. *Thank God, the kitchen.*

Jeremy stood at the back door, yanking on the door handle, but it wasn't opening. Bo grabbed a kitchen towel, wrapped it on his fist, and smashed the glass in the window, then reached through to open the door just as footsteps sounded behind him. Bo pushed the door open and shoved Jeremy. "Go!"

Spying a frying pan on the counter, Bo grabbed it and spun, brandishing it at Ezra and some big guy he didn't recognize. "Get the hell away from us."

Ezra raised his hands. "Come on, Bo, what's up? Why are you running?"

"Because I heard what you said. I don't know what you're talking about, but I'll be damned if I'm letting anybody hurt Jeremy. All we wanted to do was have some fun."

"Of course, Bo. I don't know what you think you heard, but Jeremy's long gone by now, so you don't have to worry about him."

Suddenly a wire wrapped around Bo's throat and a voice said, "Got him."

WHERE IS he? Oh God, where is he?

Jeremy huddled under the low-hanging tree branches and stared at the back door of the cabin so hard his eyes burned. *I know Bo wants me to run, but—I can't. I can't leave him behind.* For a second he frowned. *Is that because he risked his life to save me in New York?* He made a soft snorting sound. *No, it's because I love him more than my own life. Don't be a dumbass.*

Okay, so finding a way to save Bo was on tap, and his life could be in imminent danger, so no fucking around. *I could burn down the building. Yeah, how?*

By rubbing two Boy Scouts together? Better have a plan. We're outnumbered twenty to one—and I haven't seen anybody come out of the place. Mostly he wanted to go kick these people's asses and tell them to wake up. What the hell did they think they were doing? But counting on their consciences could be fatal.

Something tickled his bare arm, and he jumped. *Shit. What's creeping on this ground besides me?*

If he left the trees, he was out in the open and really exposed. His biggest regret was the fact that his cell phone was lying in the middle of the dining room rug where it had fallen when he dragged down his pants. *Shit!*

Can I create a diversion? They know I'm out here, so not likely. But what if I go to the street and start throwing rocks at their cars and making a ton of noise? This place is remote, but somebody might hear. Plus they could want to save their cars. Bet Bo could come up with a better plan. Hell, where's Bo?

His plan might be stupid, but it was all he could think of.

Skirting through the trees until he saw some bushes closer to the house, he crouched and started running. At the bushes he ducked down. The distance from where he hid to the street was two hundred yards of open space. *Whew.* He couldn't hear any noise other than trees rustling and the faint hum of traffic from some distant highway. No one moved—so he'd better.

Bent over like a scuttling animal, he took off toward the street and cleared the open space. When the bulk of the building hid him, he slowed. There were a couple of windows ahead of him, but fortunately they'd closed them so tight there was barely any light, much less visibility. *Keep moving.*

He scooted under the windows and stayed in the shadow of the building. At the edge, where the wall turned, he paused. *If someone's out there, I can take off down the street. Chances are I'm faster than any of them. If they've got a gun, all bets are off, but if they did have one, why haven't they used it? This is a sex party. No one expects anything threatening.*

Just do it. He inhaled and peeked quickly around the building. *No one. Thank you, universe. Okay, go!*

Like some iron band descended from the sky, an enormous arm wrapped around his waist and pulled him off his feet.

"Fuck!"

A low voice said, "Look what I caught. Maybe it's a leather bear?"

Jeremy struggled like mad, but the man was huge. Jeremy had seen him inside, vaguely, but had been so focused on the people he knew and thought might tell him something, he hadn't properly assessed this guy's threat. He gave a cynical smile. *Nonno would be ashamed. Hell, will I get to testify against Nonno? Without me, they've got no case.* That thought pissed him off, and he struggled even harder.

"Calm down, asshole. And I mean that literally." He chuckled at his own joke as he dragged Jeremy, still in the bear hug, up the steps of the porch.

Jeremy slammed back with his soft-sneakered foot and hit the guy's shin, which hurt him like bloody hell and barely fazed Mountain Man. The guy kicked hard backward against the door, then again, and someone opened it. "Oh my God. You caught him."

"Yeah. Aren't you glad I like to smoke?"

Somehow getting caught by a dude who went out for a smoke made Jeremy even madder.

Mountain Man hauled him through the double doors and dropped him in the living room in a heap. Jeremy instantly flipped to his feet and turned to face the scene. Everything in him froze. All the people who'd been there when he escaped were still there—including Bo. The man he loved more than life stood bound and gagged on the same footstool Jeremy had used for his oral sex—with the noose hanging above his head.

Jeremy stared, ice in his blood instantly replaced by fire. Boiling! He lost it. "What the fuck do you think you're doing? Who are you people?" He could feel the blood vessels standing out on his temples. "You're not murderers! I heard you. You didn't kill Ottersen. You just made a stupid-ass decision to hide your little sex games by dumping his body instead of reporting his death. But put Bo's head in that noose, and you'll all go to prison. Maybe some of you will be put to death."

Ezra glanced around at people's uneasy faces, then sneered, "Don't be stupid. Bo's about to do the same thing as Ottersen. He was fascinated by the asphyxiation play all evening. You know he was—we all heard him. So, oops, he slipped. Both of them are gone and no one's the wiser."

"Right. You idiot. You dumped Ernest's body to keep from being found out, and now you're going to tell everyone what you were doing? And the chances the cops won't find out are zero. You're all going down. And how are you going to kill me? You figure both of us slipped? Give me a fucking break. You haven't got the brains God gave a snail."

Jeremy's blood ran like lava and flamed out his mouth. He narrowed his eyes. "Trust me, asshole. I know murderers—intimately. And while you might not be too bright, you're no murderer." His gaze traveled

around the room. People looked way beyond nervous.
"I'm the son of a criminal and the grandson of another. I understand police, courts, law, and punishment.
You guys made a stupid mistake by listening to Ezra
in the first place. But it's very unlikely you'll go to
prison for being an accessory to stupidity. Murder Bo
and me, and you might as well kill yourself right after.
You'll ruin any chance of a future, to say nothing of
hating yourself forever. Shit. Think, why don't you?"
Calmly he walked to Bo, took his hand, and helped him
down. Like Jeremy's disgusted certainty held them all
in place, no one moved to stop him.

Suddenly the front door of the house burst open.
"Police! Drop your weapons and put your hands up."

Jeremy ripped the blindfold off Bo's eyes and
quickly stepped behind him to easily untie the awkward
knot they'd created. The people around him looked so
terrified, he half wanted to laugh. Marybeth silently
sobbed against Ezra's arm. He scowled angrily, but he
was pretty much the only one. Gen Renders had pulled
a tablecloth around her mostly naked self and was visibly shaking, while Randy had tears on his cheeks.

A SWAT team in full regalia burst into the room
and stopped—no doubt at the sight of a room full of
barely clad humans, some of them senior citizens.
O'Hara walked out of the middle of the pack of assault
rifles and body armor. He put his hands on his hips.
"Bo, Jeremy, what the hell is going on here? Why did
you call me?" His eyes dropped. "And what in the hell
are you wearing?"

Jeremy squeezed Bo's hand. He wanted to shove
every one of these people into a well or set the house
on fire with them in it, but— "Some raunchy sex games
being played here, O'Hara. Nothing illegal. However,

we tried to call you because Ezra here has something very important to tell you that will clear up your murder case."

O'Hara's brows shot up. "Oh? Seriously?"

Bo nodded.

O'Hara looked at Ezra. "Very well, sir, come with me. The rest of you, sit." He glanced at Jeremy and Bo and gave them a quizzical look.

"We'll sit." Jeremy grinned. He took Bo's hand and led him to a love seat by the wall, then wrapped Bo in his arms. "Oh God, darling. I was terrified."

Bo whispered, "I was pretty scared. I kept thinking, like you, that they'd come to their senses, but I started losing hope."

"Yeah." Jeremy pulled out of the hug and gazed at Bo's beautiful face. "Am I letting them off too easy if I don't tell O'Hara? I'd like to boil every one of them in oil."

"Tell me why you're doing it, darlin'." He smiled softly.

Jeremy wiped a hand over the back of his neck. "I could so easily have been involved in something terrible if, say, my father had made me drive him to a murder site or even participate myself. I would have desperately needed someone to see that I wasn't really a murderer. To give me another chance. But they almost watched Ezra murder you and didn't stop him. That's hard to forgive."

"I'll tell you what. When we go in to talk to O'Hara, I'll tell him about Ezra. I think he deserves an assload of punishment and an even bigger assload of scared. But I do think the rest would have backed out and might have talked Ezra out of it. Maybe. But I don't like a person capable of that much ruthlessness walking around unsupervised."

"I agree." Jeremy pulled Bo back into his arms and hugged as hard as he could.

"Jeremy?"

He looked up at Marybeth, who was still wiping tears. "Yes?"

"I just want to thank you for not telling the police we—" She made a sobbing sound. "What we did. Some of the others asked me to tell you too. We're so grateful. If we can ever do anything to repay you—anything at all—please ask."

Bo said, "You must understand that Ezra will have to suffer punishment, perhaps severe. He nearly incited people to murder."

She frowned. "Yes. I'm beyond sickened. I don't even know the man I took for my husband and rather wish I hadn't." She pursed her lips. "Thank you again, both of you. We're deeply thankful for your human kindness."

"Bo, Jeremy. You're up." O'Hara called from the hall that must lead to the back of the house.

Jeremy said, "Excuse us," to Marybeth. She kissed his cheek. He smiled at her, and they walked into a back bedroom that smelled a lot like sex all over the rumpled sheets on the bed.

O'Hara sat in a straight-backed chair, wiping a hand over his neck.

Bo said, "Glad you got my message. Did you track my phone?"

O'Hara nodded, then looked up. "That was one helluva story I got from Hamilton. Do you believe it?"

"Yes." Bo nodded.

"Choking yourself to death? Seriously? For an erection. Haven't they heard of Viagra?"

Bo nodded. "There's something you should know. Ezra tried to persuade the group to hang me tonight."

"What the fuck?"

"He thought they could give you the story of what actually happened to Ottersen and apply it to me. Jeremy came in and told them they were all crazy. He talked them down from the ledge before you got there."

"Do you think Ezra would have gone through with it?"

Jeremy shrugged.

"Bo?"

"I honestly don't know, O'Hara. He's supposed to be this big Christian. I think that's why he pushed so hard to dump Ottersen's body. He didn't want his churchgoing friends to know his penchant for group sex."

"Murder's not a Christian act."

Jeremy snorted. "No shit."

Bo said, "We came here because we'd heard that Ottersen was a member of this group and originally suspected he might have inspired jealousy and gotten killed. It wasn't until we got here we learned about the asphyxiation."

"And that Ottersen killed himself?" O'Hara asked.

"Yes, by accident. Weird irony."

O'Hara sat back. "What a mess. A bunch of people who don't protest a proposal of murder and participated in dumping the body of a self-inflicted death who like kinky sex. What's wrong with this picture?"

Jeremy nodded. "Yep. They're called people. I don't know many people who couldn't, under weird circumstances, find themselves in this situation."

"Not you. Not Bo."

Jeremy smiled. "I'm happy you feel that way."

Bo stood. "We're grateful we don't have to decide what to do about any of this—you do. But since we're wildly tired and I think Jeremy has been officially cleared, can we go home? We promise to come in and answer questions ad nauseam tomorrow or wherever you want us."

"Okay. We've got plenty to sort through here."

Jeremy took Bo's hand, and they walked toward the closed door.

"Oh, Bo? Jeremy?"

They looked over their shoulders at O'Hara.

O'Hara grinned. "Thanks for solving my case. I promise to take full credit. And I also promise not to ask how far you had to go to get this information."

Bo and Jeremy laughed all the way to the car.

CHAPTER THIRTY-FOUR

SOFT SUNLIGHT, birdies chirping, not a noose or a gun in sight, and the warm pressure of the only body he'd ever wanted next to him snuggled against his back as Bo gazed out the window in Jeremy's spartan bedroom. To quote O'Hara, what was wrong with this picture? Bo sighed so deeply his chest tingled. *Absolutely nothing.*

Jeremy peered over his shoulder. "You sound pretty self-satisfied."

Bo rolled onto his back, and Jeremy draped himself across Bo's chest. Bo smoothed that golden mane. "How are you feeling this morning?" They'd gotten home the night before and barely removed their clothes before they crashed in bed. "Not every week you get drugged, mugged, threatened with death twice, and jerked off in public."

Jeremy frowned. "Sadly, it's probably not over. There's no way to know how organized crime will react to me testifying against Nonno. Fortunately, Nonno was the last big power center in a disintegrating organization. I think without him, the Russians, Chinese, and other organized crime groups will happily fill the vacuum, but anyone could decide to take exception to my testimony." He released a long breath. "They could come after me before the trial."

Bo kissed his nose. "If we have to go into witness protection, we will."

"Witness security is the real name." His golden brows practically met in the middle. "I could never let you give up your business and your family that way. I'd rather take my chances and stay with you."

Bo lightly kissed those perfect lips. "You know what? We don't have to make that decision today. We need to talk to O'Hara and the FBI. We'll assess the risk, but whatever decision we make, we stay together." He smiled softly and let the truth suffuse his soul. "I've spent my life doing my duty. Don't misunderstand. It was my choice, my nature, and my joy. But I've thought a lot about it between brushes with death, and it feels like love is a gift. Like God, goodness, spirit—whatever you want to call it—broke off a piece of itself and embedded it in my heart. To ignore that gift in favor of some misguided intellectual exercise seems ungrateful. I choose you, Jeremy."

Tears glistened in Jeremy's eyes. "No one ever chose me before. Not Mother, Father, Grandfather—no one."

"I'm happy to be your first." He pulled Jeremy up those last couple of inches and embedded their mouths together, exploring what for him was the sweetness of the universe.

Just as the kiss started to ignite other desires, Bo's phone rang. He pulled back. "Shall I ignore it?"

"No. It could be important." Jeremy snuggled into Bo's chest.

Bo kissed his forehead and clicked his phone. "Hi, Mama."

"Bo, are you okay? We haven't heard from you for two days." Her voice sounded shaky.

"Yes. I was going to call you. I'm sorry to let you worry. Jeremy and I have had a few adventures, but we're both great. Never, ever better."

"I'm so relieved. We didn't know what to think. We really miss you."

"I miss you too, Mama." And oddly, it was true.

"When are you coming home?"

Soft sigh. "Jeremy and I have to figure out the best living arrangement for us, Mama. We'll talk to you about it."

"No, dear, it's all done. Davey and Cortina have found a lovely house to buy and have invited me and Grandpa to live with them. Blanche and Bettina are getting an apartment together. It's time you had your home back."

Well, step right up and call me gobsmacked. "That sounds like it could work well." He wanted to dance a two-step.

"They may need a little help with the down payment or something."

"I suspect that can be arranged."

"It's close enough to you that we can—" She giggled. "—meddle in yours and Jeremy's life endlessly."

Bo pressed Jeremy's face against his chest and laughed. "That sounds perfect, Mama. Just perfect."

"Okay, so get home so we can start planning the wedding."

His laugh got louder. "I have to ask him first."

"Beauregard Marchand, you can't leave that poor boy with no parents and no love in his life alone for another moment. I've taught you better than that—"

Bo broke into her lecture. "Yes, ma'am. I promise to get that done, but please let me plan it my way, okay?"

"Well, all right. But don't linger, Bo. You know how you are regarding relationships. You can be backward."

He suppressed a laugh. "Yes, ma'am. But right now, we have many pressing engagements. So how about we come by later and have a meal together?"

"That would be lovely." She sucked an audible breath. "Bo, I'm sorry for all the terrible things I've said over the years that could lead you to believe I'm anything less than proud as an admiral's buttons of you and all you do. I love you, Bo. You're a fine and honorable man, and you deserve all the happiness there is."

He blinked rapidly. "Thank you, Mama. I love you too. Very much."

"Dinner's at six. Don't be late."

"We won't. I promise." He clicked off and looked down to find Jeremy's eyes closed and his breathing coming slowly and deeply. Bo smiled at the perfection of this intimacy.

Jeremy stirred. "Everything okay?"

"Yes, wonderful. Sleep now. I'll tell you later."

"Mmm, but I want to fuck."

"Darling, we've fucked enough to last a lifetime. From here on out, we make love. And we get to do it until forever."

He sighed. "I like the sound of that."

"Me too."

They both settled into a snuggle, and Bo welcomed a bit more sleep.

Suddenly Jeremy tensed, gasped, and sat up, nearly taking out Bo's chin in the process. "Oh my God, how could I have forgotten?"

Bo's pulse hammered. "What? What's wrong?" Maybe they needed to leave now?

Jeremy clambered to the edge of the bed, climbed out, and hurried to his closet. Bo followed uncertainly.

Jeremy pulled on some jeans commando and a sweatshirt. "Quick. Put something on.

"Do I need to shower?"

"No. Anything. Hurry."

Bo grabbed his own jeans and sweatshirt and stood dressed in front of Jeremy a second later. "Okay. What?"

Jeremy extended a hand and grasped Bo's. "Come on."

Jeremy slipped on his sneakers at the door without tying them, so Bo did the same. Following Jeremy, he walked onto the porch in the cool morning air, then down the stairs.

Jeremy glanced around like a wolf scenting for prey. "See anyone?"

Bo stared around anxiously but shook his head. Jeremy walked down the steps and up the path that led to the road. He paused and seemed to listen with his whole being. Seemingly satisfied, he grasped Bo's hand again and started toward the dense trees behind the house. They stepped into the even cooler shade, and Bo wondered if they should have brought their coats, but Jeremy seemed so intent, he didn't say anything.

After a good ten minutes walking, Bo saw a shovel just lying in the dirt. Jeremy leaned down, snagged it, and kept going. After another couple of minutes, he stopped under the shade of a huge tree. He looked at

Bo with a mixture of mischief and love, then selected a spot and started to dig.

"What are you doing?"

Jeremy placed a finger against his own lips in a *shh* gesture and went back to his task. Bo stepped out of the trajectory of flying dirt.

The shovel seemed to strike something that made a different sound. Jeremy dug a bit more, but carefully. He leaned down and stared into the hole he'd dug, then up at Bo. "You know that one of the reasons my grandfather wanted to find me was to get back the money my mother willed me and my father stole from me."

"Right. The FBI guys told me. Ten million is what I heard. I explained to them that no way you could have that money, since you wouldn't have been so desperate in the face of Ottersen's attacks on you."

"Right. Although Nonno knows I'd hesitate to spend any large amount of money because it might send up a red flag that would have let him know where I was. Of course, he knew, but I wasn't aware of that."

Bo nodded, but he was torn between frowning and smiling.

Jeremy said, "Still, I told Nonno that I stole three million of my own money and started my winery with it. I figured my father must have stashed the rest offshore."

"Yes, that makes sense."

The smile lit Jeremy's face like a fine Chablis. "I lied."

As Jeremy reached for the large plastic bag in the hole, they both started to laugh. Bo guessed they'd never stop.

THREE DAYS later they sat in a favorite coffee shop that also served good tea in San Luis Obispo, with Llewellyn and Blaise opposite them. They'd opted for coffee versus Llewellyn's adored tea shop in deference to Blaise and Jeremy, who favored the bean versus the leaf.

Blaise shook his head and licked foam from his movie-star upper lip. "When you guys set out to solve a mystery, you don't mess around. Jesus, organized crime, sex clubs, asphyxiation, hanging."

"All in a day's work." Jeremy grinned.

Bo smiled but said, "We'd never represent that it hasn't been hell. But the fact that things have worked out well for us takes some of the horror away."

"Y-your f-family is really m-moving out?" Llewellyn sipped his tea latte and managed to look like it wasn't a pale substitute for his favorite brew that came from the shop a few blocks down the street.

Jeremy laughed. "Yes. Surrendering Tara to Scarlett and me." He kissed Bo's hand. "Not to say they'll ever give us a minute's peace, but hell, I could use some family that actually cares for once."

Bo returned the kiss.

Jeremy said, "We start moving me in this weekend, which won't be hard since I've lived like I might have to run for the whole time I've been here."

"W-will you be s-safe from your f-family, Jeremy?"

A slight frown clouded his face. "We hope so. But we'll also take steps to protect ourselves." The frown faded. "It would be a shame to have to abandon our combined businesses now that they seem to have a chance for big success."

Blaise said, "Maybe we can help with the early warning system. Having some snooping power in my family's journalistic business, plus one of the best researchers in the world right here, I'll bet we can even keep tabs on the underworld."

A young guy with a long braid down his back and the eyes of a wounded doe stopped at their table. "Can I get you gentlemen anything else?"

Blaise flashed his teeth. "Thank you. I think we all plan to have another, but we're happy to come to the counter to order."

"Not at all. It'll be my pleasure." He glanced uneasily at a table in the corner occupied by a dark-haired woman and two men. The people were staring at him, but then who wouldn't? The guy had an elven, otherworldly quality that set him apart instantly.

The barista piled their dishes on his tray and walked away, casting frowning glances at the trio observing him.

"W-what an amazing f-face."

Bo nodded. "I think he escaped from the Shire."

"Or Rivendell." Jeremy turned back to Bo. "He seems very uneasy with those people in the corner."

Llewellyn eyed the barista intently. "I w-wonder what his story is?"

Blaise laughed and shook his head at the same time. "Uh-oh. I think we better finish planning our wedding before some other mysterious obsession interferes."

Jeremy pulled a small notebook from his pocket. Llewellyn nodded approvingly. Jeremy poised his pen. "Okay, you now get both of us. It's the Bo and Jeremy show from here on out. So let's select a date."

Bo inhaled deeply. "Yes, we need to choose all the most wonderful details for the ceremony and the party." He could feel heat behind his eyes and blinked so he could get the words out. "And then we can use them for our wedding."

Jeremy snapped his head around so fast it was like a Disney cartoon. "What?"

"Was there something about forever you didn't understand?" He flashed the historic Marchand dimples, reached in his pocket, and extracted a black velvet box.

Jeremy pressed a hand against his mouth. "I thought you were just appeasing Mama."

"Since I got to share in Llewellyn and Blaise's engagement, I wanted them to be here for what I hope is ours." He opened the box on an old-fashioned diamond engagement ring with a huge center stone and smaller stones around it. "This ring has been in my family for generations. Of course, its design was intended for a woman. I propose we reset it any way you'd like for your hand. Together, we can bring the ring and the Marchand family into the twenty-first century and beyond." He took a gold chain from his pocket. "Until then, I ask you to wear it around your neck as a symbol of my promise to love, respect, and cherish you all the days of my life." He looked into Jeremy's eyes, leaking tears down his cheeks. "Will you, Jeremy? Please say yes."

"Oh yes, a thousand times yes!" He threw his arms around Bo's neck and kissed him wildly.

When Bo leaned back, he blushed at the rapt attention of every person in the shop, including the elven barista who stood with their drinks on a tray. He grinned, and that was a pleasurable experience. "I'd say these drinks are on the house."

Bo swept Jeremy up in his arms, swung him in a small circle, then set him down and affixed the chain around his neck. "Forever, my beloved vintner."

Jeremy looked back over his shoulder in a cheeky glance that made sweat-producing promises for what Bo could expect later. Jeremy pursed his lips in a small air kiss. "Your voracious vintner."

READ MORE IN THE
MIDDLEMARK MYSTERY SERIES:

TARA LAIN

THE CASE OF THE SEXY SHAKESPEAREAN

A Middlemark Mystery

Dr. Llewellyn Lewis leads a double life, as both an awkward but distinguished history professor and the more flamboyant Ramon Rondell, infamous writer of sensational historical theories. It's Ramon who first sets eyes on a gorgeous young man dancing in a club, but Llewellyn who meets teaching assistant Blaise Arthur formally at an event held for wealthy socialite Anne de Vere, descendant of Edward de Vere, seventeenth Earl of Oxford—who some believe was the real Shakespeare. Anne wants Llewellyn to prove that claim, even though many have tried and failed. And she's willing to offer a hefty donation to the university if he succeeds.

It also means a chance for Llewellyn to get to know Blaise much better.

Not everyone thinks Llewellyn should take the case—or the money. Between feuding siblings, rival patrons, jealous colleagues, and greedy administrators, almost anyone could be trying to thwart his work... and one of them is willing to kill to do it.

When Anne de Vere turns up dead, the police believe Blaise is the murderer. Only the shy, stuttering professor who has won his heart can prove otherwise....

CHAPTER ONE

THE MUSIC flowed through him like wine—like freedom—and Ramon threw his head back, letting the swish of hair against his shoulders tickle him as he danced. One of his partners, a big muscular stud with tattoos on his neck, leaned over and kissed Ramon's cheek. Strutting away, Ramon just laughed. *We all love our illusions, and I'm his.*

Not to be outdone, the pretty blonde girl who had also leaped onto the floor to dougie with Ramon shook her pert chest against his back. Bless her heart, she'd misjudged her target, but he gave her a butt bump in return, and she giggled.

The music crashed to an end, and Ramon swept a bow at both partners. They both looked like they'd enjoy a second act of some kind, but he tipped an imaginary hat and walked back to the bar, where that handsome dude with the silver hair had promised to save Ramon's seat. Ramon didn't get out much. Only rarely did he feel comfortable enough to go out and meet the public. He needed all the good reactions he could soak up, like fuel to keep him going until the next time.

Sure enough, there sat Silver Fox at the bar, gazing at him with open admiration while draping a very expensively clad leg over the empty barstool. Ramon gave him a grin. "For me?"

Silver Fox chuckled soft and low. "If not, I've almost lost my leg at the knee three times for nothing." He gracefully removed his appendage, and Ramon slid onto the seat, grabbing the icy craft beer the bartender had left in his absence. He wrinkled his nose. *Yuk, it's yeasty.* He flicked the hair from his eyes with a toss of his head and pushed the glass toward the bear of a bartender. "This is caca, darling. Bring me a glass of champagne instead, please." He turned on his barstool toward the crowd, where a wall of people had formed between him and the dance floor, all of them clapping and whistling like they were watching WWF with oiled fighters.

A young guy with dark, slightly wild eyes separated from the crowd and stepped toward him, staring at the floor. *Kind of cute. Kind of not.* The guy glanced up through heavily mascaraed lashes. "Excuse me. Are you by any chance Ramon Rondell?"

Ramon frowned and looked around warily, then tried to return to pleasant face as fast as possible. "Where did you get that information?"

"Uh, I saw you come in and asked the guy at the door who you were. He said your name was Rondell. I was kind of hoping. I'm a huge fan." He shrugged and extended a napkin and a pen. "May I have your autograph?"

"What if I'm not Ramon?"

The kid grinned. "You're so gorgeous, I don't even care."

Ramon glanced at him. *Caught. What can it hurt?* He laughed and scrawled his name across the flimsy paper.

The guy gazed at the signature like he'd been given an original copy of *Tom Sawyer*. "I'm such an admirer."

"I'm happy to hear it." He started to turn back to his beer.

"Are you going to write a book on the real identity of Jack the Ripper? You can prove it was somebody from the royal family, right?" The guy's voice sounded avid.

Ramon's wacko-dar tingled, and he shook his head. "I doubt it. There's a pretty extensive record of information from the time. Everyone thinks their theory is conclusive, but gathering new data's difficult, if not impossible. I confess I don't believe there's a royal family connection. It's more likely that so-called Jack the Ripper was some poor insane person who hated women and killed five in a row before he died or was incarcerated." He shrugged. "But honestly, no one wants to hear that, so I doubt I'll take on the project." He smiled to soften the blow and made to turn again.

The guy frowned darkly. "You're not gonna prove that those rich bastards used those poor women as guinea pigs? Come on, you're the one who should do it. You can get 'em."

Oh dear. "Yes, well, we all have to draw our own conclusions. Thanks for being a fan and saying hello." He turned his back on the young man and faced the bar. Sadly, writing about the mysteries of history did tend to attract conspiracy theorists and crazies. It went with the territory.

The bartender delivered the glass of bubbly, and Ramon reached for his wallet. Mr. Silver Fox put a hand on his forearm. "Allow me." He dropped a couple of twenties in front of the bartender.

Ramon raised an eyebrow at the proprietary hand, and the man withdrew it. The guy was great-looking, probably in his early fifties, wearing a lot of money on his body. Still… "You're kind, but I have just enough time to drink my champagne. Then, I fear, I must fly." He took a healthy mouthful. *Much better than the beer.*

The man leaned on his hand and gave Ramon a wistful look. "I can't persuade you to fly to my nest?"

That earned both of Ramon's raised eyebrows. "Even if I were that kind of girl, I have an early day tomorrow."

"How very sad. I haven't seen you in here before, and I'd remember, believe me."

Ramon nodded. "No, you're right. I don't come in often." Mostly because it was a four-hour drive to his real life, but no point admitting that.

"Even sadder. Perhaps I can persuade you to make a return visit soon?" Silver Fox smiled softly. "So I can determine if you *are* that kind of girl." He stuck out a hand. "I'm Martin, by the way."

Ramon shook his hand lightly. "Ramon."

"I gather you're famous. At least with one ardent admirer."

Ramon wrinkled his nose. "Only the tiniest bit. I write articles and have a popular blog."

"I'll look for them. What shall I search?"

"Ramon Rondell." He downed the last of the champagne. "Now I must go." He turned on the stool— and froze. Martin said something, but he didn't quite hear it. The crowd facing the dance floor had parted, and Ramon stared at what they'd all been watching so enthusiastically.

A male couple dancing.

No, actually it was a guy dancing, and maybe there was a partner there somewhere. The young dancer was tall, over six feet by at least a couple of inches of super-lean body that moved like he was made of rubber. Except for the ass. Holy crap, the most perfect, taut, iron-hard butt, with those irresistible dips in the side that showed even through his jeans. The only thing more perfect than those buns of steel was the face of magic—all brightness and sparkle, with heavily lashed eyes that crinkled as he laughed, dimples that could have sharpened pencils, and a flush of pink across his adorable cheeks. His blond hair flopped forward and he'd flick it back, making even Ramon's practiced head toss look amateurish. Altogether gorgeous, but more than that. The man had an energy, a charisma that captured and held every eye, and a way of grinning and ducking his head that said *Don't take me too seriously.*

"You like that?"

The voice came from over Ramon's shoulder, and he looked back. "What? Excuse me?"

Martin gazed at the dancer in cool appraisal. "Is that your type? The type you'd be 'that kind of girl' for?"

The question gave Ramon a little shiver. "I was interested in the dance style."

"Right." Martin popped a sardonic half smile. "I'm sure he goes from vertical to horizontal very quickly."

Ramon reached in his pocket, grabbed the first bill he felt, and slapped the fifty on the bar. "I like to dougie. Pay the bartender for me, will you?" He turned on his stacked heel and marched catty-corner behind the dance floor and lines of observers toward the lobby.

The weirdo who'd asked for the autograph leaned against the wall in the corner. His eyes met Ramon's and glowered almost—odd to think the word—evilly. But he didn't move. Thank God.

With a quick glance behind to be sure no presumptuous stalkers were following, Ramon slipped out the entrance and broke into a jog toward the back lot where he'd parked his car.

He ducked behind an SUV and peeked at the entrance to the lot. *No one.* Even the attendant seemed to be elsewhere. *Good.* Quickly he ran to the gray Volvo, opened the door from a few feet away, and slid into the driver's seat, then closed the door after him and gazed out through the tinted windows. Moonlight illuminated the lot, but nothing moved.

He let out a long slow breath. *Why the hell did I do this? Martin could so easily have been someone from the university. Or even that crazy conspiracy theorist. What if one of them recognized me?* He needed to retire Ramon from public view, but the idea hurt. Ramon didn't make many appearances and he was always careful to look different when he did, but those few outings were fun, dammit.

With an angry snort, he pulled the floppy-haired dark wig off and then the skullcap he wore under it, tossed them in the tote bag on his seat, and ran his hands through his totally ordinary, short brown hair. *Totally ordinary* described a lot of things. He yanked the vanity mirror down, peeled off the false lashes, fished in the tote for the plastic container and stored them away, and then squeezed out the blue contacts he used to transform his mud-brown eyes. A little lotion removed the lip gloss, mascara, and blush. *Wish I had the guts to just throw all this crap away and forget the cosplay. Ramon can write without making personal appearances.* But the idea of retiring nauseated him. Like giving up on joy.

He toed off the shoes that made him two inches taller. He just wore them for cover because he was already really tall. Then he slid off his tight leather pants, pulled his khakis from the tote, and yanked them on easily, since they bagged around his narrow hips. They felt like home. Sighing, he added the brown Oxfords and a cardigan over his shirt—that would do until he was alone—then piled some books from the well of the passenger seat on top of the paraphernalia he'd stuck in the bag. *Ready.*

He glanced in the mirror again. *Who the hell do you think you are, asshole? Easy answer. A tall, awkward, unattractive nerd, too smart to love.*

Finally he cranked the ignition, and the rumble of the old Volvo's engine vibrated through him like it was rearranging his cells. The gray of the car settled on him like a cloud, and he inhaled reality. His pulse scampered and his eyes jerked from side to side.

A minute later, Dr. Llewellyn Lewis of Middlemark University drove his Volvo out of the parking lot, pausing at the street to carefully observe the oncoming traffic.

The dark outline of a person against the next building caught his eye. *Who could that be?*

In a break between cars, he pressed the accelerator and pulled onto the street. Shaking his head, he said, "I-I've h-heard one t-too many conspiracies." *Why would you, of all people, have to jump at shadows? Especially this far from home.*

Llewellyn drove sedately onto the freeway, pointed the car south, and settled in for the long ride to San

Luis Obispo and a return to real life. Ramon Rondell could stay gone.

"MORNING, DR. L." Llewellyn's assistant, Maria Conchita Gonzalez, looked up from her computer and grinned. "Did you have a wild and crazy weekend?"

The heat started instantly, creeping up Llewellyn's neck and burning his cheeks. God, he hated it. "Uh—"

She bounded out of her desk chair in all her robust glory and planted her hands on her denim-clad hips. "Hang on, boss. Didn't we get past the blushes? Aren't we friends?"

"Y-yes." Like a lot of actors, he could only cover his stutter on the stage. When he wasn't wearing his Ramon skin, the stutter made everything harder and more miserable.

"Come on, you've got no reason to be shy around me." She held up a finger. "*A.* I'm your biggest fan."

Amazingly, that was true. When she applied for her position, she'd demonstrated an almost photographic grasp of all his scholarly works.

"*B.* I couldn't care less if your wild weekend was finding a new kind of food for your cats or hanging naked by your heels from the chandelier. Everyone gets to live as they want as long as they don't hurt anyone else."

"Yo-your opinion does represent a mi-minority view." He smiled, however.

She crossed her arms. "Yeah, well, it shouldn't."

"Besides, I d-don't think my chandelier w-would hold me."

She snorted but gave him an appraising glance. "Come on, you're lean as a fashion model." She circled back to her desk chair, then looked up through her lashes like some busty Hispanic elf. "If you decide on that chandelier trick, invite me. I suspect there are hidden treasures under those plain-Jane khakis."

He blushed again, but this time she just laughed. "By the way, the big boss wants to see you." She made quotes in the air. "As soon as you get in."

"W-what does he want?"

"Probably to waste your time on political bullshit, but he didn't consult me."

He started to turn toward the door, and she said, "Dr. L., why don't you put your stuff down first?" She nodded at his old beat-up briefcase and the cardigan sweater he carried even though the fall weather was hot. *It could change.* "Get comfortable. He'll still be there, fussing and fuming. A couple minutes won't matter."

He nodded and walked into his small, dark office. Maria complained that her assistant's desk was in a lighter, brighter spot than his desk, but he didn't really mind. Dark could be comforting. As he'd managed to discard more and more of his teaching duties in favor of his research and publishing, this dark cave had become his sanctuary. Read more. Talk less. He set the briefcase beside the desk and pulled his laptop from it. His baby. Carefully, he placed it on his battered desk and plugged it in, then walked quickly back out the door. "K-keep an eye—"

"No worries, boss. I got this." She grinned, and he returned it. What a great find she was—efficient, brilliant, talented, and so blatantly on his side it was almost embarrassing. Almost. He seldom thought to do anything for himself—well, not counting Ramon—but he'd hired Maria as a rebellious act of self-expression.

"S-s-see—"

She just flashed her dimples, an expression that said *I'll sit here and listen to whatever you have to say no matter how long it takes, and I'm always three steps ahead.*

He smiled and double-timed out the door. If he had to talk slowly, at least he could walk fast.

Skirting through the long dark halls of the old building, he passed several colleagues. This floor housed mostly professors' offices and some of their staff, no classrooms. Professor Dingleton, the only man on earth who could make French history boring and unromantic according to Maria, nodded officiously. "Lewis."

Llewellyn nodded back and kept walking. Around the corner lay "Mahogany Row," the sought-after offices of the department's crème de la crème. Llewellyn could have claimed one of those spaces by right of his research credentials, but all that exposure made him itch.

He stepped two offices down and tapped on the door of Professor Abraham "Don't call me Abe" Van Pelt, head of the history department.

"Come." Professor Van Pelt had definitely learned that response in a movie.

Llewellyn opened the door. "S-sir."

"Come in, Dr. Lewis." He gestured to one of the aggressively masculine leather chairs in front of his desk. Professor Van Pelt's accoutrements—the chairs that matched the leather patches on his jacket elbows, the pipe he never lit, the wainscoting and wooden ducks that hadn't been used in decorating since 1850—spoke more of who the good doctor would like to be than who the short, portly, balding man actually was.

Llewellyn sat. It made him secretly smile that Dr. Van Pelt jacked up his chair until the edge of the desk must have cut into his thighs and sat his guests in very low seats, making their heights closer to equal. Of course, it was hard to offset Llewellyn's gangly six-foot-one frame. He didn't speak. His stutter made Van Pelt nervous.

"Uh, Dr. Lewis, uh, Llewellyn, this coming Thursday, I and some of the other members of the history and English departments will be wining and dining several potential benefactors of our programs. These are wealthy patrons interested in supporting our research. I don't have to tell you how important these patrons are. It's so unusual to find people who want to fund something besides medical research or finding UFOs." He laughed, though it sounded strained. "Uh, I'd like you to join us."

"W-what?" Llewellyn rose half out of his seat, then flopped back when the professor's eyes widened in alarm. Van Pelt knew better. Llewellyn could manage classes when he had to, staff meetings occasionally, but fund-raising dinners? Dear God, the thought made him ill.

Van Pelt held up a placating hand. "I know. I know. But one of the potential donors is a huge fan of your work and will only attend if you'll be there. As you can imagine, we don't want to, uh, trouble you with this, but we must ask. In fact, I strongly request that you make yourself available on Thursday night."

The shaking had already started in his belly. He sucked in his gut to try to control it. "N-no. Not w-wise."

Professor Van Pelt sighed loudly. "Jesus, Llewellyn, don't you think I know that? I've had to hire two extra teaching assistants just to handle your damned classes, but this woman is important, and she absolutely insists she won't attend unless you're there and will speak to no one else. For the good of the department, I have to insist." He stood, which clearly showed how upset he was since it showed off his barely five-foot-four height. "I'm sorry, but that's final."

Llewellyn rose, not meeting the professor's eyes, and walked to the office door.

"I'll email you the necessary information."

Llewellyn just kept walking all the way to the side door to the building. Taking deep inhales, he exited to the small porch and leaned over the railing, trying to catch his breath. It wasn't just the stutter that made him a social mess. He'd entered college in his early teens, too smart and too awkward to make many friends. From there his studies kept him company, and people drifted further away in his awareness. Holding the world at bay meant he didn't have to care so much what anyone thought. *Damn, wish it worked better.*

He heard voices and looked up to see three men walking by on the sidewalk beside the building, all staring at him. One professor of English tittered behind his hand, a second teacher looked appalled, and the third man—the one with the unreadable expression—was the man who'd been dancing his perfect ass off the night before, one hundred and eighty-five miles away.

TARA LAIN writes the Beautiful Boys of Romance in LGBT romance novels that star her unique, charismatic heroes. Her best-selling novels have garnered awards for Best Series, Best Contemporary Romance, Best Erotic Romance, Best Ménage, Best LGBT Romance, and Best Gay Characters, and more. Readers often call her books "sweet," even with all that hawt sex, because Tara believes in love and her books deliver on happily-ever-after. In her other job, Tara owns an advertising and public relations firm. Her love of creating book titles comes from years of manifesting ad headlines for everything from analytical instruments to semiconductors. She does workshops on both author promotion and writing craft. She lives with her soulmate husband and her soulmate dog (who's a little jealous of all those cat pictures Tara posts on FB) in Ashland, Oregon. Passionate about diversity, justice, and new experiences, Tara says that on her tombstone, it will say "Yes!"

Email: tara@taralain.com

Website: www.taralain.com

Blog: www.taralain.com/blog

Goodreads: www.goodreads.com/author/ show/4541791.Tara_Lain

Pinterest: pinterest.com/taralain

Twitter: @taralain

Facebook: www.facebook.com/taralain

Barnes & Noble: www.barnesandnoble.com/s/ Tara-Lain?keyword=Tara+Lain&store=book

Amazon: www.amazon.com/Tara-Lain/e/ B004U1W5QC/ref=ntt_athr_dp_pel_1

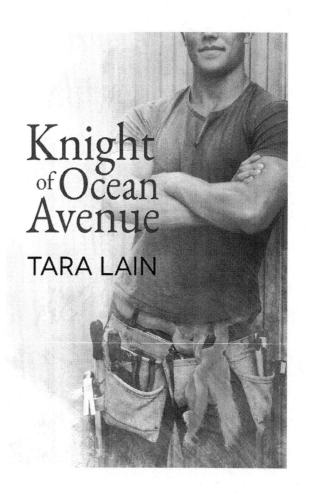

Knight
of Ocean
Avenue

TARA LAIN